Diana T. Sweeney FL 97

"Sure to ⬛⬛⬛⬛⬛⬛⬛⬛⬛⬛ ⬛s. . . .
A skillful ⬛⬛⬛⬛⬛⬛⬛⬛⬛⬛⬛⬛ ⬛d, and
fictional a⬛⬛⬛⬛⬛⬛⬛⬛⬛⬛⬛⬛ ⬛ry maneuvers a⬛⬛⬛⬛⬛⬛⬛⬛⬛⬛⬛ ⬛war as
viewed by ⬛⬛⬛⬛⬛⬛⬛⬛⬛⬛⬛ war and
a man who lived for the end of it."
—*Pittsburgh Press*

"**A vivid picture of the South at war** and the
problems behind the lines. . . . Slaughter's
fictional examination of that brilliant tacti-
cian, told through the eyes of a young surgeon attached to Jackson's troops, is as magnificent as old Stonewall's strategy."
—*Chattanooga Times*

"**The finest new fiction in recent years based
on the Civil War**. . . . The reader encounters
the outstanding figures of the time—from
Lincoln to Lee, from J.E.B. Stuart to the
leaders of the Cherokees allied with the
Southern Confederacy."
—*Augusta Chronicle*

"**One of America's leading storytellers**. . . .
The Stonewall Brigade will delight even the
most sophisticated Civil War buff."
—*Roanoke Times*

THE STONEWALL BRIGADE
was originally published by Doubleday & Company, Inc.

Books by Frank G. Slaughter

Air Surgeon
Battle Surgeon
Buccaneer Surgeon
Code Five
Constantine
Convention, M.D.
Countdown
The Curse of Jezebel
Darien Venture
David: Warrior and King
Daybreak
The Deadly Lady of Madagascar
Devil's Harvest
Divine Mistress
Doctor's Wives
East Side General
Epidemic!
Flight from Natchez
Fort Everglades
God's Warrior

The Golden Isle
The Golden Ones
The Healer
In a Dark Garden
The Land and the Promise
Lorena
Pilgrims in Paradise
The Purple Quest
A Savage Place
The Scarlet Cord
Shadow of Evil
Spencer Brade, M.D.
The Stonewall Brigade
Storm Haven
Surgeon, U.S.A.
Sword and Scalpel
That None Should Die
Tomorrow's Miracle
A Touch of Glory
Women in White

Published by POCKET BOOKS

 **Are there paperbound books you want
but cannot find in your retail stores?**

You can get any title in print in **POCKET BOOK** editions. Simply
send retail price, local sales tax, if any, plus 25¢ (50¢ if you
order two or more books) to cover mailing and handling costs to:

MAIL SERVICE DEPARTMENT
   POCKET BOOKS • A Division of Simon & Schuster, Inc.
   1 West 39th Street • New York, New York 10018

Please send check or money order. We cannot be responsible
for cash.   *Catalogue sent free on request.*

Titles in this series are also available at discounts in quantity
lots for industrial or sales-promotional use. For details write our
Special Projects Agency: The Benjamin Company, Inc., 485
Madison Avenue, New York, New York 10022.

FRANK G. SLAUGHTER

The Stonewall Brigade

PUBLISHED BY POCKET BOOKS NEW YORK

THE STONEWALL BRIGADE

Doubleday edition published 1975

POCKET BOOK edition published March, 1976

Standard Book Number: 671-80300-X.
Library of Congress Catalog Card Number: 74-2524.
This POCKET BOOK edition is published by arrangement
with Doubleday & Company, Inc. Copyright, ©, 1975, by
Frank G. Slaughter. All rights reserved. This book, or por-
tions thereof, may not be reproduced by any means without
permission of the original publisher: Doubleday & Company,
Inc., 245 Park Avenue, New York, New York 10017.

Printed in the U.S.A.

This book is dedicated to the memory of my grandfather, Stephen M. Slaughter, and my great-uncle, Richard T. Slaughter—who fought as young soldiers for the South—and to my great-great-uncle, Solomon G. Slaughter, who gave his life for the Confederacy and is buried in the National Cemetery at Petersburg, Virginia.

And men will tell their children,
Tho' all other memories fade,
How they fought with Stonewall Jackson,
In the old "Stonewall Brigade."

John Esten Cooke, *Stonewall Jackson and the Old Stonewall Brigade* by permission, The University of Virginia Press

CONTENTS

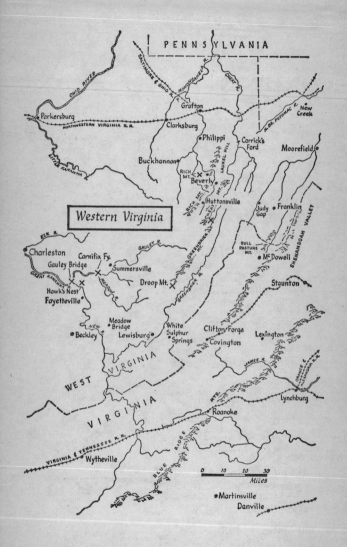

Western Virginia

Virginia

BOOK ONE

Washington

I

The sun was setting over the staid, red brick houses and three-bordered streets of Georgetown when David Preston—Doctor of Medicine by authority of the Jefferson Medical College in Philadelphia and Captain, Medical Department, U.S. Army, by commission of the President of the United States—left the City Hospital. Also known as the Washington Infirmary, the dingy hospital building was located a block north of the City Hall at Fifth and E streets in the American capital. Borne on the April afternoon breeze from the Potomac Flats, a "noxious effluvium"—more aptly characterized by less poetic observers as a "pestilential stink"—that hung over the city much of the time, assailed the nostrils of the tall doctor as he made his way down Fourteenth Street toward its junction with Pennsylvania Avenue.

In trousers of light blue, with an almost knee-length darker tunic of the same color, girt at the waist with a crimson sash and replete with two rows of brass buttons, David Preston was a handsome man. His profile was almost ascetic in its lean strength, the jaw strong and firm, the cheekbones high, setting off gray eyes that could be stern with those of his profession who jeopardized human life through ignorance or laziness, but laughing and gay with his friends.

Everything in Preston's bearing bespoke the quiet ele-

1

gance and assurance of the Virginia aristocrat he was, secure in the possession of a name fully as illustrious in his own state as Adams in Massachusetts. Prestons had sat in the House of Burgesses at Williamsburg and raised shouts of approval when Patrick Henry cried, "If this be treason, make the most of it." Prestons, too, had hunted down Shawnee war parties raiding southward through the fertile valleys of the Shenandoah and James rivers on the turbulent Virginia frontier west of the Blue Ridge during the French and Indian War, and at least one Virginia Preston in every generation had become a doctor or a minister of the strict Presbyterian faith brought southward with the migration, nearly two centuries earlier, of hardy German and Scotch-Irish settlers along the Philadelphia Way leading even as far south as the Carolinas and the hidden valleys of the Great Smoky Mountains marking the lands of the Cherokee Nation at that time.

A year of study abroad, following David's graduation from Jefferson, had included a baptism of fire in battlefield surgery during the recent European conflict, when Giuseppe Garibaldi and Victor Emmanuel II, on the one side, assisted by Napoleon III, had fought against Austrian forces on the other, seeking to oppress the Italians with their autocratic rule.

On his return home in the election year of 1860 that had won Abraham Lincoln the presidency of the United States, David Preston had accepted a commission in the tiny U. S. Army and the relatively menial assignment—for a surgeon of his skill and training——of caring for dependents of military and naval personnel on duty at the nation's capital. But however demeaning his appointment might have been considered by some, he'd not let it trouble him, welcoming instead the opportunity to put into practice some of the advances in medicine he had learned in Vienna, Budapest and other European centers. The result had been that wives and daughters of cabinet officers, the military and upper level governmental employees were now clamoring for his services. Especially after he stirred up a minor medical *cause célèbre* by asserting, in a lecture reported on by the aggressive *Evening Star,* that most cases of childbed fever arising in the hospitals of Washington came not from the fetid miasma generated by the Potomac Flats but from the failure of doctors, nurses and midwives to wash their hands before examining and delivering women in labor.

The past hour had been spent in a particularly difficult breech delivery demanding all of David's skill. He had left the hospital with the cheerful feeling of certainty that the dread stigma of puerperal fever would not attack mother or child, however, for the very good reason that he had rigidly followed the technique of antisepsis using chloride of lime solution developed some fifteen years earlier in Vienna by Dr. Ignaz Philipp Semmelweis. David himself had studied under Semmelweis in the Budapest clinic where the Hungarian physician—embittered by the rejection in Vienna of his revolutionary theories concerning the soure of infection in mothers, newborns and surgical wounds—now practiced and taught obstetrics and surgery.

With the satisfaction behind him of having successfully brought off at least a minor medical miracle, the army surgeon's thoughts at five o'clock on this warm April afternoon were logically concerned with the pleasant prospect of a drink or two of fine bourbon at the long bar of Willard's Hotel. And afterward, to top off the day, the enjoyment of a delectable dinner of *tête de veau en tortue* —a tantalizing dish for which he had developed a decided taste while traveling in France—at the establishment of Monsieur Cruchet, the French caterer and hotel master who was reputed to be the best chef in all of Washington. The prospect was made more tantalizing, too, by the probability, this afternoon of April 18, 1861—five days after the fall of Fort Sumter and the surrender of its Federal garrison at Charleston, South Carolina, to an attack by Confederate forces—that he might soon be leaving Washington and such culinary delights behind for the rigors of war; but this time wearing Confederate gray instead of Union blue.

Not many strings tied Captain David Preston to this relatively young capital of a slightly less than centenarian United States, for at best Washington was not yet a very promising metropolis. The original plan, drawn upon a

3

grid bounded by the Potomac River on the south, the Anacostia River on the southeast, Rock Creek on the west and Boundary Street on the north, was intended to create a city of "magnificent distances"; and large amounts of money had been spent upon the foundations of pretentious government buildings. But both city and structures had been stalled for many months by factionalism in Congress and now the well-designed street plan was for the most part little more than a crisscross of mud puddles. In fact, a man could easily walk over all of Washington in an afternoon, although he would have had to spend another half hour scraping mud and grime from his boots.

Even the Capitol itself, constructed to be the center of the new city, was already outdated and outgrown. Now undergoing radical surgery, it stood with the original dome removed, making the old sandstone building in the center look strangely naked and forlorn. Only the base of the new dome of cast iron was yet in place, plus the scaffolding and the towering crane that would lift the rest of it into place. On either side of the Capitol building, marble wings had begun to extend outward, but these, too, were unfinished, without even the steps in place. And the marble columns needed for completion of the porticoes were still uncapped, giving them a strangely bare and unfulfilled appearance in the warm April sunlight.

Amidst the whole stood an impressive statue of George Washington, naked to the waist but with his limbs discreetly swathed in draperies more suited to a Roman or Greek god than to the man who had inspired a "rag-tag and bobtail" at Valley Forge to turn itself into an army that had brought the vaunted British General Cornwallis to his knees at Yorktown. A much more ambitious tribute to the first President, the Washington Monument, stood in a somewhat marshy area almost directly south of the President's Park and the Executive Mansion. But like much of official Washington, it, too, was unfinished. Forlorn and oddly foreshortened at 154 feet, the truncated obelisk was bordered on one side by the Potomac Flats and on another by the no less fetid waters of the Old City Canal, more aptly described as an open sewer.

At the junction of Fourteenth and Pennsylvania, David

4

Preston turned toward the marquee extending from the curb across the brick pavement to the doorway of Willard's. Occupying much of the block, Washington's most popular hostelry was, of course, on the north—and respectible—side, with the buildings of Newspaper Row around the corner across Fourteenth Street. The broad thoroughfare of Pennsylvania Avenue, conceived originally as an esplanade extending from Capitol Hill to the Executive Mansion, was as yet little more than a miscarriage of broken paving stones. And even these were hardly ever visible, since in dry weather they were covered with red dust that rose in clouds from the busy vehicular travel and, when it rained, with a sea of mud.

The south side of Pennsylvania Avenue was lined with an aggregation of rickety buildings, shacks and tatterdemalion booths housing the City Market, gambling establishments and several brothels. Thumbing its nose at the fine shops, hotels and restaurants on the north, the south side of the avenue resembled nothing so much as a slatternly whore upending her petticoats to display a bare, but utilitarian, backside to the horrified gaze of the richly dressed young ladies and matrons streaming along the opposite side of the street, as they came and went through the doors of Willard's Hotel for the prodigal schedule of social functions displayed upon the bulletin board in its lobby.

A constant stream of vehicles was pulling up to the hotel entrance as David Preston approached. Hansom cabs, buggies, surreys, hacks and an occasional four-in-hand carriage disgorged their occupants, mainly male, for the long bar at Willard's was masculine territory.

He paused at the corner of Fourteenth Street and Pennsylvania Avenue, while one of the new Georgetown omnibuses rumbled to a stop at the corner, its iron-shod wheels grinding the red clay in the street against the cobblestones and sending up a choking cloud of dust.

From the bus a few middle level civil servants not able to afford a private equipage dismounted and entered the hotel. Several times a week they enjoyed a drink at the famed Willard bar, while picking up the latest rumor about the rapidly developing series of crises that promised

5

at any moment to explode into active warfare between the Unionist North and the rebellious—in Yankee eyes—South over slavery. Then, curiosity satisfied, they would adjourn for the evening meal to the much cheaper Harvey's Restaurant about halfway between the Capitol and the Executive Mansion.

Officers on horseback—their numbers increased sharply within the past several days by the arrival of five companies of militia from Pennsylvania and the colorful "Frontier Guards" from turbulent Kansas under the command of flamboyant Senator-elect Jim Lane, for guard duty at the capital—cantered by on the way to livery stables back of the hotel. There they would leave their mounts and join the afternoon tide of sightseers, congressmen, contract seekers, gamblers, warmongers and newspapermen bellying up to the Willard bar or carrying on discreet conversations at tables against the wall.

At the curb, David purchased a copy of the *Evening Star* being hawked by a grimy newsboy. "VIRGINIA MILITIA SAID TO BE MOBILIZING" was the headline and reading it did nothing to give him peace of mind.

The morning *Intelligencer* had carried a story on the action the day before of the Virginia Convention, which had been sitting most of the year, recommending by a vote of eighty-eight to fifty-five that the commonwealth join the seven other states—South Carolina, Georgia, Florida, Mississippi, Alabama, Louisiana and Texas—that had already seceded from the Union in anticipation of harsh action by recently inaugurated President Abraham Lincoln over the question of slavery. But with the referendum on secession for all Virginians prescribed by the convention still over a month away, and peace commissioners in Washington negotiating daily even this late for some honorable way to bring the rebellious states back into the Union, David had felt no immediate need to make a final decision concerning his own course.

Any precipitate action by the Virginian Militia, especially if it occurred before the referendum, could change David's course rather sharply, however, forcing him to choose between the United States, whose constitution he had sworn to uphold and defend when he was commis-

6

sioned in the U.S. Army, and the homeland of Virginia, to which he felt an even greater loyalty. Nor had the succession of events that spring of 1861 given him much hope that he wouldn't see once again the horrors of war firsthand, as he had viewed them briefly with the Garibaldi forces in Italy hardly a year ago.

The political discontent over slavery, seething in the United States since Congress had forbidden further importation of slaves in 1809, had come to a head, so to speak, with the election of Abraham Lincoln in November 1860 to the presidency. Lincoln's platform had advocated allowing states where slavery existed to keep that archaic institution if they chose, though forbidding it in any new states formed from existing territories. But few Southerners believed those promises would be honored, except in the breach, and Charleston fire-eaters had reacted immediately after Lincoln's election, voting on November 13, 1860, to raise ten thousand South Carolina volunteers. On November 18, the Georgia legislature had voted a million dollars to arm that state and secession by South Carolina had followed on December 20.

By the time of Lincoln's inauguration on March 4, 1861, as the sixteenth President of the United States, seven states had seceded to form the Confederate States of America, choosing ex-Senator Jefferson Davis as President, and establishing a new capital at Montgomery, Alabama, with the Stars and Bars as their flag.

President Lincoln's mollifying inaugural address on March 4, in which he once again assured all the states of his determination not to interfere in their domestic affairs, had exerted little effect upon the rebellious Southerners, although it did appear to make Virginia and North Carolina somewhat more reluctant to take the final step immediately. By that time, however, Federal forts had been seized by Confederate firebrands in most southern harbors; while post offices, arsenals and treasury offices had also been taken over in the name of the new nation being created in the South.

Only Fort Sumter in the harbor of Charleston, South Carolina, had remained under siege by April 1. And with firebrand General Pierre Gustave Toutant Beauregard, commander of the South Carolina troops, waiting for an excuse to attack, the stage was set for the final break. This had occurred on April 12, when Confederate cannon shelled Fort Sumter, and was followed the next day by surrender of the fort with its garrison.

Today the bar of the Willard Hotel, as David Preston made his way through the crowd, showed little sign of an impending war. Unless it was the increased number of Union uniforms, the rusty black suits of Yankee businessmen seeking lucrative war contracts and the relative absence of southern politicians. They, with their rumpled linens and floppy panamas had added much color to Washington before their summary departure over the past several months to assume high posts in the Confederacy and its military forces.

Very few people were in the dining rooms yet either, he saw from the lobby, but they, too, would soon be crowded, since the hotel was famous for the amount, if not the selectivity, of the food it served.

At the enormous breakfasts even *pâté de fois gras* was provided for those whose stomachs had survived late night drinking at the bar. Luncheon—also called dinner—began at eleven-thirty, when the ladies appeared, and supper— for Washington was a southern city—lasted until nine o'clock. After which, much of the hotel's male population adjourned once again to the bar, where cold cuts, pretzels, peanuts, boiled crab claws and similar viands were displayed on trays.

David was tasting his first bourbon and water, finding it considerably less satisfying in flavor than that distilled near Fincastle in his old home county of Botetourt in southwest Virginia, when a hand slapped him heartily between the shoulder blades, deviating a portion of the drink from his gullet, for which it was intended, into his respiratory passage, where it was decidedly unwelcome.

"What the hell?" he managed to splutter angrily through his choking and coughing; then a second slap stabilized things somewhat and he turned to look into the merry dark eyes of a fellow officer wearing the uniform and

8

polished boots of a U. S. Cavalry lieutenant, plus a grin that split the familiar lean visage from ear to ear.

"Lachlan!" David manged to cry happily, even in his discomfort. "Lachlan Murrell!"

II

"Present and accounted for." The other officer saluted smartly. "But how in the hell did you get to be a captain when I'm still a lieutenant?"

"Cut the parade ground manner, we're not at VMI any more." David shook hands with the newcomer enthusiastically. "While I get you a drink, see if you can find a table where we can talk over old times."

"Careful!" Lachlan Murrell's eyes danced in his dark sunburned face. "It's against the law to give firewater to Indians."

"But not to a fellow officer in the United States Army." David signaled the bartender for another whiskey and water. "How long have you been in Washington, you skulking redskin?"

"Long enough for a bath, a good night's sleep in a real bed, a meal of something besides buffalo steak and beans, and a chance to rest my boot on the rail of Wiliard's bar. How 'bout you?"

"Six months—treating smallpox and delivering babies."

No table was available in the bar so, drinks in hand, they made their way to the adjoining room and a secluded spot in the corner.

"You've got a hell of an assignment for the best cadet First Captain to ever graduate from VMI." Lachlan took a long drink from his glass and smacked his lips. "Now that's more like whiskey; you wouldn't believe the kind of rotgut the sutlers sell at western army posts, David. It isn't even fit for Plains Indians—much less a Cherokee aristocrat."

"Where were you stationed?"

"Fort Gibson, in the midst of my relations. Nobody else but the United States Army would ever think of setting

9

an Indian to guard an Indian, especially a Cherokee to ride herd on other Cherokees."

"As I remember it, you're no more than one eighth or one twelfth Indian; the rest is Highland Scotch stock like mine."

"I'm still Cherokee." The cavalry officer's voice took on a strong note of pride. "And a Southerner."

"Then you're not going to keep on wearing the blue uniform?"

"I wouldn't be wearing it now, if my great-uncle, John Ross, wasn't principal chief of the Cherokees."

"Isn't he here in Washington? I seem to remember reading something about him."

"Uncle John's been at the National Hotel since the inauguration, talking to the President and some other people about keeping the Cherokee Nation neutral. Aunt Mary and my sister Araminta are with him but, if he ever gets well enough to travel, we'll be heading for Indian Territory. There's a Confederate captaincy waiting for me in Stand Watie's Cherokee Brigade."

"The Cherokees already have a treaty with the United States Government that makes you almost an independent nation," David reminded him. "Why join the Confederacy?"

"With one plantation on the Arkansas River, another in Louisiana and shipping interests at New Orleans, how could we do anything else? What about you?"

"I'll go with Virginia—when she makes up her mind."

"Judging by the headlines in the *Evening Star,* that could be soon."

"I'm afraid so."

"You don't sound very enthusiastic about joining the forces of your native state." Lachlan Murrell gave his friend a quick, appraising look.

"I was a field surgeon with the Garibaldi forces in Italy for nearly six months. There's not much glory in war—"

"Or in setting an Indian to kill Indians. And the way things are going, that may happen in the Five Civilized Tribes before long," Lachlan added. "The Choctaws have already joined the South and a southern faction among the Cherokees wants to take us into the war—"

"Then you believe there will be one?"

"Those weren't popguns that captured Fort Sumter, my friend. And with the Virginia Militia already mobilizing even before the referendum, it could be that somebody in Richmond realizes a surprise attack is half the battle."

David smiled. "We learned that much from Professor Thomas Jonathan Jackson at the Institute—if nothing else."

'Old Jack's a prime strategist, all right. I've seen his theories work more than once in the border warfare the U. S. Cavalry is always having to fight. Did you know Jackson's going to Richmond?"

"As commander of the Virginia Militia?"

"Hardly that. Besides, Colonel Robert E. Lee already has that job."

"Lee's a general since yesterday. It's in the *Evening Star*."

"Virginia didn't waste any time in recognizing what a prize it got when Lee went over," said Lachlan Murrell. "Is it true that General Winfield Scott and President Lincoln offered him the post of General-in-Chief of the U. S. Army?"

"That's the scuttlebutt, and I'm pretty sure it's true. But what's this about Jackson?"

"The VMI seniors are going to Richmond—"

"How did you learn that?"

Lachlan grinned. "Everything that happens in Richmond is known here the next day, maybe sooner."

"And vice versa, I suspect. After all they're barely a hundred miles apart."

"The VMI seniors are going to act as drillmasters for the Virginia Militia," said Lachlan. "Which means that, as Commandant of the Cadet Regiment, Old Jack is pretty certain to go with them. He and Lee knew each other in Mexico, too! I've heard him speak of an engagement they fought together down there. So Jackson might give Lee some good advice about surprise attacks."

"Jackson talks a good battle but fighting is something different. Until you've been in a real hot campaign like

11

the ones I saw in Italy, you can't realize how many things can go wrong with even the best plans."

"There's one that couldn't miss, I'm sure. Remember the fancy artillery outfit in the militia down at Lexington that used to go on maneuvers with the cadets?"

"Sure—the Rockbridge Artillery. The commander is a minister in Lexington named Pendleton."

"And half the personnel are professors; I'll never forget the way they nursed those fieldpieces on maneuvers. Or how they could shoot."

"They made us cadets look like rank amateurs, all right," David admitted.

"Well, five will get you ten that, if Lee would put the militia, the VMI cadets and the Rockbridge Artillery on trains and route them into Alexandria by way of Manassas Junction and the Orange and Alexandria Railroad tonight, he could take Washington tomorrow morning."

"Maybe he will."

"Not unless he does it by late afternoon," said the Cherokee officer. "The Sixth Massachusetts is due here tomorrow, with the Seventh New York not far behind. And by Monday, there'll be enough militia in Washington to defend the city."

"Do you think John Ross can really keep the Cherokee Nation in the Union?"

"The talks have gone well. Before Sumter fell Uncle John was about ready to leave the National Hotel and start back to Tahlequah—where the Ross and Murrell plantations are close together at Park Hill. But Uncle John became ill a few days ago and now Dr. Thaddeus Wilson says he's dying."

"From what?"

"Congestion of the lungs according to Dr. Wilson. Mr. Cameron, the Secretary of War, and W. P. Dole, the Indian Commissioner, arranged for Dr. Wilson to treat Uncle John. We're told he's the best doctor in Washington."

"He has a high social rating here."

"Are you saying he's not much of a doctor?"

"I don't know much about Wilson, but his practice

12

includes a lot of important people in government and in Washington society."

"I guess the doctor is right about Uncle John, at that," said Lachlan. "I can see the swelling has increased, just since I got here yesterday."

"What kind of swelling?" David's voice was suddenly alert.

"Ankles mainly; they're nearly twice as large as they were the last time I saw him. He sleeps most of the time, too, but even then has to be propped up in bed to get his breath." Lachlan shook his head sadly. "I asked for transfer here so I could take Uncle John back to Cherokee Territory, but it looks now like he'll go in a coffin. And with him gone, the southern faction will take over the Cherokee Nation."

"Isn't that what you want?"

"What I want doesn't matter, David; it's what's best for Uncle John and the Nation. He was responsible almost singlehandedly for the school system that allowed young Cherokee men and women to go to schools like VMI, Yale, the Mount Holyoke Female Seminary my sister Araminta just graduated from, and a lot of others. Right now, improving my uncle's health and getting him back to the Nation are the most important things in my life, but neither is very promising. And besides, if it looks like the Cherokees will choose the Confederacy, the Federal Government might decide to hold him as a hostage for the neutrality of the Nation."

"Then you really do need to get him home as quickly as possible."

"That's why I'm in Washington." Lachlan poured the last of the bottle of wine they had been having with their dinner and lifted his glass. "Here's to victory—for whoever deserves to win. But after what I've seen on the way from Fort Gibson here, it doesn't sound like we'll have the short war a lot of people are expecting."

"I've never thought it would be."

"At least you can be sure of having a home to go back to in southwest Virginia. Kansas Jayhawkers have been trying to push the Cherokees out of Indian Territory for years so they can take our lands along the Arkansas

13

River. Now we'll probably have to make a stand or find another 'Trail of Tears' westward, as we did in 1839, when Andrew Jackson sold us down the river."

"Then why take sides in this war?"

"If the North wins, we'll be pushed west and have to fight the Plains Indians for land that isn't worth plowing for corn, tobacco or even grass for cattle. If it's the South, we'll at least have the possibility that the Confederate Government will keep its word and leave us alone."

"Not much of a choice, I'd say."

"We can come through, with men like John Ross to lead us. The trouble is, I wonder where we'll find another if he dies here in Washington."

"I could be looking at him right now," said David.

III

By nine the next morning, David had finished his daily visit to the Smallpox Hospital. Pausing on the porch for a moment, he let the breeze sweeping across the promontory called Greenleaf's Point, where the Anacostia River entered the Potomac, blow the reek of the pesthouse out of his clothing and his nostrils. As he was walking across the hospital yard toward the hitching rack where his horse was tied, he saw Jedediah Thorp, his orderly at the Washington Infirmary, approaching at a gallop.

"Colonel Lawson wants you at the bureau right away, Doctor," said Jedediah as he pulled his horse to a stop beside the rack. "A message just came to the hospital marked 'Urgent.' "

"I'm on my way." Gathering up the reins David swung himself into the saddle with the lithe movement of an experienced horseman. "Tell the matron at the hospital I'll be a little late."

Where Pennsylvania Avenue made a detour around the Executive Mansion, David cross the President's Park on one of the many bridle paths and tied his horse at a hitching rack in front of the formidable red brick building marking the War Department. Making his way to the floor that housed the Medical Bureau, he was ushered

14

into the office of Colonel Thomas Lawson, the Army's Surgeon General, who looked up sourly and returned his salute.

"You took your time getting here, Captain." Lawson had insisted on military rank for the army surgeons, who had simply been called "Doctor" before he managed to ram through an act in 1847, giving them ranks of captain or major depending on their period of service and, even more important, their political connections in the capital. But eighty years old and firmly resistant to any change, Lawson was still in the Dark Ages compared to David's own enlightened medical viewpoint.

"I was at the Smallpox Hospital, sir. Two new cases—"

"I've got enough trouble, Captain, coping with this hornet's nest Jefferson Davis has stirred up, without a smallpox epidemic on my hands."

Suddenly the old doctor's face brightened. "A small epidemic might be a blessing in disguise, though, if it drives some of these contractors trying to skin the bureau out of town—at least until their vaccinations take."

"We're going to need a lot of drugs and other medical supplies when war comes, sir."

"*If* war comes," Colonel Lawson corrected him. "President Lincoln is smart enough to figure out a way to avoid it and still let those fire-eaters down in Charleston keep face. Somebody once said South Carolina is too small to be a nation but too large to be an insane asylum. And from the way they've been acting since Lincoln was elected, I guess that's about the size of it."

"In the Italian war—"

"That wasn't a war, Captain, it was a skirmish," said Lawson severely. "You should have been in uniform when we went after Santa Anna." The old doctor shuffled some papers on his desk. "What was it you wanted, Captain?"

"You sent for me, Colonel."

"Oh, yes. The Secretary of State wants you to see that Indian chief, John Ross, he's so busy trying to keep on our side—in consultation with Dr. Thaddeus Wilson."

"Did Dr. Wilson ask for me, sir?"

"*Ask* for you?" Lawson gave a short bark of a laugh.

15

"Wilson hit the ceiling when he got the message. Says Ross is dying."

"But he's only supposed to have a slight lung congestion—"

Lawson looked up sharply. "Have you been trying to get Ross away from Dr. Wilson, Captain? You know I frown on army doctors engaging in civilian practice on the side."

"Lieutenant Lachlan Murrell is the chief's nephew, Colonel. We were classmates at VMI but I hadn't seen him for almost five years, until I met him again yesterday afternoon at Willard's."

"Maybe you're innocent then, but Dr. Wilson stormed out of here not more than a half hour ago, vowing not to see anybody in consultation with a doctor nobody ever heard of."

"I can assure you that Lieutenant Murrell and I did not discuss the question of my treating his uncle, sir."

"Maybe not, but apparently Chief Ross has had a backset; so you'd better get over there right away. Let's see—he's staying at—" Lawson rummaged in the papers on his desk. "I've got it somewhere here."

"Lieutenant Murrell mentioned that his uncle was sick at the National Hotel, sir."

"That's the one. Let's hope it isn't another epidemic of the National Hotel Disease."

At the inauguration of President Buchanan a few months over four years earlier, a serious intestinal malady had broken out among guests at the crowded National Hotel. Hot-blooded Southerners in Congress generally favored the old hostelry located at Sixth Street and Pennsylvania Avenue because of its bar. Kentucky bourbon was a major attraction there and some had claimed the malady was part of a plot by the Republicans to poison the leaders of the Democratic Party. But in the end the outbreak had been blamed on "sewer gas," said by capital wags to be a by-product of the hotel's largely southern constituency of "congressional windbags."

"Shall I report to you on Chief Ross's condition after I examine him, sir?" David asked.

"I've got more to worry about than Indians in politics,

16

Captain. Report to the Secretary of War, but send a copy to me—"

"And to Dr. Wilson?"

Lawson shrugged. "He'd only tear it up. Good day, Captain."

IV

The day was lovely as David rode the ten blocks to the National Hotel, and Pennsylvania Avenue was very busy. Congressmen headed for the Capitol. Businessmen hurried toward the War Department, where a crash program was under way to bring the minuscule Regular Army of roughly sixteen thousand up to something resembling a respectable size. And vendors of all varieties hawked vegetables and meats in carts, from which flies rose in clouds whenever the driver flicked his whip across the contents.

At the desk of the National Hotel, David was directed to the suite of Mr. John Ross. When he knocked on the door, it was opened by the loveliest girl he had ever seen.

"Dr. Preston, I'm Araminta Murrell," she said with a warm smile. "We've been expecting you."

The fact that she seemed to know him—and obviously expected him to know her—put David momentarily at a loss. When he saw the smile fade quickly from her face, he knew he had committed a nearly unpardonable sin in not recognizing her. And yet, although her face did seem faintly familiar, he couldn't place her at all.

"Please, come in," she said coolly. "Dr. Wilson and Dr. Temple are with my uncle in the adjoining bedroom."

As he followed her across the parlor of the suite, David was racking his brain for an answer to the enigma posed by the girl's warm welcome but found none. The mental effort, however, didn't keep him from observing that she was slightly taller than the average young woman and extraordinarily graceful. In her early twenties, he judged, the light creamy tint to her skin established her as probably a granddaughter, or a niece, of John Ross. Her

17

features were just enough short of aquiline to make her
resemble one of the lovely cameos he'd seen in Italy, yet
striking enough to make her stand out anywhere. The
eyes were dark brown and very direct, with long lashes
reminding him of the wings of a hummingbird he'd once
caught in a trap, and immediately released.

"I'm Lachlan's sister," she added over her shoulder.

"I am honored, Miss Murrell," he said, and saw her
lips tighten again with annoyance, though he still couldn't
understand why.

"In case you're wondering how you came to be called
into consultation about Uncle John's condition, when
Lachlan told me you were in Washington last night, I
spoke to Mr. Seward—"

"The Secretary of State?"

"He has often visited our plantation in Louisiana and
our families have been close for a long time."

As Araminta was reaching for the knob of the door to
an adjacent bedroom, it opened and an older woman
came through; her eyes were red from weeping and she
carried a handkerchief in her hand. Mary Stapler Ross
was much younger than her husband's seventy years,
David knew, and he saw now that she possessed the quiet
aura of assurance he had seen in so many Quaker aristo-
crats while in medical school in Philadelphia.

"We've heard nothing but your praises from Lachlan,
Dr. Preston," she said graciously when Araminta introduced him. "Pray God you can help my husband."

"I sincerely hope I can."

"Dr. Wilson is in the bedroom with him now."

David followed Mary Ross and Araminta Murrell into
the adjoining bedroom. The patient seemed to be asleep
but a portly man of perhaps sixty-five was lecturing
ostentatiously to a much younger man.

"This is Dr. Preston, Dr. Wilson," said Mary Ross
graciously.

Wilson bowed but ignored David's outstretched hand.

"I'm sorry the Secretary and Colonel Lawson saw fit
to trouble you, when you must be very busy preparing
for war, Captain." Wilson made the military title sound
like an epithet of contempt and David could hardly keep

18

from smiling at the obvious playacting for his benefit and the family of the sleeping patient. "Do you know my apprentice, Dr. Temple?"

"I haven't had the honor." David shook hands with the younger doctor.

"Chief Ross is sleeping from laudanum I ordered," Wilson continued. "I would not advise disturbing him."

"I shall do nothing to make him uncomfortable," David promised, putting the small black leather bag he carried on the bedside table. "What is the temperature, Doctor?"

"He is febrile—naturally."

"To what degree?"

Wilson looked baffled and his eyes widened as David took from his medical bag a tube of wood about a foot long with a slot in the side where lay a much smaller tube of glass containing quicksilver. Pulling down the bedcovers over John Ross's chest, he slipped one end of the clinical thermometer into the sick man's armpit and drew the arm close against the body, holding it in the axillary space.

"We should know his exact temperature by the time I finish the rest of the examination," he said. "No doubt you have read the writings of Dr. Joseph Skoda in Vienna concerning physical diagnosis in conditions involving the heart, Dr. Wilson."

"Of course. But I can't see——"

Wilson didn't go on, for David was pulling up the frilled nightshirt to expose John Ross's broad muscular chest. Unlike Lachlan's and Araminta's, Ross's skin was dark, his face broad, his cheekbones prominent—all characteristic of his Indian heritage. Of medium height, he had obviously been powerful in health, for his arm and chest muscles were well developed. He was breathing quietly, but with shallow, somewhat rapid respirations.

Picking up Ross's wrist, David found the pulse there with his finger. Then, reaching across with his left hand to remove a watch from his uniform tunic, he counted the pulse for a full two minutes.

"A hundred and twenty beats per minute," he said.

19

"An experienced doctor doesn't need a watch to tell him the pulse is increased by fever," said Dr. Wilson testily.

"Undoubtedly." David's tone was still mild. "But from feeling his skin I doubt that his temperature is elevated enough to produce that rapid a pulse. Besides, you will observe that the veins of his neck are full and that his breathing is shallow."

"Also signs of pyrexia," said Wilson.

David was already tapping with the middle finger of his right hand upon the corresponding finger of his left resting upon the skin of John Ross's chest. Moving across the front he noted changes in sound, marking the points of demarcation on the dark skin with ink and a blunt quill pen Araminta handed him at his request from a desk in the corner of the room. When he saw the eyes of Dr. Wilson's apprentice suddenly widen at the extent of the outline he was drawing upon the skin, he knew that one other person in the room, at least, realized the importance of what he was discovering.

"In the hands of Dr. Skoda percussion has become an art among European physicians," David observed mildly. "Though not so much used over here yet, I believe."

From the bag he now took a cone-shaped piece of highly polished wood, obviously the work of a craftsman. One end was quite small, with a round bottom of an enlargement at the tip penetrated by an opening that extended through to the other—and coned out—end of the instrument, making it a hollow funnel. Placing the large end over the outline of John Ross's heart he had percussed out, he applied his ear to the small end, and listened for a while, moving the funnel end about as he pressed it here and there against the skin of the patient's chest. Finally, he turned John Ross gently on his side, with the help of Wilson's apprentice, and listened over the back.

Hearing what he was seeking at the base of the lungs, a spattering of sounds somewhat like shot being shaken up in a bottle, David held the stethoscope in place and looked inquiringly at Dr. Wilson, who was pacing up and down the room impatiently.

"Would you care to listen to the breath sounds?" he asked, but the older doctor shook his head angrily and turned away.

"How about you, Doctor?" David asked the younger medical man.

Temple needed no urging to put his ear to the small end. Ignoring Dr. Wilson's angry look, he listened for a long moment.

"What is it?" he asked, almost in a whisper.

"Rales; from the presence of moisture at the bases of the lungs."

"Hah!" Dr. Wilson exclaimed. "A pneumonic congestion—just what I diagnosed."

David didn't answer, but put the instrument back into his bag, and then removed the clinical thermometer from John Ross's armpit and examined the mercury column.

"The temperature is elevated only one degree," he said, putting the thermometer carefully back into the bag. "Certainly not enough to account for a pulse of one hundred and twenty."

"What then?" Dr. Wilson demanded.

Going to the foot of the bed, David loosened the covers and exposed the thick, strong ankles of the sick man. They were badly swollen, as Lachlan had told him last night. And when he pressed an index fingertip against the skin, the small pit thus created remained.

Still speaking quietly, David tabulated the findings: "A fast pulse, almost no temperature, an enlarged heart, rapid shallow breathing, and pitting edema of the ankles in a patient obviously approaching *extremis*—"

"Heart failure," said the apprentice softly, then turned to Dr. Wilson, his voice suddenly harsh. "You missed it, Doctor. Missed it entirely."

Wilson raised his hand as if to strike the younger man, then turned without speaking.

"Go pack your things and move out of my house, *Mister* Temple," he snapped over his shoulder as he left the room.

Temple looked at David and grinned a bit ruefully. "So that's that," he said with a shrug.

21

"I'm sorry if I made you lose your job, Doctor."

"What you really did was cut my bonds, Dr. Preston," said Temple on a note of gratitude. "I doubt that I could have stood listening to that sonorous windbag much longer anyway. The Medical Bureau is clamoring for stewards to work in hospitals until they can pass the examinations for a surgeon's commission. I'll make application tomorrow."

Araminta had been watching wide-eyed during the tense little drama enacted in John Ross's bedroom.

"Can you do anything for him, Dr. Preston?" Her tone was tinged with awe, and no longer angry.

"At the moment there's too much blood in his body and his heart is not strong enough to pump it effectively," David told her. "The result has been a backing up in his circulation that defeats itself, as the heart tries harder and weakens itself further."

"Would you consider strengthening his heart with digitalis leaf?"

"We will, most certainly; foxglove is, next to the poppy that gives us opium, perhaps our most valuable plant in medicine," said David. "But *digitalis folia* does take time to act, which is a drawback in a critical case like this. I think it will be best to diminish the load on the heart quickly by relieving at least part of the plethora."

"Will you bring a bowl of some kind, please?" he asked Araminta. "One that will hold at least a quart."

"Yes, Doctor."

By the time she came back, David had bared John Ross's arm and, with Temple's help, drawn him to the side of the bed. Lifting the arm, he tied his handkerchief around it just above the elbow. Then slipping in the quill he had used to draw the outline of the sick man's heart upon the skin of his chest, he twisted the loop of the handkerchief as a "Spanish windlass" to constrict the veins in front of the elbow, making them bulge sharply.

"I'll need you to steady his arm, but please stand back," he told Araminta. "I'm going to bleed your uncle and Dr. Temple will be needed to hold the bowl. Besides, I'd hate to spatter your dress."

22

"I grew up on a plantation, Doctor. We soon learned not to faint at the sight of blood."

"Good. Just keep the tension where it is." He handed her the quill. "We want to shut off the veins so they'll be full of returning blood but not shut off the artery."

While Temple positioned the bowl, David selected a small, sharp-bladed scalpel from a case marked with the name of a famous Swiss instrument maker. John Ross tried to move the arm when he thrust the pointed blade through the skin to penetrate the wall of one of the large veins visible just in front of the elbow but David held it still. Araminta gasped suddenly when a small geyser of blood arched from John Ross's arm and started to fill the bowl. But when David looked up he saw that, although pale, she had clenched her teeth together, and the hand holding the quill that tightened the tourniquet did not shake.

It took all of fifteen minutes to remove about a pint and a half of dark red blood from the circulation of the Cherokee chieftain. By that time the pulse throbbing at his temple was already perceptibly slower, his breathing less rapid and the distension of the veins visible in his neck above the collarbone had noticeably lessened.

"Bleeding often has a dramatic effect in these cases," said David as he withdrew the scalpel blade. Pressing a folded pad of clean linen against the wound, he bandaged it into place with a strip of cloth Araminta found for him. Then delving into his medical bag, he removed a small package of dried foxglove leaves and stirred them in a little brandy she brought him. Lifting John Ross's shoulders, he put the cup containing the mixture to the older man's lips and found that he was able to swallow, though still not quite conscious.

"It's a miracle!" The girl's beautiful dark eyes were shining. "We haven't been able to get him to take nourishment since midnight."

"With luck, he'll be conscious in a few hours, after the affect of the laudanum wears off," David assured her. "I will stop by an apothecary's shop and order some digitalis leaf prepared in individual packets, so you can

23

give it to him every four hours for the first day or so."

"But you'll come back later, won't you, Dr. Preston?" she asked quickly.

"Before dinner—and sooner if you need me."

"Thank you very much, Dr. Temple," David told the other physician in parting. At the door to the suite, he turned back to face the girl.

"When I came in just now, you expected me to recognize you, didn't you?" he asked.

"Yes." Her eyes suddenly twinkled with mischief. "You should, you know."

"But I—"

"Lachlan bet me you wouldn't, so when you didn't my pride was wounded. Besides, I lost the bet."

"Could you give me a hint?"

"It was almost five years ago—"

"I remember now! Our graduation from VMI. You were . . ."

"A plump girl of sixteen in a short dress, high button shoes and pigtails."

"But with a promise of rare beauty that has been more than fulfilled, I assure you."

A faint flush brightened the creamlike tint of her skin and her eyes suddenly warmed with a light that would have stirred an answering fire in a cigar store Indian, which he was not.

"For that, I forgive you," she told him.

"This bet you said you lost—can't I pay it?"

"It was dinner—at Cruchet's."

"I live there," he told her. "You and Lachlan must dine with me, as soon as your uncle is better."

"You do think he will be, don't you?" Her tone was sober again. "Dr. Wilson told us Uncle John couldn't live more than forty-eight hours longer."

"He's still quite sick, but from the way his heart responded to lightening the load on it by bleeding, I think there's a good chance of getting him back on his feet."

"The whole Cherokee Nation will be in your debt. Uncle John is all that stands between us and this horrible Civil War."

V

Senator Simon Cameron had not been President Lincoln's first choice for Secretary of War—and knew it. With a full-scale civil insurrection, in the view of the Federal Government, about to break out at any moment, a strong hand was badly needed at the helm of the rickety and considerably undermanned ship of war, but, as usual, political considerations had weighed more heavily in the choice of the Secretary of War than the national welfare. When Cameron swung the large and influential Pennsylvania delegation to Lincoln at the Republican Nominating Convention of 1860, he had made it abundantly clear that he would insist upon having the post as his reward.

Not that in the summer of 1860 anyone really expected the southern states to carry out their often repeated threat to secede from the Union if Abraham Lincoln were elected. Much more pertinent was the fact that the War Department afforded very ripe plums in contracts which could be thrown to persons who could be counted upon to be grateful. None of which, of course, was a secret in political Washington, any more than was Cameron's irascible temper. Still David Preston was hardly prepared for the coldness of the Secretary's answer to his friendly greeting when he came to make his report on the condition of Chief John Ross shortly before noon.

"Well, Captain Preston," said Cameron. "What do you have to say for yourself?"

"I beg your pardon, Mr. Secretary."

"You're not deaf, are you?"

"No, sir. I presume you would like to have my report on the condition of Mr. John Ross."

The other occupant of the room hadn't spoken, but David had recognized immediately the U. S. Indian Commissioner, W. P. Dole. Furthermore, he knew Dole was considered to have handled well, at least so far, the difficult task of negotiating with the often prickly leaders of the larger Indian nations in this time of tension. None of which, of course, explained the surly manner of Simon Cameron.

"Just what is Mr. Ross's condition, Doctor?" Dole asked.

"I have just come from examining and treating him, as Colonel Lawson instructed me. Here is my report, Mr. Secretary."

Cameron took the single sheet and tossed it upon his desk without looking at it. "What I want to know is who gave you the right to solicit a patient when a distinguished physician was already in charge of the case? In fact, Doctor," Cameron added, "I believe this action could cause you to be disbarred from your profession on ethical grounds."

Commissioner Dole had been reading David's report; now he looked up and spoke before the surgeon could answer.

"Is this a true evaluation of Chief Ross's present condition, Doctor?" he asked.

"To the best of my knowledge it is."

David turned back to the Secretary, controlling his anger with an effort. "I was instructed by the Surgeon General, my superior officer, to examine Mr. John Ross this morning at the National Hotel and report to you on his condition, Mr. Secretary," he said bluntly. "This I have done."

"That gave you no right to try to steal a dying patient from one of the most respected doctors in Washington."

"I—"

"Isn't it true that Mr. Ross is in a state of *extremis?*"

"Near *extremis,* sir, largely because Dr. Wilson's diagnosis was faulty."

"You dare to—" Cameron purpled with rage and wasn't able to go on at the moment, but the quiet voice of the Indian Commissioner filled the hiatus.

"Before you say more, Mr. Secretary, I would suggest that you read Dr. Preston's report." With the words, Dole thrust the single sheet in front of Cameron, giving the Secretary of War no choice except to read the words written on it.

Silence filled the room for several minutes while Cameron read the report. When he finally put the sheet back on the desk, his hand was shaking.

"Are you sure of what you have written here, Captain?"

"Absolutely. If the treatment—or rather the lack of treatment—I found being used on Chief Ross had been continued, he might not have lived another twenty-four hours."

"And the country could well have had an Indian war on its hands into the bargain," said Commissioner Dole pointedly.

"But Dr. Wilson said he—"

The creaking of the office door, as it was opened from the corridor outside, drowned out anything else Cameron might have been going to say. David Preston was facing the door and, recognizing immediately the tall man in rusty black who entered the room, snapped to attention in his best VMI parade ground manner.

"At ease, Captain," said the President, his eyes warm with humor.

David had never seen Abraham Lincoln that close and was struck by the stark planes of his face, the jutting nose, the high projecting cheekbones, the deep-set brown eyes beneath craggy brows, the high forehead and large ears and the overall narrowness of the skull in general.

"Mr. President!" Cameron's voice was unctuous as he came to his feet. "We are honored."

"Good morning, Senator—I should say, Mr. Secretary, shouldn't I?" said Lincoln. "And Mr. Dole. I was taking a walk this lovely spring morning and stopped by the commissioner's office to inquire about Chief John Ross. Word came to me this morning that he is dying."

"This is Dr.—Captain—David Preston from Colonel Lawson's office, Mr. President," said the commissioner. "He saw Chief Ross this morning."

"How do you do, Dr. Preston?" said Lincoln.

"I'm honored, Mr. President." David bowed. "Deeply honored."

"There are those in Washington—and elsewhere—who would disagree strongly with you." Lincoln smiled warmly. "But I thank you just the same."

Turning back to Commissioner Dole, Lincoln said, "I

thought Dr. Wilson was treating Chief Ross—at least so I was told less than an hour ago."

"Then you must also have heard that Dr. Wilson and I disagree on both the diagnosis and treatment in his case, sir," David dared to say.

"And that you were trying to steal an important patient, Doctor." Lincoln's bushy eyebrows rose expressively. "But I'm sure you already know how fast news travels in Washington."

"I was just telling the captain that Dr. Wilson is highly regarded in the city, Mr. President," said Cameron. "His diagnosis of any patient, and particularly one as important as Chief John Ross, is not to be set aside lightly."

"Please tell me exactly what you think of Mr. Ross's condition from your examination this morning, Doctor," said Lincoln.

David gave a terse evaluation of the condition of the Cherokee leader; when he finished, the President nodded.

"Your report is very encouraging, very encouraging indeed, Captain Preston. Do I understand that the request specifically for you came from Secretary Seward?"

"Lieutenant Lachlan Murrell is Chief Ross's nephew, sir; we were classmates at VMI before I studied medicine." David explained. "I hadn't seen him for several years before last evening, but he did mention that his uncle is quite ill. I imagine he requested Mr. Seward to ask for me, since the Secretary of State is an old friend of the Murrell family."

"And you found Mr. Ross dying of heart failure?"

"He *was* dying, sir—but not of the disease diagnosed by his physician."

"If what you say is true, Dr. Preston, I'm curious about how you were able to recognize his condition when an older physician of great experience failed to do so?"

"After receiving my degree at Jefferson Medical College I spent over a year of further study in Europe, sir, particularly in the clinics of Dr. Joseph Skoda at Vienna and Dr. Ignaz Semmelweis at Budapest. Dr. Skoda is probably the foremost authority in the world on physical diagnosis—"

"The tapping?" Lincoln asked.

"That and auscultation—listening to the breath sounds inside the lungs and those of the heart by means of the stethoscope. Mr. Ross's heart was considerably enlarged, the bases of his lungs were beginning to accumulate fluid and his ankles were swollen. These signs usually mean the heart is unable to pump blood around the circulatory system effectively."

"Most ingenious," said Lincoln. "Then you concluded from your findings that Mr. Ross's trouble is with his heart and not with his lungs?"

"Yes, Mr. President. But, considering the fact that very few physicians in America use either percussion or auscultation yet, it was perhaps a natural error on Dr. Wilson's part to make a diagnosis of lung congestion. Particularly when he didn't use the clinical thermometer to determine that Chief Ross had only a mild degree of fever."

"Whereas, if a true inflammation of the lungs had been present, the fever would be more pronounced?"

"Exactly so, Mr. President."

"And what, pray, did you do?"

"First, I removed somewhat more than a pint of blood from Mr. Ross's circulation to ease the burden upon his heart. Then I started him upon regular doses of digitalis, to strengthen the heart and enable it to pump more effectively."

"What would you say is the prognosis now, Doctor?"

"Treatment was begun only about an hour and a half or two hours ago, Mr. President. I was able to discern some immediate improvement in Chief Ross's condition but that may have been simply from the removal of blood. My guess would be that the next twenty-four to forty-eight hours will tell us whether his heart will be able to cope with the strains that are put upon it."

"Particularly in a man seventy years old?"

"Of course."

"If you have the instruments you spoke of with you, I should be very interested to see them."

"Certainly, sir." Moving over to a table, David opened the bag and took out the thermometer and the stethoscope. When he opened his own tunic and, placing the

29

large end of the stethoscope over the heart, invited the President to listen at the other end, Lincoln did so.

"Most ingenious, most ingenious," was his comment again. "I trust that you will continue to be in charge of Chief Ross's case, Dr. Preston?"

"If that is your wish, sir."

"It *is* my wish." Lincoln spoke firmly and directly to Dole and Cameron. "We haven't always treated our Indian wards with the sympathy and consideration they deserve and it would be a particular mark of neglect on our part if Chief Ross is not properly treated. Thank you for a most interesting demonstration, Dr. Preston. Good day, gentlemen."

VI

"I'm so happy, I could kiss you," Araminta told David excitedly when she opened the door to the Ross hotel suite that evening.

"You have my permission," he told her, but she only took his hand and led him into the parlor of the suite. Her cheeks were flushed with happiness and he was sure she was the loveliest thing he had ever seen.

"I feel like echoing Araminta's emotion, Doctor—except, of course, that we Quakers are supposed to be very reserved," said Mary Ross with a warm smile.

"We threw away the medicine Dr. Wilson prescribed," Araminta assured him. "And Uncle John has been asking for some of the seed of that miracle plant you've been giving him in the brandy; he wants to plant it at Park Hill so the Cherokee medicine men can use it."

"I expect much of the immediate effect came from the bloodletting." David followed the two women into the adjoining bedroom, one of the two the suite afforded.

"This is Dr. David Preston, Uncle John," said Araminta. "You were asleep when he was here this morning, but he saved your life."

"I owe you a debt of considerable gratitude, Doctor." John Ross was propped up in bed on several pillows, his condition obviously improved. His eyes, David noted, were blue, which surprised him, until he remembered that, despite his dark skin, Ross was still no more than one eighth Cherokee by blood, though Indian by choice.

"We're all in your debt," Lachlan Murrell had been sitting by his uncle's bed, but got to his feet now.

"I hope you won't mind my making another examination, Mr. Ross," said David. "President Lincoln was asking about you this morning—"

"You saw the President?" Lachlan and Araminta asked in unison.

"He happened to come into Mr. Cameron's office while I was reporting on Mr. Ross's case to the Secretary and to Commissioner Dole."

"You do get around, don't you?" said Lachlan.

"If you didn't spend all night playing poker, you could be seeing important people, too," Araminta told her brother a bit tartly.

"Trimming rich Yankees of their silver and greenbacks is a laudable occupation, too, dear sister," said Lachlan imperturbably. "Surely no one could expect me to live on the mere pittance the U. S. Government pays a cavalry officer."

"I've ordered a bath for five-thirty in my room across the hall, so I'd better go and get ready for the evening," Lachlan added as he picked up the saber he had propped against the chair in which he had been sitting. "It's No. 215, David. Stop by on your way out and we can have a drink together."

"I'd like that." Moving closer to the bed, David picked up the wrist of the ailing Cherokee chief, while Araminta went to let Lachlan out of the suite.

"They're a handsome pair," said Mary Ross warmly. "Actually they're Mr. Ross's great-niece and -nephew, but we feel like they're son and daughter to us."

"Everything shows improvement, sir," David told Ross after examining him. "I hope you don't mind the medicine we're giving you. I'm afraid it doesn't taste too good."

"You never had to imbide the Black Drink of the Cherokees, Doctor. And besides, this happens to be the only way I can get any brandy; the women are hard-hearted and refuse to let me have it otherwise."

"I'll tell them to pamper you a bit more. We'll be cutting down on the dose of digitalis leaf tomorrow or the next day, but you can have some brandy in between."

"I must confess to another vice—the enjoyment of a few cigars. We grow tobacco at Park Hill, but I prefer the Cuban leaf we import, and Araminta is an expert at rolling the sort of thin cigars I like."

"You should be able to smoke again in a few days—in moderation of course."

"The first thing he wanted when he became conscious again this morning was a cigar." Araminta had come back into the room. "But I wouldn't let him have it without an order from you."

"Never let a woman get the whip hand over you, Dr. Preston," Ross said fondly. "Particularly this one—she's a termagant."

"But a beautiful termagant—like Kate in *The Taming of the Shrew*."

"I played Kate when the Dramatic Society at Mount Holyoke Seminary presented that play last year," said Araminta. "Do we continue the medication as we've been doing?"

"At least until I come by tomorrow morning. You can increase his diet to include soups and soft foods, though, but without much salt. In Europe some physicians think salt is not good in cases of plethora."

VII

Lachlan Murrell had finished his bath and was almost through dressing when David Preston knocked on his door and was admitted. The cavalry officer had put on a freshly pressed uniform and his boots were polished until they shone like mirrors.

"Is Uncle John's condition really as good as it appears?" he asked.

"Everything I know about medicine says it is."

"Then he can travel soon?"

"In a week, if there's no backset. But why the hurry?"

"As long as Secretary Cameron and Commissioner

Dole think Uncle John can keep the Cherokee Nation neutral, they'll let him go and come as he pleases. But if they suspect that he may not be able to keep the Cherokees from joining the Confederacy, they could decide to hold him as a hostage."

"Why would the Cherokee Nation choose the South, when it was Georgians and Tennesseans who talked Andrew Jackson into having you transported to Indian Territory?"

"Some of us—not the Murrells—still own slaves. Besides, the Confederacy has offered to pay us for our Neutral Land." Lachlan abruptly stopped polishing his buttons and, going to the door, opened it and looked up and down the hall outside before closing it again.

"I had a letter from a relative in the Nation today," he said in a lower tone. "He says Confederate sentiment is gaining rapidly south of the Arkansas River. I also played poker last night with an officer who came through the Nation about a week ago from Fort Smith. He reports the Arkansas militia may seize the fort any day and that would bring the Lower Towns, at least, in on the Confederate side."

"Then a split is really imminent in the Cherokee Nation?"

"Maybe not imminent—yet. But Stand Watie and Elias Boudinot are leading the Confederate faction and they're gaining every day."

"You seem to have picked up a lot of information."

"That's why I requested assignment here, that and Uncle John's illness. If I didn't owe him my education and my commission, I'd leave for Indian Territory tomorrow. But the Nation owes him even more than I do; so it's up to me to see that he has an opportunity to tell the National Council—that's our equivalent of the U. S. Congress—what he thinks we should do."

"It looks like you're caught between two fires."

"And both of them getting hotter every day. The Murrell family holdings in Indian Territory and in Louisiana will be subject to seizure if we choose the North. But we also have our own shipping fleet in New Orleans, transporting our cotton to New England spinners and

33

weavers, which puts us in an even greater bind. Once the war begins, some smart Union officer in Missouri is bound to see the advantage of driving down the west bank of the Mississippi, cutting the South in two and stopping all Confederate shipping by water. So, whichever way the cat decides to jump, we need to be there with a bag to catch it."

"Doesn't that come under the head of playing both sides again the middle?"

"An Indian dealing with white men learns to be pragmatic—or he winds up starving." Lachlan gave his boots a last flick with the polishing cloth and picked up his gloves. "Well, I'm off to relieve some government contractors of their ill-gotten gains. By the way, I've been given a military assignment commanding the militia guarding the Long Bridge."

"The one at the foot of Maryland Avenue leading to Alexandria?"

"Yes. The talk about the Virginia Militia mobilizing put a scare into the War Department, but believe me I've more to fear from my own men than from any Virginia troops attacking Washington."

David laughed. "I can understand that. The Georgetown and Washington Militia were drilling in the President's Park this morning, and a half hour later I had to treat one of 'em for a bayonet wound in his backside."

"That's one reason I joined the cavalry. You're always getting tossed off a horse, but at least you can be pretty sure you won't have your tail perforated by bayonets in the hands of your own men."

From outside, the high-pitched cry of a newsboy floated through the open window and Lachlan went to it. He listened for a moment and then turned back to David, his expression troubled.

"The Sixth Massachusetts was attacked in Baltimore this afternoon by southern sympathizers," he reported.

"But everybody knows southern sentiment is strong there."

"That's not what concerns me. If the southern element in Baltimore seize the B&O Railroad, Washington could be cut off from the rest of the Union. Then, even though

Uncle John is getting better under your treatment, we'd have no rail transportation to the Ohio River."

"There's always the C&O Canal. And with Western Virginia against secession, the railroad would certainly keep running west of the canal terminus at Cumberland in Maryland, even if the eastern terminus is seized."

"That could be one way," Lachlan conceded. "We could always take a ship to New Orleans, too, and a river steamer up the Mississippi to the Arkansas. Right now the most important question is, how long before Uncle John will be able to travel?"

"I still wouldn't advocate it in less than a week, possibly ten days."

"We can live with that," said Lachlin. "Especially if you go with us as far as the Ohio River."

"But—"

"Virginia's going to secede, David; it's just a matter of holding the referendum. And you'd be going home anyway before long to get your commission in the Confederate Medical Service, so why not with us?"

"Right now I've got to concentrate on getting Chief Ross out of the woods," said David. "Maybe this Baltimore thing isn't as important as it sounds."

But the Baltimore Riot, as it was already being called only hours after it happened, was very serious indeed, as David learned from reading the *Evening Star*. As in many cities served by two rail lines, the stations in Baltimore were a mile or more apart. When the 6th Massachusetts Regiment—having detrained from the Pennsylvania Central Railroad that had brought them from New York after a triumphant parade through that city the day before—started to march across Baltimore to the B&O station on the west side of town, it was attacked by a howling mob. Early reports said at least four soldiers and nine civilians had been killed, with many times that number wounded. And emotions in Baltimore were said to be at a fever pitch, too, with outraged citizens demanding that the Maryland legislature immediately pass an ordinance of secession.

Another column, almost overshadowed by the black headlines, contained an account telegraphed from Harpers

35

Ferry, Virginia, stating that elements of Virginia Militia had moved into that very important rail junction point and canal way station on the heels of the retreating garrison that had been guarding the U.S. armory. Almost no fighting had been involved, the account said, but the invaders had been so close behind the U.S. troops that most of the fires started with the intention of destroying the munitions factories and denying their use to the Virginia forces, had been extinquished, leaving a considerable number of rifles along with large stores of ammunition to be captured by the attackers.

Of the two events, the one that concerned David Preston most was the Harpers Ferry seizure. Taken on face value it meant the Richmond authorities were confident the coming referendum in Virginia concerning a decision to leave the Union would indicate a choice for secession by the populace; so confident in fact that they were willing to undertake what could hardly be regarded as anything less than an act of war. What was more, the seizure of the B&O Railroad at Harpers Ferry, where it joined the Winchester and Potomac Railroad leading southward in the fertile Shenandoah Valley, was an important step toward isolating the Western Virginia counties known to oppose secession and keeping them from crippling the important state of Virginia in its inevitable role as spearhead of the southern forces.

In the face of these overt acts against the Union, President Lincoln did not hesitate to act promptly. The Washington morning papers of April 20, 1861, carried the full text of his proclamation that began: "Whereas an insurrection against the Government of the United States has broken out in the States of South Carolina, Georgia, Alabama, Florida, Mississippi, Louisiana, and Texas," and ended by declaring a naval blockade of all ports controlled by the Confederate Government. The latter, though still sitting in Montgomery, Alabama, was now reputed to be on the point of accepting an invitation to move to Richmond, Virginia, roughly a hundred miles south of Washington itself. Moreover, departure from Washington of the Peace Commission which, urged by Virginia, had been sitting for months desperately seeking a compromise, plus the resignation of Colonel Robert E. Lee from the United States Army, seemed to scuttle the last hope of prudent men that war could be averted.

VIII

John Ross was sitting up in bed reading the morning paper when David visited him Saturday morning. The swelling was gone from his ankles and no more moisture could be heard at the bases of his lungs. The heart size had diminished sharply, too, confirming David's original diagnosis of an early acute dilatation of the organ which, had it not been arrested by prompt treatment that first morning, could easily have been fatal.

When he finished the examination and came into the parlor on the way to the outside door, David found Araminta standing by a window of the suite, looking wistfully through a glass so streaked with soot and grime from the hotel chimney that almost nothing was visible.

"What's it really like outside?" she asked.

"A beautiful April day. The redbuds are starting to bloom along the riverbank and the grass is turning green."

"While I'm shut up in this prison."

"Not much longer. I was just telling your uncle he can travel in a few more days."

"That only means leaving Washington, where intrigue is everywhere, for the Nation, where it's probably even worse."

He looked at her in surprise. "I thought you and Lachlan were actively supporing the cause of the Confederacy."

"Lachlan has no doubts; he's like the knights of old who went about righting wrongs—"

"And you?"

"Cherokee women have always been very independent, David. When I get back to the Nation, I'll start teaching in our schools—if the war hasn't destroyed them by then."

"If your uncle has his way, they'll still be operating, I'm sure."

"Don't get the idea I'm not willing to do my part to

37

pay for the education I've been given, in Cherokee schools and at the Mount Holyoke Female Seminary." She flashed him a sudden smile, her mood changing like the colors of a chameleon moving from shadow to sunlight. "Isn't that a terrible name? It's a wonderful college, but I'm afraid the people of South Hadley, Massachusetts, didn't think too well of me."

"Why not?"

"On Sunday afternoons, I sometimes used to rent a horse at a livery stable near the college and go galloping over the countryside bareback, yelling like a Comanche. The inhabitants probably expected to be scalped at any moment."

"Would you like to do that again?"

"Mount Holyoke is part of the past, like my girlhood," she said on a wistful note. "And just like North Carolina, where the Cherokees came from before the 'Trail of Tears.' There are tall hills crowned with clouds and valleys so green and verdant that the cattle stand knee-deep in the grass." She shrugged. "But what's the use of pining for something you may not ever have again—like my invitation to Mrs. Lincoln's Saturday afternoon levee today. I even had a new dress made for it and now that riot in Baltimore caused it to be canceled."

David had a sudden inspiration. "I can at least furnish you an excuse to wear the dress, if you'll have dinner with me at Monsieur Cruchet's. I promised you that, re-member?"

"Oh, David! Could we?"

"I don't see why not. Your uncle doesn't need much nursing now."

"Will you hire a buggy so we can take a ride first—maybe out to Georgetown? I haven't been there since we came to Washington."

"Of course. Shall I call for you at six?"

"Make it five, so we'll have a longer ride."

Araminta was ready when he called for her at the Ross suite in the National Hotel. She was lovely in a dress of sprigged muslin with a small cape in deference to the chill of an April evening and a perky hat with the hall-marks of a Paris couturier written all over it. The after-

38

noon crowd already filled the lobby of the National Hotel and she underwent, with complete aplomb, a gauntlet of admiring male glances before David handed her into the buggy he had hired.

It hadn't rained for nearly a week and Pennsylvania Avenue was very dusty as they drove along it past the Executive Mansion facing north in the President's Park, with the grim buildings of the various cabinet departments around it on either side. Directly across from the mansion was the square brick home of Secretary Seward with its four chimney pots and its widow's walk. Not far away stood St. John's Episcopal Church with its steeple, small dome and weather vane; the Lincolns had worshiped there since coming to Washington.

They passed one of the heavy omnibuses carrying passengers between Washington and Georgetown and Araminta smiled at the chorus of approving whistles from young men hanging out the windows of the huge vehicle. Beyond the President's Park, the streets became little more than rutted country roads and the city only a scattered accumulation of houses without much pattern to their location. But when they reached Georgetown by crossing Rock **Creek on** a stone bridge, Araminta caught her breath with delight at the sight of redbud trees blooming almost everywhere.

Children were playing in the well-laid-out streets of Georgetown and banks of hyacinths, snowdrops and lilacs were in full bloom in beds bordering the staid red brick houses of this dignified old city. They rode past the well-kept grounds of Georgetown College, its enrollment reported to have been decreased to only seventy students already by the departure of Southerners for their home states.

Since it was Saturday, the militia was not drilling and the empty mouths of cannon posted on Georgetown Heights, where they could shell Arlington to the south, were the only immediate evidence of war. Only a few soldiers were on duty and they were cooking their supper over small campfires.

Araminta was enjoying every minute, her eyes shining as each new sight met them. And content to bask in the warmth of her pleasure, David paid little attention to where they were until, just before they reached the bridge leading back to Washington, further progress of the buggy was stopped by a crowd gathered around an elevated platform beside the street. For a moment he thought they might have stumbled upon a riot but, by the time he realized the real nature of the gathering, the buggy was surrounded by people and they could not move.

"What is it, David?" Araminta wasn't disturbed, although she was attracting almost as much attention as were several people on a platform perhaps fifty feet away.

"An auction." They were close enough to see that a black man and a woman of much lighter color standing on the platform were fettered at wrists and ankles. "I'm afraid we'll never get out of this crowd until it's finished."

"But here in Washington? When Mr. Lincoln has vowed to end slavery?"

"This is Georgetown," he reminded her. "Besides, the Supreme Court has ruled that Congress has no power to forbid slavery in any state where it already exists."

"We studied that in college—the Dred Scott decision."

"President Lincoln has promised not to interfere with those who own slaves either; just that it will not be allowed in the new states."

"What am I bid for this fine field hand?" The voice of the auctioneer interrupted their conversation and they turned their attention back to the auction.

Bids began to be called from the crowd and the competition was heated. The Negro man remained impassive, even contemptuous, through it all, and was finally sold to a tall sharp-featured man in a stovepipe hat for a thousand dollars.

"That's Ebenezer Stroud, the biggest slave dealer in Washington," David told Araminta. "He's bidding for the Louisiana and Mississippi market; cotton planters down there will go to fifteen hundred or even two thousand for a fine field hand."

The girl standing on the platform was almost white and very pretty. As the auctioneer led her forward, his voice took on a sniggering, oily note that implied a great deal without actually putting his implications into words.

"Amy here is a fine specimen," he announced. "Only eighteen years old and a virgin by medical certificate. She is well trained as a house servant, too, and always obedient to her master's orders."

A ripple of laughter went through the crowd at his words and the bidding began. It was spirited and the girl was finally bought by a red-haired woman whose cheeks were heavily made up with rouge and powder. She wore a large hat with an ostrich plume, none of which hid the wattles of age in her neck.

"I think we'd better go," said David firmly. "If I'd known Rose McCauley was in the crowd, I would never have stopped."

"Is Rose McCauley really a mad——?"

"She's everything you've heard about her, but she does have the reputation of being kind to the girls she buys. And octoroons like that girl often do very well for themselves."

"I've seen them in New Orleans with some of the richest men there."

"We'd better be getting to Cruchet's; I reserved our table for seven."

Cruchet's was a considerably more fashionable hotel than Willard's and the dinner was just beginning. They were ushered to a small table by an obsequious waiter who greeted David by name.

"You seem to be quite the man about town," said Araminta as she was removing her gloves after being being seated.

"I live here," he explained. "Besides, I developed a taste for French cuisine during the time I spent in Europe."

"I was going to Europe this summer. But with this terrible war breaking out and Uncle John sick——"

The arrival of Monsieur Cruchet himself interrupted her and the next few moments were spent discussing the menu for dinner. Araminta chose a speciality of the house, *canard à l'orange*—and firmly settled the question of the wine as well.

"I would like a rosé of Provence with dinner," she said. "And then some champagne." Noticing David's

41

startled expression, she added, "We often have champagne when we go to our Louisiana plantation for the winter. But I haven't had any in ages."

"Neither have I," he admitted. "My practice hasn't left much time for social affairs."

"Even if the duck is burned and the champagne doesn't fizz, I love it here, David," she said as she looked around the elegant room. "I forgive you for not recognizing me that first morning at the hotel."

"I hadn't seen you for all of five years," he reminded her. "You were a very pretty young girl then. But now." He lifted her hand from where it lay upon the spotless tablecloth and touched her fingers to his lips." *Voilà! Une jeune fille incomparable!*"

When he released her fingers, he saw that her eyes were shining with a light that set his heart to beating faster. Their wine came just then and, after the waiter served them, David lifted his glass and touched it to hers.

"A toast," he said. "What shall it be?"

"To the Confederacy—and a quick end to the war."

Dinner was everything Monsieur Cruchet had assured them it would be, and Araminta ate with the appetite of a healthy young girl, the champagne heightening the sparkle in her eyes. Watching her, David found himself forgetting his own uncertainty of purpose in the face of her firm conviction that the South must trimuph quickly and earn the right to go her own way as a separate nation.

They had finished dinner and were enjoying the champagne over a French pastry Monsieur Cruchet sent to their table with his compliments, when a heavyset elderly man, resplendent in full uniform, shiny buttons and gold-trimmed epaulettes, was assisted to a table near the center of the dining room by an aide and a valet. His towering height, plus his great bulk, made locomotion difficult at best and he was quite winded as he settled into a chair and mopped his forehead with a white silk handkerchief.

"Who in the world is he?" Araminta asked in a low voice. "Monsieur Cruchet treats him like a king."

"General Winfield Scott, the General-in-Chief of the Army."

"I thought he was dead. How old is he?"

"Nearly seventy-five, I believe."

"He looks eight-five," she said with the frankness of youth. "Uncle John is seventy but, until he got sick this time, he could outwalk and outwork most young men in the Nation."

"The general has always lived high."

"If that's a man who will command the northern army"—Araminta shook her head slowly, as if unable still to believe what she saw—"I'm certain to get my trip to Europe by *next* summer."

"The Surgeon General is eighty and the Army's full of officers who should have retired long ago." said David. "But the preponderance of deadwood isn't confined to the North. Lachlan told me a former professor of ours, Major Thomas Jonathan Jackson, is going into the Confederate Army and may even command the troops from my home area in the Shenandoah Valley. If the professor isn't any better as a military strategist than he was as a teacher, I'm afraid of what may happen."

"Isn't he the one the cadets were always making fun of?"

"There were some pranks."

"Lachlan pointed Major Jackson out to me at your graduation. He was wearing a dingy uniform then and one of the buttons was missing, but he talked to me a few minutes at the reception and I found him very sweet." She turned from her scrutiny of General Scott. "Why didn't you go into the Army when you graduated from the Institute, David?"

"By then I'd decided to be a doctor. And anyway, at that time not more than a fourth of the VMI graduates were putting on the uniform again after graduation."

"Lachlan loves military life, especially being in the U. S. Cavalry."

"Let's hope this is all over before long, anyway. Then I'll be going back to Preston's Cove in southwest Virginia."

"Where did you study medicine?" she asked.

"In Philadelphia—at Jefferson Medical College."

"Aunt Mary comes from Philadelphia and I often

43

stopped there on the way to and from Mount Holyoke Seminary. Do medical students really go out at night and rob graves to get corpses for dissection in the medical schools? I used to walk fast every time I passed the building."

David laughed. "I'm afraid that's an old wives' tale."

"But they do in England, I've read about that."

"Didn't I hear Lachlan call you by a different name once—Sequo—I'm afraid I can't pronounce it."

"Sequoyah is my middle name, it's Cherokee. Actually, Sequoyah was a great scholar and gave us the first Cherokee alphabet. I was always ahead in school so my family started calling me that." Her eyelids crinkled in a smile. "And of course the fact that I've always been a tomboy made it appropriate, even for a princess."

"I didn't know the Cherokees went in for royalty."

"Our government is a republic in form but I'm descended from a real queen, Cofitachequi."

"Don't ask me to pronounce that, please. Who was she?"

"When the Spanish under Hernando de Soto came into our country they were guided by the Lady of Cofitachequi, a queen among the Cheraws they had captured in South Carolina. She was borne on a litter by slave women and led De Soto's men along the Winding Star Trail into the mountain country."

"But that was three hundred years ago."

"Almost three hundred and twenty-five; I read the account of De Soto's expedition in college last year and it said they left the land of the Cheraws in South Carolina in May of 1539." Her tone suddenly took on a bitter note. "Exactly three hundred years before President Andrew Jackson started driving the Cherokees like cattle across the Mississippi to the lands we hold today."

"Your people have a right to be bitter," David agreed. "I often heard Lachlan tell of that journey when we were in college."

"The Lady of Cofitachequi led De Soto's men into mountains covered with clouds—"

"What are called the Great Smokies now?"

"Yes. When the expedition stopped for the night at a

Cherokee village called Guasili—it's near where Franklin, North Carolina, stands today—the Queen of the Cheraws escaped. She came out of hiding after the Spaniards left, though, and remained with the Cherokees. My family is descended from her on the maternal side."

"Which makes you a princess?"

Her eyes suddenly took fire. "Do you doubt it?"

"Not for a moment. I've seen princesses in Europe—queens, too—but not as lovely as you."

"That's the nicest thing anyone ever said to me, David." Her tone was husky with emotion.

"Then I'm glad I was the one who said it."

Araminta glanced at the clock over the door of the dinning room. "It couldn't be nine o'clock already!" she exclaimed.

"Do you think your Aunt Mary will be worried?"

"When I'm with you? Of course not. But we'd better go, just the same."

At the door to the Ross suite, she gave him her keys, but put her hand on his arm before he could unlock the door.

"Thank you for the loveliest evening of my life, David." She rose on her toes to kiss him, but what started out as a light kiss of appreciation suddenly changed to something entirely different.

"Oh!" she said when she pushed him away, her eyes wide and very very lovely. Then she laughed a little shakily. "You'd better unlock the door quick, David. Cherokee women are very romantic and if anyone came along and found me in your arms there'd be a terrible scandal."

IX

John Ross was still improving steadily when David visited him Sunday morning. There was no longer any real reason to make a daily visit, except for the chance to see Araminta, but that prospect was already making him wake up every morning feeling that a new and exciting adventure lay ahead.

45

"I'm going to tell your nurses to let you out of bed for an hour several times a day," he told Ross.

"That's a fitting tribute to your treatment, Doctor."

"And to an iron constitution as much as anything else, I suspect. Not many men your age are as vigorous as you are, sir, even without a little heart trouble."

"It's pretty important to my people that I stay well a while longer in these troubled times, Dr. Preston. The future of the Cherokee Nation and the Five Civilized Tribes could depend on the course we follow the next few months, until this conflict is ended."

"I hope it will only be a few months."

"Then you don't think so?"

"I'm not a military man, Mr. Ross, even though I did graduate from a military college before studying medicine. But it seems that wars are always a lot harder to end than they are to start."

"Araminta tells me you were with the Italians in their fight against Austria."

"Just for six months, long enough to see that war is the poorest possible way to settle differences among nations. And an even worse way to cope with political disagreements within a country."

"I've been telling my people that for over thirty years, Dr. Preston. But the Cherokees have always prided themselves on their independence—"

"Even the women, I hear."

"Araminta's high-spirited girl. And also a very intelligent one."

"As well as beautiful. I think I'm falling in love with her, sir."

"I'm sure Araminta couldn't do better—nor you. Cherokees have always married freely with whites and it has almost come to be an accepted fact that our leaders will be mixed bloods."

"You're ample proof that their choice is wise, sir."

"The people of my nation chose me as a member of the ruling council when I was nineteen, Dr. Preston. My whole life has been spent in furthering their welfare."

"Would you have had it any other way even if you could?"

"Not for a moment." Ross looked at David keenly. "Am I right in surmising that you are going through a period of difficult decision now?"

"Very much so, I'm afraid."

"Do you know yet what your decision will be?"

"I'm a Virginian, sir—and just as proud of my heritage as you, Araminta and Lachlan are of being Cherokees. When Virginia needs me, I shall have no choice except to serve her."

John Ross nodded. "I suspect a lot of men of good will, who certainly don't support enslavement of a fellow human being, will be drawn into this controversy by the same force that motivates you. But many men on the other side feel the same way about the Union, so even though brother will undoubtedly be set against brother before this is over, none of us will really have any choice."

"I shall tell Secretary Cameron and Mr. Dole in the morning that you should be able to travel by the end of the week."

"I hope we can get through to the Ohio River, after the disturbance in Baltimore and the occupation of Harpers Ferry."

"The South would have nothing to gain by offending you," David assured him. "And we already know the authorities here are anxious for you to reach the Cherokee Nation as soon as possible. So whatever happens in the war, I think some way will be found to insure you a safe journey home."

47

BOOK TWO

Harpers Ferry

I

It was late afternoon when the patient team of mules on the towpath stopped at the musical cry of "Whoa, mule! Whoa!"—part of a favorite song of the canal boatmen. The Chesapeake and Ohio Canal packet boat nudged to a berth at the Harpers Ferry landing on the north side of the Potomac some two hundred feet from the tavern and inn that offered refreshment to travelers, as well as overnight accommodations somewhat more comfortable than the three-tiered bunks on the line's most luxurious conveyance.

Traveling four miles an hour, at a cent and a half per mile, the *General Winfield Scott* was seventy feet long and thirteen feet, eight inches wide, allowing it to negotiate the four-foot-deep canal without difficulty. It had made the forty-odd-mile trip from Washington in two days, being lifted en route through a number of locks, the largest at Great Falls, just outside Washington.

Lachlan Murrell and David Preston had been sitting on the afterdeck as the boat drew to a stop at the landing; now they climbed up on the roof for a better view of the area.

"It certainly is nice to be out of that hot blue uniform." In doeskin breeches setting off a well-turned leg, black boots, a chocolate brown clawhammer coat, ruffled white shirt and silk cravat, Lachlan was the epitome of fashion turned out by one of Washington's best gentlemen outfitters.

"You look like a Mississippi riverboat gambler," said David.

"And I might just be one, at least until we get to the Arkansas. With Federal gunboats blockading the mouth of the Mississippi below New Orleans, the Cherokee Transportation Company is going to need extra funds to bribe Yankee ship captains to look the other way."

"Then you're going to try to run the blockade?"

"At least until the fall cotton crop is sold. With Abraham Lincoln calling for more troops at every new rumor from the South, New England looms will be busy and southern cotton will bring premium prices."

While the handlers were securing the canal boat to moorings along the landing, the driver unhitched the patient mules and led them toward the stables just off the towpath. Araminta emerged from the cabin and climbed the short ladder to the cabin roof where the other two were standing.

"How beautiful!" she cried.

The sweep of her arm took in the deep cleft of the triple gorge where the Shenandoah River, draining the fertile Virginia valley of that name to the south, joined the turbulent course of the Potomac, flowing eastward from its origin more than a hundred miles to the west, in the Allegheny range of mountains.

"Glad to be out of Washington?" David asked.

"More than glad, this is my kind of country."

He pointed to the narrow gorge where the Shenandoah River cut through the mountains. "There is the entrance to one of the most fertile valleys in the world—except perhaps the Nile and the Tigris-Euphrates."

Lachlan was studying the town with David's U. S. Government-issue field glasses. "I thought your famous Virginia Militia had captured Harpers Ferry, David," he said.

"So the newspapers said. Why?"

"From here I can't see more than a dozen soldiers loafing uptown where a flag is flying in front of what looks

49

like a storefront. Do you suppose that's the headquarters of the occupying troops?"

"Don't ask me. The less I see of 'em before we're safely under way again tomorrow morning for Cumberland, the better I'll feel."

From the railroad bridge, visible as it crossed high above the Potomac from Virginia and Harpers Ferry proper on the south bank to Maryland on the north, came the long mournful whistle of a freight train. A big locomotive soon appeared, pulling a long line of hopper cars eastward toward Baltimore, Annapolis and Washington. The cars were piled high with coal and the train rumbled on across the Potomac bridge with no apparent intention of stopping at Harpers Ferry.

"I'd wager that coal will be in the bunkers of Federal gunboats blockading southern ports before the week is out," said Lachlan. "If the B&O is still hauling freight, what was the point in taking Harpers Ferry at all?"

"I've stopped worrying about how wars are fought and won or lost," said David. "Didn't you get the idea before we left Washington that everybody is still concerned with business as usual——?"

Lachlan chuckled. *"More* business and *more* profits than usual. But definitely concerned——though a better analogy would be Nero fiddling while Rome was burning."

"I guess nobody wants to admit to themselves that it's really war; I know I don't." Araminta's gaze swept the rather depressing face of the town across the Potomac. "Why would the government ever build an arsenal here, so far from everything, even though the meeting of the two rivers is spectacular?"

"You need to look beneath the surface of these mountains to see the reason," David told her. "The Potomac drops steadily as it flows eastward, so there's plenty of water power here for manufacturing. And iron furnaces have been located along tributary streams since Indian days."

"Our Shawnee and Tuscarora brothers came through this gap more than once on the way to lift a few German and Scotch-Irish scalps down in the Shenandoah Valley. But at the expense of being disloyal to my Indian heritage,

David, I'm glad no Prestons were among them." Lachlan lifted the glasses again. "Oh! Oh! Your Virginia Militia seems to have waked up from their afternoon naps."

Across the river, on the sharp slope of the street leading to the main portion of the town, a small company of soldiers in Confederate gray was gathering into a straggly formation before the storefront, where the Virginia flag rippled from a makeshift flagpole.

"That trick of bringing troops in here by railroad before the Federal forces could finish burning the arsenal and the munitions factories was a masterstroke," Lachlin observed. "I wonder who thought of it."

"If it turns out to be the success it appeared to be at the time, everybody will be claiming credit," said David. "And if it's a failure, nobody will want to admit he was to blame."

"Hear! Hear!" said Lachlan. "We've got a sage for a military medical escort, Sis."

"But a nice sage, brother dear." Araminta put her hand on David's arm and squeezed it affectionately. "You're just envious because you didn't think of saying it."

Actually, David knew, the much heralded capture of Harpers Ferry by Virginia and North Carolina militia could hardly have been called much of a military victory. Getting wind of their coming, the small Federal garrison had evacuated the town just ahead of the Virginia forces, rather than being placed under a siege that could only end one way, with surrender. As a political and emotional milestone in the now rapidly approaching conflict, however, Harpers Ferry was very important indeed because of its significance to the south.

A little more than two years earlier, a renegade abolitionist named John Brown, with the support of prominent New England opponents of slavery, had tried to stir up black slaves all over the South to rebel against their white masters and destroy them. Nobody paid too much attention at first but, when Brown got together a force of his own ilk and seized the Federal arsenal at Harpers Ferry with the announced intention of arming blacks everywhere and leading them to massacre white people, a frenzied state of alarm gripped much of the South, especially Virginia.

President James Buchanan, whose tenure of office had ended with the inauguration of Abraham Lincoln, had acted swiftly. Troops under the command of Colonel Robert E. Lee had been sent to arrest Brown and he had been promptly tried and executed. Nevertheless the name of Harpers Ferry itself could still arouse anger and fear in the white population of the South and the action of the Virginia Militia in taking the town—even though the Federal troops had already gone and hardly a shot was fired—carried a tremendous emotional significance for the entire South.

Actually, Harpers Ferry had almost eclipsed the fall of Fort Sumter in southern eyes, since the action in Charleston harbor had been carried out by a state already in defiance of the Union by secession. On the other hand, the seizure of Harpers Ferry marked not only the entrance of Virginia into the war, even before approval of the secessionist resolution by the people, but at the same time destroyed a threat of black insurrections which, in truth, had never really been much more than a myth.

Much of this had been in David Preston's thoughts during the Sunday following his dinner with Araminta at Cruchet's. That night he had taken the final step of writing out his resignation from the United States Army and had carried it with him when he went to the office of the Surgeon General on Monday morning.

The taking of Harpers Ferry had replaced the Baltimore Riot in the columns of the *Intelligencer* he'd purchased when he came down to breakfast, and all around him in the dining room people were discussing the two sudden turns of events. Both happenings were unfavorable to the Union, since control of Baltimore by southern sympathizers blocked rail traffic from the North and, with Virginia troops controlling Harpers Ferry, the B&O could likewise be throttled as a rail artery from the West.

What the *Intelligencer* failed to note was the fact that a brilliant former U. S. Army captain and Mexican War veteran in Cincinnati, Ohio, named George Brinton McClellan—having resigned his commission earlier to be-

52

come first chief engineer, then vice-president of the Illinois Central Railroad, and later president of the Ohio and Mississippi—had just been appointed a major general in command of Ohio State troops for the Union. Plus the strong possibility that, being a railroad man, as well as a trained soldier, McClellan would certainly realize the importance of the B&O as a route of attack from west of the Mississippi against Virginia and particularly the lovely and fertile Shenandoah Valley.

"I shall be sorry to see you go, Captain," Colonel Lawson of the Medical Bureau had said on Monday morning, following the Baltimore Riot, as he handed back the resignation David Preston had put on his desk. "The Secretary wishes to see you in his office and, since he has to approve this, you might as well take it with you."

Secretary Cameron was busy with a stream of people pouring in and out of his office. But when told David was outside, he immediately had the surgeon brought into his office.

"What's that?" Cameron asked, when David placed the paper on his desk.

"My resignation from the Army."

"I'd forgotten you were a Virginian, Doctor. Are you sure you want to give up your commision?"

"It's not what I want, Mr. Secretary, but what honor insists that I do."

"If you ask me, there already too much of honor connected with this war and too little of tactical action. If the Virginians hadn't waited so long to start secession proceedings, they could have taken Washington by surprise any time since Fort Sumpter fell a week ago, almost without firing a shot."

"It could probably still be done."

"But not for long. By the end of this week the Seventh Massachusetts and the Seventh New York will be on guard here. The New York Fire Zouaves under Colonel Ellsworth won't be far behind either, and Brigadier General Benjamin F. Butler will be in command at Annapolis. You can be sure Butler will clamp a lid on Baltimore and, with Colonel Mansfield in command here at Washington and General Patterson in Pennsylvania, the situation will be well controlled. But enough of this, Doctor; the President anticipated that you might wish to resign and asked me to request one favor of you."

"I could hardly—"

"This involves no disloyalty to Virginia. Is it true that Chief Ross will soon be well enough to travel?"

"By the end of the week, if he has no backset."

"With the situation on the B&O as uncertain as it is, we feel he should not go by train, at least not from either Washington or Baltimore. But the Virginia troops at Harpers Ferry have shown no wish yet to interfere with canal traffic, so we hope you will postpone resigning your commission long enough to act as military and medical escort for the Ross party as far as Cumberland by boat. They can take a train there for Parkersburg and a river steamer. but it might be best for you to go on to the Ohio River with them and see them safely aboard."

"Lieutenant Lachlan Murrell will be—"

"Lieutenant Murrell resigned his commission this morning, Doctor. And since Western Virginia is largely loyal to the Union, we feel that an officer in the uniform of the Army Medical Department would be better able to insure a safe passage for Chief Ross."

"I can see nothing wrong with that, sir—so long as my resignation is accepted as soon as Mr. Ross is safely aboard ship on the Ohio."

"It will be, but I should inform you that the President was very much impressed by your knowledge of medicine and what you learned in Europe. If you choose to stay with the Union, I can offer you an immediate promotion to the rank of major, with a colonelcy not far behind."

David hadn't even paused to be tempted. "I am a Virginian, Mr. Secretary. I have no choice except to serve her."

"Looks like we might be going to have company."

Lachlan Murrell had been studying the town and the military headquarters with the field glass and his words brought David suddenly back to the matter at hand—the question of what the Virginia military authorities would do about John Ross. Through the glasses Lachlan handed him, he could see three mounted men in uniform cantering down the street. The officer was a rather solid-looking blond fellow who sat his horse rather awkwardly, and the other two were obviously far from experienced riders.

"The Pennsylvania Dutch always make lousy cavalrymen, they're too broad across the butt," said Lachlan. "I never saw one yet that could sit a horse properly."

"They're wearing Virginia uniforms."

"The valley's full of Dutchmen. So's the area west of Pittsburgh around Wheeling, but that's still Virginia, too, you know."

The military party clattered across the long bridge over the Potomac from Virginia to Maryland and turned along the towpath toward the landing where the packet boat was moored.

"Don't you have friends among the Virginia Militia, David?" Araminta asked.

"Probably. But I'm still technically in the service of the United States Government—and also in uniform."

"No telling what will happen now," Lachlan agreed. "I'm glad to be a civilian."

"What would anyone gain by holding us?" she asked.

"The company of a pretty girl, for one thing, and to some that might be reason enough," said Lachlan. "On second thought, maybe you'd better go inside the cabin, Sis."

"I'm not afraid of them." Araminta tossed her head as she started toward the door but, before she could go inside, a clatter of hooves came from the landing and the cavalrymen rode along the loading platform. The officer wore a heavy pistol and a saber hung from his belt. He drew his mount to a stop a few yards away; then, at the sight of the girl he stiffened in his saddle, preening himself, David thought, like a turkey cock at the sight of a young hen.

"Lieutenant Henry Kramer, Virginia Militia," he announced. "At your service, miss."

"Thank you, Lieutenant," said Araminta demurely. "You could serve us well by finding a room for us at yonder inn, we're accompanying my uncle, who is ill, and my aunt to Indian Territory."

"Indians?" They could almost hear the thoughts whirling inside his blond head. "Surely——"

"The young lady is Princess Sequoyah Murrell of the Cherokee Nation, Lieutenant." David decided nothing could be lost by impressing the young officer at the start. "Mr. Lachlan Murrell and I have been detailed to accompany Chief John Ross and Mrs. Ross home to Indian Territory."

"And who are you, pray?"

"Captain David Preston, Medical Department, United States Army."

"A Yankee?" The young officer fairly spat the hated word.

"A Virginian." David's tone was equally sharp. "I plan to resign my commission and join the Virginia troops after Chief Ross and his party are safely aboard ship at Parkersburg."

Lieutenant Kramer still regarded him suspiciously, obviously not accepting the explanation.

"You and Lieutenant Murrell are my prisoners, sir." He dropped his hand to the pistol holstered at his side. "I must warn you not to resist on pain of death."

"Watch it, David," Lachlan warned in an undertone. "These Dutchmen are dumb enough to shoot first and ask questions afterward."

"If you have anything to say, sir, it can be said at headquarters," said the lieutenant sharply. "Meanwhile you will both please come with me."

Leaving Araminta on the packet boat with the Rosses, David and Lachlan were marched under guard up the street to where the headquarters of the Virginia troops had been set up in a brick building that had formerly been a store. A stocky major, whose face seemed faintly familiar to David, sat behind a table, poring over a stack of papers for which he obviously had no relish. When Lieutenant Kramer came to attention with a click of spurred boots, the major looked up and regarded the trio rather sourly.

"What is it this time, Kramer?"

"I beg to report the capture of two Yankees, Major Stannard—officers in the Union Army." With his saber Kramer prodded David and Lachlan forward.

"Did you capture them singlehandedly?" Major Stannard winked at the two prisoners.

"They were on a canal boat and made no resistance, sir. Both of them claim to be conducting an Indian chief to Indian Territory."

"Indians? Here? I've heard everything."

"Chief John Ross, they say, Major. But I believe it's only an attempt to deceive us into letting them go, so they can tell the Yankees how many men we have at Harpers Ferry."

"Let me get this business straight first about the Indians, Lieutenant," said Major Stannard. "Did you see this chief?"

"Well, no." Kramer fidgeted in embarrassment. "But there was a Princess Sequoy—"

"A princess? At Harpers Ferry? And an Indian at that?"

"That's what they claimed. But she doesn't look like an Indian, sir."

"My sister and I are Cherokees, Major, and my uncle, John Ross, is the principal chief of the Cherokee Nation," Lachlan explained. "Captain David Preston has been taking care of him—for heart disease—and was detailed by President Lincoln to accompany us as far as Parkersburg, where we plan to take a boat for the Arkansas River and our home."

"And you are both officers in the Federal Army?"

"I resigned several days ago and will take a commission in the Cherokee Brigade."

"I expect to resign my commission, too, once we reach the Ohio," David added. "President Lincoln and Secretary Cameron asked me to accompany Chief Ross at least that far because he has been ill in Washington."

Lieutenant Kramer's eyes had almost bugged from their sockets at this mention of important names in the Union Government.

"Surely you're not going to believe such a cock-and-bull story as that, Major," he protested.

"It so happens, Lieutenant, that John Ross *is* chief of the Cherokee Nation," said Stannard. "And I read about a week ago in a Richmond paper that he has been in Washington for some time, trying to maintain neutrality for his people."

"But surely you're not going to accept—"

"I'm not going to accept anything without advice from higher authority. We'll just take a ride up to Maryland Heights, where they're building blockhouses for the pickets who will be on guard there, and let Colonel Jackson—"

"Is Tom Fool here?" Lachlan exclaimed.

"I knew I'd seen you somewhere before, Mr. Murrell; they don't often have Indian cadets at VMI," said Stannard, while Lieutenant Kramer looked stunned.

"Class of fifty-seven," said Lachlan. "Captain Preston here was cadet First Captain that year."

"I practiced law in Lexington before the war," said Stannard. "You're one of the Botetourt County Prestons, aren't you, Captain?"

"Yes, sir," said David. "After I graduated from the Institute, I studied medicine in Philadelphia, then spent a year and a half in Europe, most of it with the Garibaldi forces in Italy."

"If you join up, you'll probably be the only doctor in the whole Confederacy with previous experience in military medicine."

"When did Major—Colonel Jackson get here?" Lachlan asked.

"Right after Fort Sumter fell he took the senior VMI cadets to Richmond to help drill the militia," Stannard explained. "Did a good job, too, but he was champing for action, so Governor Letcher made him a colonel and sent him to Harpers Ferry soon after the militia got here. If you could see the colonel in action here, you'd never believe the cadets gave him the nickname of Tom Fool back in Lexington."

Stannard got to his feet and took his hat from a peg on the wall. "I'll take these gentlemen up to the Heights to see Colonel Jackson, Lieutenant," he said.

"Mr. Ross has been ill," said David. "Do you think accommodations for the night can be arranged?"

"I'm sure Lieutenant Kramer here will be happy to rout some of the younger officers out of the inn so the chief and the ladies will have a place to sleep. Eh, Lieutenant?"

Krammer snapped to attention. "Yes, sir."

"You can also entertain the princess, Kramer. It isn't very often that we have a visit from royalty."

Outside Stannard ordered the troopers who had accompanied Lieutenant Kramer to dismount and preempted their horses for David and Lachlan. Crossing the long bridge that carried wagons and other traffic over the Potomac, they took a steep winding road leading up to the crest of the Maryland hills above the river.

From the vantage point of the higher elevations as they climbed, the striking beauty of the deep Y-shaped cleft where the Shenandoah River joined the Potomac lay before them. High above the Potomac, whose current tumbling over rocks in midstream was in sharp contrast to the quiet waters of the Chesapeake and Ohio Canal beside it, the elevation called Maryland Heights dominated the scene from the north. To the south lay the Loudoun Heights of Virginia, while behind the town to the west were what was known as Bolivar Heights.

"I don't need to remind you two that Jackson taught artillery at VMI," said Stannard. "The way he figures it, with a few six pounder smooth-bore cannon up on Maryland Heights, he can wreck the B&O and block the canal any time he wants to do it."

"He could, too," said Lachlan. "Those guns have a range of close to two thousand yards."

"This whole area is pretty spectacular," Stannard added as they continued to climb, "but the colonel doesn't figure it would be easy to defend."

Lachlan nodded. "With those small bores on the crest up here he could smash everything around, including the munitions factories and the railroad bridge before he pulled out, in case General McClellan attacked in force from the West."

"You can bet Old Jack thought of that," said Stannard.

"But fortunately, no such army is likely to be thrown against us any time soon, with Washington almost isolated and caught between Virginia on the south and Baltimore to the north. That's why Harpers Ferry was Jackson's second choice."

"Are you saying Professor Jackson planned this attack, Major?" David asked.

"The day Fort Sumter surrendered, Jackson sent a letter from Lexington to Governor Letcher in Richmond, detailing how militia companies from Virginia and North Carolina could be mustered and put on the cars of the Virginia Central and the Orange and Alexandria railroads."

"Including the Rockbridge Artillery?" Lachlan asked.

"Yes. Why?"

"I just wondered."

"Lieutenant Murrell is being modest, Major Stannard," said David. "He described just such a plan for capturing Washington to me several weeks ago."

"Don't forget that I studied military strategy under Professor Jackson," said Lachlan. "Go on, please, Major."

"Governor Letcher could see the possibilities of the plan and let us get it started. Major John Harman, Captain John D. Imboden and I put the railway part of the scheme into action, and it worked like a charm, too, except that by the time we got to Manassas Junction, the powers that be had gotten cold feet. Somebody said it was because Jefferson Davis was afraid the scheme might backfire and, when he gets to Richmond next week to set up the Confederate Government there, Abraham Lincoln might meet him at the city gate. So we were detoured over the Manassas Gap line to Strasburg, made a short hike to the Winchester and Potomac, entrained again and got here to find the Federals had cleared out."

"Did you say Harpers Ferry was Jackson's second choice?" David asked.

"A close second. With the B&O bridges here across the river and the C&O Canal in our hands, an army—if we got one together in time—can move right into the heart of Pennsylvania. Before the Yankees ever knew what was happening, we could threaten, maybe even take, Philadelphia and Baltimore, leaving Washington out on a limb. Then the pussyfooters in the U. S. Congress would have to agree to let us alone in the South and the war would be over."

"If this was Jackson's plan, why wasn't he put in charge of it from the first?"

"I guess the politicians in Richmond were afraid he'd decide to take Washington, so they sent him to Richmond instead. But how he persuaded Governor Letcher to give him the command here at Harpers Ferry, I don't know."

"He can be very forceful," said Lachlan.

"I'll never forget the day Jackson arrived," Stannard said. "It was late afternoon and the generals and colonels in these militia units—we had almost as many of them as there were privates—were at evening parade."

"You mean retreat, don't you?" Lachlan asked.

"Four o'clock parade. Late every afternoon they'd ride up and down the streets on their fine horses, showing off their uniforms for the ladies to admire before the evening drinking started. Everybody was having a good time until Jackson turned up at headquarters one day riding the damnedest-looking horse you ever saw—must have unhitched him from a plow somewhere along the way. Nobody would believe he was in command until he produced Governor Letcher's order demoting every militia officer above the rank of captain to that level and leaving him the ranking officer. Then you could have heard 'em scream all the way to Winchester. Jackson didn't give an inch, though, and by nightfall we still had a few colonels left but no generals. I was a captain then, but I'd done some legal business for Jackson back home in Lexington, so he promoted me to major the next day and made me temporarily the brigade adjutant. He's been busy turning this rabble into an army ever since."

They had almost reached the crest of Maryland Heights now and could hear the sound of axes and the shouts of men, as trees were felled to construct blockhouses overlooking the gorge where the two rivers met. When they topped the final rise, a strange sight met their eyes.

Perhaps fifty men in every sort of uniform from the

trim gray of the 5th Virginia to the butternut—so called because the cloth was homespun and dyed with walnut husks—breeches and shirts of volunteers not yet provided with uniforms, were working like beavers. Some were cutting logs, others were carrying them into position, while still others notched the ends to form the corners of the blockhouses and lifted them into position.

"I never saw soldiers work like that before," said Lachlan. "How do you do it, Major?"

"They're bound to keep up with the colonel."

"Where is he?"

"Over there where the logs are being lifted into place."

"Good God!" Lachlan exclaimed. "He's wearing the same uniform he had on the last time I saw him nearly five years ago at the Institute."

"You're probably right—and he'll most likely be wearing the same one when the war is over."

Seeing Colonel Thomas Jonathan Jackson for the first time in almost five years, David Preston was inclined to agree. Jackson was of medium height, but he always held himself so erect, even while sitting—and some said while sleeping, too—that he seemed to tower over others at least as tall or taller than he. Always spare in build, he was even thinner now than David remembered him, and his uniform of a dingy bluish gray color was covered with fragments of pine bark and needles, as well as spots of resin.

The day was warm and most of the soldiers had stripped to the waist, but Jackson still wore his uniform tunic. Plus, David was sure, the same VMI cadet cap that had long since become a legend at the Institute. Set far forward on his head, the cap brim shaded his eyes, so they couldn't be seen until he raised his head and glanced their way. Then, however, David was struck once again, as he had been on many an earlier occasion, by the warmth and steadfastness of the spirit that shone from them. A spirit that, whatever Tom Fool's or Old Jack's—he was known familiarly to the cadets by both names—peculiarities—and these too were legion—stirred an immediate feeling of loyalty and trust in the beholder. The forehead was a bit higher from a receding hairline, it was true, than when David had last seen Jackson, the beard and hair already shot with gray. But, otherwise, he couldn't see that his old professor and commandant of the VMI Cadet had changed in any way.

Jackson and about a dozen men were lifting a log in place to form part of a blockhouse wall. Although Major Stannard drew rein not twenty feet from where the straining crew were at work, Jackson didn't acknowledge their presence with so much as a nod, until the already notched log had been fitted smoothly into position. Something about the situation seemed odd to David but he couldn't put a finger on what it was until he suddenly realized that, although the log-raising crew was composed of both burly, sweating Irishmen and stolid Germans, such as made up so much of the valley population, not a single curse word was to be heard, this a tribute to Jackson's well-known aversion to language that broke the biblical prohibition against taking the Lord's name in vain.

The three men dismounted and were waiting patiently when Jackson finally stepped away from the blockhouse wall and came toward them. All three snapped to attention, although Lachlan Murrell was not in uniform, and Jackson returned the salute punctiliously, military courtesy having been one of the several subjects he had taught at the Institute.

"I regret to see you wearing the uniform of the enemy, Captain Preston," he said. "And that you are not in uniform, Mr. Murrell."

Major Stannard smiled as the two younger men gaped in amazement at being recognized after almost five years. "There gentlemen just came in by canal boat from Washington, Colonel. They were captured as spies by Lieutenant Kramer."

"I admire diligence in an officer, Major. Please, see that the lieutenant is commended for it." A fleeting smile brightened momentarily the rather harsh pallor in Jackson's cheeks. "Besides, Lieutenant Kramer's mother and Mrs. Jackson are close friends. May I ask what brings you gentlemen to Harpers Ferry?"

"I have resigned my commission in the Regular Army,

63

sir," said Lachlan, "and am accompanying my uncle, Chief John Ross, back to Indian Territory."

"Was Mr. Ross successful in arranging the sale of your Neutral Land to the U. S. Government?

Lachlan Murrell stared at him in amazement and momentarily lacked words. "No, he was not, sir," he said at last, "but he still hopes to keep the Nation neutral in the war."

"A laudable action on his part, I am sure. But hardly a position he will be able to maintain without considerable difficulty."

"I do not share his determination, sir," said Lachlan. "But he's a kinsman and I have agreed to see him safely back home before I join the forces of the Confederacy."

"And you, Dr. Preston?"

"I was fortunate enough to diagnose and treat Mr. Ross successfully through an illness while he was in Washington, Colonel. President Lincoln and Secretary Cameron asked me to accompany him as far as the Ohio, but after that I plan to offer my services to Virginia—with your forces, if you will have me."

Jackson's smile was warm. "You were a very capable cadet officer and I doubt not that you will prove to be as good a physician. When you return, report to Dr. Hunter McGuire. He is coming from Richmond to serve as Medical Director of our forces here, and I am sure will find a place for you."

"Thank you, sir. May I assume that you will not interfere with Chief Ross's passage westward tomorrow?"

"Major Stannard will see that your departure is expedited, but first I would like to pay my respects to a man who has led his people for over thirty years. If you will permit me, I shall ride down with you."

David had forgotten what a strange figure Thomas J. Jackson made on a horse, but was not surprised to see that he still sat bolt upright in the saddle, leaning forward a little. And since the horse he rode wasn't tall—in fact David couldn't remember ever seeing Jackson on a tall horse—his legs hung farther down than was usual with a cavalry mount, making it appear that he could step down at any moment and let the horse walk out from beneath him, as was no doubt the case.

The footing was sometimes rather precarious as they descended the winding road, but Jackson did not in any way adapt himself to the position of his mount. And when they reached the level of the landing before the inn and went clattering across the plank floor, his lean frame was still rigidly formal in the same ungainly posture that had characterized it on the descent.

At the boat, Jackson accepted the salute of young Kramer, who had been engaged in eager conversation with Araminta until the appearance of his commanding officer. In descending from his mount, Jackson had been as awkward as ever but, when David introduced Araminta to him, the older man's bow somehow seemed more sincere and even more courtly than would have been the elaborate posture of a dandy.

"You are lovely, my dear," he said. "I wish my wife were here to meet you."

"I'm sure I would love knowing her, Colonel."

"Will you take me to your uncle so I can pay my respects?" Jackson offered her his arm in an old-fashioned sort of courtesy that somehow seemed entirely proper, even here on a boat landing beside the muddy waters of the C&O Canal.

As Jackson and Araminta entered the cabin of the canal boat, the whistle of another locomotive pulling a long line of hopper cars on the main line of the B&O across the river split the warm afternoon.

"That's the second trainload of coal I've seen pass here for the U. S. Navy, Major Stannard," said Lachlan. "How much longer are you going to let them through?"

Stannard shrugged. "You'll have to ask the CO; he doesn't even tell his plans to the staff officers until he's ready to put them into effect."

"That must make your job a lot harder."

"At least it keeps anybody from revealing them to the enemy. Besides, you don't complain to Colonel Jackson, you just do what he tells you to do because you know he's already worked the whole thing out in his mind down to the last detail. Besides, you know damn well that, if you don't want to do things his way, he'll get somebody else who will."

"He treated the cadets the same way," said David. "But nobody ever said he wasn't fair."

"And nobody can say it up here either. You always know just where you stand with him, and that's worth a lot."

A young officer rode across the bridge from Harpers Ferry. Curly-haired, handsome, and sitting his saddle like a young god, he looked to be about twenty years old.

"Kramer said he had taken two Yankee prisoners, Major," said the young cavalier. "But I don't believe him."

"He was both right and wrong," said Stannard. "Captain David Preston and Lieutenant Lachlan Murrell, Lieutenant Alexander Pendleton."

"Gentlemen," said Pendleton, rigidly correct.

"Sandie Pendleton is Colonel Jackson's aide-de-camp," Stannard explained.

"Is your father still in command of the Rockbridge Artillery?" David asked.

Pendleton gave him a startled look, then his face cleared. "You were both at the Institute, weren't you? I remember Lieutenant Murrell because—"

"Because nobody expected a thieving redskin to be marching in the VMI cadet regiment?" Lachlan asked with a grin.

"I didn't mean that, sir. But you're not exactly somebody a person easily forgets."

Lachlan bowed. "I accept the compliment, Lieutenant. And I could hardly forget hearing the rector of Grace Episcopal Church in Lexington preach on Sunday in his priestly vestments, and the next day watching him aim a cannon with the Rockbridge Artillery on maneuvers. Please convey my respects to him, as both minister and gunner, Lieutenant."

"I see that you're a doctor, Captain Preston," said Pendleton. "But in the wrong army—for a Virginian."

"I plan to exchange this Union blue for Confederate gray as soon as I complete a mission I'm engaged upon."

"I hope you choose the Twenty-seventh Virginia, Dr.

Preston," said Stannard. "A lot of our men are from Botetourt and Rockbridge counties, so you probably already have friends, maybe even relatives, among us."

Jackson's appearance with Araminta on the afterdeck of the boat put a stop to any further conversations. Young Pendleton's eyes bugged out at the sight of her, much as Kramer's had done about an hour before.

"Thank you for bringing fresh beauty to such mundane surroundings, my dear princess," said Jackson courteously. "And take good care of your uncle, his welfare is very important to a large number of people on both sides."

"I shall do what I can, Colonel." She inclined her head in a slight bow—but not before David saw the mischief in her eyes at the sight of young Pendleton's confusion. "Good day, gentlemen," she added demurely.

"I have given Chief Ross a note authorizing safe passage for your party from all Virginia troops, Captain Preston," said Jackson as he stepped down to the platform. "We will look forward to having you with us on your return from the Ohio."

"Lieutenant Kramer found two rooms for us at the inn that serves the canal traffic," Araminta told David and Lachlan as Jackson's party mounted and rode away. "But I'm afraid you two will have to sleep on deck."

"For which I'm sure we can thank Kramer," said Lachlan.

"Your Colonel Jackson is a lovely man, David. I can't imagine why anybody would want to make fun of him." Araminta opened the door to the cabin. "We can take Uncle John to the inn as soon as he's ready. I'll call you."

"Some people never seem to fit anywhere, until one day they find their own particular niche." Lachlan was looking acros the river, where Jackson and his aides were riding off the long bridge across the Potomac, the commander at Harpers Ferry still an ungainly, yet somehow impressive, figure in dingy gray. "I think it has taken a war to show Jackson his particular slot."

"If he's allowed to fit there," David agreed. "But I can't help wondering how the theories of military strategy

67

he taught us at the Institute will work out under battle conditions."

"Most of them have been tested in the field, one in particular around three thousand years ago," said Lachlan. "Remember Old Jack's lecture about how Joshua won the battle at Ai?"

"Vaguely. I've been through a medical course since them."

"Jackson was always reading the Bible, so it was natural that he would take some of his strategy from Holy Writ."

David shook his head slowly in mock disbelief. "I still can't believe I'm hearing a gambler and a professional ladies' man discussing the Bible."

"The Cherokee schools were founded by missionaries —Moravians for the most part—so we all had to study the Bible. What interested me most were the battles and some of the classic maneuvers of military strategy used by Joshua, particularly when he attacked the city of Ai."

"I'm afraid I don't remember it."

"That's because you were raised an Episcopalian and were taught only the Book of Common Prayer. Remember how Joshua captured Jericho by marching around it seven times and making such a racket with the trumpets that the walls fell down?"

David nodded. "That I do remember."

"Well, that's the same way Washington would have fallen, if the Richmond authorities had possessed guts enough to let the Rockbridge Artillery start a few cannon thundering across the Potomac from Arlington Heights. Joshua made a night march across the mountains and hid the main body of his army behind a ridge near Ai. Then at dawn he took a small force right up to the walls and, when the King of Ai went outside to mop them up, the rest of the Israelite Army descended from ambush to destroy the soldiers of Ai and sack the city."

"Ingenious, but not very honorable."

"When was there anything honorable about setting out to kill your fellowman just because his political convictions don't agree with yours?" Lachlan snorted. "If we Indians had kept on fighting like Indians, we'd still have our lands instead of being pushed farther west, first by the Georgians and Andrew Jackson, and now by Jayhawkers from Missouri and Kansas, who can't stand to see us prosper by the kind of hard work they refuse to do."

"And you figure the Confederacy will protect you?"

"Protect hell! All we want are guns and a license to exterminate our enemies in the name of war; that's why Stand Watie is organizing the Cherokee Brigade."

II

David was sitting in a canvas chair on the afterdeck of the packet boat the next morning, as it glided westward along the quiet waterway at the end of the long towrope. The river had turned northward after they left Harpers Ferry, leaving the railroad to the south, and the canal followed the Potomac. Squirrels chattered in the trees shading the waterway from the morning sun and the "rat-tat-tat" of a redheaded woodpecker sounded a rhythmic obbligato.

It was hard to believe they had left a scene of war behind. Or that because of the canal, the railroad and particularly the fact that this area was a major gateway into the rich farmlands of Pennsylvania to the north, it was certain that before much longer the region would know the thunder of artillery, the crack of rifles and the screams of the wounded and the dying.

He looked up with a smile when Araminta came out of the cabin, where John Ross was discussing tribal affairs with Lachlan, and took the chair beside him.

"Did Colonel Jackson really have a plan to take Washington, the way Lachlan says he did?" she asked.

"Major Stannard says so, but that's the first I'd heard of it."

"And he had to settle for Harpers Ferry instead?"

"According to Stannard, Jackson wasn't happy with the choice. It's still a good jumping off place for attacking Maryland and Pennsylvania."

"I like Colonel Jackson. And I don't think it's fair of you and Lachlan to call him peculiar."

"Eccentric might be a better word."

"What kind of eccentricities?"

"For one thing, Jackson has always carried punctuality to the extreme. Every Friday afternoon at VMI he made a report to the superintendent on the drill during that week. It was scheduled to be given at five o'clock but, if he happened to arrive early, he'd march up and down outside in front of the superintendent's office in rain, snow or hail, until exactly five o'clock."

"At least you always knew where he stood."

"No doubt about that. Another time, Colonel Smith called Jackson in late one afternoon for something and he took a seat in the waiting room while the superintendent was on some sort of an errand. As it happened, the colonel forgot Jackson was waiting and left by another door when he'd finished for the day. When he came to the office the next morning, there was Old Jack, still sitting in the waiting room."

"But that was cruel."

"Colonel Smith didn't mean to be but don't ever think Jackson couldn't be tough himself. If he gave you a dressing down for some infraction of military rules, you felt it for days afterward."

"Suppose you deserved it?"

"We usually did—except once, come to think of it. One day in class I gave Jackson an answer to a problem different from the one in the textbook and he took me apart before the class. I was pretty angry, but I knew better than to argue, so I just took it. Sometime after midnight, when I was asleep in the dormitory, he came over in near zero weather and had me awakened by the officer of the day, so he could tell me I was right and apologize."

"Uncle John is that way; the two of them hit it off right away."

"I thought they would."

"Are you really coming back to join the Virginia troops here? I heard Colonel Jackson invite you."

"Probably. One of the regiments at Harpers Ferry—

the Twenty-seventh Virginia—is made up of men from my part of the valley. Are you going to miss me?"

"Of course I'll miss you." Her eyes were suddenly luminous with unshed tears. "Do you think Indians don't have feelings?"

"I know what my feelings are for you—I love you."

"Then why didn't you tell me?"

"Women are supposed to know such things intuitively."

"We do, but we still like to be told." Her eyes suddenly glowed with the look of mischief he'd grown to know and love. "Is this an offer of marriage or are you trying to seduce me?"

"You know better than that."

She pretended affront. "Then I'm not attractive enough for you to consider that seducing me might be nice."

"It would be heaven, but stop talking about it. When will you marry me?"

"As soon as the war's over—"

"It may last a long time, and you know what they say about absence making the heart grow fonder—of someone else."

"Is that the way you think of me?" she demanded tartly. "If it is—"

"I was just making fun—"

"If I could wait for you the past five years without even knowing where you were or what you were doing, a year or two more shouldn't make any diff—"

"Wait a minute, what's this about five years?"

"Why do men have to be so dumb?" she exclaimed. "I've been in love with you since I was sixteen."

"When Lachlan and I graduated from VMI?"

"Of course. When I saw you prancing at the head of the cadet regiment, wearing that plumed cap and carrying the sword in your hand, I said, 'I'm going to marry him.'" Her eyes suddenly took fire. "And then you didn't even remember me when you saw me again in Washington."

"You're not quite the same, you know; then you were just a pretty girl, but now you're a princess. A man would need a lot of self-confidence to dare to love royalty."

"Now you're making fun of me again."

"Not this time," he assured her. "It's just that I don't want you still thinking of me as that ramrod-straight cadet officer with a plume in his cap. I'm only a very ordinary doctor who'll probably spend his life bringing babies into the world and easing the pain of the very old until they can escape from it."

"Some of those babies will be ours," Araminta said softly. "One day we'll both see one of them marching at the head of the cadet regiment, but I still won't be as proud of him as I was of you that June day five years ago."

David bent to kiss her and she responded with the passionate fervor of the lovely young woman she had become. At the thought of losing her, when he'd really just found her, David's arms tightened about her—until she pushed him away.

"That should keep you faithful," she said breathlessly.

"I'm going to put my brand on you here and now," he told her and, slipping off his VMI class ring, tried finger after finger, but all of hers were too small. Finally, she unsnapped the locket chain around her neck and, sliding the ring on the chain, dropped it into the neck of her dress.

"I'll wear it close to my heart, darling, so I'll know you'll always be safe," she promised. "Until the war is over and we're together—for good."

Watching the *Belle of Vicksburg* churning away from the landing at Parkersburg several mornings later, its wide stern paddle wheel stirring up the muddy bottom of the Ohio, David didn't leave the dock until the river steamer was only a dark spot on the horizon to the southward. And even then, he fancied he could still see the lovely slender figure of the girl he loved standing on the upper deck, waving a white handkerchief in farewell long after neither of them could distinguish the other.

"Pray God this war is over soon," he said, and wasn't conscious that he spoke aloud.

Hailing a hackney he was driven to the Baltimore & Ohio Railroad station to take the afternoon train back to Harpers Ferry and whatever lay beyond. But the sight of long trains of coal cars waiting in the yards to begin the journey east to their destination in bunkers of United States Navy ships already tightening the noose about the Confederacy by sea, through the blockade President Lincoln had ordered of all southern ports, left him with the grim portent that it would be a long time before he saw Araminta again.

III

From near Martinsburg, Virginia—some twenty-odd miles southwest of Hagerstown, Maryland—to Point-of-Rocks on the bank of the Potomac not far from Harpers Ferry, the B&O Railroad was double-tracked for slightly less than twenty miles. When David Preston reached Martinsburg late on the day after seeing John Ross and his party safely aboard the *Belle of Vicksburg* for a journey by water to Tahlequah in Indian Territory, he was surprised to see long lines of coal cars clogging the tracks.

"What's going on?" he asked the conductor, when he found the train official walking impatiently up and down beside the train, muttering imprecations into his beard.

"That damned Confederate colonel in command at Harpers Ferry complained to the railroad management that the trains through there at night interfere with his sleep. So now we can only run cars through by day."

"Can he stop the railroad legally?"

"Legally or not, he stopped it," the conductor snorted. "Did you ever hear of a wilder reason?"

"What if the railroad refuses?"

The conductor shrugged. "Do you have any idea what would happen to the B&O if Jackson blew up the bridge at Harpers Ferry, Doctor? The whole damned railroad would be shut down."

"How long do you suppose he can keep this up?"

"Your guess is as good as mine, but you can bet the telegraph wires are humming. The authorities at Richmond know blowing up the B&O could drive Maryland into the arms of the Union—a lot of people in the state own stock in this line."

"And probably as many in the Confederacy itself. Do you think Maryland will go with the rest of the South?"

"There's sentiment in favor of it. Except in manufacturing cities, most of the people are plantation folk and a lot of 'em own slaves. But the question right now is, does Colonel Tom Jackson in Harpers Ferry know it?"

"My guess would be that he's fully informed on both sides of the question."

"Sounds like you know him?"

"Jackson taught me at VMI."

"Then you ought to have some idea of what he may be up to."

"Professor Jackson always kept things pretty much to himself even then. And now that war has begun—"

"He's got plenty of reason to be even more close-mouthed." The conductor nodded. "Lord knows everything that happens on either side is known by the other almost before it begins. Anyway my job is running trains and this one, plus a lot of others, ain't going to run again 'til morning. I'm on my way to find a seat in one of the cars where I can get some sleep and my advice to you, Doctor, would be to do the same."

Promptly at 6 A.M. the train started moving out on one of the double tracks toward Harpers Ferry. And a long line of empties, headed for the coal mines of Western Virginia, soon appeared, rattling westward upon the adjoining tracks. It was a bright day in mid-May, the sun warm and pleasant, when David stepped down from the coach to the station platform at Harpers Ferry. As he moved up the street toward the headquarters of the Virginia Militia, he could see atop Maryland Heights across the river, the frowning black mouths of the cannon in position to control the rail line, the canal and the town. Major Joseph Stannard was working at the same table where David had last seen him and stood up with a smile of welcome and a handshake.

"I hope you're ready to join us, Dr. Preston."

"If you want me."

"Want you? My God, man! Half the roster has the trots already, and Dr. Hunter McGuire hasn't arrived yet from Richmond."

Stannard fumbled around in a pile of papers until he found a printed form.

"Pull up a chair and fill this in," he said. "Colonel Jackson is at Point-of-Rocks across the river, checking over the tracks there, but he'll be back in an hour or so and can approve your commission and swear you in."

"How's his health?" David asked as he started to fill out the inevitable form, without which no army would be able to move even an inch.

"Like always—something new wrong with him every day. I came into his room upstairs the other night to get a requisition approved and found him sitting straight up in a chair like a ramrod. Said he was giving his internal organs a chance to resume their normal relationships after riding most of the day."

David smiled. "His medical peculiarities were well known at the Institute—and his predilection for mineral springs."

"He hasn't lost that either. Last night he was talking about riding over to Bath for a couple of days to take the waters. Not that I blame him; the last time I was at the hotel over there, the food was out of this world."

A famous watering place, of which more than a dozen could be found along the ridges of the Allegheny range forming the west side of the Shenandoah Valley. Bath had been popular even in the time of George Washington and its hotel on the hill above the famous warm springs was world-famous as a spa.

"I would have been here yesterday, but we were held up at Martinsburg," said David. "The conductor said Colonel Jackson had issued an order not letting trains go through at night."

"I heard the railroad officials in Baltimore are fit to be tied. B&O stockholders in the Confederate Congress at Richmond are raising hell, too, judging from the telegrams we're getting, so the colonel's got to do something soon."

"Any idea what it will be?"

"You might as well ask the Sphinx, but the way I figure it, we're sort of 'twixt 'n 'tween. Richmond doesn't want any more coal trains going through than can be helped, but they're afraid to tear up the tracks of the B&O main line."

"Why?"

"For one thing, a lot of bankers and fat cats in the South own B&O stock. They don't want to make the Maryland stockholders mad either, with Maryland still uncertain about secession."

"But their legislature just voted to stay in the Union."

"The majority of the Maryland legislature come from the cities, but out in the country there's a lot of sentiment for the South. Besides, President John Garrett of the B&O is known to have strong southern leanings."

"Sounds like Jackson's got a tiger by the tail."

"A big one," Stannard agreed. "And every time he sees one of those coal trains go through, knowing the coal is going right into Federal warships, his gut gets tied in a knot. It's working though: by limiting the trains to a few hours in the daytime, Jackson's already more than cut the rail traffic in half."

"Think he can make it stick?"

"My guess would be not for long."

Jackson came into the headquarters just then and David came to attention, along with Major Stannard and the enlisted clerks already in the room.

"At ease, gentlemen," said the former professor. "Welcome back, Captain Preston, I hope you're still of a mind to join us."

"I just finished filling out an application for a commission in the Medical Department, sir."

"Good!" Jackson gave the form a quick glance, then scrawled his initials at the bottom. "Will you join us at mess?"

David was hungry and the food was much better than Major Stannard had intimated. Jackson, however, ate sparingly, chewing upon a piece of beef while he studied a small map. When David looked his way, he saw that the map was actually a chart of the B&O rail line.

"I presume you traveled by train from Parkersburg, Dr. Preston," said Jackson.

"Yes, sir."

"Did you notice anything strange?"

"Only a terrible glut of coal cars at Martinsburg, sir. The railroad people there weren't very happy about it either."

"We don't intend for them to be, Doctor. I only wish I could stop all the traffic on the road to Baltimore and Washington."

"We could use a lot of that B&O rolling stock on the Winchester and Potomac line, sir, as well as around Richmond." The speaker was Major John Harmon, Quartermaster and Transportation Officer.

"What did you have in mind, Major?" Jackson appeared to place a lot of confidence in the redheaded officer's judgment.

"It's less than twenty miles from Winchester to Strasburg, and a connection with the Manassas Gap Railroad there," said Harman. "Once that's bridged, we'd have a direct rail connection with the Orange and Alexandria at Manassas Junction and over it to Richmond on the Virginia Central."

"That's a capital idea, Major." The dark eyes of Jackson's aide Sandie Pendleton were gleaming. "It would be a dagger pointed directly at Washington."

"Or Richmond," said Jackson rather sharply, and the young aide flushed. "I hardly think my old classmates on the Union side will overlook that advantage, my boy."

"But, sir—"

Jackson reached out to put his hand on the young officer's sleeve and, seeing the warm light in the older officer's eyes, David realized the paternal feeling Jackson seemed to have for the dashing young Pendleton.

"That's the kind of thinking we need, Lieutenant," said Jackson, and turned to David Preston.

"I believe you had some experience with actual warfare in Italy, Captain Preston," he continued. "What is your opinion of our delaying tactics where the railroad is concerned?"

"You are delaying traffic all right, sir; I could see that when I was held up at Martinsburg overnight. But how long can you keep it up?"

"You've put your finger on the crux of the problem,"

Jackson admitted. "Pressure is building on both sides for the embargo on nighttime traffic to be lifted."

"But no orders from Richmond to that effect?"

"Not yet." Jackson's voice had lost its warm note and its tone was now one David remembered quite well from his student days at VMI, when someone had been guilty of even a minor infraction of the rules. Remembering how Jackson had reacted to even implied indecision, he waited for the ax to fall, not without a certain amount of trepidation, then decided to voice the thought that had suddenly popped into his mind.

"It looks like you'll have to act before those orders can arrive," he added.

"What do you suggest, Captain?" Jackson's tone was definitely frosty.

"Have you ever hunted partridges on horseback, sir?"

A sudden startled look in the older man's eyes told David that Jackson had immediately sensed his meaning. But when he spoke, his tone was casual.

"I have been on a few of such hunts, Doctor, but some of these gentlemen have not. Why don't you describe how it's done?"

"Partridges aren't afraid of animals, and on horseback you can often drive a covey as you'd herd cattle, without flushing them." David addressed the group of officers— Jackson's immediate staff—around the table. "For this sort of hunting we use a loosely woven net in the form of a tube closed off at one end and much larger at the other. The mouth of the tube is held open by means of stakes driven into the ground and wide wings of webbing about eight to ten inches high extend out from the open ends of the tube like flanks, also supported by pegs."

"Just like a fish trap?" The speaker was Captain John D. Imboden, commander of an irregular group of cavalry recruited in the area around Staunton farther up the Shenandoah Valley.

"Very much the same thing, Captain. In our part of southwestern Virginia, riders often herd a large covey right into the trap. Then when all are in, one man rides to the mouth and closes it."

"I'll be damned!" Imboden exploded.

"You certainly will, John, if you don't give up profanity," said Jackson mildly, then changed the subject abruptly.

"How much longer will it take to finish moving what machinery is usable from the munition factories to Winchester, Major Stannard?" he asked.

"Only a few days, Colonel. Some of it was damaged by fire when the Union forces withdrew as we were approaching, so it's hardly worth saving."

"I'll give you two days to finish it up." Jackson rose to his feet and the others followed. Characteristically, he hadn't asked Stannard whether or not he could accomplish his task in the allotted time. And Stannard, wise already in Jackson's ways, didn't argue to point.

"The Twenty-seventh Virginia Regiment and the Rockbridge Artillery are without a surgeon, Doctor," Jackson said as they were leaving the mess hall, a former restaurant run by a Pennsylvania Dutchman with southern leanings. "You will be posted to them and I'm counting on you to do something about the dysentery that afflicts so many soldiers."

"I shall do my best, sir."

"What the hell was all that business about hunting partridges?" Joe Stannard asked as they were waiting on the street outside the restaurant for Jackson to move on to his quarters above brigade headquarters. "For a second there I thought the old man was going to give you your walking papers, Doctor. Then all at once he was tickled pink."

David told him and the other man whistled softly. "Maybe you're in the wrong business, my friend. You should be a line officer."

"I saw the same trick used by Garibaldi on the Italian peninsula, so it isn't original with me. Besides, I have no stomach for fighting."

"Jackson certainly does," said Stannard. "I was talking to an old Regular Army sergeant last year—he served with Old Jack in Mexico before the colonel became professor of artillery at the Institute. According to the sergeant, Jackson had several citations for bravery, as did Robert E. Lee, and the two were the finest officers in the whole army fighting against Mexico. Well, I'd better get back to the damned paperwork. You'll find the Twenty-seventh in camp at the foot of Loudoun Heights. Jim Updike is CO, but he's not here right now. Captain Everett Sanders is executive officer and a good man but if the Twenty-seventh is still running true to form, you'll find most of them behind bushes with their pants around their ankles. Sanders reported a fourth of his command laid out with the trots this morning."

IV

Headquarters for the Twenty-seventh Virginia Regiment was a shack at the foot of the southernmost of the three hills looking down upon the Potomac, the Shenandoah, the railroad and the canal at Harpers Ferry. The water supply, David noted as he walked up the path leading to the shack, came from a spring near the bottom of the hill.

The men were bivouacked under bush arbors or makeshift tents, cooking their rations of bacon, beans and hardtack in groups of from four to eight over small fires. But as far as David was able to determine, while walking through the bivouac area to the headquarters, no provision at all had been made for sanitation. The men, as Major Stannard had said, relieved themselves at will, behind bushes or out in the open, especially when what seemed to be the universal military affliction caught them suddenly.

Captain Everett Sanders, Executive Officer of the regiment, was a plump man in his forties with a potbelly and a harried expression. He looked up when David came into the log hut that served as headquarters and acknowledged his salute with a limp wave of his right hand.

"You're damned lucky to be a civilian, sir, if you ask me," said Sanders. "But either way, nothing in army regulations says you have to salute me."

"I'm Dr. David Preston. Colonel Jackson just commissioned me a captain in the Virginia Militia, so I haven't had time to get a uniform."

"Take my advice and don't while you can still get out of it, Doctor. From that salute, you must have had some military experience."

"A half year in Italy, and another six months on detached duty out of the Surgeon General's Office in Washington."

"And you jumped the traces for a commission in the Virginia Militia?" Sanders' face showed his astonishment.

"Take my advice and jump right back; we've got the devil himself for a commanding officer. Would you believe he's had me drilling these mountaineers six hours a day, when most of 'em don't know a right dress from an about-face?"

David couldn't help smiling at the lugubrious account.

"It's no laughing matter, Doctor," said Sanders indignantly. "How does Jackson expect me to drill men when the best they can do is run for a bush holding a gun in one hand and trying to unbuckle their belts with the other?"

"I know Jackson's methods, Captain. I was in the cadet regiment at VMI for three years."

"I lasted six months at the Institute, got busted for smuggling a girl into the dormitory one night," said Sanders with some pride.

David laughed. "At least you had the satisfaction of doing something that was never done at the Institute before, I suspect—or since."

Sanders brightened. "They do remember me at Lexington all right. What can I do for you, Doctor?"

"I'm your new medical officer."

"Good! I hope you can treat dysentery?"

"I've had some experience; it's a pretty common complaint in most armies. How well are you fixed for medical supplies?"

"We're lucky there. When the Federals pulled out of Harpers Ferry, they were so busy putting the torch to the munitions factories, they forgot to burn an army warehouse with a lot of medicines in it."

"How about opium pills?"

"The doctor we had for a few days—he was a contract surgeon—used a lot of 'em. If a man's bowels were open when he held sick call, he gave him an opium pill. And if they were closed he gave him a lump of blue mass. The supply of opium pills is still holding out and practically nobody needs the blue mass these days. But what I can't understand is why everybody has developed the trots since we came here, unless it's like the doctor said, from some mineral in the water."

"It's probably the water, but not the minerals. How many sinks have you dug, by the way?"

"Old Jack ordered at least one for every regiment, so we dug it like he said. But the men don't like using 'em."

It was an old story to David. Army surgeons were constantly fighting the reluctance of soldiers in camp—often abetted by their officers—to follow even elementary rules of sanitation. Sinks—also called latrines—were dug under protest and used with reluctance, except where discipline was extremely strict.

"The doctor we had signed on as a contract surgeon," said Sanders. "But an order came through from Richmond yesterday that all contract surgeons had to be commissioned and he didn't want any part of that, so he lit out for home. Come to think about it, I reckon you're the only real army doctor among the Virginia Militia, Dr. Preston. What do you want to do first?"

"Do you have time to make a sanitary inspection with me?"

"Right now. The dysentery that's putting your men out of action isn't going to stop until we've located the cause —and remove it."

"You're the doctor," said Sanders with a shrug. "Let's go."

David didn't have to look far before he knew the answer to the health of the 27th. The bivouac area had been selected with a good deal of intelligence, it occupied the lower slopes of Loudoun Heights with plenty of shade from large oaks and many pines. Near the bottom of the slope, a fairly large spring burst from the rocks, with a small branch flowing perhaps fifty feet to join a larger stream. The latter appeared to come from higher up on Loudoun Heights, since he could see several small rocky falls areas where the stream poured over the rocks before circling around the bottom of the heights to form a fairly large pool. In it some men were bathing and washing clothes.

The sink that was supposed to provide sanitary facilities for the entire camp had been dug in an area of soft earth, perhaps a dozen yards up the slope above the spring behind a screen of bushes.

"Army regulations say sanitary sinks should be dug away from the main part of the camp and properly screened from observation," said Sanders proudly. "You can see that we followed the rules."

"Except for one thing."

"What's that?"

"I'd rather show you, Captain. Do you suppose you have any bluing among your regimental supplies—you know, the stuff women use in washing white clothes to keep them from getting yellow?"

"Maybe not, but the quartermaster tent is right over there and I'll send a soldier downtown to one of the stores and get some."

Before the inspection was half over, a soldier appeared with the bluing David had requested.

Captain Everett Sanders watched with lifted eyebrows as he sifted the contents of the box into the regimental sink. "I'll be damned if I can see how that will prove anything, but like I said before, you're the doctor."

"Let's finish the inspection. It will probably take a little while before the changes I'm looking for appear."

The rest of the sanitary inspection took up another hour, but before they had gone far David had a good idea of the campground and also the cause of the characteristic stench that hung over it. The sink itself, though dug strictly according to regulations, appeared to be used only by those nearest to it. The pens where chickens, pigs and an occasional cow or steer were butchered and the meat distributed to the men who acted as cooks over a hundred small fires, had been placed near the spring to make carrying water easier. And around the butchering area, the stench from the unburied offal was quite obnoxious.

All in all, David decided, the 27th Virginia was probably no better, or no worse, than most organizations he would expect to find, at least in the early months of mobilization by any army. It was almost five o'clock when they came back by the regimental sink and he saw that the bluing had disappeared.

"I'm thirsty," he told Sanders. "Why don't we stop by the spring for a drink?"

"I could use one myself," said Sanders. "But I had something a little stronger in mind."

"I'll join you, but I'd like to examine the regimental water supply first."

The spring was fairly large, almost ten feet across, and the point where the water boiled from the low rocky overhang just above it was easily detectable. Moving around to examine the boil, David motioned for Sanders to come up beside him. Easily distinguishable at the source of the main boil, before it spread out and became dissipated, was a bluish tint to the water pouring into the spring itself.

Sanders knelt and studied the water for a long moment. When he raised his head, his face was white and he stepped away from the spring to retch a few times before he was able to speak.

"Do you mean to tell me we've been drinking *that*, Doctor?"

"You saw the evidence."

"I'll be a son-of-a-bitch. What do we do now?"

"Place the sink and the spring off limits and designate an official water source from one of those pools above the spring and sink, where the main stream of the brook it connects with comes down the slope—unless more troops are quartered at a higher level."

"We're the only unit on Loudoun Heights."

"Good. I think you'll see improvement in your sick roster before forty-eight hours."

84

"I'll believe anything you say, after what you've just showed me with that bluing," said Sanders. "In fact, if you tell me carbolic acid is good for my system, I'll go right out and get some to mix with my bourbon."

V

By sick call the second morning after David's assignment as surgeon for the 27th Virginia Regiment, the number of men on the off duty roster because of illness had declined dramatically. He had seen nothing more of Colonel Jackson, who was reported to be keeping largely to himself and spending much of the time deep in thought. That seemed justified, too, for the course of events affecting the troops under Jackson's command at Harpers Ferry rapidly seemed to be approaching a crisis.

With the railroad operating daily between the Ohio River and Baltimore, even on the restricted schedule Jackson had imposed, both the newspapers it brought and the telegraph lines beside the tracks kept the commander at Harper's Ferry and his staff well informed on the course of events throughout much of the country. And these, too, were rapidly taking a turn indicating an early development of a major conflict between the North and the South.

On May 10, the Confederate Government in Montgomery, Alabama, appointed former Colonel Robert E. Lee—summarily elevated from that rank in the United States Army to the position of major general in the Army of the Confederate States of America—to command all CSA forces in Virginia. That same day saw trouble suddenly erupt in St. Louis, one of the major Mississippi port cities, as well as the key to the future events in the border state of Missouri. There, elements of the pro-Union and largely German population led by Captain Nathaniel Lyon of the United States Army, seized Camp Jackson, where the secession-favoring militia were gathering, capturing them almost without a shot. In the subsequent march through St. Louis, however, pro-southern elements

85

among the population erupted into a riot. Some twenty-eight or twenty-nine people were killed or wounded, at least one of them a child, stirring the fever of the population almost to the boiling point and presaging a real crisis.

The following day, May 11, a large pro-Union meeting occurred at Wheeling, the extreme western point of Virginia and one of the western termini of the B&O Railroad. And two days later, on May 13, Brigadier General Benjamin F. Butler, the Union commander who had earlier occupied the relay station where the main line of the B&O joined the Washington branch, marched into Baltimore and occupied that city.

The turn of these events placed Colonel Jackson in the decidedly awkward position of sitting, in command of some four or five thousand green Virginia Militia, astride the vital railroad at Harpers Ferry, with both ends of it in Union hands and his orders from Richmond still forbidding him to damage the tracks. Jackson's Negro servant, a mulatto named Jim, reported, too, that for the past two nights the commander had prayed even more than his usual custom, which, according to Jim, who had served his master a long time, meant that some important decision was in the offing.

Major Joe Stannard, Adjutant of the 1st Brigade making up the forces at Harpers Ferry, already dubbed unofficially the Army of the Shenandoah, had visited the campground of the 27th and seen the startling results David had achieved here in a few days with a strict sanitary regimen and a change in diet to include green vegetables, fruit and fresh meat. David himself had no inkling that his actions had come to the attention of higher authority, however, until noon that day, when a runner from headquarters handed him a copy of an official order which, like the few issued by Jackson, was terse and to the point:

Army of the Shenandoah
1st Brigade, 12 May 1861

Special Order No. 6
Captain David Preston, Surgeon, 27th Regiment, 1st Brigade,

is hereby appointed, in addition to his other duties, Sanitary Officer for the Brigade.

By order of
Thomas J. Jackson, Colonel,
Commanding

Joseph A. Stannard, Major
27th Virginia, Acting
Adjutant, 1st Brigade

By now, David was enough to accustomed to the peculiarities of Jackson not to be surprised at the order, but he had no illusions that the other regimental commanders would be as receptive to his orders as Captain Everett Sanders had been. As soon as the morning sick call for the 27th was finished, he crossed the creek and made his way to Harpers Ferry and the storefront headquarters of the 1st Brigade.

Major Stannard looked up from his inevitable litter of papers. "Congratulations!" he said.

"On more work?"

"The Scripture says, *'Whom the Lord loveth he chasteneth.'* For the colonel to put more work on you is a mark of favor: it shows he's quite pleased with what you've done already."

"And if I do this well, I suppose he'll give me more responsibility?"

"That's the way a successful CO works—and I don't have to tell you the inevitable results."

"Less and less people doing more and more work; I've been in the Army long enough to know that's the way it always winds up."

"Cheer up, you're about to have a chance to get some exercise," said Stannard. "How are you on horseback?"

"I grew up in fox-hunting territory."

"Draw a mount then, and a good saddle, plus a blanket and a waterproof; I'm going to let you join me for an evening canter after supper. But take enough rations for breakfast, in case we don't get back before tomorrow."

"Just where are we going?"

"Like I said—an evening canter."

"Shall I bring a medical kit?"

"Could be a good idea to have one in your saddlebags, in case somebody falls off a horse—or gets shot with his own pistol. Join me west of the town on the canal towpath just after sundown."

David had been waiting half an hour that evening when the sound of hoofbeats from the direction of Harpers Ferry told him Stannard and a detail of mounted troops were approaching. The moon was well above the trees and the towpath beside the canal was worn smooth by the unshod hooves of the patient mules pulling the barges along the almost two-hundred-mile course of the long waterway from Georgetown to Cumberland, Maryland. Joe Stannard raised his hand in greeting without halting the long file of mounted men and David fell in beside him. He couldn't tell exactly how many were in the detail for it stretched back along the towpath farther than he could see in the moonlight.

"Was it your idea to have me along on this expedition?" he asked.

"It was Old Jack's but I'm happy to have good company along. We're under sealed orders, by the way, which is like him, too. The Old Man takes seriously the biblical injunction not to let your left hand know what your right hand is doing."

"And you still don't know where we're going?"

"My instructions are to follow the towpath to a place called Hedgesville, then head southwest for a hamlet called Bedington and bivouac there for the rest of the night. At sunup tomorrow morning, I'm to open the special instructions Colonel Jackson gave me and proceed accordingly."

"Any idea what we'll be doing?"

"Quail hunting—what else? After all, it was *your* idea."

VI

It was barely daybreak when David was awakened by Lieutenant Sharpless, second-in-command of the detail.

They had bivouacked just before midnight in a wooded area away from any road, where they were not likely to be seen. And since the kindling of fires had been forbidden by Major Stannard, as far as they had been able to tell no one in the countryside realized they were there.

The breakfast of hardtack and fried bacon they had brought with them was eaten hurriedly in the misty dawn, washed down with water from their canteens, or with a shot of whiskey by those who'd had the forethought to bring it. David hadn't slept particularly well. It had been almost a year since he'd been in the field with troops and he wasn't accustomed to using a mattress of pine needles hurriedly piled up in the darkness, beneath the weatherproof and blanket in which he had wrapped himself.

"Major Stannard is ready to open the sealed orders, Doctor," said the apple-cheeked lieutenant. "He thought you might like to see them."

Chewing on the last of the hardtack, which took on more the consistency of stone the longer it was kept, David joined Stannard and Sharpless at the head of the column, shivering a little in the cool dampness of the early morning fog. Silently, Stannard tore open the sealed envelope, glanced at it and passed it on to David.

"Close the trap and keep it closed" were the seven words written in Jackson's spidery scrawl.

"Looks like you called the shots, David," said Stannard. "Now all we have to do is plug the open end of the trap."

"What do you suppose Jackson is doing?"

"Watching John Imboden close the other end of the double-track section at Point-of-Rocks and explaining to a mad bunch of B&O trainmen that the railroad won't be running for quite a while. Order the men to mount up, Lieutenant, we've got work to do."

Martinsburg offered no resistance to the descent of more than three hundred armed men upon it and, once the inhibitants were sure the invaders were Virginia troops, they were welcomed warmly. Not so, however, the crews of the long lines of empty cars stretching back along one side of the double section of railroad tracks.

The trains had been parked on one of the two tracks the afternoon before, in obedience to Jackson's orders that they were to run only during the middle part of the day. Now the rifles of a squad facing the lead locomotive waiting to pull the empties westward threatened any who might try to move the trains, while the rest of Stannard's detail were dragging logs from a sawmill at the edge of town into position on both of the double tracks to form a barrier. With the same thing undoubtedly happening near Harpers Ferry at practically the same minute, none of the coal in the heavily loaded cars making up the eastward-bound trains waiting there since yesterday on Jackson's orders was likely to get anywhere near the bunkers of the waiting warships, nor the empties back to the mines.

"Just the way you described it, David," said Stannard when the operation was complete, "like nudging partridges into a trap."

"Only this one is twins."

"Get 'em going and coming is Old Jack's way. What say we ride back to Harpers Ferry and tell him about this end of it?"

By the time David and Stannard reached Harpers Ferry, leaving Lieutenant Sharpless in charge of the detail at Martinsburg to see that the barriers were not removed from the B&O tracks, telegraph lines had been hot for hours with the news of Jackson's clever strategy. Perhaps a dozen times along the way, the riders paused on elevations overlooking the rail bed, and each time the picture was much the same—long double lines of railroad cars, none of them moving in either direction.

"This has to be the slickest trick ever pulled by a military commander," said Stannard as they rode into Harpers Ferry. "I wonder how many he's caught."

It didn't take long to learn the answer to that question. The bag for the Confederacy had been fifty-six locomotives with over three hundred cars, many of them already being shifted to the considerably lighter tracks of the Winchester and Potomac for the run southward. The first of four smaller locomotives was also being moved onto the single-track lines for transfer to Winchester but, unfortunately, the lighter rails of the W&P could not accommodate the massive engines that pulled the long trains of coal cars from the mines to the west. Jackson was therefore faced with a quandary in deciding just what to do with part of the loot.

As sanitary inspector for the self-styled Army of the Shenandoah, David now ate at the staff officers' mess and there was still much jubilation around the tables over the feat of the morning before in capturing, without firing a shot, a considerable part of the rolling stock of the B&O Railroad. The meal over, the staff enjoyed excellent coffee which the Federal troops in evacuating Harpers Ferry had put to the torch, but in their haste only managing to roast the beans to just the right degree before the Virginia troops arrived and extinguished the flames.

Jackson had been unusually merry that evening, a side only his closest intimates usually saw—until a clerk from the brigade headquarters down the street brought him a telegram. Watching him read, David saw his expression change to one of anger before he rose abruptly to his feet.

"As you were, gentlemen," said Jackson, rather hoarsely when the others started to rise, again betraying the sudden tension the message had obviously generated in the usually reserved soldier. "If you will excuse me, I shall retire to my quarters."

Passing the telegram to Joe Stannard, Jackson turned and marched from the room. When he was gone, Stannard looked at the yellow sheet, an expression of utter unbelief on his face.

"What's that all about, Joe?" John Imboden asked. "A death in the family?"

"You might call it that. Listen to this: 'Department of the Army, Confederate States of America, Richmond, Virginia, 15 May 1861. To Colonel T. J. Jackson, Commanding, Harpers Ferry, Maryland. Effective this date Brigadier General Joseph E. Johnston assigned command all troops your district. Signed Judah P. Benjamin, Secretary of War, Confederate States of America.' "

"The son-of-a-bitch," said Imboden. "How did that come about?"

"I guess too many bankers in Richmond, Atlanta and Birmingham own the bonds of the B&O Railroad," said Stannard.

"I own some of 'em myself," Major John Harman exploded. "But I damn sure don't approve letting all those cars haul coal for ships trying to strangle the South with a blockade. Who the hell is fighting this war anyway—us or the politicians?"

"Either way there's no use crying over spilt milk," said Imboden. "The question is, do we wire Jefferson Davis to keep his hands off Virginia troops and Jackson?"

"That won't do any good," said Stannard.

"Then how about appealing to Governor Letcher?"

"He probably couldn't do anything about this either; Jefferson Davis is too close to the people who'll have to dig up the money to fight this war. Besides, we don't want to get Old Jake into disfavor with the high brass this early in the game."

"Do you suppose Johnston will give the rolling stock back to the B&O?" John Harman asked.

"We won't know until he gets here, and that will be several days at least," said Joe Stannard. "Meanwhile half of it's already in Winchester—or on the way."

John Harman suddenly put down his coffee cup and got to his feet. "Then it's up to us to see that all of it we can move is in Winchester by the time Johnston does get here."

"And the rest in the river," Imboden added with a chuckle. "The colonel ordered those cars sent to Winchester as fast as we could move 'em and he certainly can't object if we move 'em a hell of a lot quicker than anybody figured we could. Let's go, gentlemen."

The impromptu strategy meeting broke up and David Preston went to his quarters in the bivouac area of the 27th. He was sound asleep shortly before midnight when the officer of the day shook him awake.

"Colonel Jackson is ill, Doctor," he said. "Jim just came to ask that you attend him."

David dressed quickly, checked his medical bag and walked the short distance to Jackson's quarters. He found the commanding officer lying on the bed, obviously in considerable distress. His face was pale and his forehead beaded with sweat.

"I'm afraid my dyspepsia is plaguing me again, Doctor," he said. "I've been in agony with it much of the time for the past twenty years."

"Let's make sure that's what it is first," said David, and started making a complete physical examination.

First, he counted Jackson's pulse, which was not increased, then took his temperature and found it to be normal. The heart, too, was not enlarged and the sounds from both it and the lungs in the stethoscope were within normal limits. Jackson didn't appear to have an ounce of fat on him, which didn't surprise David because the almost emaciated commanding officer seemed to eat next to nothing, often making a meal from a crust of bread and a little buttermilk.

The abdomen was another matter, however. It was distended and tender to the touch, although Jackson tried to keep from exhibiting any reaction to the pain of the examination.

"You appear to be having an acute attack of indigestion for some cause, Colonel," said David. "I'm going to give you something to ease the pain and also try to relieve some of the distension."

Jackson was an obedient patient, swallowing without protest a liberal dose of laudanum and the foaming mixture from one blue and one white Seidlitz powder. Meanwhile, Jim had put water to heat on the stove in the kitchen downstairs. When he brought the pan up the steps David poured a liberal amount of turpentine into it.

"Turpentine stupes often help acute dyspepsia," he explained, while wringing out a towel he had immersed in the pungent steaming solution and applying it directly to the skin of Jackson's abdomen.

"Most of the doctors who treated me in the past prescribed elixir of pepsin, but I never felt that it did much good."

"Are you taking anything regularly for your symptoms, sir?"

Jackson relieved himself of a large belch before he

answered. "Nothing seems to help so much as hydrotherapy. If there were time I would ride over to Bath for a few days; the mineral waters there always seem to help me."

David exchanged the now cool towel for a hot one and Jackson emitted a second hearty belch, with obvious relief.

"I must say, you are surely a miracle worker, Dr. Preston," he admitted. "No one has ever been able to obtain relief for me so quickly during one of these painful spells."

"I'm glad I could help, sir."

"I believe you said you spent some time in Europe after obtaining your medical degree. Might I ask why?"

"Doctors in several European capitals, particularly Vienna, have made far greater progress in medicine than we have here in the United States, sir. I wanted to study their methods, particularly a way of preventing sepsis after childbirth and surgical operations discovered by a Hungarian surgeon named Semmelweis."

"What a blessing it would be if sepsis could be prevented from developing in battle wounds." Jackson seemed to have forgotten his bellyache. "During the war in Mexico, I saw some terrible sights. And I don't doubt that we shall experience even worse before this conflict is over."

"The same thing happened in Italy during the Garibaldi campaigns. Sepsis is not a pretty thing, whether in wounds or in the childbed."

"This doctor in Hungary you spoke of. What does he do?"

"Semmelweis teaches doctors, attendants—and especially students—to wash their hands in chloride of lime, and also soak their instruments, before delivering babies or performing operations."

"Only that? It hardly seems credible."

"The answer was so simple the doctors in Vienna couldn't believe it either, sir. Actually they drove Semmelweis back to Budapest in disgrace."

"The simplest answer usually is the best, like that partridge-hunting idea of yours. But it would be very unfortunate indeed if, after we closed the trap so neatly, someone else should open it again and let the quarry escape."

Jackson was silent while David wrung out the towels he had been using and hung them on the side of a marble-top washstand in the corner of the room, where a pitcher of water stood in a large bowl with a soap dish beside it. By the time he finished, the patient appeared to be asleep, so David started to tiptoe by the bed, planning to pick up his medicine kit and leave without disturbing the other man, now that the pain had been relieved. Jackson spoke, however, before he could leave the room, his voice softer now that he was free from pain.

"What was the season when you were in Europe, Doctor?"

"I left before Christmas, sir, but I was there much of a year."

"The summer after my first wife died, I spent some time abroad." Jackson's voice had a wistful and distant note. "Long enough to fall in love with the castellated towers along the Rhine and the vineyards of Provence."

"It's a lovely area."

"I found it hard to choose between that part of the world and the mountains of Switzerland, or even the canals of Venice. It seemed I could never get my fill of paintings and sculptures, the happy people and the gaiety and freedom from rules and customs."

"The Italians certainly know how to live, I like the peasants of Italy best of all."

"The Bay of Naples, the clouds of smoke hiding the rim of Vesuvius in the early morning." Jackson seemed to be reliving a consciousness of beauty which, David thought, only someone who knew him intimately could have dreamed he possessed, this spare, seemingly rigid man whose mind appeared always to be concerned with the business at hand. "I think I shall never see anything more beautiful, not even the lovely valley of the Shenandoah and the Cumberland."

"I grew up in a beautiful cove near the James, sir— but I quite agree."

"Did you visit the battlefield of Waterloo while in Europe, Doctor?"

"I'm afraid military matters didn't interest me then, Colonel. I was more concerned with widening the sphere of my own medical knowledge."

"A man should always welcome the opportunity to broaden his horizons: without that his view of life is liable to become narrow and rigid." The spare figure on the bed stirred. "I believe I can sleep now, Doctor. Thank you for coming to my aid."

"It was both a duty and a pleasure, sir."

Jim went downstairs with David and out into the street. "You done more for the ginral tonight than anybody else has ever been able to do, Doctor," said Jackson's valet. "When he gets like this, he's pretty miserable—"

"Then it happens often?"

"The ginral has what he calls dyspepsia a lot. And it's always worse when something's upset him, like tonight."

"I notice that you always call him 'general,' Jim."

"And why not, beggin' your pardon, sir? Ain't he runnin' er army?"

"I can't argue with that, Jim."

"You just wait'n see, Cap'n. Them politicians in Richmond ain't always goin to push the ginral aside. 'Fo' this war's over, he's goin' to be runnin' this show—him and Marse Robert E. Lee."

David didn't return to his quarters immediately, although it was after midnight. Instead, he walked down the street until he could see the canal beside the river and the tracks of the Winchester and Potomac Railroad where they joined the B&O. Lanterns were moving along the tracks and the "chug-chug" of a locomotive came to his ears as it snaked a long train of loaded coal cars southward toward Winchester and the Shenandoah Valley of Virginia.

John Harman and Joe Stannard had lost not time, he saw; the task of moving the rich prize of machinery, coal, locomotives and other equipment so badly needed by the Confederacy was already well under way. Across the river, in the channel of the Chesapeake and Ohio Canal, David could see the vague dark shapes of a line of barges. From one of them a girl's laugh floated through the night to reach his ears.

Somewhere on the Arkansas River a girl would be sleeping, her dark hair spread out upon the pillow and her lovely cream-tinted shoulders bared by the thin night-gown she would wear in the warmth of a summer night. And remembering how alive and eager her lips had been beneath his own, when he'd kissed her good-by in a secluded nook on the wharf of Parkersburg less than a week ago, he could only wonder when the fortunes of this war that had barely yet begun would bring them together again—and pray the interval would not be long.

VII

If Jackson saw anything wrong in the way Major John Harman was driving every man he managed to have assigned to him to speed up the transfer of coal cars and railroad equipment from Harpers Ferry to Winchester, he made no comment. Just as he said nothing—Major Joe Stannard reported to the other officers—about his coming replacement by General Joseph E. Johnston, a former veteran officer in the United States Army and now a high-ranking member of the military hierarchy heading the new Confederate Army, recently enlarged to include all the former state militia units. In the rest of the South, however, events were moving with sometimes stunning rapidity.

Thursday, May 16, saw Tennessee admitted as a secessionist state by the Confederate Congress at Montgomery, Alabama. And on the same day Commander John Rodgers of the United States Navy was ordered to set up a Federal naval force on the rivers of the West under the overall command of General John Charles Frémont.

Particularly interesting to David Preston was the news in the Washington papers that reached Harpers Ferry daily of a proclamation from Indian Territory by Chief John Ross, announcing that the Cherokee Nation would remain neutral in the conflict developing between the North and the South. The action had been expected and the announcement proved not only that Ross and his party had arrived home safely, David's main concern, but that the secessionist movement in the Indian Nation had not been strong enough to unseat him as its principal chief.

Just how Ross's announcement would affect Araminta and Lachlan Murrell, David could only surmise, but he was certain that she would remain with her uncle because of her loyalty and her affection for him. And with Lachlan, the determining factor would always be what appeared to be best for Lachlan's own fortune, within the bounds of a strict code of honor and his loyalty to John Ross and the Cherokee Nation.

Virginians in general had hailed Thomas J. Jackson's daring in the B&O affair, a Richmond newspaper even conferring the accolade of its approval in a glowing front-page account:

The commanding officer at Harpers Ferry is worthy of the name he bears for, "Old Hickory" himself was not a more determined iron-nerved man than he. Born in Virginia, educated at West Point, trained in the Mexican War, occupied since at the Military Institute of the Old Dominion, his whole life has been a preparation for this struggle.

A brother officer says of him, "He does not know fear!" Above all, he is a devoted Christian, and the strongest man becomes stronger when his heart is pure and his hands are clean.

Ironically, this encomium appeared the very day a small group of high-ranking officers, uniformed in fresh Confederate gray that put to shame Jackson's always rusty garments, rode into Harpers Ferry by way of the Charles Town Road. Jackson himself met the new officers in front of the store that served as headquarters for the troops. David was there, too, having just finished lecturing on sanitary practices to the officers of the Virginia Volunteers, who had been pouring into the camp in droves since Jackson's fame had burst upon the secessionist scene.

The short slender man with the gray beard and stars

of a brigadier general on his collar was quite evidently the new commander, Joseph E. Johnston. Then in his middle fifties, Johnston was a native Virginian, having been a veteran officer in the United States Army serving as Quartermaster General of the United States forces, until the Monday after the Baltimore Riot. Stationed in Washington, Johnston had resigned that very day and journeyed southward, where he had promptly been commissioned a Confederate brigadier general by the newly formed Confederate States of America and shortly dispatched to Harpers Ferry to hold in check a wild colonel named Thomas Jonathan Jackson.

Jackson saluted his new commanding officer rigidly, then shook hands with Johnston, whom he already knew from the days of his military youth in the Mexican War. Nothing in his rigidly correct manner revealed his knowledge of the real reason for his being supplanted by an older man, whose service in recent years had involved neither tactics nor strategy, subjects Jackson had taught at the second most prestigious military college in the country until less than a month ago.

Two colonels accompanied Johnston and to them Jackson was considerably more cordial. They were Colonel Barnard E. Bee and Colonel Richard Ewell, both about Jackson's age and old comrades of war in the Mexican adventure. Last was a young officer with dark hair and mustache and the hawk-lean face of a Viginia aristocrat, wearing the insignia of the Medical Department of the Confederate Army on his brand-new gray uniform.

Educated at his own city of Winchester, Virginia, and the University of Pennsylvania, Dr. Hunter McGuire was a friend of long standing whom Jackson had encouraged to join him at Harpers Ferry, while he was in Richmond earlier with the seniors of the cadet regiment from VMI acting as drillmasters for the troops being trained there.

As the new arrivals were being ushered into headquarters by Joe Stannard, Major John Harman came up the street and stopped beside David Preston. Harman's face and hands were smudged with coal dust and streaked with sweat.

"I'd like to see one of 'em shoveling coal into a locomotive firebox like I've been doing," he said. "How did Old Jack take it?"

"Like a gentleman and a soldier. What did you expect?"

"Just that—but I've known him long enough to realize his gut must be tied in a knot at the thought of a quartermaster commanding an important sector like this."

"He calls it dyspepsia, and I guess that's as good a name as any. I spent a couple of hours around midnight last night, untying the knots."

"Now you can understand what he was to live with and why it sometimes affects his disposition."

"That's something I should have realized back at the Institute, when he came over one night after I had gone to sleep to apologize for bawling me out because of a math problem he thought I'd missed. Behind that front, there's a warm and very vital human being."

"Hell!" said Harman. "I could have told you that a long time ago. But I still can't really blame him for being tied up at the prospect of having a quartermaster in command."

"You're a quartermaster."

"But I ain't no strategist, and don't want to be." Harman shifted his cud to the other cheek and spat tobacco juice into the dusty street. "It's hard enough for me to keep the men that fight in food and ammunition and the trains running, without having to figure when to attack and when to retreat—not that Old Jack will ever do much of the latter."

"Bringing General Johnston in here after Jackson pulled off the biggest coup of the war still isn't right."

Harman shrugged. "How long were you in the Regular Army, David?"

"A little over six months, long enough to see how easily simple things can get fouled up."

"Don't let anybody ever tell you the Confederate Army isn't goin' to make as many dumb mistakes as the U. S. Army—or railroad people either," said the quartermaster. "Imagine building that Winchester and Potomac line with rails so light a standard B&O locomotive would smash 'em like matchsticks. That left me nothing much more powerful than a switch engine to move nearly three hundred hopper cars, most of 'em full of coal, a good twenty-five miles."

"But you did it just the same."

"With sweat and blood. By the way, who's the new medical officer with Johnston?"

"Dr. Hunter McGuire; his family and Jackson's are friends. McGuire will be medical director."

"What's wrong with the one we've got already—namely you? From where I stand, it looks like Old Jack ain't the only one whose nose is being twisted this afternoon."

David laughed. "Don't waste your time feeling sorry for me, friend. The medical director of a unit the size of the First Brigade spends most of his time doing paperwork, hearing complaints from regimental surgeons and trying to locate hospitals where they won't be captured by the enemy. I'll be perfectly happy in the field with the troops, something I've had some experience with."

"I guess you're right at that. But if Old Jack ever gets command of anything bigger'n a brigade, I hope he lets me stay where I am. Well, I'd better get a bath and rustle up some kind of clean uniform. From the looks of the new arrivals, we're in for an era of spit and polish." Then Harman brightened. "But maybe you and I'll get a break and be allowed to mess with the enlisted men."

"No such luck," said David. "Here comes Joe Stannard and five will get you ten he's going to tell us to dress formal for dinner. If I'm lucky the seamstress I hired the first day I got here has finished my uniform."

Major Stannard was grinning when he came up to where Harman and David Preston were standing.

"I've been demoted," he announced. "From adjutant to executive officer of the Twenty-seventh Virginia—"

"What about Everett Sanders?" David asked.

"Ev's got a brother-in-law in the legislature, so he's being kicked upstairs to Deputy Brigade Quartermaster. Like your crusty friend here, somebody found out he used to run a country store."

"I'm damned glad to have him," said Harman. "The one I've got don't know salt horse from kippered herring."

"The first thing I want to see," said Stannard with

101

mock severity, "is the regimental surgeon in regulation uniform instead of khaki pants and a butternut shirt."

"What about Old Jack?" Harman asked.

"Jackson is now in command of the First Brigade and Sandie Pendleton will be back from Lexington in a day or two to become his aide. Captain Hunter McGuire is to be medical director for the First Brigade."

"Who's the new adjutant?"

"Colonel Barnard Bee—and he's not very happy about it."

The change in military protocol brought about by the presence of the new commanding general was quite evident that same evening at dinner. Jackson sat on Johnston's right but barely nibbled at his food, a savory preparation of baked freshly caught fish and sweet potatoes, topped off with a rich pudding. The rest of the 1st Brigade staff sat together at the lower end of the table, and, although brandy was served to top off the meal, there was none of the jocularity that had formerly characterized the officers' mess after Jackson had retired to his quarters upstairs, now pre-empted by the new commanding general. Jim had already moved Jackson's sparse equipment that afternoon to a small house at the foot of Loudoun Heights, where most of the 1st Brigade of Valley troops were already in bivouac.

The evening meal finished, Johnston and his immediate staff remained behind to discuss strategy with Jackson, while David and Captain Everett Sanders moved out into the street with a number of others.

"What do you think of the new commanding general?" Sanders asked as they were standing outside the officers' mess.

"It's too early to make a judgment."

"Did Johnston impress you as the kind of leader that would have dared to pull off the stunt of closing the B&O at both ends?"

"Probably not. But then, if you'd asked me three years ago at VMI whether Jackson would ever do it, I would have said no."

"I guess you never know just how a man is going to turn out in any situation, until you see him in it." Sanders looked at his watch. "A new tavern opened at the foot of the hill yesterday. Want to go down and have a few drinks before bedtime?"

"Not tonight, thank you," said David. "I thought I'd write a letter or two."

"See you later then." Sanders moved on down the street and David had started toward his own quarters across the stream when the door of the mess hall opened and Dr. Hunter McGuire came out.

"Captain Preston?" McGuire called. "Is that you?"

"Yes, sir."

McGuire came across the street to shake hands. "You can drop that 'sir' business; I've an idea we're about the same age."

"Twenty-six."

"So am I. I glanced over the personnel record this afternoon and saw that you studied medicine in Philadelphia."

"At Jefferson—and abroad."

"I took my basic studies at a small medical school in Winchester, then after at the University of Pennsylvania. I was in a militia unit but Colonel Jackson and my father are friends so, when he was leaving Richmond to come to Harpers Ferry, he asked me to join him here as medical director. I assure you that neither Colonel Jackson nor I knew you were coming here then."

"I didn't know it myself, until I came through Harpers Ferry about two weeks ago on the way to Parkersburg with a patient and met Jackson again," David admitted. "He invited me to join the First Brigade, but he told me you were coming from Richmond to be medical director."

"The minute I read your personnel record, I could see that you're better qualified for a military post than I."

David laughed. "I was in the U. S. Army long enough to discover staff work isn't my cup of tea. Besides, I hope to test some ideas I have about battlefield surgery under conditions of actual warfare, and I can certainly do that far better as a regimental surgeon."

"But you will advise me, won't you? I'm terribly ignorant about anything connected with military medicine."

"It isn't all that complicated, the most important thing is being a capable doctor."

"I noticed that you're sanitary inspector of the First Brigade," said McGuire. "That's one field were I certainly have no competence."

"I'll gladly continue in that assignment if you wish."

"Fine, I think we're going to work together well, Dr. Preston."

"You can start by calling me David, my friends do."

Writing to Araminta that night, by the light of an oil lamp in his quarters, David said:

Nobody knows exactly what effect the change of command is going to have here but in my own work, I don't think I will be any worse off. Dr. Hunter McGuire, the new Medical Director, seems to be a fine young gentleman and an excellent doctor into the bargain. He is very handsome, too, and I think the girls of Harpers Ferry will take to him. Even as busy as we are trying to make soldiers out of farmhands, there's still time for considerable social activity among the people of the town and the military population. Parties are given almost every night and, if you were here, I knew you would turn the heads of all the young officers. But since I have a job to do and I'd certainly be jealous, perhaps it's just as well that you aren't.

I was pleased to note in the Washington papers, which come here by way of the canal every day, that Chief Ross has succeeded so far in keeping the Cherokee Nation at least officially neutral. But since the papers also say Arkansas has joined the Confederacy and sent representatives to the Confederate Congress at Montgomery, I wonder if there isn't going to be more difficuly for the Nation.

Knowing how much you love mountains, I'm sure you would enjoy being here now. The dogwoods, of course, have lost their blooms, but the mountain laurel is in full blossom on the lower levels of the Appalachian range all around us. Farmers in the bottom lands along the riverbanks are cutting hay and the cattle are sleek and fat from pasturing on the bluegrass that seems to grow better here in the Shenandoah Valley of Virginia than anywhere else. We're beginning to get fresh vegetables, too, and the men need them. Left alone,

I'm afraid they would eat nothing but fried pork and boiled beans, with some beef whenever the quartermaster can buy it. And, of course, chickens when they can steal them.

In this part of Virginia, the sentiment is strongly pro-secession, but in the western counties, the feelings of the people are much more strongly attached to the Union. All of which, of course, makes Harpers Ferry a very important place as far as the future of the war is concerned. I know Col. Jackson feels very strongly that it must be held, particularly as a jumping off place for an invasion of Pennsylvania, if the CSA authorities in Richmond would find him the men and turn him loose. And I heard him say that General Lee in Richmond feels the same way. Just how Gen. Johnston will feel about it, I don't know. I imagine he will be guided by the sentiments of both Lee and Jackson, who, I know, is very highly regarded by Lee for his knowledge of military strategy and tactics.

The other evening I was returning from attending Col. Jackson in one of his attacks of dyspepsia which are often quite painful. A string of canal boats was tied up for the night and when I heard a girl's laugh from one of them, I was sharply reminded of you and the joy in living you possess to such a marked degree. No one knows when this tragic division in our country will come to an end, but it will be many months, I am sure, before the differences between the Union and the Confederacy are resolved. I can only pray that the time will be short until we are together for always.

Please give my regards to Chief Ross and to your Aunt Mary. Also to Lachlan though I suppose by now he has ridden off to war. Somehow it seems appropriate to think about him in an organization with a fancy name like the Cherokee Brigade.

As always, my darling, my love goes with you in everything you do.

David

VIII

The first general order published by General Joseph E. Johnston's headquarters command for the now official

Army of the Shenandoah assigned T. J. Jackson to command the 1st Brigade, made up mainly of units from the Valley area. Major R. L. Bradley, a minister and biblical scholar from Lexington who had known Jackson very well, appeared the same day and was assigned as an aide. Young Alexander Pendleton, known to the brigade staff as Sandie, returned to be promoted to captain and assigned as adjutant. His father, Major W. N. Pendleton, was already in command of the Rockbridge Artillery, attached for the moment at least to the 27th, the same position he had occupied before the unit was mustered into service.

A particularly welcome addition to the forces at Harpers Ferry was a cavalry squadron commanded by Colonel Turner Ashby. Numbering several hundred swaggering mounted troopers, who had provided their own horses, these were assigned to Jackson to act as his scouts, along with a group of irregular cavalry under command of Captain John D. Imboden that included a few pieces of highly mobile cannon known as the "horse artillery." David Preston's orders released him from assignment as sanitary inspector for the troops and returned him to the position of surgeon for the 27th Virginia Regiment. The first order issued from Jackson's own headquarters, however, restored him to his former post as sanitary inspector for the 1st Brigade.

Although technically listed as the Army of the Shenandoah, the troops at Harpers Ferry never numbered more than about 8,000 men, divided into four brigades containing from two to five regiments each, depending upon the size of the latter. Regiments varied widely, too, from the customary four companies of roughly 250 men to much smaller units, inducted originally as militia groups.

Only later would the southern forces come to be known by divisions and corps, but these, too, varied greatly in number, particularly after a battle before the ranks were refilled by volunteers and later by conscripts. And at no point during the entire war were northern and southern units of the same designation anywhere near the same size.

However swiftly things were moving in the rapidly increasing command at Harpers Ferry, even more startling events were taking place throughout the country as a whole. Every day brought news of a tightening in the blockade being maintained by the Federal Navy outside various Confederate ports, presaging the shortages in almost all badly needed matériel of war that soon began to develop. When Fort Sumter fell, the South had a white population of roughly 9,000,000 in contrast to about 19,000,000 in the North, but it also had to maintain, and guard, a slave population of nearly 4,000,000. In industrial production, the South was hopelessly behind from the start, with the "value of annual product" at $145,-000,000 compared to almost two billion for the North.

In one field, however, the South far outstripped the North from the beginning, the conviction of the rightness of its Cause and the determination not to submit to dictation by the loyal states. The secession of North Carolina from the Union on May 20, 1861, and the decision of the southern Congress at Montgomery, Alabama, to make Richmond, Virginia, the official capital of the Confederate States of America marked a rapid strengthening of the organization. With eleven full states out of the Union, the addition of Virginia was expected immediately after the results were posted of the referendum to be held late in May. And with an occasional flare-up of actual fighting between Federal troops and secession-minded citizens in Kentucky and Missouri, a turbulent period was obviously in prospect for both states, with their later addition to the ranks of the Confederacy not unlikely.

The Virginia referendum on May 23, 1861, produced the expected results—the eastern and central sections voted heavily in favor of secession, while the western counties elected to remain in the Union. The same vote indirectly involved the actions of the command at Harpers Ferry, now daily swollen by the arrival of more troops of all kinds. From a mere action to seize a northern-owned railroad in secessionist territory in Virginia, it had now become more of what Jackson wanted it to be—the constant threat of a potential dagger thrust into the soft underbelly of the Union. General Johnston, however, growing daily more nervous at the relatively exposed

107

position, with no support troops anywhere near, seemed to consider the situation more of a threat to himself and his command than to the enemy.

Then on May 24 President Lincoln ordered the step he had promised at first not to take, but which he could hardly postpone longer if Washington was to be made at least temporarily safe. Early in the morning Federal troops moved across the Potomac River bridges into Virginia territory. With almost no resistance they occupied the city of Alexandria and the heights of Arlington, from which Washington itself could easily have been shelled by southern artillery.

Virginia had been invaded and the die was cast. Moreover, in a move to stamp out southern sentiment in the North, United States marshals seized records of all messages sent between telegraph offices during the past year, hoping to uncover hotbeds of southern sentiment and contain them, as Baltimore had already been contained by General Benjamin Butler when he practically occupied the city.

The indignation of the South over the Yankee invasion of Virginia soil was nothing compared to the next event in the tragic and inexorable progress toward full-scale conflict. Colonel Elmore Ellsworth, well known in Washington as the leader of the famous and colorful 1st Fire Zouaves of the 11th New York, had led one section of his command into Alexandria at the forefront of the invading forces. Seeing a Confederate flag flying from a staff over the doorway of the Marshall House, a hotel in Alexandria, Ellsworth and two troopers broke in and climbed to the upper story to tear down the flag. As they were descending the stairway, the hotel keeper, James Jackson, killed Ellsworth at point blank range and was immediately shot down by Private Francis E. Brownell.

Virginia now had proof of what it considered Lincoln's perfidy in breaking his promise never to invade southern soil. The Union also had its first martyr and together the two events insured that the battle had at last been joined beyond any likelihood of reconciliation between North and South.

When the Union commander at Fort Monroe held

three Negro slaves, who had crossed the Federal lines, as "contraband," thus raising again the issue of owning slaves—in which Lincoln had also promised not to interfere—additional fire was added to the already smoldering anger of southern slave owners and politicians. That same day, too, in Missouri, a former United States Army captain named Ulysses S. Grant offered his services to the Union—and received no immediate reply.

With events progressing so rapidly on the divided national scene, many of the troops at Harpers Ferry were engaged in largely housekeeping routine, but not so the 1st Brigade. With his customary vigor, Jackson was busy turning his own command into as disciplined a fighting unit as it was possible to do with volunteer soldiers—much to their disgust.

As always, when green troops were quartered together, epidemics of otherwise innocuous diseases like measles, mumps and whooping cough swept through the camp. A temporary hospital for the entire command was set up in a warehouse and, after holding sick call in his own unit every morning, David spent the rest of each day there. Nursing chores were performed by women of the town, some of whom came from as far away as Martinsburg, driven by the urge to help the Cause, plus the presence of highly marriageable young officers at the camp.

One of these—she said her name was Belle Boyd—after having been home to Martinburg over the weekend, sought David out on a Monday morning late in June.

"I must see Colonel Jackson immediately, Dr. Preston." She appeared to be very excited. "Will you take me to him?"

"Is anything wrong?"

"Federal troops are about to move down from Pennsylvania into Virginia and retake the railroad."

The news, if true, was important enough to justify disturbing Jackson. David took Miss Boyd to him immediately and the commander listened courteously to her somewhat breathless account of what she had heard.

"May I ask how you learned this, Miss Boyd?" he asked.

"An—ah—admirer of mine attends the Academy at

Mercersburg, Pennsylvania, Colonel." The girl blushed prettily. "He came home for the summer vacation on Saturday and saw some Federal troops gathering at Williamsport—"

Jackson turned to his adjutant, who had been sitting beside him at the work table. Several maps were before him, but young Pendleton's eyes were upon Belle Boyd.

"Where is Williamsport, Captain?" Jackson asked.

"About twenty-five miles away, sir." Pendleton hurriedly studied the map and located the town. "There's an old church nearby—at a place called Falling Waters; my father has preached there several times."

Jackson studied the map briefly, then turned back to Belle Boyd. "Go on, please, my dear."

"Barney—my admirer—said he saw only a few Union troops at Williamsport, sir. But some people in the town told him several thousand are expected."

"Did he know who commanded them?"

Belle Boyd wrinkled her fair brow. "A General Patterson, I believe, Colonel."

Jackson nodded slowly. "I know General Patterson."

"His presence so near Harpers Ferry could mean an attack, sir," said Sandie Pendleton.

"Quite possibly. Quite possibly indeed." Jackson walked with the fair informant to the door. "You have done well, my dear," he told her courteously. "I will mention your help in my report to higher authority."

As he stood in the doorway, apparently watching the graceful figure of Belle Boyd walking down the street toward the hospital, Jackson seemed lost in thought. But when he turned and came back to the table, his manner was brisk and purposeful.

"Has Colonel Ashby returned from the scouting expedition I sent him on yesterday?" he asked Sandie Pendleton.

"Not yet, sir."

Jackson sat down and studied a map spread out on the table for a long moment before he spoke again; and then it was to David Preston.

"I believe you accompanied Major Stannard to Martinsburg when the railroad was shut down, Doctor," he said.

"Yes, sir."

"From your experience in Europe, would you say the area around Martinsburg is defensible?"

"If Federal troops have crossed the Potomac below Hagerstown, as Miss Boyd's information seems to indicate, it probably can't be defended against any large concentration of forces, sir. But if they were surprised—"

"That's the answer—surprise." Jackson shot up like a gangling jack-in-the-box, his eyes glowing with eagerness. "General McClellan is now in command west of the Ohio and he's no fool; we served together in Mexico and he was breveted twice during the campaign. Even though he has been running the Illinois Central Railroad for the past five or six years, McClellan must remember enough military strategy and tactics to realize the importance to the Union of opening the B&O to the west. But with McClellan being occupied beyond the Ohio and General McDowell concerned mainly with northeast Virginia, preparing for a thrust toward Richmond, that could leave a hiatus—"

"General Patterson is in command of the Pennsylvania District, sir," Sandie Pendleton pointed out.

"Patterson is an old man, he will not be expecting a surprise." Jackson picked up the map. "I will go to General Johnston at once. Come along, too, Dr. Preston, you can describe the area for the general, if he needs that information."

At Johnston's headquarters, Jackson and his officers were kept waiting for nearly half an hour. The commander of the 1st Brigade showed no sign of impatience or pique at thus being left to cool his heels, however. Instead, he occupied himself by studying the map and thinking. When finally they were admitted to Johnston's presence, they saw besides the commanding general and several others of his staff, a startling figure in pristine Confederate gray with the insignia of a lieutenant colonel of cavalry on his collar.

"Colonel Thomas Jackson, Lieutenant Colonel J. E. B. Stuart," said Johnston.

111

"Your servant, Colonel." Stuart saluted smartly, then reached forward to shake Jackson's hand.

The cavalry officer's tunic was lined with silk and tiny golden spurs jingled on his high boots, which had been polished until they shone. A red rose was stuck in the buttonhole of his tunic lapel and he carried white buckskin gloves in his left hand.

"Colonel Stuart has just joined this command from the West, with about three hundred troopers," Johnston explained.

"Welcome to Harpers Ferry, Colonel." Jackson appeared to be a little awed by the dashing cavalryman. "May I ask you where you crossed the Ohio?"

"At Ashland, Kentucky, but we had to detour south in order to get around a Federal force moving on Grafton."

"I was born not too far away from theire," said Jackson.

"Then you no doubt realize the importance it has to the Union."

"Quite, General McClellan has obviously decided to move east."

"Word has just come in that Federal forces have captured Gafton and are moving toward this place." The quaver in Johnston's voice betrayed his nervousness as he added, "I have also learned that another force is moving from the Ohio up the Kanawha River toward Charleston."

"With West Virginia voting against secession, McClellan would naturally try to cut off that section and keep it for the Union, probably as a new state," said Jackson thoughtfully. "But he could be considering a drive in force eastward along the B&O to seize the Shenandoah Valley. And that would be a major disaster for the South."

"Exactly what I just finished telling General Johnston," said Stuart on a note of admiration. "With the western counties under his command, McClellan will have more than half the B&O trackage in his hands, plus all barge traffic on a large section of the Ohio River and all of the Kanawha."

"And a ready source of coal for Federal Government gunboats on the Mississippi," added Colonel Barnard Bee, who was sitting beside Johnston as adjutant for the Army of the Shenandoah.

"Which means this command cannot wait much longer before taking some action," Stuart added pointedly.

Johnston, although the commanding general, had been largely ignored during the rapid-fire discussion among the other officers, and David Preston realized now that, compared to men like Jackson, Stuart and even Bee, the commanding general at Harpers Ferry was as small in military ability as he was in stature.

"But what shall it be? What shall it be?" Johnston asked fretfully.

"I think I have the answer to that, General," said Jackson quietly. "The danger is not simply from the west any more, it's from the north as well."

"What do you mean?" Johnston's voice was edgy.

Tersely, and without elaboration, Jackson told the group what he had just learned from Belle Boyd.

"How do you know this woman can be depended upon?" Johnston demanded.

"I don't," Jackson answered. "But a combined movement by McClellan from the west and Patterson from the north appears to be logical from the military point of view. I took the liberty of sending Colonel Ashby of my command to Martinsburg yesterday with a small force of cavalry to scout out the situation there. He should return by this afternoon and we will know then whether Miss Boyd's informant was correct."

"Meanwhile, I will telegraph General Lee in Richmond, asking permission to withdraw from Harpers Ferry to Winchester," said Johnston.

"Withdraw?" Jackson's question was like a whiplash. "That is out of the question, sir."

"The want of ammunition makes me timid," Johnston confessed.

"I grant you that we may have to withdraw in time, General, but we can at least put up a fight," Jackson insisted. "The fall of Harpers Ferry would mean leaving all Virginia to the enemy."

113

"To say nothing of the moral value of attacking before we are forced to fall back" Stuart's tone, too, was urgent. "We cannot win by pitting force against force; the resources of the North in manpower and the output of its factories far exceed our own. Which means our only hope is for an early victory because our *esprit de corps* is greater than theirs and we can afford to be more daring."

"I shall act upon General Lee's advice and what our cavalry discovers, Colonel Jackson," said Johnston rather coolly. "Good day, gentlemen."

Outside, Stuart joined Jackson and his party, including David Preston. "It's a good thing you got to Harpers Ferry before Timid Joe, Colonel Jackson," said the flamboyant cavalry leader, "Else the B&O would still be hauling coal to Norfolk to fire the boilers in Federal gunboats and supply the Union forces at Fort Monroe and Newport News. Thank God Beauregard is going to command the Army of Northern Virginia."

Jackson looked startled. "Is that official?"

"So I heard in Kentucky."

Six years older than Jackson, Pierre Gustave Toutant Beauregard had preceded him at West Point by four years. Wounded twice during the Mexican War and breveted to the rank of major, Beauregard had been superintendent of West Point in 1861 but resigned when Louisiana seceded. He had been in command at Charleston, South Carolina, during the tense days when Fort Sumter was under siege, and had directed the final attack leading to the surrender of the fort by the Federal garrison.

"Beauregard and you are the only two bona fide heroes this war has produced so far, Colonel Jackson," Stuart said. "Maybe by working together, we can still create a small diversion to entertain our northern friends in this region. Do I have your permission to ride north and see what your man Ashby has discovered?"

"You're not under my command, Colonel Stuart."

"Pray God I shall soon be. But since General Johnston has apparently not yet decided where to assign me and my men, I shall act upon my own devices." Stuart had been untying the reins of his horse from the hitching rack in front of headquarters as he spoke. Now he mounted with a graceful swing of a well-turned leg, compared to Jackson's almost awkward habit when mounting a horse, and saluted with his gloved right hand.

"My men are bivouacked nearby, so I shall leave you for the nonce," he said.

"Take care, Colonel," Jackson called after him. "I think you and I shall have some adventures together before the war is over."

Stuart's men had been bivouacked at the foot of the hill. Some were busy grooming their dust-covered mounts in a small open field, while others were gathered around a fire upon which several coffeepots were bubbling, being entertained by a man picking a banjo.

"That's Joe Sweeny, my private clown," Stuart called back as he started down the street. "He keeps my men drinking coffee and singing, when they're not fighting, so they'll stay out of trouble."

Sweeny's voice, a high "whiskey tenor" floated to them from the circle about the campfire in the refrain which, in a few short months, had become almost the theme song of the Confederacy:

> *The years creep slowly by, Lorena,*
> *The snow is on the grass again;*
> *The sun's low down the sky, Lorena,*
> *The frost gleams where the flowers have been.*

As the plaintive words died away, the mounteback with the banjo struck a jarring chord. And when he began to sing again, the men around him joined in, shouting the words with gusto:

> *Just before the battle, Mother,*
> *I was drinking mountain dew.*
> *When I saw the Yanks a'marchin'*
> *To the rear I quickly flew.*

"That sounds like Johnston's theme song." Sandie Pendleton laughed and to David's surprise, he heard Jackson chuckle softly.

"We may be able to change that tune a little," he said, then added in a more sober tone, "with luck, and God willing."

IX

As it happened, Lieutenant Colonel J. E. B.—already being called Jeb—Stuart had no occasion to break camp that day in Harpers Ferry. Colonel Turner Ashby and his small troop of cavalry returned around noon with news that Belle Body's information had been correct. A small number of Federal troops were already in the neighborhood of Williamsport in Maryland, but so far not enough had yet crossed the Potomac to become anything resembling a threat to the troops at Harpers Ferry.

Meanwhile, Jackson had written his friend General Robert E. Lee, now serving as military adviser to Jefferson Davis in Richmond, pleading that Harpers Ferry be held. Lee agreed and Johnston, though still timid, was instructed from Richmond to hold Harpers Ferry as long as he felt it was suitable to do so. And to make certain the Army of the Shenandoah was not surprised, Stuart's command was dispatched to Martinsburg as a protective screen.

Since he was a more experienced horseman than any of the other regimental surgeons, David Preston was given the chore of riding to Martinsburg twice a week to hold sick call for Stuart's men. As he was returning to Harpers Ferry one morning, a shambling soldier in Confederate pants and a butternut shirt—a not unusual uniform for the volunteers—stepped out from behind a tree and lowered his rifle to bear on the medical officer.

"Reckon I'll have to take your horse, Cap'n," he said in a typical Valley drawl.

"I'm not armed, as you can see."

"I know that. And I know you're the kind of doctor the South is going to need bad before this war is over, so just don't make no false move and you won't get hurt."

"Can I keep my saddlebags? All my instruments are in them."

116

The deserter grinned. "Take 'em, Doctor. I ain't hankerin' to start practicin' medicine."

Obediently David dismounted and lifted the saddlebags from the horse's back, slinging them over his shoulder.

"Mind telling me why you're deserting?" he inquired.

"The way I figger it, doc, I volunteered myself into this Army and I got a right to volunteer myself out of it."

"But why?"

"In the first place, I can't see where prayin' and drillin' is ever gonna help whip the Yankees. And in the second place, I ain't no nigger to be told what I kin do and what I ain't 'lowed to do. If I was fightin' and killin' Yankees, it'd be different. But they's a crop to be planted back home and the way I figger it, I'll be more use to my ole woman and the young'uns there than up here gettin-calluses on my knees a prayin' and on my feet from always marchin' and never goin' nowhere."

"But desertion is a crime."

"So's lettin' your wife 'n kids go hungry when you ain't doin' the South no good, Doctor," said the mountaineer as he mounted the horse. "I know your people down in Botetourt, growed up not far from Preston's Cove. When I get home I'll send word to your mom that you're doin' a fine job here for Old Jack. In the fall, when the crops are in and I finish killin' hogs, I might come back. By that time maybe there'll be some fightin' a man can get his teeth into."

Trudging back to Harpers Ferry with his saddlebags over his shoulder and his feet getting sorer by the miles, David had time to think about what the deserter had said. And the more tired he became, the more the man's words began to make sense—until the magnificent upward thrust of the mountain ranges and the stark beauty of this dramatic meeting place of streams and mountains erased even his weariness from his mind.

More than once since coming to Harpers Ferry, he had climbed to the elevation Jefferson's Rock. And having read the third United States President's *Notes on the State of Virginia* at least once a year since he'd found a volume in the small library in a log-walled

117

Botetourt County schoolroom, he could quote the section by heart word for word:

The passage of the Potomac through the Blue Ridge is perhaps one of the most stupendous scenes in nature. You stand on a very high point of land. On your right comes up the Shenandoah, having ranged along the foot of the mountain a hundred miles to seek a vent. On your left approaches the Potomac, in quest of a passage also. In the moment of their junction they rush together against the mountain, rend it asunder, and pass off to the sea.

The first glance of this scene hurls our senses into the opinion that this earth had been created in time, that the mountains were formed first, but the rivers began to flow afterwards, that in this place particularly they have been dammed up by the Blue Ridge of mountains and have formed an ocean which filled the whole valley; that continuing to rise they have at last broken over at this spot, and have torn the mountain down from its summit to its base. The piles of rock on each hand, but particularly on the Shenandoah, the evident marks of the disrupture and avulsion from their beds by the most powerful agents of nature, corroborates the impression.

But the distant finishing which nature has given to the picture is of a very different character. It is a true contrast to the foreground. It is as placid and delightful, as it is wild and tremendous. For the mountain being cloven asunder, she presents to your eye, through the cleft, a small patch of smooth blue horizon, at an infinite distance in the plain country, inviting you, as it were from the riot and tumult roaring around to pass through the breach and participate in the calm below.

Having recently crossed the Atlantic himself, David could heartily agree with Thomas Jefferson. But although the mountains and the streams were still much as Jefferson had first seen them, he was sure that not even the far-sighted creator of Monticello had ever dreamed of seeing the double-tracked iron rails of the B&O following the riverbank. Although as a bona fide visionary, Jefferson might have planned the system of locks and dams by which the canal to the West was lifted above the fall

118

line and travel made possible even as far as Cumberland.

Even Jefferson would hardly have dreamed, however, that there would be seen here one day, not only power wheels moved by the thunderously racing current but factories for the production of instruments of death and destruction. And none more unique than the famous Harpers Ferry pistol which, with its .54 caliber barrel—actually a small cannon that must be held with both hands when discharged—was easily the most formidable side-arm in frontier America.

Halfway down the slope to Harpers Ferry itself, David came around a rocky crag and was halted by a lanky soldier holding a musket pointed directly at him, the second such experience that day.

"Halt and give the countersign," the man demanded in a typical southwest Virginia drawl.

"What countersign?"

"Where you been, Doctor?" Although thus acknowledging his recognition, the soldier hadn't lowered the barrel of the musket and David made no attempt to argue with him.

"To Martinsburg, holding sick call for Colonel Stuart's cavalry," said David shortly.

"Jeb in trouble?"

"Only by an epidemic of measles."

"Wish to hell I hadn't had 'em before I got in the Army. At least I'd have some time off."

"When I left yesterday, there wasn't any countersign," said David. "When did that go on?"

"This morning, when Ginrul Johnston decided to retreat south to Winchester."

"Retreat? Why?"

The soldier shrugged. "Don't ask me, Doctor. Ask the ginrul."

This was startling news indeed, for, although the move had been discussed by the staff, no decision had been made when David had left the previous morning and he was quite sure Stuart had no part in it. In fact, when he had left the dashing cavalry commander in Martinsburg a few hours ago, his troops had been en-

119

gaged in feeling out the Federal movement southward from Hagerstown and Williamport.

"You goin' ter give the countersign, Cap'n Preston?" the picket inquired.

"I wasn't here when the order was given, so I couldn't be expected to know the countersign, could I?" David inquired.

The soldier scratched his head, lowered his rifle and spat a stream of tobacco juice at a lizard crawling up the face of the rock, knocking it off to land on a shrub below.

"Reckon you wouldn't," he admitted. "And seein' as how I'm from the Twenty-seventh and I know you're the doctor for the regiment, I reckon you kin go on."

"Are the First Brigade troops going south too?"

"Nah!" the soldier's voice was eloquent with disgust. "We got here first and we'll go out last, I been in the army long enough to know that's the way it goes. By the way, what happened to your horse, doc? I see you're carrying your saddlebags."

"A deserter took it away from me. He was carrying a rifle and I wasn't, so there wasn't any point in arguing."

"That would be Jed Burnet; when roll was called this mornin' somebody said he'd sneaked out during the night. But Jed's from Botetourt, too, and you can be sure when he gets down there he'll take your horse around to your mother's plantation and leave it for you."

Seen at close quarters as David trudged toward the foot of Loudoun Heights, Harpers Ferry appeared to be in a ferment with men, horses and equipment in constant motion, much of it rather obviously without purpose, along the dusty street. There was an air of impending panic to the situation around Johnston's headquarters, too, that made David frown. But at those of the 1st Brigade, he found Joe Stannard at work writing orders while Sandie Pendleton, looking like a Greek god in a spotless Confederate gray uniform, shuffled constantly between the workroom and Jackson's living quarters.

"I was beginning to be afraid you'd been captured by the enemy," said Stannard. "Where've you been?"

"I *was* captured—by a deserter. Took my horse and headed south for home—in my own county, too."

"He's not alone. One company of the Fifth lost twenty men in two days."

"Is General Johnston really going to pull out of Harpers Ferry?"

"As fast as he can go; the order was issued this morning, in spite of objections from Jackson and even a telegram from General Lee. A lot of wagons have already started moving toward Winchester and troops will march in the morning, after they finish putting the torch to the munitions factories here."

"Then everybody's leaving?"

"Everybody except us. One regiment of the First Brigade will cover the pullback."

"I hope it's the Twenty-seventh."

"You guessed it. We're the smallest so we drew the honor."

"It almost looks like a rout outside there. I saw a few of those in Italy and they all smell alike."

"We had some in Mexico and it's not a pretty thing either to see or smell," Stannard agreed. "I think Johnston can keep it under control, though."

"What happened since yesterday to stir the general up?"

"Make that generals. Bee and a couple of others who came with Johnston were breveted to brigadier general yesterday afternoon when orders came by telegraph from Richmond."

"But not Jackson?"

"No."

"My guess is that somewhere along the way—maybe when they were both in the U. S. Army—Old Jack rubbed Jefferson Davis the wrong way. From what I hear, our President has a long memory when it comes to carrying a grudge."

"How's the colonel taking it?"

Stannard glanced toward the stairway leading up to Jackson's quarters and, when he spoke, it was in a lower tone. "Outwardly there's no reaction. But Sandie Pendleton's closer to him then anybody else and he says Old Jack is fit to be tied."

"Can you blame him?"

121

"Hell no! If we'd waited for Timid Joe to come here in the first place, the B&O would still be running coal through day and night and the South would have a lot less railroad cars and locomotives of their own."

"What happened to build such a fire under Johnston?"

"While Turner Ashby was on a scouting expedition, he staged one of those playacting dramas he likes to put on, this time riding through the whole Yankee camp north of the Potomac pretending to be an itinerant horse doctor. Ashby reported that General Patterson's been telling everybody he's going to cross the Potomac and drive us up the Valley. I guess Timid Joe believed him."

"I'll bet Old Jack didn't."

"You don't smell any aura of panic around this headquarters, do you, friend? If I know our closemouthed leader, he's planning right now to turn what's supposed to be only a covering operation for the main body into trouble for a Yankee general named Patterson."

Which was exactly what happened. By noon the next day, the last of General Joseph E. Johnston's main force had disappeared through the gap where the Shenandoah River, having crept along at the base of the eastern wall of the Blue Ridge for over a hundred miles, feeling out each pass, finally cut through below Loudoun Heights to join the Potomac. Even before the last wagon was out of sight on the road to Winchester, the 1st Brigade, which had been left behind to cover the withdrawal, was being mustered into position, awaiting only the thunderous explosion of the powder charges engineers had placed under the long B&O railroad bridge across the Potomac and the crash of the structure to start the march.

Characteristically, Jackson told neither officers nor men what was impending. But when the march began, with the wheels of the Rockbridge Artillery gun carriages, caissons and limbers rolling noiselessly on well-greased axles, he took his place at the head of the line. A squadron of Ashby's cavalry was scouting ahead and, if there'd been any doubt in anyone's mind about which way they were going, those doubts were quickly dispelled.

The road they took upon leaving Harpers Ferry turned sharply northwestward, a good ninety and more degrees from the route taken earlier by the main part of the command. Jackson's 1st Brigade was retreating *forward* in the direction of the enemy, a maneuver with which they were to become quite familiar in the months ahead.

X

Looked at from a strictly military point of view, the Battle of Falling Waters, fought near the south bank of the Potomac a few miles below Hagerstown on July 2, 1861, almost in sight of the bridge at Williamsport, could hardly be counted as anything more than a skirmish. In fact, both sides claimed victory, meaning neither really achieved one.

Destruction of the long railroad bridge across the Potomac at Harpers Ferry had effectually put the railroad out of operation for several months, removing a vantage point for the North. And moving directly upon Martinsburg, Jackson's men had easily pushed the few Federal troops out of the city and neatly brought about the capture of both the large and important railway yards and the elaborate repair facilities built there by the B&O.

After destroying this area, even to the extent of pulling the rails and heating them to where they could be bent around trees, Jackson obeyed an order from General Johnston, and began a retreat toward Winchester. Still chafing at the lack of aggressiveness in his superior, he took with him, drawn by teams of horses in front of the troops, a number of B&O locomotives to be repaired in the shops of the Tredegar Iron Works at Richmond, after a long journey overland to Strasburg, thence by way of the Manassas Gap, Orange and Alexandria and Virginia Central railroads to the Confederate capital.

The cavalry of dashing Jeb Stuart and Turner Ashby, ranging through some thirty to forty miles of territory between Winchester and the Potomac, brought word in the last days of June that the Federals were beginning to cross in force at Williamsport. Johnston finally decided then to move his forces along the Valley Turnpike to Darkesville, about halfway between Winchester and Williamsport. And loosed at last by his timorous commanding officer, Jackson pushed ahead with only about three hundred men of the 27th, plus several guns from the Rockbridge Artillery, commanded by Sandie Pendleton's father.

The brilliant comet that flashed across the sky on the last night in June was variously interpreted to be a sign of victory or, by a few, as a warning of disaster. Each of four men saw it as significant in his own life—though differently. And as it happened, each was wrong.

Pierre Gustave Toutant Beauregard saw the comet as a sign of heavenly favor, for had not the Lord already smiled on all his endeavors? He had become a southern hero overnight simply by virtue of being in command at Charleston during the attack upon Fort Sumter, although in itself that victory had required little except more guns, more ammunition and more people than the small garrison of less than a hundred Union soldiers. Transferred from Charleston to command the Army of Northern Virginia in the early summer, Beauregard burst upon the Virginia scene and promptly began to amass a force at Manassas Junction, northwest of Richmond, with the avowed purpose of seizing Washington. Fiery, colorful, impetuous and filled with energy, Beauregard at forty-three was in the prime of life and at the peak of his military career, so how could the sudden burst of glory in the evening sky be anything but a good omen to such as he?

George Brinton McClellan, a Philadelphian and a West Pointer, had resigned his captain's commission in the Regular Army in 1857 to become chief engineer to the Illinois Central Railroad and later its vice-president. Appointed a major general in the United States Army in 1861, he had directed the successful advance of Federal troops into Western Virginia, against little organized opposition, laying the ground for the planned separation of that section of Virginia into another state within the Union. Handsome, self-confident and even then certain of his own high destiny, the comet could only be a sign of heaven's favor to a man obviously so well fitted for military and political leadership.

Major General Irvin McDowell, as Assistant Adjutant

General of the regular U.S. Army, had been active in preparing for battle since the fall of Fort Sumter swept the few lagging states, particularly Virginia, into active participation in the Confederacy. Working as best he could under the not always understandable orders of the aging U.S. General-in-Chief, Winfield Scott—himself barely able to walk but nevertheless planning military campaigns with great gusto from his bed and pointing to the maps along the wall with a cane pole—McDowell had been handicapped from the start.

The same age as Beauregard and in the same class with the fiery Louisianian at West Point, McDowell possessed little of Beauregard's color and almost none, it seemed, of his daring. A major at the outset of the war, McDowell was immediately made a brigadier general of volunteers, but was not a favorite of General Scott. Sensitive, a lover of music, gardening and often absentminded in appearance, McDowell was not one to fit very well into the turbulent life of Washington immediately after war began.

With military prudence, McDowell had taken the precaution of expediting the occupation of the Virginia bank of the Potomac just across from Washington and had made General Robert E. Lee's old home in Arlington Heights the army headquarters there. He had been busy, too, throughout the spring and early summer of 1861 trying to consolidate the varied forces in and around the capital into a homogeneous fighting army. This in spite of interference by President Lincoln and various members of the Cabinet, as well as amateurs in the volunteer army with political influence enough to guarantee themselves high commissions for which they were rarely suitable.

By late June McDowell had been able to prepare a map of his proposed campaign and present it to the military council made up of the President and the Cabinet. A bold venture, it was designed to strike directly into Virginia east of the Blue Ridge Mountains, cut the Manassas Gap Railroad to the Shenandoah Valley and isolate Richmond, where his former officer friend, Jefferson Davis, was now President of a young and still tottery nation.

One thing in particular about McDowell's preparations for war had caught the attention of the public, too—a hot-air type of observation balloon prepared by Professor T. S. C. Lowe. In it observers were able to ascend high above a battlefield and watch the movements of an opposing force, telegraphing information directly by means of a trailing wire to campaign headquarters.

At his headquarters in the abandoned Lee mansion, commanding an army of some thirty-two thousand men, many of them, it was true, poorly trained, General Irvin McDowell had every reason to think, at the beginning of July 1861, that the comet which had appeared across the heavens the night before augured the beginning of an equally blazing campaign, the success of which would make him a national hero overnight and end the war by capturing Richmond, the very heart of the rebellious Confederacy that aspired to be a separate nation.

To a fourth observer named Thomas Jonathan Jackson, watching the blaze of light across the sky from a bivouac in the lovely Valley region north of Martinsburg, with laurel and rhododendron still in bloom high on the mountainsides of the Blue Ridge, the comet could hardly seem other than an omen of failure, however. With some three hundred men from the 27th Virginia and a few cannon at his call, Jackson could hardly consider himself much more of a threat to the massed thousands of General Robert Patterson's well-shod, well-equipped and much better trained Union army moving into the Valley, than were the flies buzzing lazily around the sleeping men and the grazing horses of the Rockbridge Artillery.

Almost three months into the war, Jackson was still a colonel, although he had captured part of one of the nation's most important railroads—and that without a shot. Moreover, the former professor seemed destined always to work as the lackey of higher command, moving ahead of the main body of troops to bear the brunt of attack in danger, guarding the rear in retreat yet always yielding the reward and credit to others when it was over.

Watching his commanding officer sitting bolt upright, as always, on a log beside the smoking campfire that served more to keep off flies than any other purpose, it being hot and still this night of July 1, David Preston heard the whispered words of a prayer and understood that Old Jack was busy talking to the only person with whom he seemed able to commune at will, his God. But whether he was praying for victory or for his own soul, not even his closest companions ever knew.

It was 4:30 A.M. and the sun had not yet risen above the serrated ranges of the Blue Ridge to the east when Jackson ordered the bugle blown for reveille, albeit softly in case any Yankee pickets had moved that far south of the main body of Patterson's command. For about an hour there was a stir in the camp and the smell of bacon as rations were cooked and eaten—the best place to carry them when possibly going into battle, most soldiers had already learned, being in their stomachs.

Although some arms and ammunition had been retrieved from the partially destroyed arsenal and munitions factories at Harpers Ferry, Jackson's men were still poorly armed for a major fight. Muskets, only a few of them breechloaders, fowling pieces, pistols—a motley group of weapons by any standards—were their only arms, except for bayonets and knives. Knapsacks had quickly proved to be too cumbersome for use on the march and the only equipment most of them carried, beside weapons and ammunition, was a blanket roll covered with a waterproof sheet and whatever toilet articles they chose, again only a minimum, secreted inside.

Breakfast over, the column began marching north. The few cavalry disappeared at the beginning of the march, their purpose being to serve as eyes and ears for troops going into battle. Jackson's marching orders were quite simple and remained so, five minutes of rest out of every hour, the men flopping to the ground in their tracks when the halt was called. David Preston was on horseback like the other officers, with his medical equipment in a small case and surgeon's tools in his saddlebags.

Two hours past the bivouac, Colonel Turner Ashby, the cavalry commander, suddenly appeared in the road ahead and the column came to a halt while Jackson, Major W. N. Pendleton, Lieutenant Sandie Pendleton, his son, and the two company commanders conferred ahead. When the parley was finished Sandie Pendleton rode back with the company commanders and his father,

127

who immediately began to supervise the removal of the cannon to a position away from the road, from whence they could enfilade the way ahead.

"Colonel Jackson wants you to establish a dressing station immediately, Captain Preston," said the young adjutant.

"What's up, Sandie?"

"A Yankee skirmishing party numbering several hundred men is moving this way. The colonel hopes to catch 'em unawares and pile 'em back on the main column. Falling Waters Church is just ahead."

The troops, almost all of them mountain men experienced in stalking deer and bear, had already begun to melt into the forest and, by the time David got his makeshift dressing station located, hardly anyone could have told troops were around. Since the battle had not yet begun he went forward to report that the dressing station was ready.

Major W. N. Pendleton was supervising the placing of his battery, with the cannon angled to sweep the narrow road ahead. David was surprised to find Jackson there, until he saw that the spot gave a clear view of the road and the white clapboard church only a few hundred yards ahead.

"Stay and watch, Doctor," said Jackson. "You have studied some of the European battlefields and seen troops in action, so you may be able to give us some advice."

David moved up to a position behind Jackson but was careful to stay out of the way of the elder Pendleton. A taciturn man, the minister-turned-artilleryman was sighting fussily along the barrel of a Parrott gun, with a waterproof sheet drawn over it to keep any reflection of the sun from warning the enemy of its presence.

For nearly half an hour there was no sound, save the chatter of birds and squirrels from the trees, the occasional distant shout of a human voice and once or twice the report of a rifle being discharged. Then, at the edge of the churchyard, three men on horseback suddenly appeared, riding as if the devil himself were behind them. The front rider, David recognized as Colonel Ashby by his lean face and small pointed beard. He was followed by the two other troopers.

"There's the bait, Captain Preston," said Jackson softly. "We ought to see our quarry any moment now."

From the woods beyond the church came a sudden burst of firing, proof that Ashby and his troops had been seen. And as they disappeared into the woods encircling the clearing, the sound of heavy footsteps met the ears of the small waiting group.

"Here they come," said Jackson. "Steady, gentlemen. Fire only on my order."

Glancing down at the cannon, David wasn't surprised to see a number of bags of grapeshot piled beside it. At this distance and with troops concentrated in such a small area, grape could be a murderous weapon indeed against the Federal troops, their bright blue uniforms and polished weapons making sharply etched targets in the bright morning sunlight. As they crossed the clearing around the church, David could see at least a few among them were regulars from the way they spread out, instead of bunching together as green troops often instinctively did for support, making them an ideal target for cannon fire.

The Union soldiers, David saw, carried the dependable Enfield type rifle manufactured in munitions factories all over the North. A burly sergeant, distinguished by the bright slashes of the hash marks and insignia of his rank on his sleeve, led several of them in a quick examination of the church itself. Not a sound or a movement came from the woods through which the track led southward in a sundappled pattern of lights and shadows across shallow ruts in the sand. And calling to the others to follow him, the sergeant led them into the clearing.

The senior Pendleton crouched over the cannon, his position so intense with expectation that the fingers clutching the lanyard by which it was fired were actually trembling. And when he looked at Jackson, David saw that, for once, the spare frame was not bolt upright as usual but he, too, was leaning forward, his head in the dingy barracks cap that formed his constant headgear pressed forward, giving him much of the look of a turkey buzzard startled by an alien sound.

"Colonel!" Even in his excitement, Sandie Pendleton kept his voice to a whisper. "Look at the sergeant's weapon."

Jackson turned his head and David saw that the deep-set eyes were glowing with a fanatic light, as if he were anticipating with almost vulpine satisfaction the crack of the gun and the murderous hail of the some fifty or sixty small iron balls making up the charge of grapeshot within its barrel, as it whipped the clearing like the fabled tide of death itself. Just so, was David's startled thought, the eyes of the spectators in the Roman Coliseum must have glowed when they gave the thumbs down verdict of death for a defeated gladiator.

"That's a fifteen-shot repeating Henry rifle the sergeant's carrying," said Sandie Pendleton urgently but still in a whisper. "You can load one on Sunday and fire it the rest of the week."

"He's worth ten soldiers in the open," Jackson agreed. "Stop him, Sandie."

The young officer was already moving before Jackson finished speaking. The Sharps carbine he carried in a holster at the front of his saddle when on horseback was leaning against a tree no more than two yards away. Seizing it, Pendleton glanced at the pellet of the fulminate cap which, when struck by the hammer as the weapon was fired, would ignite the powder charge and send the bullet hurtling toward its target. The paper tape covering the cap was dry, proving that it had not been dampened by the heavy dew on the ride from the bivouac area of the night before to Falling Waters. Dropping to one knee, he lay the barrel to the Sharps across the waterproof sheet covering the Parrott gun his father was waiting to fire and centered the sight upon the broad chest of the sergeant leading the advance party. At just that moment, however, more blue uniforms appeared on the far side of the clearing and Jackson reached out quickly to put a restraining hand on Sandie Pendleton's arm.

"Hold your fire," he said, and David was amazed by the calm in his voice even in this important moment. "I'll tell you when."

Below them, the sergeant had stopped to look back over his shoulder at the new arrivals.

"Any sign of Johnny Reb?" one of them asked in a thick Pennsylvania Dutch accent.

"Nah!" said the sergeant contemptuously. "They skedaddled out of this part of the country soon as some real soldiers started after 'em the same way they left Harpers Ferry. Come on."

The latecomers, a couple of dozen strong, started across the clearing as the noncommissioned officer leading the party turned again toward the path. Perhaps forty men were in the churchyard now, bunched together because of sheer numbers.

"Now, Sandie!" said Jackson softly.

At the crack of the rifle, a puff of smoke from the gas leak at the breech as the powder charge ignited—a characteristic of all Sharps—momentarily obscured the target. The smoke disappeared quickly, however, and in the instant before the elder Pendleton jerked the lanyard of the three-inch rifled Parrott gun, David saw a crimson stain appear like a tiny sunburnt on the breast of the blue tunic just before the sergeant started to pitch forward.

"Excellent shooting, Captain Pendleton! Capital shot —" Jackson's words were cut short by the flash of the cannon as grapeshot sprayed the clearing, sending blue uniforms tumbling like pins in a bowling alley with a strike.

David felt a sudden twinge of nausea at the sight but Jackson was smiling with approval as the gun crew swabbed out the barrel of the deadly weapon with a "sponge" made of a cylinder of wood covered with sheepskin on the end of the long rod. Punching a powder charge home, they rammed in another bag of grapeshot, while the elder Pendleton was screwing the powder-filled small copper tube of a friction timer into the vent hole of the cannon.

The troops hidden among the trees began to enfilade the area with musket fire as the Union soldiers—less than half now able to remain on their feet—scurried from the open space for the relative safety of the underbush around it, many throwing away rifles and equipment in

131

their panic. And with a chorus of rebel yells, the Confederate troops poured after them.

"I'll be needed at the dressing station, Colonel," said David.

"Of course." Jackson's voice was distant now as he watched with no sign of emotion on his sallow countenance the carnage taking place in the clearing below. "It has pleased Almighty God to give us the victory today, Doctor. The enemy will be needing you more than our gallant soldiers."

As he hurried through the trees along the hillside toward the dressing station, David asked himself what sort of God could possibly find pleasure in watching those created in His own image being cut down, often in youth, by a hail of iron balls propelled by a fortuitous combination of charcoal, sulphur and saltpeter. And yet there was no doubting that Jackson, a pious and God-fearing man, believed just that.

Before the battle the yellow flag used to mark field dressing stations and infirmaries had been hung from a limb of a tree projecting over the road leading to Falling Waters Church. A path had also been blazed up the hillside for about two hundred feet from the roadway, so the station would not be under fire if the situation changed quickly.

Just as David reached the dressing station, the first patient arrived, a gangling youth who gave his name as Private Hal Perkins. He used his musket for a crutch as he limped painfully up the slope, and his lack of familiarity with warfare was evident by the fact that the weapon was loaded. David carefully took the gun and leaned it against a nearby tree before easing the youth to a seat on a rock with the trunk of the tree at his back.

A glance at the boot and the neat hole through it had already told David the story; such evidence had been as damning in Italy as it was here at the foot of the Blue Ridge in Virginia. But remembering his own nausea moments ago, when he'd watched the slaughter of the blue-uniformed soldiers in the churchyard at Falling Waters, he felt only sympathy for the young soldier whose determination had obviously failed him when it came to killing his fellowman, leading him to turn the musket upon himself.

"Where are you from, Perkins?" David asked as he removed the boot, with neat holes through both upper and sole.

"Winchester, Doctor—I mean, Captain. I was studying medicine at school there."

The wound was clean, too, located between the base of the big toe and the adjacent second toe. A brief examination showed that the bullet had missed the long bones—the metatarsal shafts—of both toes, damning evidence in itself that the injury was self-inflicted.

"Is it bad, Doctor?" the boy asked in a voice that quavered a little.

"No. But you will have a hard time explaining it to a court-martial."

"I don't know what came over me, Doctor." The words tumbled over themselves in the young soldier's eagerness to confess to a seemingly sympathetic listener. "When Fort Sumter fell, practically everybody in my class enlisted right off the bat and—"

"You should have stayed on and finished your medical course. The South is going to need doctors very badly."

"I know that now, but we all got carried away. They were talking about taking Washington and hanging Abe Lincoln and stuff like that."

"Then you saw this morning what war is really like?"

"I wasn't fifty feet from that Union sergeant. Had my sights right on him but I couldn't pull the trigger." Perkins' voice broke for a moment. "And when that bullet knocked the big hole in the sergeant's chest and his blood came gushing out—I guess I lost my mind for a minute."

"That could be the medical explanation." David was applying a dressing of scorched linen. "But you won't find much sympathy from a court-martial, especially when you took the trouble to reload your rifle."

"I guess that was a fool thing to do. But—"

"You figured if it wasn't loaded, somebody would suspect you did it yourself. Is that it?"

Perkins nodded and wiped his eyes with his sleeve. "I guess that makes me a coward, doesn't it?"

133

"To some people—yes. How old are you, Hal?"

"Nineteen. I lied to the recruiting officer."

"You were willing to—" David stopped, for a heavy crashing sound had come from the bushes nearby. Thinking some more wounded might be arriving, he quickly finished bandaging Hal Perkins' wound and tossed the incriminating boot into the underbush where it wouldn't immediately be visible. He was tying the ends of the bandage together when the crashing sound stopped and he looked up to see, not ten feet away, a tall soldier in a blue uniform, blood streaming down across his face from a wound in his scalp and his eyes glazed with pain and fear.

"God-damned Rebels!" he shouted as he steadied himself against a sapling and lifted the Enfield rifle he carried. He was close enough for David to see that the cap was in place, the hammer cocked back with his right hand and his right index finger curled around the trigger. Transfixed by the menace of the cocked rifle in the hands of the Union soldier, David didn't try to move but, instead, braced himself against the impact of the minié ball he expected to strike him at any moment. He could only pray the wavering of the barrel might be great enough to make the ball miss its target in the center of his body. When the sound of the powder charge detonation came, however, it had an oddly double character, as if followed immediately by its own echo.

Waiting for a stab of pain to tell him where the bullet had struck—and not feeling it—David wondered by what miracle even a wounded and fear-crazed man had managed to miss him at such close range. Only then did he see that, where once had been a shallow bloody trench in the Yankee soldier's scalp, a section of his skull the size of a child's hand had now been blown away, leaving the oozing red pulp of the brain surface exposed beneath. And he understood at last that Hal Perkins had somehow managed to reach his own musket in time to pull the trigger and send a minié ball crashing into the other soldier's skull, an instant before the cocked hammer of the Enfield had descended. But that had been time enough for the movement of the Union soldier's body as

134

he staggered backward from the impact of the bullet to elevate the muzzle of his weapon and send the minié crashing harmlessly through the pines beside the stream.

"I couldn't just sit here and watch him kill you, Doctor." Hal Perkins' voice was almost apologetic. "Not after you treated me so well."

"You saved my life!"

In that moment David realized what he must do—and quickly—if the youth medical student were not to give his life for his own failure in a moment of panic. Moving quickly to his saddlebags, he reached inside for his scalpel case and its three finely tooled blades of the best Swedish steel.

"Get the bandage off your foot, Hal," he ordered. "And hurry!"

Private Perkins needed no urging, he ripped off the bandage while David was taking one of the shining blades from the scalpel case.

"I'm going to convert that bullet wound into the kind of wound you would have sustained if you had blundered upon a bayonet on the rifle of a dead enemy," he explained. "Get a good hold on that rifle stock, this will hurt like hell."

Setting the point of the scalpel against the entry wound on top of the boy's foot, with the blade pointing toward the ends of his toes, David drove it down through the flesh to the other side. Then, pushing the razor-sharp blade forward in a single slashing stroke, he cut through the some half to three quarters of an inch of flesh between the toes.

Perkins gasped as blood spurted from small vessels severed in the skin and the tissues beneath, but made no other sound. David allowed the blood to flow, washing out any bits of wadding that might have been carried into the wound, while he picked up Hal Perkins' musket and moved into the underbrush where he'd thrown the boot. Setting the heavy shoe upright, he jammed the joint of the bayonet through both upper and sole, slashing through the leather to duplicate in the shoe the wound he had already made in Perkins' foot.

Bleeding from the new wound had almost stopped

when David finished destroying the damning evidence against Hal Perkins, so he applied a fresh dressing to it, bandaging the cut at the end of the foot snugly and drawing the edges of the skin together. Unless sepsis intervened, the wound would heal quickly by first intention.

"How can I ever thank you, Dr. Preston?" Hal Perkins' voice was husky with emotion. "You probably saved me from a firing squad."

"Stick to the story I gave you and you'll probably come out all right."

"Would you let me work with you when my foot heals? I'll be your slave—"

"Orderly will do for a while. With that year you had in medical school, plus the experience we'll be getting before long, maybe you can pass the examination for hospital steward one day. We're going to need a lot of them, too, before this is all over."

"Whatever you say, I'll do, sir."

Working at the dressing station as the few men wounded in the affair at Falling Waters Church trickled back for treatment, David could soon tell from the intensity of the firing to the north that Jackson's small force had apparently run into at least the advance guard of the Federal main body. He wasn't surprised, therefore, when Sandie Pendleton came up from the road, with orders from Jackson to load the wounded into wagons for immediate transferral back to Darkesville. Jackson himself appeared soon afterward, riding a nondescript-looking sorrel horse captured from the enemy. And, before the sun went down, the entire skirmishing group was back with the main force.

Upon arrival at the temporary base camp, David started working in the field hospital set up near 1st Brigade Headquarters. Dressings and splints applied at the forward station had to be changed and the leg of one soldier, the main section of his femur in the thigh shattered by a minié ball, had to be amputated, always an unpleasant choice.

As surgeon for Jackson's command, Dr. Hunter McGuire performed the amputation. David assisted him and

136

although McGuire lacked experience in field surgery, David could see that he had been well trained. Afterward, David cleaned up a number of wounds, removing torn flesh and bits of uniform from them before washing them out well with hot water. He was busy applying a splint to the leg of another fracture case, this one fortunately not compounded, when he heard a footfall close beside him and looked up to see Colonel Jackson standing by the fire, where water had been heated for washing the wounds and preparing soup and coffee for the injured.

"Go on with your work, please, Captain Preston," said Jackson when the surgeon started to rise from where he was kneeling beside the litter on which the wounded man lay. "It is more important, I am sure, than military custom."

"I'll be finished in a few minutes, sir."

"What is that device you're using, Doctor?" Jackson customarily used military and medical titles indiscriminately.

"A combination splint for applying traction to fracture cases, sir. The traction overcomes the tendency of the muscles to contract and make the bones override."

"Ingenious. I hope a Confederate surgeon thought of it."

"The splint itself was devised by Dr. Nathan Ryno Smith at the University of Maryland Medical School quite a while ago, sir. The traction device was first put together by a New York surgeon, Dr. Gordon Buck."

"We are told in God's word that 'They who are whole need not a physician; but they that are sick.' So I am sure our Heavenly Father would not want the healing gift to be withheld from anyone."

"In the Oath of Hippocrates, subscribed to by all physicians, we say: 'So far as power and discernment shall be mine, I will carry out regimen for the benefit of the sick and will keep them from harm and wrong,' " David told him. "I have never felt that it discriminated between friend and enemy."

"Our blessed Lord once said: 'Love your enemies, do good to them which hate you.' " A smile softened the

137

normally grim line of Jackson's lips. "But in the heat of battle, I am afraid I do not always heed."

"The engagement this morning was brilliantly executed, sir. I hope the results satisfied you."

Jackson stroked his beard for a moment before he answered, long enough to make David wonder whether he had been presumptuous in asking the question.

"I am rarely satisfied with anything I attempt, Captain Preston. Today we drove an advance party back and slowed the movement of a column of perhaps fourteen thousand—"

"That many?"

"So Coloney Ashby told me before we undertook the skirmish. When you think of attacking fourteen thousand with three hundred men and three cannon, it does sound a bit like David of old going against Goliath, doesn't it?"

"More like taking on the whole Philistine Army, sir."

Jackson smiled. "We tossed our three stones and withdrew with forty prisoners of war, perhaps a hundred rifles, according to Captain Pendleton, and less than a dozen casualties of our own."

"I would call that a victory, sir."

"Not exactly, Doctor. You see, with three thousand instead of three hundred, and perhaps thirty cannon, instead of three, I could have sent Coloney Ashby's and Colonel Stuart's cavalry in a flanking attack to destroy the bridge at Williamsport. Then I could have thrown the enemy back against the barrier of the Potomac and destroyed the effectiveness of his forces probably until next spring, giving me time to train and equip my army for the real battle that must come."

It was the nearest David Preston had ever come— except as a student at VMI—to hearing Jackson explain his philosophy of military strategy. And from the complaints of staff officers that their taciturn commander never told them anything, he doubted very much that even they had ever heard as much.

"But that," Jackson added, "would have meant committing the entire force with the probability, if we lost, that the enemy could not be kept from driving southward through the Shenandoah Valley, cutting the rail lines to the west and outflanking Richmond. So General Johnston was probably right in deciding the attack this morning should be only a skirmish to feel out the enemy."

Jackson's use of the word "probably" told David something he'd never realized before—that beneath the drab exterior, the oddities and peculiarities that made Thomas Jonathan Jackson stand out so sharply from other men, there also beat the heart of a lover of adventure, a man of flash and daring, fully as distinct a personality in his own way as Jeb Stuart, with his polished boots, his plumed hat and his scarlet-lined tunic.

"Good night, Doctor." As Jackson turned to go to his own tent a familiar figure strode into the circle of light cast by the coals of the small fire. It was Colonel Turner Ashby and from the happy look on the lean face of the cavalryman when he saluted, it was obvious that he brought good news.

"We rode north to the telegraph line between Martinsburg and Harpers Ferry so Sergeant Holbein of the Signal Corps could tap it, Colonel," said Ashby. "General Patterson telegraphed General Winfield Scott in Washington that you attacked this morning with thirty-five hundred troops. He is recrossing the river at Williamsport tomorrow to regroup his forces."

Jackson chuckled. "Imagine a colonel of infantry commanding that many men."

"It's unheard of, sir." Ashby's guffaw of delight rang through the clearing. "Holbein is still tapped into the wires in case any more messages pass between Williamsport and Washington. Shall I have him send General Patterson a message from you, telling him to keep out of Virginia from now on?"

"The temptation is great, Major, but the Book of Proverbs says, 'Boast not thyself of tomorrow; for thou knowest not what a day may bring forth.' Thank Sergeant Holbein for me and keep in touch with him by courier."

"I've left orders for that, Colonel. The wires are going to be humming between General Patterson and the War

139

Department tomorrow. Who knows what we may learn?"

"I hope something of what General Beauregard will soon be facing on the other side of the mountain." Jackson's voice was sober now. "If I were General McDowell, I would certainly attack Beauregard before he can accumulate a large army between Washington and Richmond."

XI

The next morning the Army of Shenandoah returned to Winchester, the spirits of both officers and men considerably buoyed by news of the Yankee withdrawal northward across the Potomac. What had at first appeared to be an abortive raid at Falling Waters was now taking on many aspects of victory, a victory climaxed by an order from Richmond dated July 2, announcing the belated promotion of Colonel Thomas Jonathan Jackson to the rank of brigadier general in the Army of the Confederate States of America.

The same mail brought a letter to David from Araminta Murrell. He took it to his tent in the bivouac area of the 27th, outside the town, so he could read it in privacy.

Park Hill, Cherokee Nation
June 14, 1861

Dearest David,

Your letter from Harpers Ferry reached me in two weeks but this one may take longer, for the situation here in the Nation grows more troubled every day. Our trip from Parkersburg to Fort Smith by steamer was tiresome but uneventful. Just getting back home has given Uncle John strength, but Aunt Mary has never thrived away from her beloved Philadelphia and is poorly much of the time.

I went ashore in Memphis, as you suggested, and was lucky enough to buy a good supply of the powdered digitalis leaf from a large apothecary shop there. The proprietor of the shop gave me a picture of the foxglove plant you mentioned and Uncle John recognized it immediately. Cherokee medi-

140

cine men, he says, have been using the foxglove for years to make a tea they give to patients with dropsy—so you can see that we Indians are not such a primitive people after all.

David stopped reading to picture Araminta sitting at an escritoire in the Murrell home as she wrote, her dark head bent over the paper and her facile fingers wielding the pen. He couldn't help smiling, too, at the thought of anyone thinking of her, or Lachlan, as "primitive." She, the product of at least a thousand years of Cherokee traditions and customs joined to the sophistication of her three years at Mount Holyoke Female Seminary. And Lachlan, a military product of VMI, where men from the best families in the commonwealth traditionally strengthened their Virginia heritage against the demands of both war and politics, never really far apart in either strategy or purpose.

Sitting there with the breeze of evening blowing through the open flap of his tent, David could almost hear Araminta chuckle to herself as she penned the thrust at the pretensions of white men alone to supremacy in every field.

Lachlan has gone south to obtain his commission and also gain as much information as he can on the situation there, particularly the intentions of the agents of the Confederacy who are trying to get the Cherokee Nation to choose the South. Mr. Albert Pike, Mr. David L. Hubbard, the new Indian Commissioner for the Confederacy, and Brig. Gen. Ben McCulloch from Texas came to Tahlequah on June 5, and visited Park Hill trying to persuade Uncle John to favor the South, but he stood firm.

You have heard me speak of the schools that were established years ago, mainly by Uncle John and other leaders of the Cherokee Nation. They cost a lot of money and the Treasury of the Nation has been depleted ever since, so Uncle John offered sometime ago to sell the Federal Government eight hundred thousand acres of what we call the Neutral Land, a strip about twenty-five miles wide extending some fifty miles north from our boundary. He asked a half million dollars, plus interest on that amount since 1835, when the land was given to us by the government.

When Mr. Pike and Mr. Hubbard were here, they assured Uncle John that the Confederate Government would buy the Neutral Land for the half million dollars and also pay interest back to 1835, if he would make a treaty with the South. Uncle John told them the Cherokee Nation would remain neutral in this war, but I can see that he is troubled by the number of Cherokees who would like to join the other Civilized Tribes in supporting the Confederate Cause. He feels that Indians can only lose, no matter what side they are on, because the government, whether North or South, never really honors its treaties with our people. And I owe Uncle John enough and love him enough to put aside my own feelings where he is concerned.

Everything is beautiful here at Park Hill in the spring and early summer, almost as beautiful as New England in what they call Indian Summer. I wish we were all together here in peace and I know you would love it for I know how much you care for your own homeland.

I told you before we parted at Parkersburg that I've been intending to marry you ever since I first saw you in that fine uniform parading at VMI when I was sixteen. I'm even more determined now than ever, so when this horrible war is finished, you can be sure I'll be coming back to Virginia to put my brand on you again, this time for good.

Take good care of yourself. Remember you belong to me, too.

All my love,
Araminta

At the sound of a footfall outside, David put the letter in his pocket but even before he saw the glow of a cigar in the early dark, the aroma of it had identified the owner; nobody in the 1st Brigade smoked such strong cigars as Major Joe Stannard.

"Can I come in?" Stannard asked.

"Not with that cigar; I'll come outside where I won't be asphyxiated."

"With the Federal blockade growing tighter every day,

even tobacco is getting harder and harder to find," said Stannard. "I bought some good brandy in town, though. Care for a snifter?"

"I'll join you there—willingly." David took a drink from a bottle Stannard held out to him. "But don't let General Jackson catch you."

"Jackson's not quite the teetotaler he makes himself out to be. I once heard him tell Doctor McGuire he loves the taste of whiskey so much he refuses to let himself have it. Like a monk putting on a hair shirt, I suppose."

"The general certainly doesn't favor himself." David sat on a tree stump while Stannard settled himself comfortably on the ground, with his back against a stunted oak. The aroma of burning pine knots filled the air and from the distance came the sound of a man's voice singing the plaintive ballad of a soldier who had left his girl behind.

"I've got a daughter about as old as that girl in the song would be," said Stannard. "She's got black hair, too, like the Indian princess you brought to Harpers Ferry."

"I had a letter from her today."

"How are things in the Cherokee Nation?"

"Troubled, according to Araminta. John Ross is trying to keep the Cherokees out of the war but it's a tough job."

"Keeping people from making damn fools of themselves is always tough," said Stannard morosely. "If a bunch of tobacco- and cotton-growing politicians in South Carolina and Alabama—and a few around Richmond, too, plus Jefferson Davis, hadn't fired everybody up, we might have been able to work this thing out without fighting. After all, farmers in southwest Virginia proved a long time ago that slavery in our kind of agriculture isn't profitable."

"We've had the same experience in Botetourt County farther south."

"Your ancestors must have come up the James River from Tidewater like mine," said Stannard.

"A Preston was sheriff in Botetourt when the county extended all the way to the Mississippi in the West and north as far as what is now Chicago."

"And John Ross's people were here long before any of us. Do you think he'll be able to hold them together?"

"Araminta thinks not. She says the pro-Confederacy and pro-Union factions in the Cherokee Nation are already snapping at each other, so open warfare could break out at any time."

"With a lot of white settlers in the border states being caught up in it," said Stannard. "I firmly believe the spark that really lit the whole powder train leading to secession was when John Brown and a few stiff-necked New England abolitionists tried to capture enough rifles, by seizing the arsenal at Harpers Ferry in 1859, to arm Negro slaves and kill off a lot of white people."

"Like Nat Turner did in the Southampton insurrection of 1831, here in Virginia. But Turner got himself hanged."

"So did John Brown. It's sort of the irony of fate, too, that a colonel named Robert E. Lee was in charge of the troops that went to Harpers Ferry and seized him."

"And Major Thomas Jonathan Jackson led the VMI cadets to watch the hanging and make sure there was no uprising at Charles Town when Brown was executed. It looks like everything adds up."

"Eventually," Stannard agreed. "Which just goes to show how badly things can get mixed up when civil war breaks out inside a country. What's more, the ones who shout the loudest for war are often the first to scream when they get in a tight place."

"Like who?"

"Beauregard, for one. Because he lobbed a few cannonballs into Fort Sumter, when the Federal garrison could have been starved out in a few more days anyway. Lucky Pierre was handed the most important military job available, that of holding off the Union Army when McDowell makes up his mind to attack Richmond, instead of Robert E. Lee, who deserves it. So Beauregard settled down at Manassas Junction, because it's the most important rail concentration point in the whole area of northern Virginia and only about twenty miles or so from Washington, a fact, incidentally, that Old Jack pointed out months ago. And now that McDowell finally appears to be getting up enough courage to start the Union Army moving toward Richmond, what does the famous Frenchman do? Attack like Old Jack did at Falling Waters?"

"I take it the answer is No."

"You're damn right it's No. Beauregard is screaming for the Army of the Shenandoah to rush to his aid but what the hell does he suppose Patterson will do with his almost twenty thousand men when he discovers, as he's bound to do, that Old Jack scared the hell out of him with only three hundred men at Falling Waters?"

"He'll come slamming along the Valley Turnpike to keep the Army of the Shenandoah here at Winchester while McDowell chops Beauregard up into chunks small enough to make that bouillabaisse the Louisianians are always bragging about."

"For a doctor in uniform, you catch on quick. Which brings us to another thing: why isn't the only doctor in this army who's had any military experience at all Medical Director of the First Brigade, instead of a bright young fellow who's never smelled cordite?"

"Don't sell Hunter McGuire short, Joe. He's a very capable surgeon."

"And what kind of an administrator?"

"That we won't know for a while, but you're missing the main point. I'm a doctor, Joe—a surgeon—and I don't want to be anything else. By being attached to General Jackson's staff, McGuire will have to be more and more of an administrator and less of a doctor as Jackson is given more important commands, so I don't envy him."

"He'll be promoted faster."

"I'll be promoted when I earn it. After all, Jackson got his star because of Falling Waters."

"Don't you believe it," said Stannard. "Old Jack deserves two stars for scaring Patterson into believing three hundred were thirty five hundred, but his promotion was decided by Virginians and VMI alumni. They persuaded Jefferson Davis against his prejudices to pro-

145

mote Old Jack, because they've got a lot of influence in the Confederate Government."

"No matter how Jackson got his BG, he deserved it," said David. "What I'm most interested in right now is what's going to happen to Beauregard. If he's thrown back toward Richmond this early in the game, the war's as good as lost."

"The worst part is, I'm not too sure I won't be better off if that does happen—and you too."

"So what are you going to do?"

Stannard shrugged. "Fight like hell for Virginia—the same as you're doing, when you could easily have had a commission as a major or even a colonel in the Union forces. Anyway, there's one consolation."

"What?"

"The whole question is going to be decided in a few weeks. Beauregard didn't have to go to the trouble of infiltrating spies into Washington to learn McDowell's plans. I hear the city is full of 'em, and the leader is a Mrs. Rose Greenhow."

"I met her at some social function while I was in Washington. She's got plenty of acquaintances in high places."

"Low ones, too, from what I hear—like beds. According to the scuttlebutt, McDowell can't turn over in his sleep without Beauregard knowing it by daylight, but what good does it do the Confederacy? I tell you, doc, if Old Jack were in command of that army at Manassas Junction, Lincoln would have long since gone scuttling back to Illinois, or wherever he came from."

"The question is, do the Confederate authorities know that?"

"If you had been at the strategy conference this evening, you'd say they're beginning to. Remember how Joe Johnston and his staff used to treat Jackson when they first came to Harpers Ferry?"

David nodded. "Like a country bumpkin, who didn't know which way was up."

"They don't treat him that way any more, my friend. Like always, our glorious leader doesn't tell anybody what's on his mind but, if anybody can keep General

146

Pierre Gustave Toutant Beauregard from having his face pushed around to where his backside is now, it's Brigadier General Thomas Jonathan Jackson. And I wouldn't miss seeing how he does it for the world."

BOOK THREE

Manassas

I

By late June, the Army of the Shenandoah was spoiling for a fight—and no part of it more than Jackson's 1st Brigade, oldest in point of service of the units now making up Johnston's command of slightly less than twelve thousand men. A timid move southward by Patterson's Union army had reached Bunker Hill on June 15, nine miles north of Winchester on the Valley Turnpike, and Jackson had pleaded for permission to attack the enemy with the 1st Brigade. It was a logical move, too, for timorous as Patterson had already proved himself to be, a vigorous drive could throw him back across the Potomac once again, removing the Union threat to the Shenandoah Valley for many months and, even more important, leaving the Valley troops free to bolster Beauregard's heavily outnumbered forces at Manassas Junction some fifty miles to the southeast across the Blue Ridge.

Much to Jackson's disgust—as reported to David Preston by Captain Sandie Pendleton, who had developed a slightly infected hip, which he was treating—Johnston agreed only to sweeping cavalry thrusts by Jeb Stuart's and Turner Ashby's mounted troops. Nevertheless these, delivered with the usual dash and verve by the two cavalry commanders, were enough to shake Patterson's nerve and send him scuttling eastward with some eighteen thousand troops.

Patterson stopped near Charles Town, about ten miles west of Harpers Ferry, from which point, he apparently assured himself, he could hold the Confederate Army of the Shenandoah in check and prevent it from moving east to strengthen Beauregard at Manassas Junction. The Valley troops would be badly needed, too, when McDowell's planned thrust was launched along an obvious invasion artery, the Orange and Alexandria Railroad from just south of Washington to Gordonsville, where it joined the Virginia Central line leading through Charlottesville, Staunton and Covington in the heart of southwest Virginia. But there, too, Patterson was mistaken, for instead of anchoring Johnston's army in the Valley, his failure to attack freed it for the sort of swift maneuver Jackson and the 1st Brigade loved.

Reports filtering into headquarters of the Army of the Shenandoah at Winchester indicated that Beauregard had learned from his faithful feminine spy in Washington, Rose Greenhow, that the long awaited attack by McDowell's 35,000 troups against Fairfax Courthouse—only fifteen miles from Washington itself—and Manassas Junction, some ten miles further to the southwest, would be launched on the night of July 16. Beauregard immediately called on the Valley Army for help, but, with 12,000 Union troops less than twenty miles away, Johnston hesitated at first to move across the crest of the Blue Ridge in a fifty-mile march to help defend Richmond. Convinced, at last, by Jackson and his staff that Jeb Stuart's cavalry could keep Patterson occupied, Johnston finally issued the orders to march. But at Jackson's insistence, the troops were not told at the beginning of the march where they were going, lest the news somehow find its way to Union headquarters at Charles Town.

July 18 dawned cool and fresh with the tendrils of fog that often hung about the crest of the Blue Ridge to the east still visible along the summit. The fields were rich and green, the corn almost knee-high, and in the orchards along the way the limbs of apple trees were already show-

149

ing the green fruit that would be harvested in the fall, bright red, firm and ready for storage against the rigors of winter. Reapers were in the wheat fields, too, and in the lowlands along the river, shocks of cut winter wheat were stacked in rows of military precision.

Some ten miles to the south, the crest of the Massanutten Range of mountains, dividing the fertile valley of the Shenandoah longitudinally for a distance of roughly thirty-five miles, jutted broadly upward in the morning sunlight. Hal Perkins' wound was almost healed and, at David's request, he had been reassigned as orderly and driver of the light wagon that carried the medical supplies of the 27th.

David himself was on horseback and, as he rode along the line of the regiment marching at the point of the 1st Brigade, he was watching for anyone who fell out from the heat which increased steadily as they marched further southward. The sweating, angry faces of the Emerald Guards—a group of Irishmen already famous for their skill as fighters in battle and drinkers and carousers in camp—told him the apparent movement away from the enemy did not fit well with these brawling warriors.

"Hey, doc!" The speaker was a soldier with a bandage around his head underneath his cap, David having sewn him up a few days earlier following a brawl in a Winchester tavern. "What the hell is Joe Johnston doin' runnin' from a pack of Yankee krauts?"

"The general knows what he's doing, O'Brien. When he's ready, he'll tell you."

"It ain't him knowing what he's doin' we're worried about, Doctor," said the man behind O'Brien. "It's what Jefferson Davis is telling him to do that bothers us. If he don't let us know soon, we're gonna march right smack into Massanutten Mountain, and I sure don't want to bust my head open agin no rock."

"It won't make no difference, seein' as how you already got rocks in your head," said a rangy fellow with a long-barreled fowling piece over his shoulder and the lanyard of a powder horn slung over his arm.

A ripple of laughter ran down the line of men and Hal Perkins grinned broadly when David pulled his horse to a walk beside the wagon. Hal was driving with his still bandaged foot propped against the whip socket.

"If you had time, Cap'n, I'd take you home for a breakfast of hot biscuits with Virginia ham and eggs floating in red-eye gravy," said Hal. "Our farm's only about two miles off the turnpike at the foot of the mountain."

"Maybe we'll stop by on the way back." David tightened the reins in his hand as a sharp order was sounded somewhere ahead. "Better pull up, Hal. Looks like the column has been halted."

As the order was passed back, the long line of marchers came to a halt, unit by unit. The men stood leaning on their muskets, some cutting off chews of tobacco from plugs in their pockets. If the halt was as much as an hour, David knew, they would manage to get some gambling going. It was the favorite pastime, in camp or on the march, where pools were made every day on how far they were going. In a few minutes, Major Joe Stannard rode back along the line to where the 27th had halted, holding a sheet of paper in his hand.

"I heard some of you griping about where you're going, so hear this,' he said. "It's General Johnston's order of march."

Stannard began to read in a tone loud enough for all to hear:

Our gallant army under General Beauregard is now attacked by overwhelming numbers. The general commanding hopes that his troops will step out like men and make a forced march to save the country.

Signed: Joseph E. Johnston
Major General CSA
Commanding
Army of the Shenandoah

"He still didn't tell us where we're goin', Major," somebody objected.

"It's the junction point where the Manassas Gap Railroad going east across the Blue Ridge meets the Orange and Alexandria," said Stannard. "The Yankees figure to wipe out the Army of Northern Virginia there and take Richmond, so it's up to us to help stop 'em."

"Then what the hell are we waitin' for?" a voice with the twang of the Allegheny Mountains demanded. "The way I hear it, them Yankees always take a lot of whiskey with 'em when they go into battle. So the sooner we git thar and lick 'em, the quicker we kin start drinkin'."

A cheer went up from the long line of troops in the 1st Brigade when the familiar figure of Jackson, sitting bolt upright, as usual, on the small sorrel called Fancy that had become his favorite mount since the Battle of Falling Waters, turned east toward Ashby's Gap. Penetrating the Blue Ridge mountain range at a maximum elevation of only eleven hundred feet, compared to the four-thousand-foot crest of Stony Man, some miles to the south, the gap was almost due west of Washington, about fifty miles away.

For a while, the route of march led across fertile farm-lands and pastures. Cattle were grazing on the lush green bluegrass of the bottomlands bordering the Shenandoah River in the broad expanse of the Valley, which, far back in the prehistory of man, had once been a vast lake. Still retaining much of the fertility imparted to it by a million years or more of submersion, the soil here was extremely rich and the bluegrass a lush pasture.

The ground was only mildly rolling now in the foothills of the Blue Ridge and the dark mass of the Massanutten Range to the south grew less distinct, when a thunder-cloud began to form across its face, bordered with a lin-ing of brilliant gold by the sun shining behind it. From an occasional elevation in the land, David glimpsed the green emerald of small valleys where sprawling tributaries of the Shenandoah, tumbling downhill from the slopes of the Blue Ridge, traced a series of S's on the way to join the larger stream. Behind them a long pillar of dust, its end quite invisible to the north and west, marked the route of march.

Past small farms the troops marched hour after hour, across arched bridges spanning creeks whose waters were tinted a golden hue from acid used in iron and copper mines upstream. Now the road traversed a narrow gorge where trees growing beside it formed a leafy tunnel with the sun sprinkling through to form patterns of lacy beauty upon the earth below.

Word of the army's approach sped along the road before them as Ashby's cavalry ranged ahead to form a moving picket line, in the unlikely possibility that a Federal scouting force might have penetrated this far south and would dare to try an ambush. Jeb Stuart's cavalry had been left behind to create diversions and convince General Patterson that the Army of the Shenandoah was still in the Valley from which it took its name.

Girls in bright-colored dresses met them with gifts of fruit, fresh baked bread, cakes and other viands. Since many of the soldiers came from this part of Virginia, greetings were often exchanged, but, fearing the wrath of their beloved Old Jack, no one dropped out to gorge themselves. Instead, they grabbed a quick cup of milk without stopping, handing the empty cup to the next group to be filled again, and stuffing cakes or pieces of pie into their mouths while marching on.

Every hour, Jackson called the usual five-minute halt for rest. And since the 1st Brigade was in front and the rest of the long column could hardly walk over men sitting beside the road or sprawled in the middle of it, the entire column had perforce to rest also. Late afternoon found the long line of marchers wading the Shenandoah River in water up to their armpits; shortly the road began to climb and the going got harder.

The artillery bringing up the rear with the supply train was in three batteries. Theoretically two guns formed a section commanded by a lieutenant. But, since the militia officers rarely had significant training—except the elite Rockbridge Artillery—the gun crews had been organized on something of a pickup basis and would have to learn as they fought.

Each gun was towed by a limber drawn by six horses, with a chest of ammunition lashed to the limber. Additional supplies and ammunition were carried on a caisson, which was also drawn by a limber with its six-horse team. Each gun and limber, plus the caisson and limber, formed a unit called a platoon, under the command of a sergeant

153

with a crew of nine men. Three of these rode the horses on the left side when the weapons were being moved from place to place.

Jackson's favorite artillery piece was the six-pound Napoleon smoothbore in a gun-howitzer combination cast in bronze. The tube itself weighed eight hundred and eighty-four pounds and the carriage roughly the same, so it was no light combination. Capable of being fired several times per minute at an effective range of roughly two thousand yards, the six-pounders were versatile weapons, largely because of their great mobility. And nowhere was this more true than when they were backing up a line, firing a deadly hail of grapeshot or shrapnel directly over the heads of advancing troops into the ranks of the enemy.

The going uphill in the steady climb for the crest of the Blue Ridge, which must be surmounted before they could reach the lower ground around Manassas Junction on the eastern side, was hard for the troops and even harder for the artillery. Long before the head of the column passed through Ashby's Gap and started down the other side, stragglers had begun to fall aside.

Some simply faded into the protective covering of the thick screen of woods bordering the rough track. More at home here than on the road, they would simply disappear like the deserter who had taken David's horse on the way back to Harpers Ferry from Martinsburg. Safely away from the route of march, they would kill a rabbit or a squirrel and broil it over a fire in some secluded spot by a spring. Then, perhaps when the battle was over, they would turn up east of the Blue Ridge as scavengers to share in the spoils of war.

David's main concern was for men, many without shoes, who were determined to march on in spite of blistered feet, painful muscles and coughs made worse by the cloud of dust that almost enveloped the long line except at the very point. All afternoon, he rode back and forth along the line, stopping to bandage blisters with a soothing ointment from his saddlebags, hoisting a soldier no longer able to walk behind him for the short ride to the medical wagon, now with half a dozen occupants beside Hal Perkins, the driver.

154

When a halt was finally made for supper just over the crest of the Blue Ridge, David was saddlesore and weary. But there was still much more to be done, dressing cuts, lancing "stone bruises," treating all the minor ailments that afflicted troops on a forced march in hot and dusty weather. By the time the chores were finished, the tantalizing smell of frying bacon told him Hal Perkins was busy with a skillet over a small fire near the brook that tumbled down the mountain beside the route of march. And when he approached the fire, he wasn't surprised to see several mountain trout, already cleaned, filleted and laid out on a flat rock beside the fire, while a slab of bacon sizzled in the skillet, and a pot of dried beans was bubbling over the coals to one side.

"Don't tell me you're a cook and fisherman in addition to your other talents, Hal," he said, dropping to a flat rock beside the stream.

"You'll be able to judge how good a cook I am in a few minutes, Cap'n. I never had much time for fishing, though, so I just use the gig." Reaching across the rock where the fish lay, Hal picked up a small three-pronged fish spear he had attached to a slender pole about five feet long.

"With a pine knot torch and one of these, I can rustle a meal in almost any mountain stream. You'll have to make out with hardtack for bread, but I'll heat it up in the bacon grease to soften it after I finish frying the fish. It sure would help though if I had a ham hock to cook with the beans."

Picking up a trout fillet, Hal dropped it into the pan, where it sizzled tantalizingly. "If I had an egg and some onions, I could cook up some hush puppies that would melt in your mouth," he added. "Maybe I can get some of the makings tomorrow when we get to Piedmont, at the foot of the mountain."

The supper was everything the aroma of its cooking had promised. Even the hardtack, normally like stone, was softened considerably by cooking in the hot bacon grease. David and Hal had barely finished eating when the bugle blew for the troops to fall in once again and,

155

amidst much grumbling, they started down through the eastern foothills of the Blue Ridge.

The going was better by far than it had been climbing to Ashby's Gap after wading the Shenandoah River that afternoon, but it was more difficult for the artillery. In many cases, wheels had to be locked by thrusting a fagot through the spokes in order to put a brake on the caissons and limbers, and a cannoneer was injured coming down the mountain when a spoke snapped in a wheel of one limber. While trying to keep the vehicle on the road, the foot of the artilleryman had been caught under a wheel, and David temporarily splinted the crushed bones by binding the foot against a short board taken from a fence beside the road.

If was after midnight when the 1st Brigade came to a halt at the edge of a tiny settlement called Paris. Before unrolling his own blanket and waterproof, David applied a more effective metal splint from Hal Perkins' wagon. The camp was quiet by the time he finished, the weary soldiers having stacked arms where they were when the order to halt was sounded, before dropping down along the roadside or in haystacks.

"Did you hear about the battle over near Manassas Junction this morning, Cap'n?" Hal Perkins asked as they were making the injured cannoneer as comfortable as possible in the medical wagon.

"Where?"

"At some fords across a creek called Bull Run. We won it, too."

"How in the world would you know that, when we're still thirty miles away, maybe more?"

"A couple of fellows came from over there tonight— on the way back to Carolina. Got here just after we made camp."

"Couriers?"

"Not so you'd notice it, sir." Hal grinned. "They were real careful not to let any officers see 'em."

No matter how strict the prescribed punishment, deserters always managed to leave if they wished. A man would drop out to obey nature's call—and with the diet on a forced march limited largely to hardtack, bacon and

156

the pickled beef called salt horse, the calls came quite often—never to be heard from again as far as the Army was concerned. Many of the troops were volunteers, too, and had signed up for three months, so, with the period now nearing an end, they considered themselves more or less free to go and come as they wished.

"Did the deser——, the soldiers know any details about the battle?"

"They said our troops withdrew from around Fairfax Courthouse when the Yankees started pressing 'em a couple of days ago, and set up a line along this stream they call Bull Run. Apparently General Beauregard has decided to make a stand along that creek, and when the Federals sent out an advance party to feel our lines out, there was a right smart skirmish at a couple of crossings. I think the two fellows said at Mitchell's Ford and Blackburn's Ford."

"I'm not familiar enough with the lay of the land east of here to recognize the names," David admitted.

They said some captured Yankees told 'em the enemy units came from Tyler's division and Richardson's brigade. Anyway General Longstreet's brigade trapped 'em and cut a whole Yankee regiment to pieces."

This was good news, not so much because a skirmish in which an advance regiment was defeated was so important in the overall battle for Richmond, but because it probably meant an extra day before the main engagement. And hopefully the Army of the Shenandoah could join the Army of Northern Virginia under Beauregard in time to be effective.

"You think maybe Old—General Jackson—might like to know about this, Cap'n?" Hal asked.

"I'm sure he would. You don't know what organization the men you heard talking were from, do you?"

"They didn't say." Perkins' tone was slightly wary.

"Are they still in camp?"

"They ate and moved on, sir." Hal's tone of regret sounded genuine but David had been in uniform long enough to know better than to expect his orderly to break the code that forbade the betrayal of one soldier to an officer by another.

"I'll go over to brigade headquarters and see if they know about this already. I'll check on the patient in the wagon before I go to sleep, too, so you might as well get some sleep, Hal."

As David made his way toward brigade headquarters by the light of a pine knot torch they had been using for illumination while at work, he had to step over and around officers who hadn't bothered to wait for their orderlies to put up tents. Exhausted as the enlisted men, they had wrapped themselves in the blankets and waterproofs everyone carried and lay down where they, too, had halted. He finally found the sleeping form of Captain Sandie Pendleton, Jackson's aide, and was on the point of awakening the young officer when a voice called to him softly.

"Dr. Preston." It was Jackson. "Did you want to see me?"

"Yes, sir." David moved to where Jackson was standing outside the only tent that had been erected in the headquarters area. "I didn't intend to awaken you, sir, but I have some information you might want to hear."

"Let Captain Pendleton sleep, Doctor. I realized just now that I hadn't ordered a sentry to stand watch for the rest of the night, so I'm taking the duty for myself."

"I'd be happy to relieve you, sir."

"If I lay down to sleep after riding all day, Doctor, I would probably wake up in the morning stiff as a board and my staff would have to lift me into the saddle." David wondered if he was really hearing the usually austere Jackson chuckle to himself. "That wouldn't be a very good example, would it?"

David quickly gave Jackson the information he had gained from Hal Perkins. When he finished he could sense excitement in the way the older man moved to the open flap of his tent. When he came out seconds later he was carrying a map.

"Bring your torch over to this stump, Dr. Preston. Perhaps we can verify what young Perkins heard." With David holding the pine knot torch, Jackson spread the map out on a large stump.

"I thought I remembered the course of Bull Run from

158

my visit to Richmond in May," he said, putting his finger upon a spot on the map. "Here are the two fords, listed with the same names the deserters used. I don't know much about General McDowell's army, so I can't be sure of the organizations they mentioned, but I served with him during the Mexican War and he's a very cautious man. A cautious commander would look upon the defeat of an entire regiment as indicating a superior opposing force and think twice about throwing his entire army in a frontal attack even across a small stream like Bull Run." Jackson was still studying the layout of the map. "Under the circumstances I would say General McDowell would be more likely to carry out a holding action against the abatis and other fortifications an energetic and experienced soldier like General Beauregard would certainly have thrown up along the course of Bull Run, and choose another area for his main thrust."

"Perhaps a flank attack to try to get behind our troops and cut them off from reinforcements and supply?"

"Exactly, I'm pleased to learn you still remember my course in strategy from the Institute, Doctor. Just such an attack was carried out by Captain Robert E. Lee at Cerro Gordo, by mounting a flanking column that swung around the Mexican position and cut the National Road while a frontal action kept the defenders occupied. Scout, flank, pursue was the formula we used during the Mexican War and I have yet to see any military operation that surpasses it.

"Now comes the crucial question." Again Jackson bent over the map. "If you were in General McDowell's place, Doctor, which flank would you try to turn?"

"Our left, sir—to the west," David said promptly.

"For what reason?"

"For one thing, sir, our left flank is on the opposite side of Manassas Junction from Richmond, so I would expect it not to be as strongly defended by Confederate forces. For another, if General McDowell should manage to flank Manassas Junction entirely, not only would he cut the rail line from Strasburg in the Valley, over which reinforcements could come, but he might also succeed in cutting the Orange and Alexandria below the junction, putting himself between General Beauregard and Richmond."

"Capital, Doctor! But you haven't considered one thing. What about the Army of the Shenandoah?"

"McDowell no doubt thinks we're still in the Valley, sir, blocking any movement by General Patterson southward."

"Let us hope and pray he keeps on thinking just that, at least for two more days. Now you had better get some sleep, Captain; we will move out early." Jackson took out a large gold watch from a pocket of his uniform tunic. "Only a few hours from now in fact."

"You haven't had much sleep either, General."

"I shall be quite busily occupied until reveille, but you can leave me your torch, if you will."

Jackson hadn't disclosed his own strategy but David was fairly certain he knew what that would be. A direct thrust across Bull Run against the troops defending the position, weakened as they would be by McDowell's shift of forces for a flank attack against the Confederate left, could throw the enemy into confusion.

To David it seemed that he had only just fallen asleep when the bugles blew for the camp to break. Nor was he surprised when the 1st Brigade got under way immediately, while the other three units prepared for a somewhat more leisurely departure. Somewhere ahead, perhaps less than a day's march, the preliminary skirmishing preparatory to a major battle was going forward and Old Jack showed every intention of being involved in it. Nor did the fact that the reported Federal strength was roughly twice what the Confederacy would expect to throw against the enemy deter the commander of the 1st Brigade.

As the grumbling men swung out across the valley separating them from Bull Run Mountain, a range of hills lying at the headwaters of the creek of that name, David drew his own horse to a halt beside the road. He was waiting for the wagon driven by Hal Perkins to follow in the wake of the twenty guns making up the entire artillery contingent of the Army of the Shenandoah. Nor was it happenstance, he was sure, that all of the artillery was traveling with Jackson's swift moving brigade. As he sat his horse there in the bright morning sunlight, Major Joe Stannard pulled his mount off the road and reined in beside him.

"It's damned frustrating not to know where you're going." Stannard's voice had a note of bitterness David remembered hearing from other commanders to whom Jackson had failed to reveal the overall pattern of battle he always carried in his head. "Do you perchance know, David?"

"I think so." He rapidly recounted his after-midnight conference with Jackson.

"There's a railway station at Piedmont, a short distance to the southwest, I remember passing through it on the way to Strasburg and Harpers Ferry back in April," said Stannard. "My guess would be that Jackson plans to use the railroad to move the brigade to Manassas for the battle."

"Do you think we'll make it?"

"If Old Jack says McDowell will avoid attacking across Bull Run because one of his regiments got chewed up there yesterday, you can be damn sure it will probably happen that way." Stannard rubbed his chin. "The unerring way our commander has of being able to predict just how other people will act would almost make you think all that praying he does has gotten him the ear of the Lord, wouldn't it?"

David laughed. "If he sets the brigade marching around the next place we attack, blowing trumpets seven times like Joshua of old, I wouldn't even be surprised when the walls start falling down."

Halfway to Piedmont and the railroad, the sound of cheering was heard coming from the rear of the long line of soldiers, whose bayonets glittered in the morning sunlight as they marched. The sound moved along the line, growing in volume as more and more of the men became aware of its cause. David was riding beside the medical wagon when he saw the reason, a large horse bearing an officer wearing a broadbrimmed, shallow-crowned hat. It was fawn colored with the right side of the brim pinned to the crown by a gilt star, and a large ostrich plume

161

attached to the right side waved as the officer galloped along beside the line of troops.

The newcomer wore a spotless gray uniform with collar and cuffs edged in white serge. His riding gauntlets were also white and the insignia of a colonel on his sleeve was in such bright gold braid—"chicken guts" in the parlance of the foot soldiers—that it had obviously been polished that very morning. Behind him rode an equally dashing cavalry troop, waving their hats and shouting insults at the foot soldiers as they passed the plodding line.

The appearance of J. E. B. Stuart, already a legend in the Army of the Shenandoah, buoyed the spirits of the tired troops like nothing else could have done—except perhaps the sight, a short time later, of the long line of railroad flatcars on the track at Piedmont with steam hissing from the boiler of the waiting locomotive.

As the infantrymen began climbing on the flatcars, where they perched, legs hanging over the sides and rifles lying flat, Sandie Pendleton rode back to where David was tying his horse to the back of the medical wagon. It would continue on toward Manassas by road while he rode on the train, in case there was fighting before Hal Perkins caught up with the brigade later that day. Pendleton drew rein beside where David was standing.

"General Jackson wanted me to tell you that Colonel Jeb Stuart intercepted a telegraph message from General Patterson to General McDowell yesterday afternoon," he said. "It stated that the Army of the Shenandoah is still in the Valley, where Patterson is keeping some 25,000 of us pinned down near Winchester."

II

By four o'clock that afternoon, the men of the 1st Brigade were lined up beside the railroad about twenty miles east of Piedmont, and the train was disappearing in the direction from which it had come, on the way to transport more troops. Jackson had ridden ahead to confer with General Beauregard, acklowledging with an uplifted gauntlet the cheers of the crowd lining his route.

The conference with Beauregard lasted no more than half an hour and David was quite sure Jackson was urging upon the Louisianian just a direct attack across the fords as they had discussed the night before near the settlement of Paris. But when Jackson came back from Beauregard's headquarters, the 1st Brigade moved into position between Mitchell's and Blackburn's fords, and bivouacked in the woods there, proving that, for the time being at least, Jackson's arguments had been ignored.

Hal Perkins and the medical wagon at the end of a train of artillery caissons and limbers, and an even longer line of supply wagons, arrived around midnight. By the afternoon of July 20, three of the four brigades of the Army of the Shenandoah were in reserve between Mitchell's and Blackburn's fords, waiting to parry any serious thrust across the stream, should McDowell decide to make it, or launch their own attack if he did not. The 4th Brigade of Alabama and Mississippi regiments under General Kirby Smith had not yet reached the field, nor had the rest of the Valley troops, it was said because a traitorous railroad engineer had managed to wreck some cars upon the track and block the line.

Though outranked by General Joseph E. Johnston, who had come upon the scene late that afternoon, Beauregard was directing the Confederate forces because he was more familiar with the terrain. Shortly after midnight, news received from a spy indicated that McDowell had finally decided, as David had predicted, upon a shallow crossing at Sudley Ford and the Warrenton Turnpike to form two converging arcs—the main prong under General Burnside and the second driving almost due west along the Warrenton Turnpike—McDowell obviously hoped to circle the Confederate forces between Manassas Junction and Bull Run and destroy them.

To counteract the Federal movement, Beauregard finally decided to attack the Union left flank, as Jackson had urged, by throwing the 1st Brigade across the fords of Bull Run, creating a circular movement from which troops could be swung quickly into any opening that presented itself.

In order to be ready for an expected stream of casualties, once the attack got under way, David and Hal Perkins moved the medical wagon on the night of July 20 to a spot beside the road from Mitchell's Ford, planning to establish a dressing station there. But when by two hours after daylight David heard no sound of major firing nearby, he left Hal Perkins at the dressing station and climbed a rather sharp hill nearby to see if he could find out what was happening.

The elevation, David discovered when he reached the top, was already occupied—by a single officer, whom he didn't recognize, perched atop a thirty-foot tower of two-by-four pine scantling. A fairly large brass telescope, obviously more useful than the glasses used by most officers who could afford them, lay on the platform atop the obviously hastily erected tower and a wooden case containing what looked like several flags was propped against a rather flimsy-looking railing around the platform.

"Hope I'm not intruding," David called up to the occupant of the tower. "I'm Captain David Preston from General Jackson's brigade."

"Captain E. P. Alexander, General Beauregard's signal officer," said the observer pleasantly. "Climb up, if you like, Captain; we'll have a grandstand seat for the action, once it begins."

Surveying the vista that lay before him from the vantage point of the signal tower, David saw that it was remarkably like the map he had examined three nights before with Jackson by the light of a pine knot torch. The snakelike course of Bull Run was easily traced, as were the fords and the narrow Stone Bridge where the turnpike to Warrenton crossed the creek. In the near foreground he could see Confederate troops moving among the trees and could also make out several units traveling northwestward—the wrong direction for them to be taking, according to the last battle order he had seen.

"What unit did you say you were with, Captain?" the signal officer asked.

"Twenty-seventh Virginia."

"From Johnston's Army of the Shenandoah?"

"Yes, Jackson's brigade."

164

"You made a fast march to get here. General Beauregard was afraid the Secretary of War and President Davis had delayed too long in sending in reinforcements."

"I see some troops there to the northwest," said David. "But the order I last saw didn't indicate a concentration in that area."

"General Beauregard changed those orders after midnight." The signal officer reached for a map lying on a stump and pointed to a heavy black line crossing it in a slightly southward direction. "Here's the Warrenton Turnpike going toward Gainesville—"

"We passed that town on the railroad before reaching Manassas Junction."

"Then you're roughly familiar with the lay of the land." Alexander extended the telescope, focused it and handed it to David. "Center on the Stone Bridge across the north fork of Bull Run, it's easy to see."

David leveled the glass and made out the arch of what was called the Stone Bridge—for obvious reasons—on the Warrenton Turnpike.

"You can see another bridge a little over two miles away," Alexander continued. "In the new orders, two small brigades under Cocke and Evans are to hold the Yankees back at that point, while General Ewell and General Holmes at the extreme left of our line east of Blackburn's Ford swing around west and attack the right flank of the enemy."

"That's certainly a switch of orders."

"A last minute switch. I'll bet the men affected are grousing at having to march so far before they can fight."

"What about the Army of the Shenandoah?"

"Your troops are still in the neighborhood of Mitchell's and Blackburn's fords." Alexander pointed to the map. "But they're supposed to follow Ewell, once he's clear of the area and moving west."

"Suppose the enemy launches a thrust in strength across the Stone Bridge? Couldn't our forces there be split in two?"

"That's what I'm up here for. From this elevation I can see for several miles in any direction, though not as

165

far as Professor Lowe up there." Alexander pointed northward, to where a large captive balloon tugged at its moorings high above the enemy sector.

"If the Yankees start moving in the center," he continued, "I'm to signal another tower like this one at General Johnston's headquarters, so your Army of the Shenandoah can be concentrated at the bridge to reinforce the two brigades there."

"It all seems to have been planned well."

"Very well," Alexander agreed. "So far there's been a fair amount of action at the bridge but no sign of a major troop movement. What worries me is that General Ewell's troops seem to be taking so long to get into position to turn the enemy's flank."

"Do you see any sign that the brigades from the Army of the Shenandoah have started moving into place?"

"They're still in reserve, ready to move toward the Stone Bridge if the action increases there, or support Ewell on the left flank when he starts to strike the enemy."

"I'm no military strategist, Captain," said David. "But I've seen actual fighting in Europe and I'm always afraid of such complicated maneuvers before a battle. The sort of mistake that failed to notify me my regiment can be expected to fight some distance away from my dressing station, leaving them without medical support, could also result in units not being where they're supposed to be at the right time."

"I share your fears," Alexander said with a frown. "According to the new battle plan, Ewell should be launching his attack already and that would be the signal for General Johnston's forces to support him. But I see no sign of it from here."

While he was speaking, Alexander had been studying the terrain with the telescope, the brass tube pointing at an angle roughly north by northwest. Now he stiffened suddenly.

"I can see movement on the enemy side in the neighborhood of Sudley Ford, but can't tell whether the troops are theirs or ours." He handed David the telescope. "See what you make of it."

When David focused the powerful glass until the field of vision was sharp and clear, he could see individual soldiers but at that distance in the haze of a July morning, the difference between the blue of the Yankee uniform and the grayish blue of the Confederate was very difficult to distinguish. Then suddenly, a tall man appeared upon the round stage encompassed by the telescope lens; and, though David could see only the upper half of his body, that was enough to identify him beyond question.

Only one organization in either the Union or the Confederate Army wore loose red blouses and *bersaglieri* hats—a New York detachment, made up of Swiss, Hungarians, Italians and a half dozen other nationalities, with a few Cossacks. Known by the colorful title of the Garibaldi Guard, it had been the most colorful part of the long parade at Lincoln's inauguration less than six months ago.

"Those are Union troops!" David exclaimed. "I saw them last spring in Washington."

"Are you sure?" Captain Alexander took the telescope and studied the moving spot of color David pointed out to him.

"Absolutely."

"Some of the Zouave companies among Confederate units have pretty fantastic uniforms," Alexander said doubtfully.

"Not like this one. It's the Garibaldi Guard from New York. Mostly they're a bunch of ruffians. But if they fight in battle like they fight in barrooms, they'll be hard to beat."

Captain Alexander didn't argue further but reached into the wooden case for his signal flags. Each on a short staff so it could be handled easily, the flags featured a bright red square standing out in the center of a white field so it could be easily seen. Busy studying the distant movement of men in the telescope, David had no time to watch the signal officer wield his flags in this new and strange method of communication. But since Alexander spelled out the letters of the message verbally, as he moved the flag to communicate with General Beaure-

167

gard's headquarters, David understood the urgent message:

L-O-O-K O-U-T F-O-R O-U-R L-E-F-T; Y-O-U A-R-E
T-U-R-N-E-D!

The message was repeated several times before a distant answering signal indicated that it had been received.

"I've never seen that method of communication before," said David when Alexander, sweating from the effort of moving the flags up, right to left and return to signify "One"; up, down and up right for "Two" and so on, following a prearranged code—put the flags back into the case.

"I'm not sure it was ever used in America before," said the signal officer. "But I hear Professor Lowe has figured out how to dangle a telegraph wire from his balloons and communicate directly with the arm below. Compared to that, using a high hill, a telescope and signal flags is about like comparing a bow and arrow to a Sharps rifle."

III

As it happened, Captain Alexander's fear about the battle being lost almost became a reality, because of the mix-up in orders following Beauregard's change of plans as late as midnight on July 21. Fortunately, by the time David and Hal Perkins harnessed the two mules that drew the medical wagon, Colonel Evans at the Stone Bridge had finally decided the thrust at that crossing was a feint. Leaving four companies behind at the bridge to defend it—like Horatio of classic fame—Evans took the ten companies remaining in his command and crossed the Warrenton Turnpike in a forced march to pit them against the Federal column of Colonel Ambrose E. Burnside at the point of the attacking flank movement, in the neighborhood of Sudley Ford and Matthews Hill, a short distance to the south.

Considerably ahead of the main left wing of the Confederate Army, Evans' troops thus suffered the brunt of

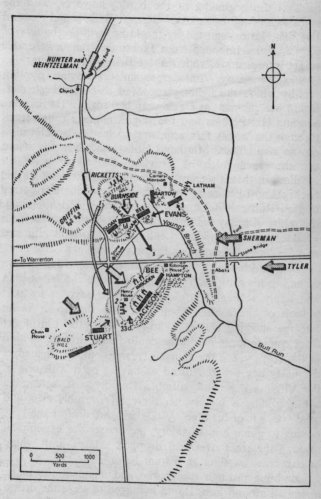

*The Battle of First Bull Run or First Manassas,
July 21, 1861*

the attack when the Federals attempted to turn the Confederate wing. His forces were able to hold the enemy back at the beginning of the battle, however, with the assistance of the brigades of General Bartow and General Bee. The latter, assisted by the horse artillery battery of Captain John Imboden from Jackson's troops, were able to get into position, with the 1st Brigade in reserve.

With so many Confederate units changing position rapidly where the fighting appeared to be thickest, confusion was rampant as David searched for the 1st Brigade. Sending Hal Perkins and the wagon along a rough track through the woods that appeared to lead to an elevation on the map labeled Matthews Hill, from which the sound of firing seemed to be heaviest, David cut across a meadow in that direction with a light medical kit on his back. Almost before he knew it, after crossing a tributary of Bull Run called Young's Branch, he found himself in the midst of heavy fighting at the edge of the woods, with a melee of blue and gray uniforms all around him and minié balls whistling uncomfortably close.

Ahead he saw a soldier fall with blood spurting from a wound in his arm and ran to kneel beside the fallen man and apply a rough tourniquet, using a bayonet to twist a loop of the soldier's belt and stop the flow. As he finished showing the man how to keep the tourniquet from coming loose before he could find a dressing station at the rear, where the spurting vessel could be ligated, a drummer boy he recognized as having been with one of the Virginia regiments stumbled blindly past, screaming while holding a bloody handkerchief over his eyes and what was left of his face. As David started after the boy, hoping to guide him to safety, the crack of a cannonball through the trees overhead dropped a large limb where he had been standing an instant before.

Stumbling through the smoke and flame of the battle raging all around him, David managed to seize the drummer boy's sleeve. But, blind with pain and fear, the youth fought even against help, until the sudden dull thud of another minié shattered his temple. Dead before his body started falling, the boy careened against David, smearing his shoulder and arm with blood and brains and setting a sudden spasm of nausea clutching at his insides.

"Which way, Captain? Which way?" David hadn't even realized the soldier with the arm wound was following him until the man's voice, little more than a screech of pain and fear, sounded in his ear. Even then the words were barely audible above the roar of battle and the screams of the wounded.

"I don't know," David answered. "I can't see the sun for the smoke and the trees."

"I crossed a road a few yards back there just now," the soldier managed to say, even as a small tree, cut down by cannon fire, forced them to turn quickly to one side.

"See if you can make it then," David told him. "There must be other wounded around here."

Even as he spoke David stumbled over a body, but a brief examination showed him the blue-clad figure was beyond medical help, half his torso torn away by the charge of grapeshot that had struck him full in the chest.

"Doctor!" Vaguely David heard the man with the wounded arm call. "I've found the road. It's over here."

Moving toward the voice through the trees, ducking instinctively at the angry hum of the bullets that filled the air, although he realized that any missile really intended for him would have dropped him before he could duck, David staggered toward the road, still invisible in the pall of smoke from the trees and underbrush set fire by the artillery barrage sweeping the woods. When he came upon it, he barely had time to scramble aside as a team pulling a limber attached to the carriage of one of the light cannon popularly known as the "horse artillery," although usually drawn by mules, almost ran him down. The artilleryman riding the left-hand lead mule pulled it away just in time to keep David from being struck down by the hooves of the wildly plunging animal as the gun rolled on.

"What the hell are you doing here, Captain Preston?" a familiar voice snapped, and David looked up while scrambling to his feet in the dirt beside the road to see the blazing eyes of Captain John Imboden. Reining in his horse, Imboden warned the driver of a second limber to one side so as to pass without injuring David.

"Looking for the battle," David heard a strange voice croak, then realized that it was his own.

"You're going the wrong way, this is a retreat." Reaching down from his saddle, Imboden pulled David to his feet. "Get up behind me before the Yankees catch us."

Imboden's horse was already moving as David seized the saddle and was swung up behind the husky officer.

"I was following a soldier with a tourniquet—"

"He grabbed a seat on the limber that almost ran you down. The Yankees have been pounding us to pieces on Matthews Hill and General Bee ordered a retreat."

"Where's Jackson and the First Brigade?" David managed to ask, while holding on with all his might to keep from being thrown from his precarious perch behind Imboden, as the artillery unit raced on down the winding country road away from the battle raging behind them.

"God only knows but I sure wish He'd tell me. Evans, Bee and Bartow were swept back from Matthews Hill when they got ahead of the main body. If somebody doesn't put on the brakes pretty soon, this is going to be a rout."

The cavalcade of two guns suddenly shot out of the woods into a small clearing just behind the top of a wooded hill. As Imboden ordered the unit to halt, David slid from behind him. He had no trouble recognizing the officer sitting like a ramrod in his saddle a few yards away, while troops of the 1st Brigade streamed by him on both sides, evidently going into position near the top of the hill.

"Dammit, General!" said Imboden angrily. "The Yankees have been beating the hell out of us."

"You don't have to swear, Captain," said Jackson severely. "Unlimber your battery. I'll support it here behind Henry House Hill."

Just then General Barnard E. Bee, who commanded the 3d Brigade of Johnston's Army of the Shenandoah, rode up to Jackson. Bee's sword was in his hand and his uniform was covered with dust and soot from having ridden through the burning trees and underbrush, where

172

the heavy fighting was still going on. As Bee pulled his horse to a sliding stop, scattered remnants of his own men came running out of the woods, many without weapons or equipment and none stopping to salute the two generals, proof that Imboden had been correct in identifying the situation as a near rout.

"They're beating us back, General!" Bee shouted to Jackson.

"Then, sir, we will give them the bayonet," said Jackson calmly as he directed his own men to form a line on the eastern edge of the elevation, which David remembered now from the map was called Henry House Hill. As he was turning, Jackson saw David and his eyes suddenly blazed with anger.

"Captain Preston!" he snapped. "Where is your wagon?"

"I don't know, sir. I sent it around by the road."

"The road's at the bototm of this hill behind us. Get down there and set up your dressing station; you'll be receiving casualties soon."

David saluted and started down the hill, but not before he saw General Bee ride into the stream of his retreating troops, breasting it as he shouted to an aide—in what sounded to David at the time distinctly like a tone of exasperation: "Look! There's Jackson standing like a stone wall!" And then in a tone of resignation, Bee added: "Rally behind the Virginians."

That Bee was hotly indignant at what appeared to be Jackson's refusal to move forward could not be doubted. But only when he found Hal and the medical wagon at the base of the hill was David able to move to a spot where he could see the position that had aroused Bee's exasperation.

Jackson's 1st Brigade had moved forward by then and occupied the top of Henry House Hill. Calmly arranging his men and his artillery near the crest of the elevation with a fringe of pines to protect them, Jackson had selected a place of battle where he would have a considerable advantage over the enemy. He appeared determined to stay there, too, until the Federals reached the spot and he could engage them on his own terms.

Searching for a protected spot for the dressing station in a position of relative safety behind the 1st Brigade, David could see Jackson himself riding up and down on Fancy behind the front line of troops. As calmly as if he were on maneuvers, Old Jack was directing the placement of Imboden's small mule battery, lining them up beside the Rockbridge and Leesburg artillery units at the most critical point yet reached in a battle that could well settle the fate of the Confederate States of America within the next few hours.

When he counted twenty-six guns in line just behind the crest of Henry House Hill where the Yankees would not be able to see them easily, David realized that, in the midst of what had almost become a rout, Jackson was calmly laying a trap for the exultant enemy soldiers who would come charging up Henry House Hill at any moment, sure of victory. He could even hear Jackson giving the artillerymen instructions to put short fuses on the shells so they would explode close to the advancing troops, after being fired directly over the heads of his own men lying just behind the crest of the hill, from which position they could send a hail of bullets against the Yankees. And he could understand, too, why General Bee had been exasperated by Jackson's insisting on keeping his position of preference—literally like a stone wall —instead of moving forward to relieve Bee's hard-pressed troops.

David saw Jackson throw up his left hand with his open palm forward in a characteristic gesture, as he gave the artillerymen some instructions. When the general suddenly jerked his hand back and a spot of blood appeared on one of his fingers, he knew Jackson was wounded. But when he instinctively started forward to help, Jackson saw him and his face darkened with anger as he spurred Fancy down the slope toward the medical wagon.

"Your place is at the rear, caring for the wounded, Captain Preston!" he said sharply. "Stay there."

"You're wounded, General," David started to protest, but Jackson shrugged it off, his eyes blazing with the same hot glare David had seen in them during the brief fight at Falling Waters Church.

"Only a scratch! A mere scratch!" Pulling a handkerchief from the pocket of his uniform, Jackson wrapped it around the finger and galloped back to where the artillery batteries were being made ready.

Hearing the freshly loaded guns of the three batteries discharge almost in unison, and feeling the earth shudder, David felt a moment of intense exhilaration at the realization that Jackson's plan was working like a well-oiled machine—until he remembered the drummer boy and the body of the Union soldier he'd found in the woods and thought of the enormous carnage that must be resulting even now, as the shells with their short fuses exploded almost in the faces of the advancing Federals, spraying them with lethal grapeshot and shrapnel.

For the next several hours, David was far too busy caring for the wounded that poured down the back slope of Henry House Hill to wonder how the battle was going. Here and there, however, a less severely wounded soldier was able to describe something of the horror being enacted on the other side, allowing him to keep some track of what was happening. At the height of the battle for the strategic hill, the 33d Virginia Regiment, hidden until then by a copse near the left end of the line, had charged the Federal batteries that were shelling Jackson's position. Somehow the enemy had mistaken the charging Virginians for their own men and had held their fire.

Screaming the rebel yell, itself calculated to strike terror into the heart of an enemy, the regiment, composed mainly of mountain men from the wilder areas of the Allegheny Range, had come over the hill firing and jabbing with bayonets as they ran. And long before they could fire their cannon in their own defense, the Union artillerymen had been annihilated, leaving the battery helpless.

Severely battered and already half decimated by the massed cannon of Jackson's artillery on the hill before Henry House, as well as by a slashing charge of Jeb Stuart's cavalry from the left flank of the Confederate forces, the Union troops gave ground. They managed to rally once, keeping themselves briefly from being driven off the hill, but, sensing that near defeat was now on the point of being turned into victory, Beauregard had ordered a general advance. And, when the Confederates charged again, the Union troops were driven in confusion across the Warrenton Turnpike and Young's Branch.

At the climax of this charge, both Johnston and Beauregard appeared upon the field, David was told later, riding forward with the standards of the 4th Alabama beside them. Meanwhile, from the position atop Henry House Hill, Jackson's artillery was still pounding the retreating Federal troops. Progress was halted briefly by a daring charge of the Fire Zouaves of the 11th New York in their blue and scarlet uniforms with white turbans. And backed by two artillery batteries, their desperate counterattack might have stopped the Confederate advance, had not Jeb Stuart and his cavalry come racing across from the left flank, charging the Zouaves and riding them down at the same moment the 33d Virginia went through them jabbing and shouting.

Working at the dressing station less than a thousand yards back of the heavy fighting around Henry House Hill, David Preston could hear the din of battle quite clearly all that afternoon. The sharp chatter of small arms fire was easily distinguishable from the almost constant booming of the cannon Jackson had carefully located behind the crest of the ridge. But, except for the occasional crash of a cannonball or the explosion of a shell in the surrounding woods, the dressing station might as well have been miles from the battle.

Since the various units of the 1st Brigade had been concentrated in one position by virtue of their crucial role in stopping the Federal advance, this one dressing station served as a central point for the wounded of the entire brigade. Two other surgeons were helping but David, by virtue of his considerable experience on the battlefield, which none of the other possessed, had assumed charge of the busy unit from the very first.

One surgeon had been dispatched as soon as casualties began to arrive, to the roadway leading into the dressing station area to sort the wounded. Anyone able to return to the front after his wound was dressed was given first priority because of the desperate need at the battlefront

176

for those able to shoot. Others who, with preliminary dressings, could walk back to the brigade infirmary operated under the direction of Dr. Hunter McGuire at Manassas Junction, a little over two miles to the south, were quickly treated and sent on their way to the rear. A third group, the severely wounded, needing immediate surgery to save life, David treated himself, stopping bleeding, occasionally ligating an artery which, spurting in an otherwise non-fatal wound would have been fatal. He also splinted fractures and otherwise prepared patients for the journey back by ambulance or wagon to the brigade infirmary.

By late afternoon the flow of casualties had slackened to where the other two doctors were able to care for them, and David decided to investigate the question of whether the dressing station should be moved nearer the scene of actual conflict. Carrying a temporary pack containing dressing materials, opiates and a few instruments and ligatures, he circled Henry House Hill toward where Young's Branch crossed the Warrenton Turnpike and quickly found himself surrounded by scenes of bloody carnage such as he had not witnessed even in the most sanguine skirmishes between Garibaldi's partisan troops and the Austrians.

The ground was littered with dead men and cast aside or partially wrecked equipment, both Union and Confederate. Here and there, men wandered about dazedly, staggering over bodies, falling sometimes over equipment or blanket rolls, crawling when they couldn't walk. In one shallow ravine the fallen, both gray and blue, lay in well-arranged windrows, a macabre military formation quite as horrifying as it was strange. Ahead and off to the left, where Jeb Stuart's cavalry had cut them down, the fallen bodies of New York Fire Zouaves resembled a row of bright-colored patches across the pattern of a crazy quilt, each representing a life ended summarily here on a dusty battlefield two hundred and fifty-odd miles from their regular small spheres of existence as members of the New York Fire Department.

To the right, past Henry House Hill itself, David thought he could distinguish some cannon of John Imboden's batteries still firing and, moving toward the sound, found himself almost immediately in a stand of pines that had obviously taken the brunt of the artillery barrage. Trunks and branches were scarred and torn from shell fire until the whole area looked oddly like the path a small tornado had taken across the countryside of Botetourt County, far to the southwest, when he was a boy.

There was still considerable firing in the area and, with the sun not much more than an hour high, the woods were full of dark and menacing shadows. Stumbling over a blue-clad body here and there among the trees in the near dusk, David was startled to see a light area visible through the forest ahead and moved toward it. But when he came to the edge of the small open space he could hardly believe his eyes.

The clearing—it could hardly have been as much as an acre—could have originally served any one of a dozen functions: a potato patch, a corn, wheat or tobacco field, even a cabbage or collard garden. Right now it contained a small hospital under the canvas roof of a large tent, the sides of which had been rolled up to allow free passage of air on the hot July afternoon. A Union flag was tied to a sapling at the front of the tent and perhaps two dozen wounded men, some in blue, some in gray, lay on the several rows of cots filling the covered space. A second banner, below the Union flag, bore the identifying insignia of the unit, which David didn't recognize.

A Union medical officer was moving along the line of cots, staggering sometimes as if dazed by the holocaust into which this unit of mercy had somehow been thrust, bending over here to give a wounded man a drink of water and pausing there to adjust a bandage. At the edge of the clearing David could see several wagons, brand new and of a spring type he had never seen before, the horses that had apparently drawn them tethered to a pole running between two trees. He was at the edge of the clearing when the Union medical officer looked up and raised his hand.

"Don't shoot!" he said wearily, as if it really didn't

make much difference. "I'm a medical officer and a non-combatant."

"Jess Bayard!" David cried.

"David Preston!" The two men had been fellow students and roommates at Jefferson Medical College but hadn't seen each other in the two years since graduation.

"What the hell are you doing here?" Bayard asked as the two doctors shook hands.

"I'm regimental surgeon of the Twenty-seventh Virginia."

"They must be part of the group of Rebels that came tearing by here a couple of hours ago and set all our troops running."

"That sounds more like a bunch of fighting Irishmen called the Emerald Guards. But what's all this?"

"A new type of field hospital designed to work close behind the front lines, but I still can't figure out how in the hell we got ahead of 'em without moving an inch." Major Bayard shrugged. "Well, we're your prisoners, David. What are you going to do with us?"

"Damned if I know; nothing in regulations covers this. Of course I could take a chance and accept your parole—"

"Oh no!" said Bayard. "The way our troops were running, they're probably halfway to Washington by now. I'd be sure to get killed before I could find our lines."

"Have all your patients been treated?"

"All who needed surgery have had it." Major Bayard nodded toward a refuse pile a few yards away, where a half dozen arms and legs spoke for themselves. "And so have I."

Sinking into a canvas chair beside a medicine chest that formed the main office for the portable hospital, the Union doctor reached inside the chest and brought out a pint bottle of whiskey. Taking a long pull, he handed the bottle to David, who took a liberal drink before selecting another camp chair for himself.

"How long has the Union had this sort of an outfit? he asked.

"This is the first," said Bayard. "After we graduated, I went over to the University of Pennsylvania Hospital

179

to study more surgery. One day I read about those tent hospitals the Austrians were using in Italy—"

"I saw some of them in operation."

"I wish I could have, maybe I'd have done a better job with this one. Anyway, as soon as it looked like we were going to have war, I got busy at the hospital and put this thing together. The War Department accepted it on a sort of provisional basis, you know how slow the Medical Bureau is to approve anything new."

"From here it looks like it turned out all right."

"It's a neat little hospital. Worked perfectly as long as I had somebody to help me here, but, when shells started whistling through the pines around noon, most of my personnel went north. At that, they were only about two jumps behind a newspaper reporter who came down with us to write a story about this new departure in caring for the wounded. I doubt if *he'll* stop until he crosses the Potomac again."

David was examining the surgical equipment in a smaller, adjoining tent. It included a collapsible operating table, oil lamps with reflectors to concentrate light upon the operating field, a stove for heating water and a surgical chest, the interior of which could be lifted up to form a rack with a half dozen metal trays, making the instruments easily available.

"This setup is devised to make excellent surgical care available very near the fighting," Bayard explained. "The whole thing can be ready to move in those special wagons in less than an hour, too—if your personnel don't cut and run the way mine did."

"Are the wagons built to serve as ambulances, too?"

"Yes. The litters slide into special racks."

"You certainly did a good job."

"You'll have plenty of time to examine it." Bayard took another pull at the bottle. "As of now it's yours and I'm your prisoner."

"I'll take you back with me and see what the medical director wants to do about you," said David. "Since you were working at the University of Pennsylvania, you may know Dr. Hunter McGuire."

180

"Sure. McGuire's one of the smartest young doctors who ever studied at the university. Why?"

"He's General Jackson's personal physician—and medical director of the First Brigade."

"What about you?"

"I'll stay with the troops in the field—and with one of these hospitals if I can swing it."

"Like I said, this one is your as of now."

"I still have to persuade the Medical Department in Richmond that a field hospital like this is badly needed."

"This battle is proving that. By the way, who's winning?"

"I don't think anybody knows yet."

"Why don't we both stay here until they decide and maybe we can figure out which one of us is going to be the prisoner of the other?"

The idea was enough to start them both laughing but they stopped suddenly when a chunky man with a craggy face and deep-set, intelligent eyes, rode into the clearing. Pulling his horse to a stop, John Imboden dismounted and looped the reins around an overhanging limb.

"Evenin', Dr. Preston," he said, as imperturbably as if he were meeting David in the front yard of his home. "Need any help?"

"Major Jesse Bayard, Captain John Imboden," said David. "Jesse was a classmate of mine in medical school, John."

Imboden shook hands with the Union officer. "I'm not too sure that's the best sort of a uniform to be wearing around here right now, Major," he said. "The fighting seems to be over for today, but the 33rd found an abandoned sutler's wagon about a mile away with a lot of whiskey on it. Apparently half of Washington came out to see how quick the Union troops would destroy the Confederacy and brought the materials for a celebration."

"I had to pull my wagons off the road a half dozen times day before yesterday to make way for a senator and his carriage or some crony of Abraham Lincoln's," said Bayard with feeling. "Since your army has captured me and my hospital, the medical supplies belong to you."

Taking another bottle of whiskey from the chest, he handed it to the artilleryman. "Drink, Captain?"

"Nothing like good whiskey at the end of a day." Imboden took a long drink and wiped his mouth with his sleeve. "Now that you've captured a prize singlehandedly, David, what'll you do with it?"

"Major Bayard and I had just decided to stay here until tomorrow morning and see who's going to be who's prisoner."

"I'm afraid nobody knows the answer to that quite yet," Imboden admitted. "We seem to be winning at the moment, but we had almost lost the first phase at Matthews Hill this morning when Colonel Evans' command was hard pushed. General Bee went to Evan's rescue against his better judgment and, as a result, all of us were being pushed back when I found you this morning, David. It could have been a rout if Old Jack and the First Brigade hadn't made a stand just behind the crest of Henry House Hill. I was down to three rounds per gun by then."

"I heard General Bee tell Jackson the enemy was pushing him back but all Old Jack said was, 'Then, sir, we'll give them the bayonet.'"

Imboden nodded. "Bee didn't like the implication that his troops should have made a stand, but he did manage to stop them."

"I heard Bee accuse Jackson of standing like a stone wall in that position just back of the crest of Henry House Hill while his own troops were being cut to pieces," said David.

"The men have already named him Stonewall Jackson," said Imboden. Then he added soberly, "But I'm afraid we'll never know exactly what General Bee meant. He was killed late this afternoon."

"Too bad. He was a brave man."

"A lot of brave men have died here—on both sides. I've done more amputations today than I would do in a year of civilian practice," said the Federal medical officer. "The worst part is that in Philadelphia at my own hospital, I'm pretty sure I could have saved half of those limbs."

Imboden looked at the sun, now barely visible through

182

the trees. "I'm on my way back to General Beauregard's headquarters to report for General Jackson," he said. "Can I take a message or anything?"

"You can do more than that." David suddenly saw an answer to the question of what to do with his prisoner. "Would you mind taking Major Bayard back with you and turning him over to Hunter McGuire? They're old friends and McGuire can see that he gets decent treatment."

"What about you?"

"I'll stay here but you can stop at my dressing station back of Henry House Hill and tell Hal Perkins to move everything up here. If I know Jackson, he'll be attacking again in the morning and this looks like a good place for me to work."

"Some of my patients ought to be moved back," said Bayard.

"We'll load two of your wagons, if Captain Imboden has time. You can drive one, Jesse, and that will clear some space for more casualties if there's any more fighting."

David felt a bit lonely as he watched the two wagons pull out and move south, the more so because Imboden had taken him aside before leaving and told him a full-scale attack was to be launched shortly after three in the morning. Which meant that he might be a Union prisoner himself before tomorrow was ended.

David was busy for the next several hours, caring for the remaining wounded prisoners. During the time he could marvel at the thoroughness with which the field hospital had been planned and equipped. It consisted of the surgery tent he had already examined and a storage area under canvas, plus the main ward tent housing thirty-six patients and capable of being expanded by using several other similar-size tents. The whole had obviously been planned with great care and an adequate supply of dried food in the two supply wagons could be prepared easily by adding water and heating in nested pans upon a field range fired either by kerosene or by wood, insuring that the patients would be well nourished.

The morning attack began with the thunder of artillery, and the first group of casualties arrived just as dawn was breaking with news of heavy fighting, when northern troops of the 1st Rhode Island Regiment, commanded by Colonel A. E. Burnside, rallied sharply. Once again, however, the Confederate artillery that had proved so effective the day before broke up the rally and shortly it was reported that the entire Federal front had been thrown into confusion.

When a Confederate shell struck a bridge over Cub Run, one of the tributaries of Young's Branch and Bull Run, at midmorning, a wagon crossing the bridge was overturned and the route of retreat blocked for some time. Adding to the whole state of confusion, too, was the presence of many civilians who had driven out from Washington to see the rout of the Rebel forces, and what could have been an orderly retreat of McDowell's superior army soon became a rout. Long before noon, the Federal forces were in full retreat toward Washington, completing the debacle.

Packing up the field hospital on its special wagons, David took it to the rear and presented himself at Jackson's new headquarters near Centerville with a request in writing for reassignment from the position of surgeon to the 27th Virginia Regiment to command of the new field hospital serving the entire 1st Brigade. Approved by Major Hunter McGuire and General Jackson, his request was forwarded to General Johnston, who was once again commanding the Army of Northern Virginia, now that the fighting at Manassas had ended in a sharp defeat for the North.

Actually it was a month before the authority David had requested came through. And then he was instructed, because of the shortage of doctors among the Confederate forces, to function still as regimental surgeon for the 27th Virginia in addition to operating the 1st Field Hospital of the 1st Brigade in the Army of the Shenandoah. But, since there was no fighting now and only the minor illnesses and wounds of troops in bivouac on the now dormant front needed attention, he did not fret about the delay.

Writing to Araminta from the camp near Centerville and Manassas Junction, as the long hot days of July drew to an end, David was thankful that, as yet at least, mail was not censored, and he could speak his innermost thoughts in written words:

The first great battle of this terrible war is over and I am afraid proved nothing. Except perhaps that the South has one of the most capable military tacticians of history in the person of General Jackson—and that an obscure professor of military science and philosophy from VMI is now the hero of two armies, North and South. I am not certain myself just why General Barnard Bee likened him to a stone wall that day, but the title was earned and both Jackson and the Brigade will be known by that name for the rest of the war, I am sure.

The Richmond papers made much of my capturing a new type of highly mobile hospital singlehandedly. The truth is that I stumbled upon it accidentally and was fortunate to find it commanded by an old friend from medical school, whom I took prisoner. The most important thing to me is that I have been given command of the hospital and that I can now give those unlucky enough to be wounded the kind of service I would want to receive if I were struck down myself.

Life in camp is very dull as we wait to see where the Federal forces will strike next. Malaria is always prevalent during the summer in eastern Virginia and I have suffered a mild attack myself. Fortunately we captured a large amount of medical supplies, including quinine, at Manassas and I am using it freely, so our roster of sickness from that cause is not unduly high. What it will be when our supply is exhausted, I dread even to think, for medical supplies are already short among many Confederate units.

But enough of such dull subjects as sickness and drugs. Another thing we captured at Manassas was a Federal mobile library and I have been reading poetry—shall I confess that romantic poetry seems to interest me more than any other?

185

It does for, when I read, I think of you and wish that I could manage sonnet and verse as well as I can scalpel and stethoscope. But alas the Muse refuses to obey my commands and so I must repeat "I love you' over and over, until I'm sure you are tired of listening.

When I remember the Saturday afternoon we drove to Georgetown, our dinner at Cruchet's and the lovely evening when I first kissed you outside the door of your uncle's suite at the National Hotel, I find myself wishing more than anything else for this senseless conflict to end. Then you and I can take up, under such pleasant circumstances as that lovely evening, I hope, the pleasant task of learning to know each other. Until that happens, you can be assured of my complete devotion.

All my love,
David

V

Early August brought news that set the Confederate camp, drowsing in the muggy heat near Centerville, only twenty miles from Washington, agog. The Richmond *Examiner* trumpeted in bold headlines: "GREAT VICTORY AT WILSON'S CREEK, MISSOURI." The *Enquirer* gave a somewhat more restrained report of the first major battle west of the Mississippi. But, however reported, no one denied that an important engagement had been fought on August 10 among the rolling hills a few miles southwest of Springfield, Missouri, in a state considered crucial for the Confederate Cause—ending in a Union defeat.

The most exciting aspect of the report, as David Preston read it in the Richmond papers, was the presence on the Confederate side of a sizable number of Cherokee Indian troops under Colonel Stand Watie, of whom Araminta and Lachlan had often spoken. Watie's Indians, the Confederate battle dispatches claimed, acquitted themselves remarkably well, capturing almost an entire Federal battery and presaging the strengthening of the Confederacy when the Five Civilized Nations joined the southern Cause.

Reading the account, David wondered what part Lachlan had played and was pleasantly surprised several weeks later to receive a letter from his old VMI classmate:

Araminta wrote me some time ago that you are now the surgeon for the 27th Virginia. I was in New Orleans arranging for a shipment of some cotton to Nassau on a British vessel, when the Battle of Bull Run—or Manassas—was fought. The New Orleans *Times-Picayune* said your regiment played a prominent part in Old Jack's victory there, so it sounds as if our old professor covered himself with glory at Manassas Junction. Which, incidentally, is quite an accomplishment in a battle directed by that dashing hero of Fort Sumter, General P. G. T. Beauregard, who seems to have a positive genius for attracting attention to himself.

I now hold the rank of captain in the Second Cherokee Mounted Rifles, commanded by Colonel Stand Watie, a kinsman of both the Ross and Murrell families, but a bitter political enemy of Uncle John. I have taken no part in Cherokee politics but I will fight for the Confederacy, since it appears to offer more to the Indians than the Union has ever done or is likely to do.

You have no doubt heard of our little skirmish at Wilson's Creek, about ten miles southeast of Springfield, Missouri, on August 9 and 10. Ours was a small engagement compared to the battle at Manassas, but fortunately the Federal commander made more mistakes than we did. Had someone of Old Jack's caliber been in command for the Union, I suspect we would have had our ears pinned back pretty severely.

The Cherokee Mounted Rifles are receiving much praise in southern papers for capturing some Federal artillery, which was actually left in our hands following a brief skirmish by the retiring enemy. I'm afraid some of my Cherokee brothers let their enthusiasm for warfare get the best of their judgment, with the result that some Yankee casualties were conspicuously lacking in hair.

David paused to chuckle at Lachlan's choice of phrase. He could picture his dark-skinned friend now, over a bottle and a cigar, reciting with gusto the gory details of the battle. The letter continued:

The coastal blockade grows steadily tighter, and I don't know how much longer we are going to be able to sell our cotton through New Orleans. We can, of course, haul it across Texas to the Mexican port of Matamoros, where Yankee buyers from New England snap up every bale they can, but that will be very expensive. So far, though, I have been able to arrange through contacts in the North for the sale to England not to be disturbed, but this, too, may not last.

Please give my respects and congratulations to General Jackson. I'm afraid he never had a very high opinion of me as a soldier and certainly not as a student, but I am more than pleased to see his undoubted qualifications as a military leader being fully utilized by the South.

With warmest personal regards,
Lachlan

VI

Fuming with indignation at what he considered the dilatory tactics of President Jefferson Davis and Secretary of War Judah P. Benjamin in failing to strengthen the forces between Richmond and Fairfax Courthouse, where the 1st Brigade was stationed that summer so they could keep a close eye on Washington, Stonewall Jackson continued to have trouble with his wounded finger.

Some signs of chronic inflammation had developed but, fortunately, the equipment of the field hospital David Preston had captured singlehandedly for the Confederacy included a metal tub in which a foot or an arm could be immersed for hydrotherapy. Attached to the side of the container so it projected over the edge and down into the water was a small paddle wheel on a shaft turned by means of a belt, pulley and treadle, which anyone using the apparatus could operate with his foot.

The first time Jackson came by the hospital and saw the apparatus, he had asked that it be used in treating his injured finger. And, when David added some chloride of lime to the hot water in the tub, Jackson quickly became impressed with the relief the apparatus gave him from pain and formed a habit of stopping by almost every day for a treatment.

David was not always at the hospital when Jackson came by, but he instructed Hal Perkins to keep the bath always ready and the solution in a demijohn, from which it could be poured into a pot and heated very quickly to the temperature favored by Jackson. At this time, the 1st Brigade was bivouacked within a mile of Fairfax Courthouse and the 27th Regiment had moved as far toward Washington as Munson's Hill, only five miles from the Potomac. From this elevation, with field glasses, they were actually able to watch the people moving about on the streets, as well as Federal pickets on the south side of the river, who occasionally exchanged shots with them.

Although he'd been given a brevet, or temporary, promotion to major after the Battle of Manassas, it was still David's custom to ride up to the area of the 27th every morning and hold sick call, following which he would return to the hospital. As he tethered his horse outside it one day, he saw Jackson sitting beside the metal container with his hand and arm in the lime solution, while he methodically pedaled the device that turned the paddle wheel inside it and provided a flushing movement of the solution.

"I'm sorry I wasn't here when you arrived, General," David apologized when he came beneath the canvas shelter that protected Jackson from the sun. "I hope your finger is better."

"Thanks to your ministrations, Doctor, it is. If I could just soak it in the warm spring at Bath, I know it would soon be well." Jackson looked up from the basin. "If you were free to choose where we should fight next, Captain, what would your choice be?"

"In the Shenandoah Valley, of course, sir. The apple trees will soon be heavy with ripe fruit and in the farmer's gardens fresh tomatoes will still be on the vine."

"With twenty thousand men"—Jackson appeared almost to be speaking to himself—"I could cross the upper Potomac and drive northeast to outflank Baltimore and

189

take it, forcing the Federal Government to evacuate Washington by ship. You know General McClellan has replaced General McDowell in command of the Union Army Division of the Potomac, don't you?"

"I read it in the *Enquirer*."

"If McClellan hasn't changed since Mexico, he will take time to build up a tremendous army before trying to take Richmond. Meanwhile, we could be driving into western Pennsylvania to take Uniontown and perhaps even Pittsburgh, and if the move is made before winter sets in, the army can even live off the land. By the time General McClellan in Washington realizes he's outflanked, Western Virginia, Kentucky and Tennessee would be cut off entirely from the North. It would be a body blow to the enemy, Doctor, a real body blow."

"Surely President Davis can see that, sir. After all, he was Secretary of War in the Cabinet of President Buchanan before the war and a United States senator before that, as well as a graduate of West Point."

"A military man in politics, particularly such a position as Davis finds himself in, tends to become overcautious." Jackson lifted his hand, pink from the heat of the water, and studied it abstractedly. "Did you know that a council of war was held not long ago at Fairfax Courthouse?"

"No, sir. And you were not invited?"

A wintry smile came and went on the bearded face. "The commanding officer of a brigade does not speak for a division or an army."

"But that brigade saved the Confederacy from defeat at Henry House Hill, sir."

"It *was* a grand battle." Jackson's voice was distant again, as if he were once again riding up and down before the ranks of his men just before that moment of glory— and carnage—cautioning them to hold their fire. Just as another officer named Israel Putnam, when the scarlet wave of the British regulars swept forward, had cautioned his green troops at Bunker Hill with the words:

"Wait 'til you see the whites of their eyes! Then get up and tear out their bellies!"

"Well, good day, Major Preston," said Jackson. "And

thank you again for thinking of using hydrotherapy for my finger."

Major Hunter McGuire rode into the hospital yard shortly after Jackson left. "Has the general been here?" he asked. "He wasn't at his headquarters when I stopped by on the way back from Richmond."

"He left a while ago. What's new in Richmond?"

"The *Enquirer* carried a story yesterday saying McClellan is trying to convince Lincoln the next attack on Richmond should be made along the peninsula between the York and the James."

"It would put an army almost on Richmond's doorstep—if he succeeds."

"Without ships on the James, the South would have to fight the Federal army when it tried to make a landing," said McGuire. "How were Jackson's spirits this morning?"

"He seemed depressed. I didn't ask him why."

"Then you didn't hear about the promotions?"

"I had to ride up to Munson's Hill; only got back about an hour ago."

"The government in Richmond has just announced the promotion of Samuel Cooper, Albert Sidney Johnston, Robert E. Lee and Joseph E. Johnston. They confirmed the battlefield promotion Jeff Davis gave Beauregard at Manassas—all of them to be full generals."

"And nothing for Old Jack—who's worth more than the whole kaboddle—except maybe Lee?"

"That's the size of it."

"No wonder he was so depressed and wanted to go back to the Valley. I wonder what bad news he'll hear next?"

Marking time in camp, much of it near Centerville, that summer as the "dog days" of August wore on toward September, General Stonewall Jackson was not alone in feeling that valuable time was being wasted. Both the Army of the Shenandoah and the Army of Northern Virginia shrank steadily in numbers from desertion and disease, for Jackson's malaise affected the entire Stonewall Brigade, always peculiarly sensitive to its leader's moods.

When Jefferson Davis himself came to the camp near Fairfax Courthouse to review Beauregard's command on the first day of September—one day after announcement of the promotion of the five generals—Jackson sought Davis out. And watching the tableau from the 1st Field Hospital, which the President of the Confederacy had just inspected and given his hearty approval, David could hear enough of what Jackson and Davis said to know the tenor of their conversation.

"May I ask how the war goes in Western Virginia, Mr. President?" Jackson asked just before Davis was leaving the camp.

"Not good, General Jackson. Not good at all."

"I was born and grew up in the Clarksburg area," said Jackson pointedly. "My first job, at the age of fourteen, was on the Parkersburg-Staunton Turnpike."

"So? I didn't know that, General."

"With Morgantown, Virginia, and Cumberland, Maryland, in our hands, the whole Federal position in western Pennsylvania and the Monongahela Valley would be in danger. In fact, just the threat of a possible flank attack eastward through Maryland and Pennsylvania against Washington would certainly cause General McClellan to move some of the forces now concentrated for the next drive against Richmond westward."

"An interesting theory, General," Davis' voice was noncommittal as he moved away with his staff.

As David discussed the interchange between Davis and his now most famous general over one of Hal Perkins' matchless culinary efforts that evening with Joe Stannard and John Imboden, all followed by a bottle of fine old brandy with which a luckless U.S. senator had planned to celebrate the expected victory at Manassas, Stannard asked the obvious question: "You studied under Jackson for three years at VMI, David; was he telling Davis how to run the next phase of the war?"

David laughed. "The one thing you can expect from Jackson is that he'll probably do what you *least* expect. But when you analyze it later, you discover that the logic

192

was so simple you couldn't see the forest for the trees."

"Actually, the whole thing is like a giant chess game," said Imboden. "Lincoln badly wants to take Richmond and end the war—"

"And Jackson could have taken Washington a month ago right after Bull Run," said Stannard.

"We'll never know for sure and besides it's too late now, with McClellan building the biggest army in U.S. history," said the cavalryman. "Obviously, Lincoln wants Richmond badly, but he's afraid to expose Washington to attack in order to capture it. On the other hand, Jefferson Davis is afraid to launch a major attack anywhere else because it would mean depleting the forces guarding Richmond. I wonder if any other major war was ever fought with the opposing capitals less than a hundred miles apart?"

"Of the two Presidents," said David, "I guess Jefferson Davis is the least secure, with his forces numbering less than half what Lincoln's giving McClellan."

"If the Union battle plan is carried out," Imboden agreed, "Richmond will be attacked from two directions and we could lose a war before Christmas—unless Jefferson Davis somehow manages to pass a miracle."

"A miracle named Thomas J. Jackson might do it," David suggested.

"Maybe he could bring it off," Imboden conceded. "But with Jackson already a hero to the people of Virginia and Richmond, Davis can't afford to give him an opportunity to become even more of a hero by wrecking McClellan's plan before the Federals can launch their main attack. A lot of people in the Confederacy didn't think Jefferson Davis was the best choice for President in the first place—me among them. And if a Confederate Napoleon named Jackson suddenly appeared, our President might just have to take a back seat—which I don't see him doing."

"So what happens?"

"If I were Jefferson Davis, I'd try to create a diversion that would scare Lincoln into holding back a lot of troops to defend Washington."

"Maybe that's why Lee was sent to Western Virginia."

"It probably was, but Lee doesn't seem to be getting anywhere. What Jefferson Davis really needs at this moment—and the Confederacy too—is a one-man army to threaten Washington from the west."

"And God bless his cantankerous fighting soul, I hope Old Jack makes it," said Joe Stannard.

VII

On October 7, 1861, Generals James Longstreet and Thomas Jonathan Jackson were promoted to the rank of major general. And on October 21, Secretary of War Judah P. Benjamin wrote Jackson, announcing his assignment as commanding general of the II Corps, the third of the three armies set up under the reorganization of the Department of Northern Virginia, with General Joseph E. Johnston in overall command. The first two were the District of the Potomac, District of the Aquia, covering the Peninsula up which McClellan was planning to advance on Richmond. A finger of land lying between the York and James rivers, both navigable from Chesapeake Bay almost to Richmond, the Peninsula was the vulnerable backside of the Confederate capital.

Sandie Pendleton, Jackson's chief aide, showed David the letter from Benjamin naming Jackson to command the troops in the new District of the Valley. It read:

The exposed condition of the Virginia frontier between the Blue Ridge and the Allegheny Mountains has excited the deepest solicitude of the government, and the constant appeals of the inhabitants that we should send a perfectly reliable officer for their protection have induced the Department to form a new military district, which is called the Valley District of the Department of Northern Virginia.

The choice of the government has fallen upon you. This choice has been dictated, not only by a just appreciation of your policies as a commander, but by other weighty considerations. Your imminent knowledge of the country, of its population and resources, render you peculiarly suited to assume this command. Nor is this all. The people of that district, with one voice, have made constant and urgent appeal that to you, in whom they have confidence, should their defense be assigned.

General Order No. 15 from the Adjutant and Inspector General's Office in Richmond, dated October 22, established the new department, with Jackson in command of the Valley District, between the Blue Ridge and the Alleghenies. General Beauregard was given the Potomac District, in the center of the front, and Major General T. H. Holmes, the Aquia District, in the east. A special order assigning Jackson to the Valley District was dated October 28, with instructions to leave on November 4.

"I guess we can call ourselves a couple of prophets," said Joe Stannard when he sat down beside David Preston in the officers' mess on the evening of October 28. "You said Davis needed a one-man army in Western Virginia and damned if he didn't select the only man who could qualify."

"When will the Stonewall Brigade be marching?"

Stannard's face sobered immediately. "The brigade isn't going, only Jackson and his staff. And when he gets to the Valley he'll have less than two thousand men—most of them militia without any weapons much better than flintlock."

"What about you and me?"

"I'm staying here with the Twenty-seventh, and you and your hospital are assigned to the brigade—which also stays. Major McGuire will go with Jackson, of course, as medical director of the new district."

"Then it looks like this time Old Jack's going to have to pass a real miracle and make something out of nothing," said David soberly. "I'd sure like to be there when he does it."

VIII

As exciting as were the events of September and October 1861, with Jackson's promotion and his being ordered to the Valley, even more interesting to David Preston was another event reported with jubilation by the Confederate press. This was the signing on October 7, at Park Hill in Indian Territory, of a treaty between the Cherokee Nation and the Confederate Government. Chief John Ross, it was reported jubilantly in the Richmond press, signed for the Nation, along with a number of other principal chiefs.

David wasn't surprised to receive a letter from Araminta about two weeks later; what did surprise him was its tone. Knowing how strong were her sentiments toward the South and its Cause, he had expected jubilation. Instead, her concern for John Ross and the welfare of the Cherokee Nation was apparent in every paragraph.

> Park Hill, Cherokee Nation
> Indian Territory, CSA
> October 10, 1861

David, my dearest one,

You no doubt know by now that on October 7, Uncle John finally had no choice except to sign the treaty with the Confederacy, though much against his will. In fact, he only signed because the loyal portion of the Nation was in grave danger of finding itself at the mercy of the southern faction led by Stand Watie and Elias Boudinot, as well as the Choctaws, Chickasaws, the Lower Town Creeks and some of the Plains Indians.

You have only to look at a map to realize that if the Cherokee Nation had remained neutral, we would have found ourselves besieged by our own people on the south and west and on the north by Jayhawkers from Kansas and Missouri, who are really nothing but thieves and plunderers. Even before the treaty was signed many of our plantations had been attacked and our cattle and horses stolen to be sold.

It is no secret that Stand Watie and the Boudinot faction intend to take over the government of the Nation, backed by General Ben McCulloch's Confederate troops and the Cherokee Brigade. Actually Uncle John finally signed more to foil them than because his sympathies are with the Confederacy. We hope the Territory will now stay quiet, but reports of the victories by the South at Wilson's Creek in

Missouri and at Manassas, where you are, in Virginia, have fired up many who were formerly our friends, in favor of this union with the Confederacy. For that, as well as other reasons, those of us who support Uncle John in whatever he does, must always be careful of what we do or say in public. And I have no doubt that soon even our mail will be censored, seeking evidence to use against us when the Boudinot faction consider themselves strong enough to bring charges of treason against Uncle John. We Cherokees have always prided ourselves upon our sacred honor and the fact that our word has always been as good as our bond, so it is a terrible thing to see even that whittled away as distrust of each other mounts.

News of General Jackson and the Stonewall Brigade reaches us regularly in the newspapers from Little Rock and Memphis, as well as through the New Orleans *Times-Picayune*. And my heart threatens to burst with pride when I tell people that you belong to the gallant Brigade that fought so well at Bull Run. Lachlan still ships cotton downriver to New Orleans, so we sometimes get Mr. Horace Greeley's New York *Tribune*. I was much amused to read how he urged President Lincoln "On to Richmond" just before the Battle of Manassas, but after the Union was so badly defeated there, Mr. Greeley's voice was one of the loudest calling for a negotiated peace.

Before this war is over, I am sure a lot of Yankees will wish they had let us go our way here in the South, and I pray daily that you and others I love will come safely through this terrible conflict. When I read about what a Miss Clara Barton and some other women are doing in one of the hospitals in the North, I only wish I could work with the wounded in Richmond, but Uncle John needs me here. I not only act as his nurse, making him take his medicine and the daily rest you prescribed, but I am also his secretary and there are many letters to write, so I stay busy.

I love you,
Araminta

David stood holding the letter as he looked out across the cornfields around Centerville, long since shorn of the ripening ears by soldiers in search of grain to roast in the shucks among the ashes of their campfires. Less than twenty miles separated him from the city where he had first met Araminta, and a week ago he had stood with the pickets on Munson's Hill and looked down across Georgetown, where they'd witnessed the slave auction that Sunday afternoon, it seemed now long ago.

Nothing looked quite the same now, however, for Federal engineers had turned the aqueduct by which the C&O Canal had crossed the Potomac into a bridge and over it part of the advancing army had moved to Manassas. Across it, too, but in reverse, streams of soldiers and civilians had fled in panic the next day after the galling defeat of the Union Army.

Now a war separated him from the girl he loved, two wars, in fact. The larger one had literally set brother against brother across the face of the land and scourged too much of it already with fire and sword. Now, almost a thousand miles away, a smaller war was liable to break out at any moment, setting Indian against Indian and possibly engulfing his beloved.

"Why so pensive?" The voice was familiar, and David looked up to see Major Hunter McGuire standing a few yards away.

"I've been reading a letter—from my fiancée."

"Don't let me interrupt."

"I just finished."

The two doctors had become close friends in the five months since McGuire had joined Jackson's troops at Harpers Ferry.

"Is your fiancée in the Valley?" McGuire asked.

"The valley of the Arkansas River—a long way from here."

"That's Indian Territory, isn't it?"

"She's an Indian." David was not surprised at the startled look in his friend's eyes. "A niece of John Ross, Chief of the Cherokee Nation."

"I saw Ross once in Philadelphia. Didn't he marry a Quaker lady there?"

"His second wife is Mary Stapler, a Philadelphia aristocrat. Ross is an eighth-blood, I believe, and so is Araminta."

"What a lovely name."

198

"She was named for Araminta Ross, a relative of John Ross's, but my Araminta is a Murrell. She graduated from Mount Holyoke Female Seminary in Massachusetts last spring."

"Look!" McGuire was obviously embarrassed. "I didn't mean any——"

"I know you didn't, Hunter." David slapped the tall, dark-haired doctor on the back. "We Virginians can boast the bluest blood in the country, but Araminta's ancestors were chiefs of the Cherokee Nation hundreds of years before Columbus stepped ashore on San Salvador."

"And look how we've treated them," said McGuire. "I came to ask you to dine with General Jackson and some members of the staff this evening."

"I should be honored. What time?"

"About six o'clock—at his quarters."

IX

Clean-shaven and wearing a uniform Hal Perkins had hurriedly sponged and pressed, David presented himself at Jackson's quarters promptly at six o'clock and was introduced to Lieutenant Kyd Douglas, newest member of the staff, and Brigader General Charles S. Winder, slated to command the Stonewall Brigade after Jackson's departure. Several other members of the staff, some celebrating recent promotions, were there too: Colonel John Harman, Colonel John Imboden, Major Sandie Pendleton and the Reverend Major John L. Dabney, a rather dour divine recently appointed to be Jackson's chief of staff.

The meal prepared by Jim, the general's mulatto orderly, was a triumph: roast turkey, oyster dressing, mashed potatoes as soft as the snow in the Valley in winter, cranberry sauce, hot biscuits with butter and honey—plus a magnificent chocolate cake for dessert. The conversation was light, with no talk of war except Jackson's reminiscences about the Mexican campaign, when he and then Captain Robert E. Lee had served together, along with a number of others now high in the military councils of the Confederacy, as well as some fighting for the Union.

David was seeing a side of Stonewall Jackson he'd been given only an intimation of before, a highly educated philosophical observer of life who found much to admire in everything. Afterward, he walked back to brigade headquarters with John Imboden and, when he spoke of Jackson's charm as a host, Imboden smiled.

"We've all known for a long time the real Stonewall was there," said the cavalryman and mobile artillery specialist. "But the Jackson who obeys the orders of a superior to the letter—even against his own convictions—and the one who can plan to the last detail and execute a maneuver of his own making are two different people. Unless I'm entirely wrong in my estimation of General Jackson—and I've known him for many years—we are about to see the emergence of a great military figure."

"Unless he's merely being tossed to the Federal wolves by sending him into the Valley to keep McClellan from concentrating enough forces against Richmond to take it on the next try?"

"That's a possibility," Imboden conceded. "Especially when you consider that the most Jackson will have to fight with there are three small brigades and some militia. Actually we'll be lucky if one man in ten in the Valley District is armed with anything better than a flintlock musket."

"Joe Stannard says Jackson will have to be practically a one-man army."

"It won't be the first time he's had to operate that way. If you'd been at Manassas Junction on April 18—only six days after Fort Sumter was fired on—you'd have seen three makeshift troop trains northbound on the Orange and Alexandria Railroad, carrying the Albemarle Rifles, the Monticello Guards and a lot of Virginia Militia, bound for Harpers Ferry. We transferred at the junction to the Manassas Gap line and headed for Strasburg in the Valley."

"That must have been the first major troop movement by rail in the U.S."

"I don't know about that; I was too busy with the presidents of the Orange and Alexandria, the Manassas Gap and the Virginia Central railroads for two days at the Exchange Hotel in Richmond, making arrangements for the militia units to be picked up all the way from North Carolina and southwest Virginia to Manassas Gap. I wired the commanders of the units in towns along all the lines about noon the day before to put their men on board the cars and the first train was actually moving out by sundown. That afternoon I arranged for ammunition and supplies from the Richmond Arsenal to be loaded on freight cars."

"It was quite an operation."

"We put the whole thing together at Manassas on the morning of April 18, but one thing we hadn't figured on —an engineer who was a sympathizer. About five miles out of Manassas he stopped the lead train on a grade and decided not to go on—until Joe Stannard put a pistol to his head."

"Was the plan really Jackson's, as Joe claims?"

"I never saw it put down on paper in Old Jack's handwriting, but it's just the sort of thing he would think of." Imboden's tone grew sober. "I hope he's got his thinking cap on again, because where we'll be going there'll be plenty to do."

"And the right man to do it, I'll bet on that."

"Don't forget that even Robert E. Lee fell on his face out in Western Virginia, when Jeff Davis sent him there to drive the Federals out cf the Cheat Mountain area— and *he* could have commanded the Union army if he'd chosen the other side. But I'm counting on Jackson to manage, by hook or by crook, to scrape together an army in the Valley large enough to scare the hell out of Abe Lincoln and George McClellan and relieve some of the pressure on Richmond."

"So you don't agree that he's being thrown to the wolves?"

Imboden gave a short bark of a laugh. "Wherever

Jackson goes, action soon follows. If anybody turns out to be the wolf, he'll be the one, and you can bet there'll be a lot of torn sheepskins before spring."

A few days later, parading the 1st Field Hospital unit with the rest of the Stonewall Brigade at the rear of the II Corps camp at Centerville, David thought of what John Imboden had said about scaring Lincoln and McClellan and how much Old Jack would relish the idea. But only a deeply earnest note could be heard in the rather sharp voice as the shambling figure with his cap pulled forward crookedly almost over his eyes, spoke from the saddle of Little Sorrel. And not a man in the brigade but knew their former commander meant every word:

Officers and men of the First Brigade, I am not here to make a speech but simply to say farewell. I first met you at Harpers Ferry in the commencement of the war, and I cannot take leave of you without giving expression to my admiration of your conduct from that date to this—whether on the march, in the bivouac, in the tented field, or on the bloody plains of Manassas, where you gained the well-deserved reputation of having decided the fate of the battle.

Throughout the broad extent of country over which you have marched, by your respect for the rights and the property of citizens, you have shown that you were soldiers—not only to defend, but able and willing both to defend and protect. You have already gained a brilliant and deservedly high reputation throughout the army and the whole Confederacy, and I trust in the future, by your own deeds on the field, and by the assistance of the same kind Providence who has heretofore favored our cause, you will gain more victories and add additional luster to the reputation you now enjoy. You have already gained a proud position in the history of this our Second War for Independence; I shall look with great anxiety to your future movements, and I trust whenever I shall hear of the *First Brigade* on the field of battle, it will be of still nobler deeds achieved and higher reputation won.

Jackson paused, but not a sound came from the massed thousands of men to whom their commander was saying farewell. Then he raised himself in the stirrups and lifted his gloved right hand, palm outward, in the typical gesture all of them had seen him make so often. And when his voice rang out again, there was a new urgency in its tone, a new assurance of his eternal affection for them, from the lowliest private to the highest-ranking officer:

In the Army of the Shenandoah you were the *First Brigade!* In the Army of the Potomac you were the *First Brigade!* In the Second Corps of the Army you *are* the *First Brigade!* You are the *First Brigade* in the affections of your general; and I hope, by your future deeds and bearing, you will be handed down to posterity as the *First Brigade* in our Second War for Independence. Farewell!

As Jackson settled back in his stirrups and turned Little Sorrel's head away, the cheers of the assembled men rose in a mighty roar that continued long after the oddly slight-looking figure upon the sorrel horse had grown small in the distance.

Stonewall Jackson was going back to his own love, the Shenandoah Valley of Virginia, on orders from Confederate headquarters in Richmond, but leaving behind him his personal army, the Stonewall Brigade.

X

The arrival of Major General Thomas Jonathan Jackson at Winchester, near the north end of the Shenandoah Valley, was not hailed quite so joyously by the Confederate military establishment already in southwest Virginia. At a time when many Confederate volunteers did not consider themselves obligated to fight outside their own states, the former—many of them militia officers—considered Jackson a symbol of the power given to Jefferson Davis. The civilian population, on the other hand, saw in him a savior from the Yankee strength gathering for seizure of this important breadbasket for Richmond, as well as Richmond's most vulnerable source of Federal attack.

General Nathaniel P. Banks, having taken over command for the Union from aging General Robert Patterson, who had been ingloriously outfoxed by Jackson and Jeb Stuart that summer, was preparing to move from Pennsylvania across the Potomac along the traditional invasion route of the Shenandoah Valley. In Western Virginia, however, Robert E. Lee had been quite unable, even in the face of a Yankee invasion of Virginia, to persuade two warring political figures, Henry A. Wise and John B. Floyd, to join in an effort to save a new state from being created in this area. There the enthusiasm for slavery in the Virginia referendum of the past spring had been less than lukewarm, and a new force of Federal troops was gathering to attack from the West, as well as along the valley of the Great Kanawha River farther to the south.

With winter coming on, the mountaineer troops of the Virginia regiments could see little reason for fighting under such arduous circumstances when those around Richmond appeared to be marking time, so several factors were against Stonewall Jackson. Nevertheless he set about much the same task he'd embarked upon at Harpers Ferry roughly six months earlier, that of molding a mass of men with practically no training, varied interests and little enthusiasm for military discipline, into an effective fighting force. And this with the enemy already in possession of the vital center of Romney, just across the easternmost ridge of the Allegheny Range from the Valley itself, with that fertile area and its towns and railroads only a few days' march away.

With characteristic vigor, Jackson sent for his trusted allies, the Stonewall Brigade. And, recognizing from Lee's reports the disorganization now rife in Western Virginia, Jefferson Davis released the famous unit of Valley troops to help its namesake. Crossing the Blue Ridge and descending into the lovely, fertile Valley, the brigade was shortly the central factor in a typically swift Jackson foray against the enemy.

Moving into their old haunts in the Martinsburg area early in January 1862, in spite of the rigors of winter,

Jackson's small army of about 9,000 struck hard at the recently repaired B&O Railroad at Martinsburg and also destroyed a number of dams furnishing water for the Chesapeake and Ohio Canal, now a major freight artery. Turning south then in bitter winter weather, Jackson fairly easily drove the Federal troops occupying Romney farther back into Western Virginia and seized the town, a vital transportation center.

To hold Romney and help protect the Valley, Jackson placed the town and area under command of General William W. Loring. That done, he moved back to Winchester to take up winter quarters with, he thought, his western flank amply protected by Loring's troops. But here what was perhaps Jackson's greatest weakness almost betrayed him; he had failed to confide to an envious Loring the exact reason why Romney was such an important post for protection of the vital Shenandoah Valley against attack from the west.

Shortly there occurred one of the more bizarre incidents in a war characterized by more than its share of such misunderstandings, when Jackson received at Winchester a peremptory order from Secretary of War Judah P. Benjamin at Richmond, directing him to return Loring and his troops to Winchester at once. The grounds, as stated by Loring in a private letter to Benjamin, had been that he and his men were being discriminated against by being stationed at Romney in favor of the 1st Brigade, largely because of the more favorable climate in the Valley.

Stonewall Jackson was not one to disobey an order from a superior, even if a civilian. Loring and his men were promptly ordered to Winchester and, almost in the same post, a letter went from Jackson to Benjamin with his resignation and the request to be reassigned to the faculty of the Virginia Military Institute at Lexington.

The prospect of losing the Confederacy's best-known and most effective general created a sensation in Confederate political and military circles. Particularly when about the same time information gained by spies in the Union camp revealed that a massive army under General

John Charles Frémont was already starting to move westward. The intent was obvious, to apply pressure upon Jackson in the Valley, while Banks drove upon him from north of the Potomac.

Both maneuvers in turn were designed to keep Jackson from moving to the aid of the armies now defending Richmond from attack by three forces: Frémont from the west; McClellan from the Peninsula, where he was about to launch his long-planned waterborne invasion along the land route between the York and the James rivers; and McDowell, whose forces were poised once again just south of the Potomac and Washington, eager to erase the stain of their humiliating defeat at Manassas some six months earlier.

For once politics and military expediency joined forces and moved expeditiously. Personal letters from General Joseph E. Johnston in overall command, and from Secretary Benjamin in the political sector finally mollified the outraged Jackson and persuaded him to reconsider, while Loring was relegated to the military limbo. Meanwhile, however, valuable time had been lost in Jackson's opinion in preparing to defeat the Union campaign to clear the Confederates out of Virginia west of the Blue Ridge.

Early in March, David received the news that his mother, living alone except for the Negroes who farmed the plantation at Preston's Cove, was ill. Granted leave, he took the Valley Turnpike south—up the Shenandoah Valley since that river ran north—and reached home to find her somewhat improved under the care of Dr. Buxton, their old family physician.

From the Cove, just before returning to duty at Winchester, he wrote Araminta:

You will no doubt be surprised to learn that I am at Preston's Cove, on leave because of the illness of my mother. She is better, though frail, and I shall leave for Winchester and duty starting tomorrow. I am sure spring is already farther along where you are than it is here but I wish you could see what it is like in the Valley at the beginning of April. The snow has melted on the mountaintops and the pools where the streams descend to join the James are full of trout. Just yesterday, our black majordomo, Jake, went fishing with me and we caught a fine mess which we had for supper.

This is one of the loveliest times of the year here at Preston's Cove, with the full promise of spring quite evident everywhere, but the reality not yet arrived. My love for you makes me selfish enough to wish we could be here together, where we could forget, at least for a little while, the horrors of war and the sufferings of people for want of so many things that are absolutely necessary to life. Even at that we are far more fortunate here at Preston's Cove than the people in Richmond and other cities of the South, where shortages of food are beginning to be felt very sharply indeed and the lack of vital medicines makes even a minor illness potentially fatal.

Yesterday I saw a stag, a six-pointer, with his doe, drinking from the spring that bursts from beneath a cliffside near the house. They were so beautiful and so much a part of the loveliness of this Valley, where my ancestors built their home before the Revolution, that I didn't have the heart to shoot either of them. The ground is covered with snow and, in the face of all this natural beauty, it saddens me to think that, with the coming of spring only a few weeks away now, the ground itself may soon be torn and stained with blood and that the pines covering the lower slopes of the mountains with a mantle of green may be struck down and burned by the fires of war.

The night I arrived here, young Ellen, who is married to Jake, went into a difficult labor. May, the midwife who brought me into the world some twenty-six years ago, was not able to cope with the problem but fortunately I had brought my instruments with me, and was able to use the forceps to deliver the baby without damage to either it or the mother. I couldn't help thinking, as little Jake gave his first cry, how much more fitting it is for a doctor to use his skill in bringing life into the world than as a part of war, which entails so much death and suffering—even though he destroys no life himself.

In a few weeks spring will be coming with the dogwoods

and redbuds blooming upon the hillsides. I pray that, by next summer, I can show you all of this beauty I love so much and which, I am sure, you, too, will come to love as I do. Until then, my fondest affection is for you,

> My dearest love,
> David

BOOK FOUR

The Valley

I

Late winter and early spring of 1862 had not been an easy time for General Jackson or the Stonewall Brigade. Food, shelter and equipment were already short throughout the Confederacy and even during the coldest part of the winter many of the brigade were without shoes. As spring approached, bringing the certainty of another Union campaign in Eastern Virginia, General Joseph E. Johnston, commanding in the area north of Richmond, had asked Jackson to keep an eye on the Federal troops under General James Shields located north of Winchester in the Valley. The purpose of this precaution was to prevent reinforcement of the substantial army now poised under General Irvin McDowell south of Washington and, it was hoped, to keep Lincoln from sending more troops to McClellan for the Peninsula Campaign.

Jackson naturally responded with his favorite weapon, attack. Informed by his usually reliable cavalry commander, Colonel Turner Ashby, that much of Shields' Federal force had started eastward across the Blue Ridge to join General McDowell, leaving only a small number of Union troops from the command of General Nathaniel

209

P. Banks north of Winchester in the Valley, Jackson attacked on March 23 at the small village of Kernstown with thirty-five hundred troops.

This time, however, Ashby's information proved to be wrong and Jackson found himself fighting nine thousand Federals. Facing an irreparable disaster for the Valley Army, Jackson relieved the commanding officer of the Stonewall Brigade, General R. B. Garnett and placed himself in the thick of the fighting, inspiring his men even in the face of obviously greater numbers. Fighting desperately the Confederates extricated themselves from the trap into which they had stepped.

As they withdrew southward, each side claimed victory, with some justification, for the toll of casualties was almost even. In terms of the single engagement, nobody won, but judged by the effect upon overall Union strategy, Kernstown turned out to be a resounding victory for the South—although the evidence took some time to develop.

During the next several weeks the Army of the Shenandoah, now more popularly called the Army of the Valley, retreated slowly southward. Meanwhile, Ashby and his cavalry carried on a constant harrassment to the cautiously advancing enemy, leading Shields to report to Lincoln that fifteen thousand Confederates had been involved at Kernstown, roughly five times the true figure.

By April 18, Jackson finally started establishing his base of operations in Elk Run Valley, about fifteen miles east of Harrisonburg, with the steeply rising range of the Massanutten Mountains between him and the Valley Turnpike. Here an arterial road crossed the Blue Ridge at Swift Run Gap, giving access to Charlottesville and Culpeper, toward which the eastern prong of the Federal attack by McDowell was expected to be launched.

At nearby Conrad's Store, Stonewall Jackson set up his headquarters and there the mass of information about enemy movements that had been pouring in during the weeks of slow retreat southward from Kernstown was digested. Included was information gathered when Ashby alone carried out one of his characteristically flamboyant ventures by pretending once again to be an itinerant self-made horse doctor, crossing the lines to treat the mounts of a Federal cavalry detachment, and listening all the while.

Ashby came into the dressing station David Preston had established beside Elk Run to have a small cut on his hand dressed one morning and handed the surgeon a copy of the Washington *Evening Star* of two days ago.

"Thought you might like to see a Yankee paper, Major Preston. They're making much of General Jackson relieving Garnett from command of the Stonewall Brigade—"

"The men aren't very happy about it either."

"What do you think?"

"The brigade fought well at Kernstown and General Garnett only ordered them to retire when they ran out of ammunition."

"But Old Jack wanted them to fight on with the bayonet."

"Three thousand against nine thousand? That sort of odds might be all right with cannon and grape, but hardly with bayonets."

"We lost a lot of men that day, some of it because I made a mistake," said Ashby. "And we could have lost a lot more, if the brigade had kept on fighting with only bayonets, so you're probably right. Jackson never had to retreat from a battlefield before, either, so I can understand how he felt, but I'm glad he's withdrawing the charges against Garnett. It'll help the morale of the Stonewall Brigade and that means a lot with the kinds of odds we'll be facing in the next month or so."

"Sandie Pendleton told me the staff is evaluating the final effect of Kernstown. Have you reached a conclusion?"

"On the best evidence, Williams' division of eight thousand Federals from Shields' command was almost to Manasses Junction to support McDowell before the battle of Kernstown. The day after the battle they hurried back to Winchester and General Banks himself returned to take charge. General Blenker's Federal division of roughly ten thousand was slated to join McClellan on the Peninsula, too, but has been rerouted to Western Virginia to strengthen Frémont's army."

211

"Which is now advancing toward Staunton, according to what I hear."

"I suspect that's the main reason why we're holed up here in Elk Run Valley, where the general can pounce on either Frémont, Banks or Shields, depending on which one gets closest," said Ashby. "Kernstown threw another stink bomb into McClellan's playhouse, too. McDowell was supposed to send thirty-seven thousand men to the Peninsula Campaign to make sure the Federals could drive right through to Richmond from the southeast; now they've been held back to help defend Washington."

David whistled softly. "With forty-five thousand bayonets withdrawn from the Peninsula, I imagine McClellan's about to have a nervous breakdown."

"Couldn't happen to a more deserving fellow," said Ashby cheerfully. "But McClellan's got another reason to be chewing nails about now. Lincoln reorganized the Union defense of Washington again and now they've got four independent armies in Virginia: Frémont in the west; Banks and Shields north of us in the Valley; McDowell in northern Virginia; and McClellan on the Peninsula. And all of 'em take orders from a couple of civilians named Lincoln and Stanton, the new Secretary of War, with nobody wanting to weaken himself to help the others."

"Don't underestimate Stanton. In Washington he's got the reputation of being tough."

"Maybe so, but any way you look at it, I'd say Old Jack has every right to be proud of what he did at Kernstown with only three thousand men."

II

David had been conscious that Hal Perkins was moving about within earshot while he and Ashby were talking. Now Hal, his sergeant's stripes sewed on since a recent promotion, came up to where the surgeon was preparing to wash his instruments.

"Let me do that, sir," said Hal. "One of the scalpels needs honing anyway, you dulled it on the skull of that corporal from the Emerald Guards that got his head broken the other night during the fight at a tavern in Elkton."

The Emerald Guards, Irishmen to the core, were something of a trial to their surgeon. But they were so effective as fighting men that one could hardly begrudge them an occasional binge at taverns in the neighboring towns, even though Jackson had expressly forbidden any such debauchery.

"You're going to need these instruments pretty soon, Major," Hal added as he poured hot water into a basin. "When the general decides it's time to attack General Frémont."

"So it's to be Frémont?" David wasn't really surprised; it wasn't the first time Hal had appeared to know Stonewall Jackson's plans before anyone else became privy to them. "Mind telling me why?"

"I read my Bible, sir, and General Jackson's battle plans usually follow Scripture. Remember how David used the Philistine city of Ziklag as a base from which to spite his enemies?"

"I'm afraid I never was much of a Bible student, Hal."

"When King Saul tried to kill David because the prophet Samuel had anointed him to be King of Israel, David was forced to flee. He settled in the Philistine city of Ziklag on the border with Israel and made lightning raids into enemy territory from there."

"I can see the parallel."

"So does General Jackson, I'm sure, sir. David kept the enemy forces from joining up and overcoming him by catching different groups off balance, just like General Jackson has been doing here in the Valley. So it would be logical for him to attack the elements of General Frémont's Union army that are now approaching Staunton from the west."

"Maybe you should be at headquarters, Hal, instead of behind the lines with a hospital."

"Oh, no, sir!" The look of horror on the younger man's face was almost comical. "My place is with you, I'd never want to be anywhere else."

"Are you telling me you figured all this out yourself?"

213

Hal Perkins grinned. "General Jackson's orderly, Jim, has a brother who belongs to our family. When I asked him what part of the Bible General Jackson was reading these days, he showed me." Hal's voice grew more earnest. "I'm sure this regiment will play an important part in the coming battle, sir. The whole thing about David is described in the twenty-seventh chapter of First Samuel."

But when Jackson did make his move, it seemed—for a while at least—that Hal Perkins was wrong.

III

On April 19, 1862, the Union commander in the Shenandoah Valley, General Nathaniel Prentiss Banks, started his army on a ponderous movement to close one jaw of the pincers designed to crush and obliterate the Army of the Valley. Moving southward from Winchester and Kernstown, after Jackson's retreat to the protection of Elk Run Valley some sixty miles to the south, Banks was confident that he outnumbered by several times the Confederate forces opposing him. He therefore felt safe in launching what was intended to be the beginning of the expected grand battle plan of the Union. And with McClellan thrusting inland toward Richmond through Yorktown along the Peninsula, McDowell attacking near Manassas and crossing the Rappahannock River, while Frémont menaced Jackson's rear by way of the Lewisburg Turnpike through Staunton, while Banks pressed from the north, Armageddon seemed inevitable for the Confederate forces north of the Carolinas.

The ponderous Federal movement had one effect which none of the Union commanders could have desired, nor which, as events developed, they had foreseen. It set the stage for one of Stonewall Jackson's lightninglike raids, logically aimed—as Hal Perkins had pointed out to David Preston—at Frémont's Union force, now moving cautiously eastward toward the Shenandoah Valley through the Allegheny mountain range.

Through the daring of Colonel Turner Ashby and his

cavalry, Jackson knew at all times exactly where Banks' forces were and in what strength; never again would Ashby make the mistake of underestimating the enemy's spies and potential. From the elevation of Swift Run Gap, where the road between Harrisonburg, Stanardsville, Charlottesville—and eventually Richmond—crossed the Blue Ridge, Jackson, with six thousand men, was watching every move. Moreover he was in constant communication with General Richard S. Ewell and his division of eight thousand veterans poised near Manassas, ready to move in either direction as they were needed.

Meanwhile, on the Valley Turnpike, separated from Jackson's hideaway in Elk Run Valley only the southern promontory of Peaked Mountain at the extreme southern tip of the Massanutten chain, General Banks, with 19,000 Federal troops, moved south to New Market. He traveled slowly and cautiously, wary of Jackson's capacity to sting but obviously planning to continue southward toward Harrisonburg, with the intent of boxing the Valley Army into a position between the Federal forces, the Blue Ridge and the only route of emergence southward toward Staunton. And there the Federal force under General Robert H. Milroy, an advance guard of thirty-seven hundred men from Frémont's army, opposed a small Confederate army of only about twenty-two hundred under the command of General Edward Johnson. Thus Jackson faced odds of almost two to one, even with Ewell's division in reserve. As usual, however, he told no one his plans.

On a lovely evening near the end of April, Major Hunter McGuire came to David's tent located in a clump of trees near the bank of Elk Run. Hal Perkins had gone fishing that afternoon and they'd had fresh mountain trout for supper, with "corn dodgers"—onions chopped up with cornmeal and eggs—fried in bacon grease with the fish.

"If I'd known you were going to have real Virginia food, David, I'd have come earlier," said the dark-haired medical director.

"Name the day and we'll catch a fine mess of trout

for you," David told him. "You might even bring the general if you can."

"He'd like it, I'm sure," said McGuire. "I've been so busy since we evacuated Kernstown that I haven't had time to thank you for your fine work during the battle. But I did prepare a letter of commendation to Surgeon General Moore in Richmond. And when I asked General Jackson to sign it, he added a postscript."

"My men deserve as much credit as I do," David protested. "Especially Hal Perkins. Has the general told you what he plans to do next?"

"Not a word. Jim doesn't know, either, so I sometimes wonder whether Jackson does."

"I doubt that. Even at VMI he always knew exactly what he was doing—except maybe once."

McGuire smiled. "He told me about the time he woke you in the middle of the night to tell you he'd been wrong."

"The funny part is, he really wasn't. There were two ways to solve that problem: my way gave the solution, but only through a roundabout and involved procedure that added several extra steps. But Jackson's solution went right to the heart of the problem—as always."

"He has a habit of cutting through unessentials, like the letter he sent to Richmond about you." McGuire took a sheet from the pocket of his uniform coat and started to read:

Major Preston captured a Union field hospital at Manassas and has improved upon it steadily since that time. With the spring and summer certain to involve large military operations with many casualties, it is suggested that Major Preston be ordered to temporary duty in Richmond for the purpose of explaining his methods to brigade and divisional surgeons.

"Leave the Stonewall Brigade?" David exclaimed.

"Only for a week or so; the general wouldn't give you up permanently." McGuire handed him the letter. "General Johnston endorsed your assignment to detached duty in Richmond and General Lee has also approved it. Can you leave in the morning?"

"At dawn, if that's necessary. I'd like to get this over with before Jackson decides to pull something out of the hat and confound the enemy again."

"This time we'll need all the confounding he can manage," said McGuire soberly. "McClellan is supposed to have massed a hundred thousand men for the Peninsula Campaign around Yorktown, and McDowell probably has another fifty thousand poised to cross the Rappahannock. If those two come together while General Banks keeps us here in the Valley—"

"Do you really believe the Yankees can keep Old Jack anywhere except where he chooses?"

"They almost did—at Kernstown. By the way, a courier just arrived. There was a letter for you in the headquarters packet and I brought it along, in case you leave before the mail distribution in the morning."

David didn't have to open the letter to recognize Araminta's strong slanting strokes.

As McGuire started to leave, he turned back. "While you're in Richmond get some fresh medical supplies, if you can. I've an idea we're going to need them."

As soon as the other doctor left, David opened Araminta's letter.

Darling,

I read of General Jackson's defeat at Kernstown in the St. Louis *Post-Dispatch*—a Union newspaper—and I have also watched the casualty lists being published in our own papers, praying I wouldn't find your name listed there.

By now, I'm sure you have heard about the Battle of Pea Ridge, fought the middle of March at Elkhorn Tavern in Arkansas. Union papers, particularly the one published by Horace Greeley in New York, made much of the behavior of the Indian troops upder Captain John Drew, an old friend and compatriot of Uncle John's. Perhaps they did yell like savages in the midst of battle and, if they used bows and arrows instead of muskets, it was because none had been issued to them.

David paused, remembering how only a few months earlier Stonewall Jackson had ordered a thousand pikes from Richmond to arm the new recruits for whom there were as yet no rifles. And he doubted very much that even the yelling of Indians could be much more blood-curdling than the rebel yell with which he'd heard Confederate soldiers go into battle more than once.

Besides, Cherokee soldiers had not been issued uniforms, nor had they been paid. Uncle John was very angry at General Van Dorn and Major Pike, who are in charge of the Indian tribes that joined the Confederacy, for ordering our troops away from Indian Territory, where they were only supposed to act as home guards. Lachlan writes, however, that Stand Watie's men acquitted themselves very well at Pea Ridge. We have set up a little hospital here and try as best we can to help the victims of outrages, mainly by Jayhawkers, and those who are starving for lack of food. But we don't have very much ourselves, except what we are able to raise, or the fish we catch in the river.

Until just recently, Lachlan had been able to sell cotton through New Orleans and Matamoros in Mexico in spite of the blockade. Even though the Yankees claim to be so pure and high-minded, merchants in Boston have been arranging for vessels loaded with cotton to escape the blockade and reach the Bahamas or Bermuda, where the cotton is resold for the mills of New England. Lachlan tells of balls and extravagant social affairs in Texas and Arkansas, but there are none such here on the Arkansas River.

When I think of the receptions and levees I attended in Washington and Boston, I can't help longing a little for a change from what we have. But then, I see people all around me hungry and sick, lacking medicines and even clothing and I feel guilty for my thoughts. Actually I suppose I'm far better off than either you or Lachlan, although I must say he seems to get pretty much anything he wants.

You will remember how I have always rolled the cigars Uncle John likes to smoke. By some miracle, Lachlan still manages to have tobacco imported from Cuba so Uncle John can have his cigars, and I am growing the foxglove plant for his digitalis here in the garden. Other medicines are very scarce, though, particularly quinine, which we always took in the spring, when the fever settles upon the area, and many

218

people are suffering from the ague. In the old days, we Murrells used to go to the Great Smoky Mountains when the fevers started, but I'm afraid this year we will have to make out the best way we can.

Lachlan has been here for a few days but is leaving in a few minutes, and I must end this letter so he can take it on the boat with him and mail it at Fort Smith. He sends you his regards. Lachlan, of course, has always been a romantic and, in the beginning I am sure he enjoyed the experience of war. But now that he is seeing what it does to the people who have no real responsibility for it, I know he realizes the bitter truth that nobody really wins, except perhaps the politicians who gain power. And that would certainly seem the least of reasons for starting a conflict.

In closing, I can only say again how much I love you and how much I wish to be with you.

Always,
Araminta

IV

David awakened just before dawn to see a familiar drab figure silhouetted by the moonlight in the open flap of his tent.

"General Jackson," he stammered, reaching for his clothing.

"Take your time about dressing, Major Preston." Jackson was fully dressed, even to the dingy gray cap shoved forward, as always, until the brim almost covered his eyes. "That bacon Sergeant Perkins is cooking smells so good, I am going to have breakfast with you."

When David came out of his tent, carrying a pair of saddlebags in which were stored the clothing and other necessities he would take to Richmond, Jackson was sitting on a flat rock nearby. The general had a tin plate in his lap and was eating with more relish than David had ever seen him exhibit for food, considering the chronic dyspepsia that was his nemesis. Crisp bacon, fried cornmeal mush and coffee disappeared into his beard with astonishing rapidity.

"Capital rations, Major Preston! Capital!" said Jackson as David accepted a plate from Hal and chose another rock. "I'll have a position as cook and caretaker for the headquarters staff waiting, if you ever release Master Sergeant Perkins."

Hearing Hal Perkins' exclamation of surprise at this sudden elevation in rank, Jackson added, "The Bible says, through the mouth of Job, that God setteth an end to darkness and searcheth out all perfection. Should I not make note of perfection when I have the power?"

"Sergeant Perkins and I will hardly argue against that, sir. But I'm sorry you weren't here last night for supper; the mountain trout was delicious."

Jackson put down his empty plate and finshed his mug of coffee. Then, taking an envelope from the breast of his uniform tunic, he passed it to David.

"This letter is for General Robert E. Lee," he said. "I desire that it go directly to him, outside of military channels." From the same pocket he extracted a small sheet. "This pass will insure that you will see General Lee directly."

Knowing Jackson's reluctance to share his plans of battle with anyone else, David was quite certain the envelope contained a sketch of the next proposed action for the Army of the Valley. With General Joseph E. Johnston in the Manassas-Rappahannock area and General James Longstreet on the Peninsula crying for men and supplies, he could understand Jackson's wishing to deal with Lee directly, even though, as military adviser to Jefferson Davis, the latter's position was still somewhat ambiguous. By sending the letter in the custody of a relatively non-military courier, however, Jackson could avoid arousing the suspicion of either of the other two generals that he had gone behind their backs in contacting Lee.

"I'll leave at once, sir," David promised.

"Take the train from the Mechum's River Station on the Virginia Central, Major. I'm counting on you to deliver that letter to General Lee sometime this evening."

It was barely dusk when David reached Richmond, having left his horse with a livery stable owner at Mechum's River and a deposit for its keep. Taking a hackney, he was driven directly to the Capitol. Nor did he have any trouble in being admitted to the presence of General Robert E. Lee, once he presented the pass Jackson had given him.

Earlier in the war, the courtly Virginia aristocrat, who had rejected the highest military position the Union had to offer to accept command of the Virginia Militia, had seen that post vanish when the local troops were brought under control of the new Confederate Government. After brief missions in Western Virginia and the Carolinas, however, Lee had been brought back to Richmond, this time in the post of Jefferson Davis' personal deputy in supervising the war. His great capability in keeping the brilliant personalities of the often prickly tempered generals in charge of the main Confederate forces in Virginia in harmony had already begun to erase much of the stain of failure attending the campaign in the Alleghenies, but the supreme command of the troops defending Richmond still remained with General Joseph E. Johnston.

"I remember seeing you in Washington once, Major Preston," said Lee courteously when David presented the letter from Jackson. "As I remember it, you were with a remarkably pretty young lady."

"That was my fiancée, Miss Araminta Murrell, sir. She is a niece of John Ross."

"The principal chief of the Cherokees?"

"Yes, sir."

"A very remarkable man, Ross. He has worked tirelessly for the welfare of his people over many years. I hope he is well."

"Chief Ross has some heart trouble, but I've been able to control it with medication."

Lee smiled. "I remember now hearing about some dissension over the case before I left Washington. Dr. Wilson had friends in high places."

"Fortunately, so did Chief Ross."

"Many of us have had to choose between conflicting allegiances, Major, particularly we Virginians who have never felt that slavery was a cause worth fighting for." Lee picked up the letter from Jackson but did not open

221

it. "I see by your orders that you are detailed for duty at the office of Surgeon General Moore. Do you know where you will be staying?"

"I came directly here from the railroad station, sir, but I hope to find a room at the Spotswood Hotel."

"The Spotswood is very popular and usually filled, but perhaps I can help you; the manager is an old friend." On a pad Lee quickly wrote a few lines, tore off the sheet and handed it to David. "That should get you a room, Doctor. When is your first lecture scheduled?"

"I don't know, sir. Colonel Moore will probably tell me."

"I'll ask him to notify me, too; the idea of a medical flying squadron has always intrigued me. Good day, Major Preston."

Lee's request for a room proved perfectly valid; without even consulting his reservation list, the clerk gave the register to David to sign. Passing through the lobby of the Spotswood on the way to his room, he could almost believe he was once again at Willard's in Washington. There was the same ornate decor, the same throngs of top-hatted businessmen in dark suits and officers in dress uniform, neither apparently suffering any lack of rations or thirst, as they lined up at the long bar of polished mahogany.

True, the uniforms were gray instead of blue, but the pipings and facings were ornate and colorful. The loud talk, too, was familiar; the boisterousness produced by whiskey, of which there seemed to be none of the short supply already beginning to be felt in the field, where spirits were a favorite medicine; the endless boasting of victories won, though usually he suspected not by those doing the talking; the description of deals consummated—all appeared to be the same, whether North or South.

The prospects of a drink and a leisurely meal downstairs were enticing, but a bath was even more, so David took time for that. After scrubbing away the grime from the ride down the slope of the Blue Ridge from Swift Run Gap and the journey of several hours by train from the Mechum's River Station to Richmond on the Virginia Central, he put on a clean shirt and underwear. Dressed again, he decided that he was fairly presentable, though certainly not in comparison with the bemedaled and smartly uniformed officers who had crowded the lobby and the bar when he came in.

At the bar, he worked his way in between two lieutenants who were trying to outbrag each other, and ordered whiskey and soda, causing the young officers to stare at him as if he were a creature from another world.

"Learned to like it in England, you know," David said in an amused tone, and the two stared at him for a moment longer, then bowed and made room for him at the bar.

When David finished his drink and moved into the adjoining dining room, he saw that it was still almost filled, in spite of the late hour. By now he was prepared for almost anything in this city of contrasts and a fine dinner of roast guinea hen, fluffy sweet potatoes, green beans from Georgia and hot biscuits—plus a bottle of an excellent Chianti—did not disappoint him.

After breakfast the next morning David climbed the stairs to the hotel roof for a look at Richmond, before reporting for duty at the Office of the Surgeon General. It was hard to believe a Union army of more than a hundred thousand—probably equal to the entire Confederate force in Virginia—was bivouacked a short distance to the east on the Penninsula. And still another of half that strength was less than fifty miles to the north, while life went on in the capital city of the Confederacy, much as if no threat existed.

The morning breeze had dissipated much of the fog that so often shrouded this city's seven hills, leaving a muggy heat that would grow worse as the day wore on. Malarial heat, David thought, causing an increase in the intermittent fever that plagued armies in such areas. And particularly difficult to treat, with a chronic shortage of quinine as the blockade tightened its noose inexorably around the Confederacy.

The brown flood of the James flowing in its bed at the southern edge of the city and the canal that crept along beside it were roiled sluggishly when the lock gates were opened for a chain of muledrawn canal boats he could see moving slowly along. When conceived, the waterway had been intended to traverse the Blue Ridge and Allegheny ranges to join the Great Kanawha River in Western Virginia and empty its freight boats eventually into the Ohio. But construction had stopped at Buchanan, just south of Lexington and almost two hundred miles west of Richmond, victim of the rapid growth of the far more effective railroads.

The voice of a street vendor floated up to him, crying vegetables grown in the lush rich river bottoms between the James and the Rappahannock and still farther south, toward Petersburg. And from the Tredegar Iron Works smoke from a half dozen furnaces rose skyward in lazy patterns. David had read in the morning edition of the *Enquirer* at breakfast that the cannon formerly occupying places of honor along the curbs since the Revolution had recently been dug up and were now being melted down to form the smoothbore Napoleon cannon favored by Jackson and other fighting leaders to back up the infantry in combat.

Around and between the seven hills sprawled Richmond itself, spilling out across river and canal to the opposite bank of the James. Islands studded the stream here and there and on one of the largest David could see the sprawling structure on Belle Isle Prison. It was always overflowing, he had read, in spite of the almost daily exchange of prisoners, since the fighting for Richmond had begun—could it possibly have been almost a year ago?—with bloody Bull Run, or Manassas.

Nearer by in its twelve-acre square stood the state Capitol, designed to resemble the Maison carrée, which had attracted the admiration of Thomas Jefferson almost a hundred years earlier, while Minister to France. Richmond was lovely by any standard, a city with grandeur, tradition and a quiet dignity—a strangely quiet dignity today, David thought, as he turned to the stairway leading down to the ground floor of the hotel. Yet beneath he sensed a feeling of tension extending even to the height of the hotel roof.

With McClellan's blue-clad army moving thunderously northwestward along the Peninsula from tidewater in the

Chesapeake Bay and McDowell slowly closing another arm of the giant Union pincers from the north, Richmond had good reason to feel itself doomed. Yet something about the tension that gripped the city told David fear of conquest was not the only threat. He'd seen men die from within, perhaps with a hemorrhage from an apoplectic stroke destroying the brain, or a cancer eating its way into the vitals. Now a city seemed to be dying, too, from a cancer he could not yet name, and the appearance was much the same.

Leaving the Spotswood Hotel for the War Department, David decided to walk in order to take a closer look at the beleaguered city. To his surprise, he saw strangely few vehicles even on Broad Street, the wide thoroughfare that almost bisected the city. Plenty of people were abroad, but not the richly uniformed military or the top-hatted merchants and politicians he'd seen in the Spotswood Bar the night before. Instead, these were the common people, a strangely grim and at the moment uncommunicative throng.

An iron worker, his face smudged still by soot from the furnaces where he'd worked during the night, marched along, unsmilingly, carrying his lunch basket. A young woman with a shawl over her head clutched a baby, its tiny features peaked and drawn from what David recognized as the symptoms of malnutrition. A painted whore from the new bordello in front of the hospital for wounded soldiers operated by the Young Men's Christian Association, switched along, unable to relinquish her habitual provocative walk, even though she was making no attempt to accost the masculine contingent. Old men shuffled through the dusty street, rheumy eyes fixed on the shining white reproduction of the Maison carrée, posed majestically at the head of the mile-long plain stretching from the river to the Capitol. An adolescent boy followed, not old enough to be eligible for military duty but finding nothing in the daily ritual of school to attract him in a time of war.

Standing out so remarkably from the rest of the crowd that it naturally fell into line behind her was a giant of a woman wearing an apron stained from the carcasses of

225

beefs and hogs she had butchered, but whose meat she probably could not afford.

From the slopes and the summits of the seven hills, streams of people converged upon the capital, of both a proud state and a would-be nation. A few paused momentarily to shout obscenities at the iron gates of the Executive Mansion occupied by Jefferson Davis, where armed guards stood twenty-four hours a day. Some even spat upon the gateposts marking the former home of Chief Justice Marshall, built in 1725 and now occupied by General Robert E. Lee and his family. "Evacuating Lee," tart-tongued newspapermen had dubbed the general after his failure in the mountains of Western Virginia and few still thought of him as anything more than a lackey for Jefferson Davis.

As the crowd gathered before the Capitol, the guards posted there eyed them speculatively, not certain yet whether to interfere. Only when a sizable mass of angry people had accumulated beneath the linden trees shading much of the grounds, did the guards start fingering their muskets hesitantly, obviously wondering whether they would have the courage to shoot into the ranks of unarmed women, old men and children, if ordered to do so.

As yet the people were silent and sullen, milling about restlessly, as if uncertain of just why they were there or what they were expected to do. But even their uncertainty was a threat, for, should they decide to act in concert, they could easily overpower the guards. Only when the rhythmic sound of marching feet sounded nearby and a sergeant at the head of a new detail of soldiers swung through the wrought-iron gate before deploying his men before the mansion, did the crowd begin to build itself into a tangible—and frightening—horde.

"People of Richmond!" Startled by the shout, David turned to locate its owner and found that the huge woman in the butcher's apron had taken charge, much as Madame Defarge had stimulated revolutionaries in another time and another land to destroy their oppressors.

"How long are we going to stand for drunk officers and swindlers in beaver hats stealing our bread from us and from our children, leaving them to starve?" the big woman demanded.

"No longer!" came the cry from several parts of the crowd, while others began to repeat the slogan, "Down with profiteers! Down with conscription!"

"Feed our babies!" shouted the young woman with the wizened child and at the sound the infant began a high-pitched mewling cry, as if it lacked the strength— and no doubt it did—to make a more lusty protest.

"How long must our sons be killed to protect the damn politicians that keep Jeff Davis on his throne?" the female butcher shouted. "How long will you let generals feed like pigs at the Spotswood Hotel while we starve to pay their salaries?"

"Bread! Bread!" came a cry from another part of the crowd, and the rest picked up the chant, in a rhythm that had all the menace of an army's cadenced tread.

"Money! Bread!" The big woman raised her hand and silence fell over the crowd.

Here was a natural leader, David recognized, a Judith come to save her people from the enemy within, often more dangerous than those without, a Joan of Arc reborn to fire them with the spark of rebellion.

"Are we goin' to let the profiteers get rich while we starve?" the Amazon demanded, and shouts of indignation arose from the crowd.

"Then let's go!" Stepping down from the hitching block where she had harangued the crowd, she started toward Ninth Street, shoving aside a guard who tried momentarily to deny her passage, and daring them all to shoot.

Into Ninth Street the crowd poured behind her, solemn and purposeful, a tide of grim, angry faces that grew ever larger as those who had been standing on the outside of the crowd, lured by the possibility of plunder, hurried to join it. Clerks and minor officials stared down at them from the windows of the War Department but the townspeople in general had already scurried to the protection of their homes or shops. Behind the bloody-aproned leader hurried the young woman with the hungry baby, whose wailing had even stopped now, as if it, too, sensed that at last measures to assuage the hunger of the starving populace were being taken.

Even the rheumy-eyed old men were marching proudly, like the soldiers some of them had been long ago. And the pale-faced boy ran beside the crowd, calling to friends he saw on the sidewalk to join him. And though his own destination had been the War Department and the Surgeon General's Office, David found himself hurrying along the sidewalk from which he could see the leaders caught up in the drama of the occasion.

By the time the mob crossed Main Street and headed into Cary, where the war-rich had their stores, they were seizing carts, drays and whatever vehicles they came upon. Battering down the doors of shops, the crowd poured in one side and out the other, carrying everything they could lay their hands on. Hams, bacon, flour, cornmeal, syrup, cheese, everything was seized and carried out into the street. Some of the plunder was loaded in the carts, but many stopped to eat, tearing ravenously at smoked sausages, dried beef and pickled pig's feet.

The glass front of a bakery was smashed and the tide poured in, seizing loaves of bread, boxes of cookies, round cartwheels of yellow cheese, everything that could be taken out. It did no good for store proprietors to close their establishments against the angry mob for fragments of paving stones and whole bricks from the streets easily smashed glass storefronts, giving access to all. Some were cut by slivers of glass while scrambling through the smashed windows, but, in the frenzy of looting, ignored their wounds and staggered heavyladen from the stores, blood from the cuts staining the dust of the street and the loot they were carrying.

It was the first time David had ever watched a mob in full cry and he could not have turned away if he had tried, so gripping was the horror—and yet the excitement—of the scene. On Main Street, the more expensive stores and shops had been quickly closed by their proprietors but this did not deter the crowd in their frenzy of looting. Smashing windows, they carried out bolts of fabric, plumed hats—even a corset the pale-faced boy laced about his body, laughing with insane glee at his own appearance.

With the mob still in full cry, no one noticed the sound of a bugle in the distance, until the cadence of marching feet reaching them at last through the cobblestones finally warned that official action to control the riot was about to be taken. Not wanting to be seen in uniform in the crowd by the guards, David climbed the steps of a small hotel where a number of onlookers had gathered.

"Have the Yankees been sighted, Major?" an obviously scared man asked in a shaken voice.

"This is a riot, not an invasion."

"But what do our own people have to riot about?"

David stared at him in amazement. "Food, they say."

The man only shook his head. "There's plenty of food in the stores."

"Money then, I suppose." David couldn't help thinking of the classic speech made by Marie Antoinette in another, and not very dissimilar situation, when she'd said, "Let them eat cake." He felt a twinge of guilt at the memory of the succulent guinea hen he'd consumed last night. And the bacon and eggs and hot biscuits he'd had for breakfast now turned into a lump inside his stomach.

Around the corner came a Home Guard company marching—albeit somewhat timorously—with lowered muskets and fixed bayonets. The bugle sounded again and a man, whom David recognized from newspaper pictures as Governor Letcher, climbed to the podium of a hitching block and shouted for order. The part of the crowd nearest to the governor was silent now, but at the other end the leaders continued to shout and only when the governor gave a command to the guard and the bugler blew a loud blast, was the looting halted.

"Read the Riot Act," Governor Letcher ordered the anxious-looking clerk who accompanied him. But as the man began to read, hoots of derision and cries of "Louder! Louder!" drowned him out.

"You have five minutes to disperse," Letcher told the crowd angrily. "After that the guards will shoot."

The people were uncertain now, halted at last but still

grim and in no mood to give up the booty they had gained. The Amazon at the head of the pack was thrusting her way back through it now, shouting threats at the governor and Home Guards as she went. Behind her, a knot of men and some women, inspired by the courage of their leader in defying even the authority of the state, gathered strength as they followed. They were almost at Letcher, their demeanor leaving little doubt that they meant to attack him, when a carriage whirled around the corner. A slender figure was standing up in it, holding only to the whip socket, and the set of the small man's jaw, the complete absence of either fear or hesitation on his part, cowed even the Amazon momentarily.

"God-a-mighty!" said a voice from the crowd. "It's Jefferson Davis himself!"

The carriage stopped and the President of the Confederate States of America jumped down, elbowing his way through the edge of the crowd to where a dray, half loaded with goods taken from one of the looted stores, stood near the curb. Climbing upon it, Davis looked down at the crowd.

"This is worse than a Yankee victory!" His voice was like a whip, lashing them with fury. "Are you mad that you steal from your own people!"

"Bread! Bread!" someone shouted in the crowd.

"Do you think farmers will bring their meal and flour into the city if they know you are waiting to seize it before they can be paid?" Davis' voice was sharp with contempt. "What you have done here will only make bad matters worse."

"They couldn't be no worse than they already are— with babies starving." Seizing the baby from the girl who had been holding it and lifting it above her head, the Amazon pulled away the blanket to expose the wizened little face, the tiny body, skin loose and pallid from lack of food.

"Look at this baby, Mr. President!" she shouted as the mewling cry began again. "Look at it and puke next time you dine on soft-shell crabs and champagne at the Spotswood Hotel."

"If you are in need, I will provide for you from my

own purse." Davis raised his hand when the catcalls began and they subsided quickly in the face of his obvious sincerity and conviction. "Let us bear hardships the same way our brave soldiers bear the dangers and privations of battle."

Roving across the crowd, Davis' gaze settled on David Preston where he stood upon the steps in front of the hotel. "You there, Major," he called. "What is your organization?"

"First Brigade, Army of the Shenandoah."

"General Jackson's brigade—the Stonewall?"

"Yes, sir."

"I recognize you now, sir." Jefferson Davis' voice was suddenly warm. "Here's a real hero, folks. Dr. Preston captured a Yankee field hospital singlehandedly during the Battle of Bull Run and is now using it to save the lives of our brave men under General Jackson's command. Would you have him take back to them the news of your disgraceful actions here today?"

Even the small patch of supporters around the big woman was cowed now. And as her following began to melt away, Davis spoke again, but in a milder voice, like a father soothing a rebellious child.

"Return to your homes, your work. You have my assurance that the hungry shall be fed, the naked shall be clothed."

"It's a good thing there isn't a body of water around or that son-of-a-bitch would try to walk on it," said a voice in David's ear, and he turned quickly, laughing, to find a tall man with a saturnine face and a prominent nose standing beside him.

"And from the way he broke up this riot singlehandedly, I'm not at all sure he wouldn't make it," the tall man added.

"It took courage to do what he just did."

"Nobody ever accused Little Jeff of not having that. Judgment? Maybe not. But gall? That's something else." The speaker held out his hand. "Name's Ed Mattox, Richmond *Enquirer*. I think my brother Jake may have been at VMI when you were there, Doctor."

"I remember him well. Where's Jake now?"

"Back home in Chase City, wearing a diaper and rolling around in a wheelchair. A minié ball cut his spinal cord at Bull Run and left him half a man—or less." Mattox's voice was bitter. "If Jeff Davis and the rest of the southern states had left Virginians alone, we could have lived with Lincoln in Washington. Now we're going to lose everything unless, when this is over, Old Abe can beat Stanton and the rest of 'em in Congress who want to destroy us and steal everything we have. Can I buy you a drink, Doctor? This hotel has a bar."

"Not this early, Mr. Mattox—but I'll take a rain check. I was on my way to the War Department to report for duty when I saw the crowd. I guess we mountain people are naturally curious."

"Good thing you are," said the newspaperman. "If Little Jeff hadn't been able to shame the rioters by pointing you out as a war hero, there could have been hell to pay. In fact, Virginia might have been out a governor and the Confederacy, a President. Where are you staying, by the way?"

"The Spotswood."

Mattox grinned. "That female butcher could have been talking about you. Well, I'd better be off to write the story of what happened here the way Jeff Davis wants it written; he's calling all the shots these days. But if you'll join me at the Spotswood Bar around five-thirty, you can exercise that rain check."

V

Through streets littered with debris and broken glass, David made his way to the War Department and reported to Colonel Samuel P. Moore, Surgeon General of the Armies of the Confederate States of America. Colonel Moore welcomed him without much enthusiasm.

"I'm not at all certain I approve of your describing for our medical officers a type of hospital we can't possibly manage to manufacture for another year or maybe longer, Major Preston. But General Jackson and General Lee are enthusiastic—" Moore shrugged and David understood that he was being accepted only on a temporary basis.

"The hospital we captured was designed by Major Jesse Bayard, a former classmate of mine at Jefferson Medical College, Colonel. It's highly effective in battle, but I'm already having trouble because we can't find wheels that fit the wagons. I'm hoping to get some new axles turned and put into place somewhere out in the Valley."

"I like the idea of using the wagons interchangeably to haul medical supplies and equipment, and as ambulances for the wounded," Moore admitted.

"The ambulance problem is grave, sir. Major Hunter McGuire is working on that now."

"McGuire's a good man." Moore had thawed perceptibly. "I gather that you get along very well together."

"His job is largely administrative, while mine is purely treating the wounded, sir. And that suits me fine."

"You're fortunate, Major," said the older doctor somewhat wistfully. "We have you scheduled for three lectures during the next four days, the first one this afternoon at four o'clock. I see by your service record that you've had only one short leave in almost a year, so I suppose you would like to stay in Richmond awhile and enjoy yourself before going back to the field."

"I'll stay here as long as you need me, sir. But I'd like to get back to the Stonewall Brigade before the next battle."

"Which could be soon from what I hear. Are your quarters satisfactory?"

"They're luxurious compared to the field, sir. But something about Richmond troubles me."

"Everything about Richmond troubles me, Major. You saw one of them just now." Moore gave a short bark of a laugh. "One of my officers saw you from the window here about an hour ago being swept along in the crowd of rioters."

"I'm afraid my curiosity got the better of me, sir."

"People are starving while war contractors get rich, Major, so incidents like that will be more and more common as the Yankees tighten the noose around us with the blockade. I'll have orders sent to your hotel four days from now, returning you to your organization, so try not to make my officers too discontented with their lot. Good day, Major."

"Good day, sir. And thank you."

It was five o'clock when David finished describing to a small group of about fifty medical officers how the 1st Field Hospital of the Stonewall Brigade operated. A brief flurry of discussion had occurred when he described how antiseptic field surgery had saved many limbs in the Austro-Italian war that would otherwise have been amputated. But in answer to pointed questions, he was forced to admit that, during the engagements he'd participated in so far, the rush of casualties had been far too great to allow use of the ideal treatment very often. And he was forced to admit that, because of the dangers of sepsis in such wounds, amputation still seemed to provide a more certain method of saving life.

Judging by the press of the crowd at the Spotswood Bar, one would hardly have guessed that Richmond had survived a serious riot by its civilian population less than twelve hours ago. David was working his way through the crowd when a hand tapped his shoulder and he looked up to see the tall form of Ed Mattox beside him.

"I've got a table over in the corner and they keep a brace of juleps on ice here for me every afternoon at this time, Major Preston," said the newspaperman. "I owe you at least two drinks for helping me make up my mind at last."

"So?" David asked, but Mattox didn't answer until he had directed his guest to the table and they had touched the two frosted glasses already standing there with a sprig of mint resting in each one.

"To our friendship, Major Preston. Long may it continue."

"I'll willingly drink to that, but what have I done to deserve such an honor?"

"You gave me the courage to write my last news story the way Jefferson Davis demands, instead of the way it really happened. Take a look at these instructions from our beloved leader." Mattox took a sheet of paper from his pocket and spread it out on the table:

To the Richmond Press, Gentlemen,

Since it is possible that the unfortunate disturbance which occurred today may be interpreted by some not familiar with our situation as evidence of dissatisfaction on the part of a few citizens of the Confederate States with our Cause, you are requested to avoid any reference to such occurrences either now or in the future, lest you thereby give aid and comfort to the enemy.

Furthermore, the telegraph company is being instructed not to allow transmission of any dispatches regarding this or future occurrences of this type.

Jefferson Davis,
President CSA

"What you're seeing, Dr. Preston, is censorship of the worst kind," said Mattox bitterly. "We've been expecting it for some time and there it is."

"Isn't censorship always part of war?"

"Usually—but from the generals, not the civil government. No newspaperman worth his salt would admit there's ever any real justification for withholding non-military information. But, cravens that we are, we've been writing what Davis wants, which is almost as bad."

Mattox unfolded a sheet of copy paper. "Here's part of what I wrote about this morning's affair—if Davis will ever let us print it. I leave it to you to decide which is worse, to say nothing or to whitewash the truth."

Solemnly Mattox read:

A handful of prostitutes, professional thieves, Irish and Yankee hags, gallows birds from all lands but your own, congregated in Richmond with a woman huckster at their head, who buys veal at the toll gate for one hundred and sells the same for two hundred and fifty in the morning market.

Swearing that they would have goods at government prices, they broke open half a dozen shoe stores, hat stores and tobacco houses and robbed them of everything but bread, which was just the thing they wanted least.

Mattox looked up from the sheet. "Doesn't that make you want to vomit?"

"It's well written, I'll give you that."

"But true?"

"No."

"I wrote it this afternoon, Doctor. Then I went to my editor and asked to be accredited to the Valley District as a war correspondent—"

"Why?"

"If Stonewall Jackson is the kind of man who can earn the unquestioned loyalty of someone like you, he'll let me write the truth—even about his failures."

"He doesn't have many failures, you know."

"So much the better. When are you going back to the Valley?"

"In about four days."

"Good. It may be that long before the War Department gives me the accreditation I need. If they do, we can travel together."

"Why would there be doubt about your getting it?"

"I've made no attempt to hide my feelings about censorship, so Jeff Davis knows very well where I stand. My guess is he'll be quite happy to have me out of Richmond."

"How much danger is Richmond really in?"

"McClellan is pushing up the Peninsula, screaming all the time to Washington that he needs more men and McDowell is doing the same thing as he moves down to cross the Rappahannock. Any way you look at it the situation appears well-nigh hopeless, but don't forget that a year ago, the North was convinced it would take no more than two days to capture Richmond, until Old Stonewall brought his troops from the Valley and saved Beauregard's skin. Maybe he can do it again."

"I don't think Jackson has Richmond in his immediate schedule right now," said David. "With Frémont, Banks and Shields all converging on us in Elk Run Valley, we're going to be pretty busy."

"Then why sit there when that's not Jackson's usual way of fighting a war?"

"Did you ever see a Frenchman fight?"

"Can't say I have."

"He strikes, kicks and butts. I like to believe Old Jack is waiting for the Yankees to get close enough for him to hit 'em from every angle."

"And overpower an enemy that outnumbers him two to one?"

"Three to one, or even more, is probably nearer correct. But I'm still betting on Jackson."

"So are a lot of other people," said Mattox. "Let me know when your orders come through and maybe we can take the same train west. I'll be damned glad to get away from that Yankee observation balloon, makes you feel like somebody's looking over your shoulder all the time."

VI

The train had left Richmond early that morning, but it was close to noon when it drew to a halt at Mechum's River Station about ten miles west of Charlottesville on the Virginia Central Railroad connecting the Confederate capital with Staunton in the southern part of the Valley. Ed Mattox had met David at the Sportswood Hotel for an early breakfast before they were driven to the station in a hack. On the way to Mechum's River Station, they'd been forced to pull off on a siding several times to allow trains loaded with war materials to pass.

"We'd better find some food," said David as they stepped down from the car in which they had been riding. "I left my horse here but we're certain to have trouble finding one for you. In Jackson's army they're even scarcer than medical supplies."

"How *do* you get them?" Mattox asked.

"Mainly it's a case of beg, borrow or steal—the latter case usually confined to Yankee cavalry units, when we're lucky. Of course a lot of men brought their own when they enlisted but it's a continual problem. Come winter, too, forage is going to be scarcer than hen's teeth."

The food in the station dining room was plentiful—and good. As the two men were leaving, a flurry of hoofbeats sounded outside and a half dozen officers in Confederate gray pulled their mounts to a halt at the hitching rail. All of them were dusty, as if they had ridden many miles. The leader was a rather short, bald man with prominent eyes and the truculent look of a bantam rooster. David didn't need to see the twin stars of a major general to recognize Richard S. Ewell.

Jackson's senior at West Point by six years, Ewell was an infantry commander in the classic mold. Intensely bright, cocky, with prominent eyes, he was known to be capable of rapid movement and attack when needed. Given to profanity at times and a slight lisp when excited, Ewell was the antithesis of the cool, calculating, but equally intense, Jackson.

When David came to attention and saluted, Ewell regarded him with an angry look for a moment, before returning the salute.

"Major Preston, isn't it? I remember you from Manassas."

"Yes, sir."

"Why aren't you with General Jackson, Major?"

"I've been in Richmond a week, sir—on detached duty at the Surgeon General's Office lecturing on field hospitals."

"Did Jackson send for you?"

"No, sir. I'm on the way back to Elk Run Valley."

"Jackson's not there any more."

Startled, David asked, "Are you sure, sir?"

"No, I'm not sure." Ewell's eyes bulged even more than usual. "Why else would I ride twenty miles down here from Stanardsville trying to find out what that crackpot commanding general of yours is up to?"

"I'm sure I don't know, sir. General Jackson rarely tell his plans to anyone."

Ewell controlled himself with an effort. "Two days ago a lieutenant named Douglas, I forget his first name—"

"That would be Kyd Douglas, sir. He's just joined General Jackson's staff."

"That was the name, General," said one of the aides.

"This lieutenant appeared at my camp near Culpeper with an order from Jackson to proceed to Elk Run Valley by way of Stanardsville and Swift Run Gap. But when I got to Stanardsville last night, they said Jackson had been here at Mechum's River Station."

Ewell purpled again. "So if everybody in this part of Virginia already knows about Jackson being forced out of Elk Run Valley, Major Preston, would you be so kind as to tell me why in the hell he didn't let me know? Or does he want me to go barging in there and be ambushed by Federal troops?"

"General Jackson doesn't push easily, sir," said David. "I suspect he's on the way somewhere and is keeping his destination a secret so the Federals won't know until he strikes them."

"The major may be right, Dick," said a brigadier general on Ewell's staff. "The message Jeb Stuart's telegrapher intercepted from General Banks to Secretary Stanton in Washington yesterday morning said Jackson's on the run."

"Which is probably exactly the impression General Jackson wants to create, sir," David added.

"But my orders are to move into Elk Run Valley," Ewell fumed. "Why would that be, if he's preparing to fight somewhere else?"

"Elk Run is an important place, with natural fortifications," David explained. "I'd say General Jackson wants you to hold it while he strikes somewhere else."

"What you say does make some sense, Major Preston," Ewell conceded, his anger apparently giving way to more rational thought. "But I would still like to know where Jackson went."

"He'll be heard from, you can be sure of that."

"I suppose I'll have to go on that," said Ewell. "Let's get some food, gentlemen, we've got a long ride back to Standardsville this afternoon. Thank you for your help, Major Preston; I hope your general doesn't put me where I'll wind up in that fancy hospital of yours I've been reading about in the Richmond papers."

"So that's 'Fighting Cock' Ewell," said Mattox as they were walking back to the train. "Boy, was he mad."

David stopped short. "How much of what Ewell said did you overhear?"

"All of it."

"And how much do you remember?"

Mattox grinned. "Not a word.

"See that you don't have a sudden recall, then. If I catch you around a telegraph office before Old Jack finishes whatever he's up to, I'll place you under arrest myself."

"Don't worry," said Mattox. "If Stonewall is about to pull off another of his stunts, I want to be in on the whole show."

The train was not yet ready to depart, so the two men stretched their legs with a turn of the graveled area that served as the station platform alongside the tracks. It was considerably longer than normal, in order for the troops being loaded or unloaded here to have access to the cars. At the end of the graveled walk, David stopped suddenly and stared at a wagon without wheels elevated on some wooden blocks.

"That looks like a hospital wagon," he told Mattox. "Let's take a look at it."

"Get your pant legs full of beggar lice if you wish. I'll go back to the train and tell 'em to hold it, in case they decide to leave before you figure out where Stonewall went and decide to follow."

Even at a distance, the wagon had looked familiar. And when David examined it at closer range, the remaining pieces of the puzzle about Jackson's visit to Mechum's River Station suddenly fell into place. Crossing the grassy field to the freight office, he stepped inside. The clerk who was working at a desk looked up.

"Anything I can do for you, Major?" he asked.

"I like the looks of that abandoned wagon frame out there on the blocks. Do you know where I could get some wheels for it?"

"Not for that wagon, Major. Them're Yankee wheels."

"I suppose General Jackson had to leave it here when his troops boarded the train," said David on a casual note.

"Yeah. They arrived here yesterday morning with one

of them new-fangled hospital wagons barely able to go, so the sergeant in charge took the wheels off that one and put the others on the train." The clerk stopped suddenly. "That's supposed to be secret, Major; I'll catch hell if anybody finds out I blabbed."

"I'm a doctor with General Jackson's forces in charge of that field hospital," David assured him. "I've been in Richmond for the past week and didn't know exactly where my unit was. This way I can go on and join them."

"You'll be more than a day late, Major. We loaded the troops on the morning train for Staunton early yesterday. They were due to get there before dark."

General Ewell and his staff had given their orders but the food hadn't been brought yet when David entered the dining room.

"Could I speak to you outside, General?" he asked.

Ewell rose immediately but neither spoke until they were outside the station, where no one would overhear.

"What is it, Major?" Ewell asked. "I'm pretty hungry."

"I know where General Jackson went, sir. And I thought you might like to know."

"You mean you've decided to tell me, don't you?" Ewell's tone was sharp.

"I just discovered it myself."

"How in hell—?"

"That's one of the wagons from my field hospital." David pointed toward the wagon frame. "We've been having trouble with the wheels and some more must have given way coming across the Blue Ridge night before last. When they got here my sergeant took the good wheels off that one and put them on some of the others."

"Did you figure that all out yourself, Major?" Ewell's manner was much less truculent now.

"The railroad clerk helped, after I recognized the wagon out there and trapped him into telling me General Jackson loaded the Army of the Valley on the cars yesterday morning."

"For Richmond?"

"For Staunton. The general must have felt he should get there as quickly as possible, or he wouldn't have moved on Sunday."

Ewell nodded slowly. "Which means Frémont's forces are moving on Staunton and General Edward Johnson needs help."

From the locomotive came a sharp whistle blast and the conductor called, "All Abo-a-r-d!"

"I've got to go, sir," said David.

"Don't miss the train, Major." Ewell held out his hand and David gripped it hurriedly. "Tell General Jackson I'll hold Elk Run Valley for him. But I'd a lot rather be with him scaring that bastard Frémont out of his drawers."

VII

The morning of May 8, 1862, was bright and sunny. Having joined his old organization two days earlier at Staunton, David was once again in charge of the 1st Field Hospital with the Stonewall Brigade. The afternoon before, the Army of the Valley had advanced along the Lewisburg Turnpike westward from Staunton, with Brigadier General Edward Johnson's brigades from the Army of the Northwest, reinforced by the 12th Georgia, at the head of the long column.

When information had reached Jackson that Frémont had divided his forces, with Milroy's brigade moving toward Staunton, Schenck's brigade at Franklin—over thirty miles to the north—and a substantial force at Romney much too far away to help the other two, Jackson had decided to attack the Federals west of the Valley Turnpike.

The military situation was an ideal one for Jackson's favorite strategy of divide and conquer. Federal pickets had been contacted late on the afternoon of May 7 and driven back toward the small village of McDowell, a few miles ahead, where the troops of Federal Brigadier General R. H. Milroy, thought to be only about three thousand strong, had made their headquarters.

As the Confederate forces moved out early on the morning of May 8, with the 1st Brigade at the rear, followed by the bright-uniformed VMI cadets, who had marched from Lexington to join in the fray, Major Hunter McGuire rode back to where David was riding beside his wagons.

"General Jackson wants you at the front to help locate a good site for the hospital," he said.

"I was beginning to think about just that. Take over here, please, Hal, I shouldn't be very long."

By the time the two doctors reached the head of the column, it was already moving toward the top of Bull Pasture Mountain in a Shenandoah range of the Alleghenies forming the western boundary of the Valley of Virginia. Looking down upon the small village of McDowell, with the entire Federal force encamped around it, David could see the wisdom of Jackson's insistence on secrecy. The troopers of Colonel Turner Ashby's cavalry, Hunter McGuire told him, were spread out as a screen to the north, where the forces of General Banks waited at Harrisonburg, to keep the enemy from learning the main body of Jackson's troops intended to pounce on General Milroy's forces before the latter could be reinforced by Frémont.

David had told Jackson on the night of his arrival at Staunton about what Ewell had said concerning the message from General Banks to Union Secretary of War Stanton intercepted by Jeb Stuart's telegrapher. Jackson had thanked him, but his manner had still been reserved.

"I'm not certain you did us a favor by bringing Mr. Mattox back with you from Richmond, Major Preston," he said.

"I warned him I will arrest him myself if he breaks a pledge of secrecy, General. And I think we can depend upon his keeping his word."

"I shall hold you responsible in any event, Doctor," had been Jackson's only other comment. Now, as he sat his horse within earshot of the two generals and their staff, David wondered how Mattox was faring as driver of one of the hospital wagons, for which task he had volunteered.

"If we hold the top of the mountain and Sitlington's Hill here close to the turnpike," Jackson pointed out to

General Edward Johnson, who stood beside him, "we ought to be able to bottle General Milroy in."

"It looks like an excellent position, if we can keep the Federals from realizing you're here, too," Johnson agreed. "As long as Milroy thinks he's still opposing only my two brigades and the Georgia troops, he might do something foolish."

"We'll help him all we can," said Jackson. "Now, if you will have your troops move into position, General, with God's help we will win a victory here today."

The town of McDowell lay in a narrow valley traversed by a branch of the Cowpasture River. David had selected a sizable clearing on the riverbank, where there was an adequate supply of water, as a location for the hospital. Now he led the wagons off the road beside the stream and supervised the erection of the tents under which the unit would function. With Hal Perkins, Mattox and the half dozen men, many of them recovering from wounds, assigned to the hospital unit, he had barely finished making preparations when the sound of firing ahead warned that at least the preliminary stages of the battle had begun.

A little after four in the afternoon, the firing became very heavy, and casualties soon began to pour into the hospital, most of them Deep Southerners from Georgia whose soft twang betrayed their origin. General Edward Johnson was brought in shortly after five o'clock with a musket ball through his arm. David gave him a hypodermic injection of morphine and washed out the wound, which was through-and-through, with chloride of lime solution.

"Milroy almost outfoxed us," Johnson admitted somewhat ruefully while the wound was being dressed. "We were trying to outflank his position, but he was reinforced by part of Schenck's brigade. Those Ohio and Western Virginia troops fought like tigers."

"I've been seeing a lot of shrapnel wounds," said David, "as if the enemy is using long-range artillery."

"They are—and very effectively. General Jackson has tried to keep our forces under the protection of the hilltop."

"He used the same strategy at Manassas—"

"It would have worked here, too, but those Georgia boys kept rushing to the front. The Yankees just picked them off with those Sharps rifles or lobbed over long-range shells with the Parrott guns they use so much, exploding them just over the crest of the hill and spraying us with shrapnel."

"We didn't come all the way from Georgia to Virginia to run away from no Yankees, General," a tall soldier with a bandaged head called across a row of cots.

"Martial spirit is fine," said Johnson. "But when it takes the place of judgment—"

"What's the situation now, sir?" David asked.

"Pretty close to a standoff. With regiments from Schenck's brigade in the battle, the Federals now outnumber us, but we've taken a heavy toll. If General Jackson succeeds in sending a force around by a back road he's learned of to outflank the Federals, they will have to fall back."

"Then he's found the road?"

"Just before I was wounded, a scout came in with news of the route, but it means quite a long forced march and these mountains are no place to find your way through after dark. The general will have to wait until morning to lead that force."

"Lead? Surely he isn't going to do that?"

"Sometimes you don't have any choice, Doctor. Jackson doesn't have much confidence in the colonels commanding two of the other three brigades—"

"So he'll lead the flanking march himself and take the risk."

"Would you expect anything else?"

"I guess not," David admitted. "But I'd feel better about his chances of coming through this war alive if he occasionally showed some sign of fear."

By dark the fighting had died down to an occasional sharp report of a Parrott gun, which could fire at fixed range even after darkness and thus hold the southern troops at bay. No casualties had appeared at the hospital for over an hour by the time David had finished a meal of hardtack and dried beef, which Hal Perkins had managed to make into a stew with potatoes and onions filched from somewhere to make an appetizing dish. Leaving Hal in charge, he climbed the hill to Jackson's command post on the summit.

Lieutenant Kyd Douglas, Jackson's new aide, was writing a letter. Young and handsome, Douglas was a lawyer, born, David had heard, at Shepherdstown, a river crossing on the Potomac some eight miles almost due west of Martinsburg. When he stopped beside Douglas, the young officer started to scramble to his feet.

"As you were, Lieutenant. I had an interesting conversation about you a few days ago at Mechum's River Station."

"But I'd never been to Mechum's River Station, Major, until we boarded a train there on Sunday."

"This was with General Dick Ewell. He was trying to find out where General Jackson was going."

Douglas laughed. "He tried to pump me at Gordonsville. But I didn't even know myself, so I couldn't tell him."

"He spoke highly of you, though."

"I guess I must have looked like Paul Revere at the end of his ride. Actually mine was a bit longer—all the way to Gordonsville, about fifty miles from Elk Run, and back in forty-eight hours."

"You must have been dead in the saddle."

"Part of me certainly was. It rained the whole time and, when I rode up to General Jackson's headquarters at Conrad's Store in Swift Run Gap the second night, I was soaked to the skin. I went into the general's room to report that I was back and found him lying on the floor wrapped in a blanket on a mattress. I even had to wake him to make my report, but all he said was, 'Very good. You did get there in time. Good night.'"

Douglas chuckled at the memory. "I'm afraid I behaved like a schoolboy who expected a reward and General Jackson must have realized it. He sent for me the next morning and I found him sitting on a camp stool by a small fire reading a dispatch. I started to apologize for the night before but before I could find the right words, he stopped me.

" 'Mr. Douglas,' he said, 'Major Baylor leaves me today to take command of the Fifth Regiment of the Stonewall Brigade. I want to assign you to duty as assistant inspector general on my staff.' " The young officer smiled. "Can you tell me what are the duties of an assistant inspector general, Dr. Preston?"

"I don't know what the military Tables of Organization say, but in the Army of the Valley, he does whatever General Jackson wants him to do—like the other members of the staff."

"I've learned that much, and I guess I'll learn more tomorrow when I accompany him on that flanking movement." Douglas looked away for a moment, then back at David. "Have you ever been under fire, Major Preston?"

"Several times."

"Frankly I'm scared stiff."

"Everybody is—and not just the first time. But if you're with Jackson, you'll come out all right, Lieutenant. Can I see anything from the top of this hill? I was so busy today that I didn't get a chance to study the field after the battle started."

"The whole terrain is there before you," said Douglas. "I'll go out with you."

From the top of Sitlington's Hill they looked down upon a vast sea of darkness, dotted with the campfires of the Union army resting there for the night.

"The first reports placed General Milroy's forces at less than three thousand," said Douglas. "But from the looks of those fires, there must be a half million of 'em down there. Brave men, too, Major; you should have seen the way those Ohio troops charged up the hill this afternoon. I thought they would overrun us for sure but the Georgia boys fought 'em off every time."

"I could tell that from the number of casualties we were receiving, but tomorrow should be better. When General Jackson gets to the Yankee rear with that flanking movement, the Federals will have to withdraw or be cut to pieces."

"You mean *if* he gets to the Federal rear, don't you, Major?"

"That's something else about the Army of the Valley,

Lieutenant; we don't use the word *if* where General Jackson's plans are concerned, only *when*. Good luck in the morning."

"Thank you, Doctor. I'm afraid I'm going to need it."

As it turned out, the young assistant inspector general didn't need good luck. When the sun rose and the morning fog cleared from the valleys beyond Bull Pasture Mountain, only the blackened coals of hundreds of campfires, many of them still smoking, remained. The Federal troops had withdrawn from the entire area during the night, moving northwestward to join the much larger force of General J. C. Frémont with the barrier of the eastern bulwark of the Allegheny Range between them and the Shenandoah Valley itself.

Ed Mattox was driving one of the ambulance wagons and had been busy all during the day before. When Mattox came back to the battlefield for his final load of evacuees around noon, Hal Perkins was performing his favorite task, cooking a pan of trout he'd caught in the branch of the Cowpasture River beside which the hospital stood, using worms and several set lines he'd put into one of the pools during the night. Invited to share the meal with David and Hal, Mattox ate with obvious relish.

"You're a better cook than the chef at the Spotswood Hotel, Hal," said Mattox after the meal of trout fillets, hush puppies and golden fried potatoes, with coffee, disappeared. "If you want to open a restaurant after the war, I'll organize a syndicate in Richmond and stake you."

"I'm going to be a doctor, Mr. Mattox."

"More's the pity, food, like this would do far more to prevent stomach trouble than a dozen doctors could do to cure it. But you're probably wise at that; I hear the medical college at Richmond is going to start a shortened course to train more doctors for the armies." He turned to David. "Did you hear about the telegram Jackson sent to General Lee and General Johnston this morning?"

"No. Didn't I warn you about hanging around the telegraph office?"

"The operator at the railroad station has been telling it all over Staunton that he wired, 'God blessed our arms with victory at McDowell yesterday' to Richmond. And yet Jackson won't let me send a word about the battle."

"Maybe he has good reason."

Mattox gave David a sharp look. "Do you know something I don't know?"

"No, but I can give you a hint. The troops we defeated yesterday were only part of the Federal forces at or near the Valley. Actually three armies are poised within range of no more than a hundred miles, Frémont's, Banks' and Shields'."

"Even Jackson can't hope to beat them all alone."

"General Jackson never fights alone, Mr. Mattox," said Hal Perkins. "Remember the message he sent to Richmond?"

" 'God bless our arms.' " Mattox shook his head slowly. "No wonder he always wins. A man in partnership with the Almighty can't lose."

VIII

May 16, 1862, was decreed by Jefferson Davis as a day of prayer and thanksgiving for the victory at Mc-Dowell. Ironically enough it was also the day the new Conscription Act, placing every man between the ages of eighteen and thirty-five in military service—unless he could produce a satisfactory reason for being excused—was to be signed in Richmond by Davis, according to a separate proclamation.

Jackson's forces had pursued the Federal troops retreating from McDowell as far as Monterey, in a beautiful valley that reminded David of a lovely area in Switzerland—thence north along the south branch of the Potomac almost to Franklin. But learning that Frémont had thrown up breastworks in the area, he turned his army eastward toward Harrisonburg, on the Valley Turnpike.

The sixteenth was warm and pleasant, but when David awakened in the bivouac area of the 1st Field Hospital at the rear of the Stonewall Brigade, now under command of Brigadier General Charles S. Winder, he sensed immediately that something was wrong—and knew where to find out what it was.

"What's going on, Hal?" he asked when he finished washing up in a nearby branch.

"It's the Twenty-seventh, sir. The word is that some units will refuse to muster for morning roll call."

"Why?"

"With conscription about to go into effect, a couple of companies in the regiment don't think they're subject to that new law."

A bugle sounded just then and the units of the 27th began to gather for the morning muster—except a group of about a hundred men who still lounged around their campfires, making no move to pick up the stacked rifles and join the formation.

"There goes Colonel Grigsby to brigade headquarters now," said Hal, as a grim-looking officer with a colonel's insignia on his collar strode through the bivouac area. Grigsby wasn't gone long and, when he came back, his expression was even more grim than before.

"I wonder what General Jackson told him?" said Hal.

"Whatever it is, you can't bet it wasn't pleasant."

A succession of sharp commands came from the area where the 27th was encamped and it wasn't long before they found out.

Throughout the bivouac area company commanders were barking orders and the other companies of the regiment were falling in as usual, with their rifles. Only the two companies who had mutinied—it could hardly be called by any other name—failed to obey the order to fall in for the morning report to Colonel Grigsby, who stood at one side, with the regimental adjutant in front of him and a drawn sword in his hand.

"You men there," he called to the loafing soldiers. "Didn't you hear the order to fall in?"

"Our 'listment 'spired yesterday, Colonel," a mountain man drawled. "We're going home as soon as we git our pay."

"I order you to fall in."

"We done finished our 'listment," said another. "Somebody else can fight Jeff Davis' war for a while."

250

"Present arms!" Grigsby ordered the troops who were already in formation.

"See here." The spokesman for the mutineers was obviously disturbed. "You don't have no call to—"

"Prepare to fire!"

"Jesus Christ!" the man shouted. "Are you goin' to shoot us down like dogs?"

"Like deserters!' Everyone here recognized the rather high-pitched voice and all eyes were turned upon Jackson, who had come up unnoticed and was standing about ten feet away from Grigsby.

"Look here, General—"

"Ready! Aim!" snapped Grigsby.

There was a moment of tension, and the clicking of cocked hammers was loud in the tense silence as several hundred rifles were leveled upon the unarmed men. Then a sudden rush to the stacked arms ended the brief mutiny and, in two minutes, every man was in formation, with his weapon.

"Report your companies," Colonel Grigsby told the commanders and taking of the roll began immediately. When the mutineer companies of the 27th were reached, their response was as sharp as any of the others, perhaps sharper. And at the end, the regimental adjutant wheeled, saluted and reported, "All present or accounted for, sir."

"Dismissed!" As the command was passed along by the company commanders and the men fell out of rank, Colonel Grigsby took a handkerchief from his pocket and wiped his forehead, where great beads of sweat had popped out, although the morning was cool.

"Thank God!" he was heard to mutter under his breath.

"It will take Divine Intervention to get Grigsby out of the doghouse for going to Jackson with this little affair." The voice was familiar and David turned to find Colonel John Imboden standing beside him.

"Did the general tell Grigsby to do this?"

"He *ordered* him to do it," said Imboden. Then as Ed Mattox, who had been standing a little way off watching the dramatic scene, moved up with them, he added, "Good morning, Mr. Mattox."

"Hello, Colonel," said the newspaperman. "I don't think I've seen you since that morning you got those trains together outside Richmond and headed for Harpers Ferry."

"That was a long time ago. A long, long time ago."

"Do you think General Jackson would really have had those men shot if they hadn't obeyed the order?" Mattox asked.

"He would have anybody shot who doesn't obey a lawful order, Mr. Mattox," said Imboden. "Don't you agree, David?"

"No doubt about it."

"I'm beginning to understand why Jackson's soldiers are so loyal to him," said the reporter. "He isn't afraid to share their danger, but he expects the same sort of courage and devotion from them."

"And gets it, don't forget that," said Imboden. "Well, I'd better be going, there's a lot to be done."

"I wonder if anybody in the Confederacy right now realizes just how much does have to be done," said Mattox soberly as he and David were walking back to the hospital area. "After a full year of fighting, this army of Jackson's is about the only one that isn't in a bad position. General Albert Sidney Johnston was wounded in battle at Shiloh, Tennessee, last month and his army driven from the field. New Orleans has been captured by Farragut's gunboats, closing the mouth of the Mississippi, and the upper part of the river north of Memphis is now under Federal control."

"Except the area around Vicksburg."

"Ulysses S. Grant isn't going to stop until he takes that too," said Mattox. "Here in the East, McClellan has over a hundred thousand men marching up the Peninsula; the last report I heard he's at White House on the Pamunkey River, twenty miles from Richmond. And on top of that, McDowell has got something like forty thousand near Fredericksburg, where he can jump either toward Richmond from the north or reinforce McClellan. Besides that, Federal gunboats are far enough up the James River to menace Richmond."

"Are you saying we're defeated?"

"I'm saying Stonewall Jackson and the Almighty had better get together real soon and cook up some miracles or the capital of the Confederacy is going to have to start moving back toward Montgomery. And the worst part of it is that Jackson won't let me send a word out of here to Richmond."

"All of which could mean he's already planning his part of that miracle you were just talking about," said David.

IX

"Didn't I tell you Old Jack knows what's he's doing?" David asked Mattox a few days later. As he always tried to do on Sunday, Stonewall Jackson had halted his troops for a day of rest at Mount Solon, about twelve miles southwest of Harrisonburg and somewhat less than that distance west of the Valley Turnpike. "You recognized the officer who just rode into camp, didn't you?"

"Nobody could miss Dick Ewell. But what's it all about?"

"Banks has already started withdrawing from Harrisonburg toward Strasburg and Winchester; Sandie Pendleton told me that this morning when the dispatches came in from the couriers."

"Can you blame Banks for not wanting to fight so far from his base of supplies at Winchester and the B&O at Harpers Ferry?"

"Hardly. But if he runs true to form, he's doubled the size of both Jackson's and Ewell's forces in his reports to Lincoln and Stanton. We probably have about fifteen thousand now, so Banks has convinced himself that he faces thirty or thirty-five thousand men."

"If Ewell and Jackson join up together."

"You may be a good newspaperman, Ed, but you're a damned poor military strategist." David shook his head in mock pity. "I'll lay you ten against five that right now Jackson and Ewell are hatching a plan that will put Banks between them."

"No bet," said Mattox. "I'm going to soak my feet in

some of that alum water Hal recommends. Unless I miss my guess, Stonewall Jackson's famous 'Foot Cavalry' will be doing a lot of walking in the next few days."

At the morning church service the Reverend Major J. L. Dabney, chief of staff and private chaplain for Jackson, preached his usual fiery sermon. After the noonday meal, cooked and served by Jackson's body servant, Jim, Ewell and his staff rode east again toward Conrad's Store and Elk Run Valley.

True to Mattox's prediction about walking, some two hours after dawn on Monday morning, the Army of the Valley marched into Harrisonburg to the cheers of the people. Wagon trains were already converging upon the city, which was obviously being turned into a supply base for this new campaign. And when the order was given to deposit their packs at the courthouse, a cheer went up from the veteran troops.

"What's that all about?" Mattox asked Hal from the seat of the hospital wagon where he'd been riding, after his feet gave out some five miles beyond Mount Solon.

"When the order's given to drop packs, it means they're going into battle," Hal explained.

Late the next afternoon, the 1st Field Hospital pulled off the road between Harrisonburg and New Market when the strains of band music sounded behind them. Shortly afterward, a colorful column of marching men appeared. Three thousand strong they were in fresh gray uniforms with white gaiters, the dying rays of the afternoon sun flashing from their bayonets and the colors displayed on the guidons.

"What unit are you?" Hal Perkins called to the sergeant marching at the back of the second column.

"Louisiana Zouave Brigade, Ewell's division," the sergeant answered with a distinctly French accent. "General Richard Taylor, son of a President, commanding."

"And no stragglers," said Hal in a tone of awe. "By the time General Jackson rode into New Market this afternoon, the Stonewall Brigade was stretched out for five miles along the pike."

"How far have you come today?" Ed Mattox asked the Zouave sergeant.

"Keezletown Road, six and twenty miles."

Just then the band started up a waltz, and without breaking cadence, a company of swarthy Acadians in the column began a rhythmic dance step.

"Good God!" said a burly Irishman from the Emerald Guards. "A bunch of dancin' masters."

"I've seen some accounts of the way those fellows fight, Sergeant," said Ed Mattox. "Get into a scrap with one of them and his feet will be in your face before you know what hit you."

"I can go home now," said the Irishman. "I've seen everything."

A short distance out of New Market the next morning, with the morning mists still shrouding the mass of the Massanutten Range, the head of the column turned sharply east toward Luray and a pass leading through the range that split the Valley lengthwise here for roughly forty miles. Soon the column crossed the South Fork of the Shenandoah River flowing north to join the Potomac at Harpers Ferry.

"I wish you would tell me where in hell we're going, David," said Mattox.

"We'll probably end up splitting General Banks at Winchester from General Shields at Front Royal." David, too, was mystified by the sudden change of direction.

"Or cross the Blue Ridge to get behind McDowell at Manassas and attack Washington," said Mattox. "I'm betting on Washington."

"I'll take the Valley route."

"My boss in Richmond will drop dead when I send a dispatch telling how Stonewall Jackson captured Abraham Lincoln and Secretary Stanton and ended the war at one shot," said Mattox.

By the end of the second day of hard marching, the "Foot Cavalry" was through the Massanutten Range and into the narrow, but lovely, Luray Valley separating it from the massive heights of the Blue Ridge. The higher range, in turn, stood between the Valley army and Piedmont, Virginia, where the Federal Army under General Irvin McDowell was menacing Richmond. While farther

255

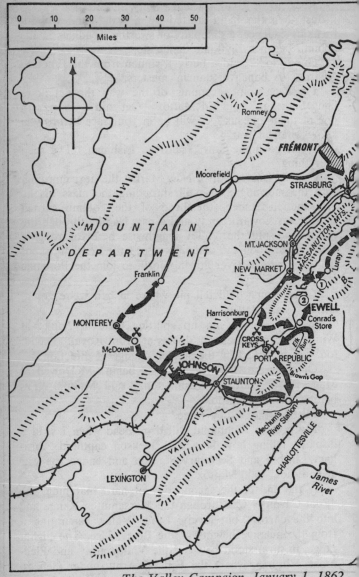

The Valley Campaign, January 1, 1862

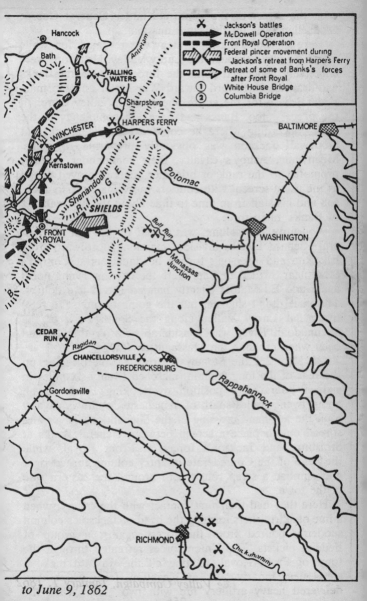

Legend:
- ✕ Jackson's battles
- ▶ McDowell Operation
- ▶ Front Royal Operation
- ⬚ Federal pincer movement during Jackson's retreat from Harper's Ferry
- ⬚⬚▶ Retreat of some of Banks's forces after Front Royal
- ① White House Bridge
- ② Columbia Bridge

Hancock

Bath

FALLING WATERS

Antietam

Sharpsburg

WINCHESTER

HARPERS FERRY

BALTIMORE

Kernstown

Shenandoah

RIDGE

SHIELDS

Potomac

Bull Run

FRONT ROYAL

B L U E

Manassas Junction

WASHINGTON

CEDAR RUN

Rapidan

CHANCELLORSVILLE

FREDERICKSBURG

Gordonsville

Rappahannock

RICHMOND

Chickahominy

to June 9, 1862

east, the Army of the Peninsula under General George McClellan, was on the same mission.

Here Jackson's master strategy was revealed, for, while marching north through the Luray Valley, his troops were effectively concealed from the forces of General Banks withdrawing northward toward Winchester and the main Federal base for the entire Shenandoah Valley there. In the process, too, Banks had been left completely in the dark concerning where he could expect the attack that Stonewall Jackson was obviously preparing to make. Meanwhile, Ashby's cavalry, their commander recently promoted to the rank of brigadier general, moved ahead as the usual screen, with couriers reporting back to Jackson and his staff from time to time about the whereabouts of Banks' main force.

At Luray, the column was joined by the rest of General Richard Ewell's division, marching northward from Elk Run and Jackson's former headquarters at Conrad's Store near Swift Run Gap. Here the column swung north again and Ed Mattox silently handed David five dollars. The pace didn't slacken, but the going through the relatively flat Luray Valley along the South Fork of the Shenandoah River was considerably easier than it had been when crossing the Massanutten Range.

On May 23, the Stonewall Brigade, still bringing up the rear of the long column, marched twenty-six miles in sixteen hours to a position overlooking Front Royal, about twenty miles south of Winchester. Ashby's cavalry took the left-hand crossing of the Shenandoah River and spread out to place a screen between General Banks at Strasburg and Jackson's forces at Front Royal, while the head of the Confederate infantry column turned right and climbed a steep rough path around the eastern side of the town.

Here they had their first contact with the enemy, when a line of skirmishers forming the head of Jackson's column suddenly poured from the forest against a group of Federal pickets. The Union forces retreated through the town of Front Royal, fighting all the way, to make a stand near the river on an elevation, from which they delivered heavy artillery fire with two guns. When the

258

Confederate cavalry moving westward from the town began to threaten the Federal rear, however, the Union troops burned the bridges across both branches of the Shenandoah River, which united just north of Front Royal, and began to retire.

David had ridden forward at the sound of firing ahead and arrived in time to see the brightly clad Zouaves under General Taylor beating out the flames of the two bridges as they poured across to attack. At the same time Stonewall Jackson urged the 6th Virginia Cavalry into the river to pursue the retreating enemy, riding hard himself in their midst. With the inevitable cap pushed forward across his eyes until from the rear he seemed not to have any head at all, Jackson looked, David thought, remarkably like Washington Irving's famous Headless Horseman.

The skirmish—it was hardly more than that—lasted only a short time before the cavalry returned with some six hundred prisoners, perhaps a hundred horses and a store of grain for them, plus the two Parrott guns that had caused most of the trouble at the Shenandoah crossing. By the time darkness fell, the Federal rout at Front Royal was complete. About seven hundred and fifty prisoners, most of them Marylanders from the regiment of Colonel J. R. Kenly, had been taken and the entire force was so nearly captured that there was a possibility General Banks might still think that little more than the Confederate cavalry screen which had harried his retreat all the way from Harrisonburg was involved.

Well before dawn the next morning the entire force was put in motion once again toward the Valley Turnpike and Winchester. A vast supply of food and other supplies had been captured by Ashby's troopers, who, like most of the army, had been traveling fast on short rations. When they stopped to plunder and eat, Jackson himself caught up with them and lashed them into motion again, but it was too late. Some of the fleeing Union troops managed to escape and warn General Banks at Strasburg that his old nemesis, Stonewall Jackson, was after him in full cry.

When David Preston reached the Valley Turnpike with his hospital unit in the wake of the Stonewall Brigade, a strange sight met his eyes. As far as could be seen, the captured Federal supply train stretched southward along the highway. Some wagons were burning, but far the larger number had been seized intact. Hardly any troops were free from battle and available to secure the supplies from looters, both military and civilian, so people were swarming over the booty everywhere.

Ahead, where Jackson's flying cavalry had cut off the train, isolated piles of human and animal bodies indicated points where the Federal cavalry screen supposed to protect the wagon train had dared to engage the attackers before being cut down by the Confederate juggernaut. At one point a couple of wagons had been placed under a row of giant oaks off the road and a group of camp followers—retreating, too, from Harrisonburg, but changing sides en route—had set up a temporary brothel, before which lines of men waited under the trees.

"There's your human interest story, Ed," David Preston told Mattox as they rode by, the newspaperman having appropriated a Federal cavalry mount by that time for his own transportation.

"There's no point in writing that one for quite a while, if at all," said Mattox. "Jefferson Davis couldn't let it be published."

"Why?"

"He's been doing everything he can to close up the whorehouses in Richmond, but a new one opened across the street from the YMCA Hospital just a few days before we left. One of the doctors at the hospital told me he treated more cases of clap the week after it opened than he'd seen before in his whole professional life."

"Life goes on, you know. I suppose you're going to write a book when this is over."

"I'm not sure I even believe what I've been seeing," said Mattox. "Until Ewell's division joined Stonewall, I doubt if the Army of the Valley ever had as many as five thousand men. Yet Jackson's already defeating his second Federal army of at least twice that number in not much more than a month. I'm wondering now whether they'll stop him short of the Potomac."

"You had him taking Washington a few days ago," David reminded the reporter. "Losing confidence?"

"No, I'm just wondering what would happen if Jeff Davis would put the whole war in the hands of Lee and Jackson."

The Stonewall Brigade was in the forefront of the action against Winchester, with David following close behind, rendering aid to the busy regimental surgeons whenever he came upon the dressing stations they set up along the turnpike. But with the column moving rapidly forward and a succession of small vicious battles-in-miniature breaking out almost every mile, plus the probability that before he could get his tentage up the action might be miles away, there was no time to set up a hospital near the front.

On Sunday, May 25, 1862, Winchester fell to Stonewall Jackson's advancing Army of the Valley and was occupied the following day. While the rest of the army celebrated, however, David Preston was busy. The lightning-swift Valley Campaign had not been accomplished without considerable casualties on both sides. And, with Banks' army in flight across the Potomac and some probability that his own unit could function normally for a few days at least to take care of the wounded, David set up the 1st Field Hospital under canvas, as he preferred, at the southern edge of Winchester.

Unwilling to let Banks and his troops rest short of the Potomac, Jackson sent forces in pursuit the following day and Ed Mattox went with them. He returned, however, two days later.

"I finally got Jackson's permission to write the story of the Valley Campaign for my paper," he reported to David at the hospital. "And what a story it is."

"Have you already put it on the wire?"

"Not yet, too many of the telegraph wires away from the Valley Turnpike are still in Federal hands. I'm going to ride across the Blue Ridge at Swift Run Gap and catch the train for Richmond at Gordonsville. By tomorrow this time, I should be in Richmond and writing like mad."

"But saddlesore."

Mattox shrugged. "That alum water of Hal Perkins works wonders for feet, so I hope it will do as well for the rump. After I get to Richmond and see my story set in type, I'll mix me up a big tub of alum solution and sit in it for a while."

"How far north did you go with the troops?"

"All the way to Harpers Ferry with the Stonewall Brigade. It even occupied Loudoun Heights—"

"The Twenty-seventh was bivouacked there when I joined them about a year ago. My first job was to stop the latrine from draining into the spring they used as a source of water."

"Some units chased Banks as far as Martinsburg, but he got across the Potomac," Mattox added. "The crossings are heavily defended, though, so they made a strategic retreat, after destroying a lot of stuff and capturing all the wagon trains that could be turned around and driven back here. That telegrapher named Holbein Jeb Stuart lent to Ashby tapped the wires between Martinsburg and Washington just outside Harpers Ferry. I've been given permission to use some messages General Banks sent to Washington explaining what happened."

Mattox took several sheets of paper from his inside coat pocket. "Listen to this one from Banks to the War Department:

"A portion of the troops passed through Winchester in some confusion, but the column was soon reformed and continued its march in order. My command had not suffered an attack and rout. It had accomplished a 'premeditated' march of nearly sixty miles in the face of the enemy, defeating his plans and giving him battle wherever he was found."

Mattox looked up from reading. "You think Secretary Stanton will fall for that?"

David shook his head. "I never met Stanton but I know something about his reputation in Washington. He's hardheaded enough to recognize the truth."

"It would be pretty hard for anybody except General Banks to ignore the evidence of Jackson's skirmishers attacking the hills around Harpers Ferry, even though he didn't try to take them," Mattox agreed. "Not that the bombproofs in Richmond didn't have us doing it. I got hold of a copy of my old paper when we rode through Charles Town. The feature story announced that Jackson has already crossed the Potomac into Maryland in considerable force, and is headed for Philadelphia."

"Any fool ought to know he's got more sense than that—with Frémont's army in the west and General Shields' on the east still not badly hurt."

"I imagine Frémont's still in a little pain after McDowell, but what Jackson has accomplished these past few weeks is still enough to make a hero out of him and I'm certainly going to do everything I can to help. I've already sketched the opening paragraphs of my story:

"Audacity—and mystery—these are the qualities that stand out most in General Stonewall Jackson, the Confederacy's first bona fide hero. During the period of about three weeks this reporter spent with Jackson, I had an opportunity to see, and admire, both qualities in him more than once. In that brief period, the audacious Jackson of mystery confused both enemy and friends by crossing the Blue Ridge eastward from Elk Run Valley, where General Banks thought he had the Valley Army trapped, and embarking his troops at Mechum's River Station near Charlottesville. He then promptly recrossed the Blue Ridge again, westward by rail this time, at Waynesboro and headed for Staunton and McDowell, where he administered a stinging defeat to Union Generals Frémont and Milroy.

"In the days following the defeat of General Frémont's troops, Jackson next moved north to the Valley Turnpike and occupied Harrisonburg before pressing on to New Market. At that point he crossed the Massanuttens eastward to join General Ewell's army, again mystifying the enemy, and moved rapidly north to flank the retreating Federal army under General Banks and take Front Royal. From there, Jackson moved westward again to the Valley Turnpike, cut-

263

ting the Federal wagon trains in half and seizing a tremendous amount of booty, much of it badly needed medical supplies and food for the Army of the Valley. Continuing to push General Banks northward, Jackson again defeated the Federal army at Winchester, driving it to the Potomac and beyond.

"Jackson's exploit in defeating General Banks' much larger army and driving it from the Valley caused the Union Secretary of War to turn a sizable force under General Shields back across the Blue Ridge, where Shields could no longer support General McDowell's Union Army of the Rappahannock. This daring feat may well have saved Richmond from attack this summer by a superior Federal force, both from the east and from the south along the Peninsula. Meanwhile, the difficult question has been posed for the Union commanders—and the Secretary Stanton as well as Mr. Lincoln—of deciding just where this Napoleon of the South will strike next."

"Jackson will like that 'Napoleon of the South' idea," said David. "Though you'd never get him to admit it."

"He was quite affable when I told him good-by this morning," said Mattox. "Sandie Pendleton showed me the reason, a letter from General Johnston, which I copied."

Mattox smoothed out another piece of paper and began to read:

"Hd. Qrs. Dept. North Va.
May 27, 1862

Gen'l.,

I congratulate you upon new victories and new titles to the thanks of the country and of the army. If you can threaten Baltimore and Washington, do so. It may produce an important diversion.

McClellan is near and McDowell reported advancing from Fredericksburg.

Your movements depend, of course, upon the enemy's strength remaining in your neighborhood. Upon that depends the practicability of your advance to the Potomac and even crossing it. I know of no hostile force to prevent either.

Most Respectfully,
Your Ob. Servant
J. E. Johnston
General

P.S. Time will be gained and saved by addressing me always instead of the government.

J.E.J."

X

May 25, 1862, had seemed like Doomsday to much of the North. On April 30, when Stonewall Jackson left Elk Run Valley to begin his now famous Valley Campaign, newspapers in New York, Philadelphia, Boston and Washington had been predicting a speedy end to the war. McClellan and his massive Army of the Peninsula were within sound of the church bells of Richmond. McDowell was preparing to move south across the upper Rappahannock River upon Richmond. Shields was on the way from the Winchester area to help sweep the Confederates out of the eastern foothills of the Blue Ridge. Frémont was also moving on Staunton from the Alleghenies and the vital link of the Virginia Central Railroad there, while the mighty Banks was as far south as Harrisonburg, ready to destroy Jackson and his pestilent Army of the Shenandoah.

Four weeks later, however, Banks was fleeing across the Potomac to refuge in Maryland; Frémont was recovering from the defeat at McDowell; Shields was hurrying back to the Valley; and General Irvin McDowell was now afraid to move against Richmond with the invasion route Stonewall Jackson had wanted to follow so long into Maryland and Pennsylvania seemingly opened wide by Banks' rout. As for McClellan's invasion by way of the Peninsula, Lincoln's demand for troops to protect Washington and Maryland from Jackson had turned that well-organized plan into a shambles.

But Jackson was too smart a general to overextend

himself in the enthusiasm of victory. He had made the mistake once, at Kernstown, and—in his eyes at least—had been defeated. He didn't propose now to be caught in a trap of his own forging by three sizable Federal forces poised to west, north and east of his new prize, Winchester. So calling the Stonewall Brigade back from Loudoun Heights at Harpers Ferry and the units watching on the south bank of the Potomac from that area, he began a strategic withdrawal, which northern newspapers, desperately seeking some news to counteract the terror that had seized the Northeast with the word that Jackson was on the south bank of the Potomac, quickly named a retreat and then a rout. What they failed to remember, however, was that, while Stonewall Jackson frequently withdrew to fight again, usually after inflicting serious wounds on the enemy, he had never retreated in the full sense of the word.

Nor did he now.

From partisans in the area, Jackson had received word that McDowell was even then implementing a plan to catch him at Strasburg, less than twenty miles south of Winchester, and destroy the army and the general who had just finished administering a series of stinging defeats to the Union. Twenty thousand troops under Shields were already crossing the lower ranges of the Blue Ridge toward Front Royal while Frémont, with 15,000, was moving toward Strasburg from the west and another 20,000 were being rapidly organized from Banks' scattered forces north of the Potomac.

With the prospect of being forced to pit some 16,000 Confederates against 55,000 Yankees, Jackson started south along the turnpike, leaving the Stonewall Brigade to make a forced march from Harpers Ferry. At the same time he sent a small force east to make a demonstration before Shields and dispatched Ashby's cavalry westward to hold off Frémont's army. The race to reach Strasburg began on May 31, and was hampered by the impediment of over 2,000 prisoners, plus long wagon trains of badly needed supplies, captured from General Banks' retreating army less than a week before. Plus

266

hundreds of badly needed horses and mules that also had to be fed on the way south.

On the night of May 31, Jackson's army was bivouacked at Strasburg between the two Federal armies of Shields and Frémont, but safely out of cannon range. On June 1, Ashby and Ewell managed to sting Frémont's forces on the west enough to hold them back for a day while the Stonewall Brigade, footsore and weary after marching thirty-six miles from Harpers Ferry without food, caught up with the main force. And late that night, Jackson moved south again, leaving the Federal generals, who had been so sure of trapping him, empty-handed.

By now it was obvious to friend and foe alike that the elusive Jackson was heading for his old haunts in Elk Run Valley, about fifteen miles east of Harrisonburg. Seeking to thwart him, Shields sent a Federal force down Luray Valley, east of the Massanuttens, but Jackson's mountaineer cavalrymen burned the bridges across the South Fork of the Shenandoah River, closing that route. Even so, the Federal generals were sure they had Jackson trapped and on June 8, Shields wrote to Frémont urging him to "thunder down on his [Jackson's] rear" from Harrisonburg, which Frémont had reached by June 7. Both generals thought Jackson was retreating in disorder, while in reality he was laying another trap.

It was a surprisingly simple trap: Ewell's division was to hold off Frémont, while Jackson's main force destroyed Shields, after which Jackson would help Ewell smash Frémont, removing at one stroke all threats to the Confederate army in the Valley except the timorous Banks, who, mindful of previous experience, was moving cautiously southward. In preparation for these events, Major Jed Hotchkiss, Jackson's map specialist, was ordered to watch both areas closely from an observation post on Peaked Mountain, at the southern end of the Massanutten chain.

As it happened, however, the operation of the plan was not quite so simple, mainly because some of Shields' forces made a skirmish at Port Republic and almost captured Jackson himself before the plan went into effect. Meanwhile Frémont made a timorous advance which ended in a resounding whipping from Ewell, so in the end the results were the same. Both Federal armies were defeated in two days of fighting at Cross Keys and Port Republic and the threat to Jackson in the Valley was over—at least for several months.

Moreover, the spare, often awkward-seeming professor had become the hero of the Confederacy for a second time, having saved Richmond from capture when McClellan's advance along the Peninsula had to be halted to provide troops for the defense of Washington and McDowell was forced to send Shields west again in the frantic race to destroy Jackson—which, too, had failed.

On every count, the summer of 1862, which had promised to bring victory, was now a black one for the North.

XI

Weyer's Cave, Va.
June 14, 1862

Darling Araminta,

I hope you will not consider me remiss for not writing to you since I left Richmond in May. But knowing you read the newspapers regularly, I am sure you have already realized that events here in the Shenandoah Valley have been moving with startling rapidity. I understand that Ed Mattox's story of his three weeks as an observer with us has now appeared in a number of papers and it is quite possible that you have seen it, too.

In a period of about five weeks we traveled around four hundred miles, fighting a least every other day. In five major battles, the Army of the Valley defeated four enemy armies, completely routing two of them. In addition to many much-needed weapons, about four thousand prisoners were taken—and all of this with the loss of less than one thousand men killed, wounded or missing, surely as remarkable an accomplishment as any victory of Alexander the Great or Napoleon.

The Shenandoah Valley is beautiful at any time of the year but never more so than in these first weeks of June, with everything green and the mountain laurel in blossom, as well as the rhododendron. For the Battle of McDowell, we were joined by the Cadet Battalion from VMI, and although I was surprised that Jackson would let the boys be subjected to danger, he wisely kept them at the rear of the battle, where they had little chance of coming to harm. Yet because the Stonewall Brigade was also held in reserve, the students would not feel they were being denied a part in the battle because of youth.

You would find cause for amusement, I am sure, if you could see Jackson's chief of staff, Reverend John L. Dabney, who holds the rank of major. He usually wears a Prince Albert coat and beaver hat, instead of a uniform, and he often holds up a large umbrella to shade himself from the sun. The men like his fiery preaching and so does the general. They are constantly making jokes about him, though rarely to his face, for fear of incurring Jackson's wrath, which can be like the proverbial fire and brimstone Reverend Dabney is always preaching about.

Amazingly enough, war sometimes has moments of high humor, although I suppose we laugh more than we might to hide from ourselves and others how scared we often are. Much of the time though, it's nothing but hardship and not a little suffering. In winter the men nearly freeze because few of them have enough clothing or decent shoes. And in summer, half the muster is liable to be sick at any given time, many with malaria, which we have difficulty in treating because quinine is almost impossible to get any more.

Never more than when I take pen to write you am I so completely frustrated by the knowledge of my own inadequacy to express my feelings and my gratitude for the completely undeserved miracle of your love for me. But alas, I am a poor scrivener instead and can only say in ordinary words that I love you more than anything else in life. And that I look forward, with a passion that sometimes makes me afraid because of its strength, to holding you in my arms when all of this is ended. Until then you can be assured of

All my love,
David

David posted the letter to Araminta at Port Republic the next day, and on June 17 the Army of the Valley

269

broke camp and headed for Brown's Gap, a few miles south of their former headquarters at Conrad's Store. Sweeping down the east side of the Blue Ridge in a long column of marching men, wagons and artillery, they came into the Piedmont section of Virginia to meet an old enemy—drenching rain.

No one had doubts about their destination this time. Jackson had crossed the Blue Ridge ahead of them several days before, taking elaborate precautions to keep anyone from recognizing him, for the purpose of planning the coming battle to save Richmond with General Lee, now virtually in full command of Confederate forces operating in Virginia.

On July 18, almost a month later, while encamped at Hanover Junction, less than twenty miles north of Richmond on the banks of the Pamunkey River, a tributary of the York and a junction point on the railhead to Fredericksburg, David was handed a copy of the Richmond *Enquirer* for that morning by Hal Perkins. Marked was a brief story on the inside page, and he had only to glance at it to know why Ed Mattox wished to bring it to his attention.

CHEROKEE CHIEF CAPTURED BY NORTH

Tahlequah, Indian Territory, July 15—Chief John Ross of the Cherokee Nation was captured without resistance today in his home at Park Hill, near Tahlequah, capital of the Nation. The small Union force that took Mr. Ross prisoner was under the command of Capt. H. S. Greeno and made up of one company of whites and fifty Cherokees. It is part of an Indian expedition under command of Col. William Weer, organized in Kansas about six months ago for the purpose of holding the northern part of the Indian Territory for the Union, if at all possible.

Among those captured with Mr. Ross and his wife, the former Mary Stapler of Philadelphia, were a young niece, Miss Araminta Murrell, some body servants, and several Cherokee aides. Mr. Ross, it will be remembered, signed a treaty with the CSA about a year ago to keep his people out of the conflict, but has been suspected of having Union leanings.

It is said that Chief Ross, who had been ill for some time, will be paroled to live in Philadelphia and has promised to take no further part in the politics of the Indian tribes involving the CSA agreement. Miss Murrell and Mrs. Ross will live in Philadelphia with Mr. Ross during the time of his internment at a home he maintains there, formerly the property of his wife.

The Federal force that reached Tahlequah and captured the Cherokee Chief withdrew in advance of the arrival of Col. Stand Watie with his Indian company known as the Cherokee Brigade, which has been helping to hold the area for the South.

Across the bottom of the page, just below the article, Ed Mattox had scrawled: "Tough luck, David. But after a few more victories like those in the Valley, the war will be over anyway. Best, Ed."

BOOK FIVE

Antietam

I

The Stonewall Brigade was happy—and so was the commander. For Stonewall Jackson was at long last engaged upon the adventure he had wanted to undertake a year earlier, at the end of the Battle of Manassas.

It had taken a long summer of fighting against the huge armies McClellan and McDowell had thrown against Richmond, plus the somewhat inconclusive results of that conflict, to convince the timorous Confederate War Department finally that something more daring than the seesaw battles for Richmond was needed to turn the tide now flowing steadily against the southern Cause. And who was better qualified to carry out such a daring feat than the general who, with only 16,000 troops, had managed to outwit and create consternation and fear in 175,-000 Yankees, causing confusion and a shifting of Federal forces that had largely insured the failure of McClellan's ambitious scheme to crack Richmond and the Confederacy like a nut between the jaws of the armies on the Peninsula and the area around Culpeper south of Washington?

"If they will only give me 60,000 men, I will go right on into Pennsylvania," Stonewall Jackson had written Congressman Boteler after the Battles of Cross Keys and Port Republic in early June of 1862 had almost destroyed any Federal threat in the Valley. "I will not go down the Valley; I do not wish the people there to be harassed. I will even go with 40,000 if the President will give them to me, and my route will be east of the Blue Ridge. In two weeks I could be at Harrisburg."

But the War Department and General Robert E. Lee, at last in full command, had been too concerned earlier in the summer with the threat of McClellan's forces, then within five miles of Richmond itself, to see that Jackson's proposed move was the only sure way to create consternation in Washington and cause complete abandonment of the Peninsula Campaign that had brought Union guns almost within cannon-shot of the Confederate capital.

Purely as a feint, Lee had sent two divisions westward, apparently as reinforcements for Jackson. But the action was only designed to deceive the remaining Federal forces in the Valley, largely those under General Frémont.

In a letter, dated June 17, 1862, Lee had written to Jackson while the latter was still in the Valley at Weyer's Cave:

From your account of the position of the enemy, I think it would be difficult for you to engage him in time to unite with this army in the battle of Richmond. The present therefore seems to be favourable for a junction of your army and this. If you agree with me, the sooner you can make arrangements to do so the better. In moving your troops you could let it be understood that it was to pursue the enemy on your front. Dispose those to hold the Valley, so as to deceive the enemy, keeping your cavalry well on their front, and at the proper time suddenly descending on Pamunkey. To be efficacious, the movement must be secret.

Since the Pamunkey was a branch of the York River —itself dividing into the North Anna and South Anna, which crossed the tracks of both the Virginia Central and Richmond, Fredericksburg and Potomac railroads around Hanover Court House, about fifteen miles from Richmond—Jackson knew exactly where Lee wished him to be. Obeying fully the injunction for secrecy, he

273

began the sort of elaborate game of hocus-pocus that had worked so beautifully when he had crossed the Blue Ridge twice on two successive days that same spring to attack Milroy's Federal force at McDowell.

David Preston had become involved in one aspect of the deception at the very beginning of the game, and befort the move to Richmond, when Colonel T. T. Munford, who, following the death of Turner Ashby, had taken command of Jackson's cavalry, came to him in Harrisonburg shortly before the move into the Richmond theater of war. David had been there for several days, arranging for a group of Federal surgeons and ambulances to evacuate the Federal wounded northward to Strasburg and Winchester, where Fremont's forces had retreated after the Battle of Cross Keys.

"Do you have time to join me in a short walk, Major Preston?" the cavalryman asked.

"Of course." To David's surprise, Munford took him to a house he had commandeered for his headquarters, where the Federal surgeons were also quartered.

"I told the Yankee doctors several hours ago that I had sent a courier to General Jackson to find out whether he wants the wounded sent North," Munford confided. "He should be here shortly."

"But Jackson's at Port Republic, close to fifteen miles away. It would take a courier all day to get there and back."

"We know that—but *they* don't," the cavalry officer confided. "Jackson wants me to send them back empty-handed, so they can warn Frémont that he's about to launch an attack on the lower Valley by way of the turnpike."

David gave him a searching look. "Another Mechum's River Station operation?"

"You could call it that. We all trust you implicitly, Doctor, so I want you to be a witness. But you had to know what will really happen or you might give the deception away."

They had mounted the stairway to Munford's room, adjoining the apartment where the Union surgeons were quartered and separated from it only by a thin wall. At the door of the apartment, Munford stopped and looked inside.

"I should have word from General Jackson soon, gentlemen," he told the Federal medical officers. "I trust that your needs have been attended to, as our somewhat inadequate facilities allow."

"We're comfortable, Colonel," said a bearded Yankee doctor. "But we would like to get under way."

"It won't be long, I promise."

In Munford's room, the cavalryman threw his plumed hat on the bed and nodded toward a chair for David. "I'll be glad to know what General Jackson is planning myself," he said loudly. "You know how secretive he is."

David didn't answer, for just then they heard a jingle of spurs ascending the stairs. And when the wearer came into the room, he wasn't surprised to see Mr. William Gilmer, a civilian famous in the area for his practical jokes. Gilmer was dusty and hot, as if he'd just dismounted from a long ride.

"Well, sir," said Munford, in a tone so loud that David understood it was intended to be heard in the adjoining apartment. "What did General Jackson say?"

"He told me to tell you the wounded Yankees are not to be taken away." Gilmer, too, spoke loudly. "The surgeons are to be sent back with the message that the general intends to take care of their wounded men in his own hospitals. He's coming right on, himself, with heavy reinforcements. Whiting's division is up; Hood's is coming. The whole road from here to Saunton is lined with troops, and so crowded that I could hardly ride along."

"Excellent," said Munford. "Dr. Preston, please inform the Union surgeons of General Jackson's decision and arrange for them to leave at once under their flag of truce."

Crossing the Blue Ridge beside the wagons transporting the 1st Field Hospital several days later, David saw a dust-caked courier passing the long column of troops toiling up the road and recognized one of Colonel Munford's troopers. A half hour later, when the hospital wagons reached the crest and started down the other

275

side, he saw Sandie Pendleton sitting his horse beside the road. When Pendleton beckoned, David pulled off and they rode about a hundred feet away from the column out of earshot.

"Your bit of playacting the other night worked like a charm, David," said Pendleton. "We just had a message from Munford that Frémont has pulled out of Strasburg, moving north because of an expected thrust toward the Potomac by our army."

"Do you have any idea where General Jackson is now?"

"Somewhere around Richmond, he rode ahead to go over the plan of battle with Lee."

"Somewhere," as it turned out when the reinforced Army of the Valley, now officially called the II Corps, reached the Richmond area, had been just outside the Confederate capital on Nine Mile Road.

Meanwhile General George B. McClellan, poised almost within cannon-shot of Richmond on the banks of the Chickahominy River and fuming over the way Jackson's lightning-swift Valley Campaign had thrown his entire elaborate plan of battle badly out of kilter, was at last ready to throw the most formidable army ever assembled on American soil against the southern capital. Numbering more than 160,000 troops, it was also the best-equipped and -trained army ever put into the field in the Western Hemisphere.

And yet the Union commander had already made one vital mistake before the fighting actually started: he had divided his force with one part, the larger, south of the Chickahominy River, and only one corps, the V, under General Fitz-John Porter, north of the stream and the swamplands through which it flowed. This portion Lee had chosen to attack, following Jackson's strategy of divide and conquer.

The Seven Days Battle around Richmond had brought McClellan's Peninsula Campaign to a bloody halt when, after losing 16,000 men, 50 cannon and 35,000 muskets, McClellan had to undergo the humiliation of being forced to retreat to the protection of U. S. Navy ships on the James River, southeast of Richmond.

The Stonewall Brigade had been almost decimated by their long campaign in the Valley, and during much of the Seven Days Battle, fought only using reinforcements who were not accustomed to Jackson's way of fighting. Jackson himself was ill, too, and unable to function with his usual coolness and daring. Moreover, Lee's generals, particularly the two Hills—A. P. and D. H.—Longstreet, Ewell, Jubal Early, Magruder, Holmes, Stuart and Jackson, had never fought close together before, so a number of mix-ups had occurred. In the end, however, what victory there was could be claimed by the South, with McClellan retreating to the James and Richmond relieved. But controversy raged hotly in Richmond for months over who had failed whom, with the blame naturally centered on the one from whom the most had been expected—Jackson.

Hospitalized in Richmond by a severe attack of malaria, following the Seven Days Battle of June 26 to July 2, 1862, David could only read about these and succeeding events, in the newspapers. And the later, as usual, overdramatized the exploits of Jackson, as they had criticized him earlier for not singlehandedly winning the early portions of the Seven Days Battle.

On the Federal side General John Pope, called from his successes in Mississippi to command the forces of Federal Generals McDowell, Sigel and Bowles north of Richmond—now grouped as the new Federal Army of Virginia—had arrived too late to play much part in the Seven Days Battle. Hailed as the savior who would punish the South for the debacle on the Peninsula by driving upon Richmond from the north, Pope announced, upon assuming command, that he would show his troops only the backs of their Confederate opponents in retreat.

Setting out immediately to outflank the defenders of Richmond and cut Jackson off from his base in the Valley by taking the Manassas Gap Railroad and driving through Centerville, where the Stonewall Brigade had spent much of the previous summer, Pope planned to go on to Gordonsville and Charlottesville, cutting off all rail connection between Richmond and the Valley.

Included in Pope's command were Jackson's old enemies Banks and Shields, drawn east to help cut him off from the Valley. But at Cedar Run and again at Manassas Junction, Lee and Jackson—now a formidable combination after General J. E. Johnston was wounded before Richmond—were able to use Jackson's brilliant flank march technique to cut the Federal troops off, defeating Pope's forces of some 70,000 marshaled against the Confederate army of less than 50,000 in what came to be called Second Manassas. And at Chantilly, not far away, the humiliation of the no longer boastful Pope was completed on September 1, 1862, with the end result that, of all the Union commanders who had played their roles in that bloodiest of theaters between Washington and Richmond, each confidently predicting total victory, Pope's tenure was the shortest—from July 27 to September 3, 1862, a total of thirty-seven days.

II

The happiness of the Stonewall Brigade this fine morning in early September was not so much because of their strategic or material accomplishments, as from the fact that they were once again headed for their beloved Shenandoah Valley. Their number was smaller then ever; equipment was still poor, uniforms were usually makeshift, composed of bits of Union uniforms, butternut shirts, denim trousers and, if the soldiers were lucky, shoes. The supply of shoes had been limited in the South from the beginning of the war because the major shoe factories in the United States were located in western New York, around Binghamton, and Confederate soldiers rarely obtained any except from captured prisoners, or from the dead left lying on the battlefields.

Though long since accustomed to receiving strange orders from their sometimes eccentric commanding general, even the Stonewall Brigade had been at a loss at the start of the march to know where they were going. And

278

since their leader rarely told anybody anything about his plans, they could not know that General Lee had agreed at last to try Jackson's often advocated strategy of a drive into Pennsylvania to cut the railway to the west at Harrisburg before swinging east to menace Philadelphia, Baltimore and Washington.

It was a daring plan, shrewdly calculated, even if it failed, to draw General McClellan—once more in command of the Virginia Union armies with the humbling of the bumptious Pope but now a source of much unrest in the North—into pursuit and thus relieve the pressure on Richmond. At the same time, Lee's move was shrewdly calculated to cause political disruption in the North, now approaching an off-year congressional election, and further decrease the waning voter strength of Abraham Lincoln.

Crossing the Potomac into Maryland by way of the fords near Leesburg, Virginia, Lee pushed his army to Frederick in Maryland, and paused to allow stragglers to catch up and his men to rest. He needed time, also, to patch up several quarrels between his generals, particularly Jackson and A. P. Hill, plus the problem of General J. B. Hood, who had been put under arrest for refusing to give up some ambulances captured by his men. As the armies moved deeper into Maryland and it became apparent to Jackson's II Corps and the Stonewall Brigade that they were not headed for the relative comfort of winter quarters in the Valley, desertions—always a major problem with what was largely a civilian army—increased markedly.

Wtih his army already deep into Maryland north of the Potomac, Lee had expected the Federals to evacuate outflanked Harpers Ferry, but General Henry W. Halleck —since July 23 the Union General-in-Chief—ordered the garrison to stand. And since a force of more than 12,000 could hardly be left intact in the rear of the Confederate army, Lee had no choice except to send a division under General Lafayette McLaws and a brigade under General G. B. Anderson to approach the critical rail and canal junction point from the north by way of Maryland Heights. General J. G. Walker's division was ordered to parallel the river and destroy an important aqueduct of the C&O Canal, before crossing into Virginia and seizing Loudoun Heights. Meanwhile Jackson's forces were to sweep west across the Potomac at Williamsport and drive south of Martinsburg, forcing the garrison there to retreat to Harpers Ferry and driving a cork into the bottleneck of the Valley to cut off all the small number of Federal forces there.

The plan worked like a well-oiled machine as far as Harpers Ferry was concerned, with the Federal force there surrendering on the morning of September 15. But although 12,500 prisoners, 1,300 small arms, seventy-three cannon and several hundred wagons were captured, valuable time had been lost. And during that period McClellan managed to amass an army and arrange rail transportation north of the Potomac, while an increasingly nervous Abraham Lincoln urged almost frantic haste. Meanwhile, too, Lee had been forced to split the army with which he had intended to drive through western Maryland and into Pennsylvania like a juggernaut, slowing his advance almost to a crawl between Frederick and Sharpsburg, thirty miles away, as the crow flies, while he awaited the outcome of the attack on Harpers Ferry.

Still weak from his long bout with malaria, David Preston helped treat the less than a hundred casualties of the Harpers Ferry attack, carried out almost entirely by artillery bombardment from the heights overlooking the river and rail junction. And when, about noon on the day Harpers Ferry fell, he saw a tall, dark-skinned man in civilian clothes, dusty from travel, dismount from his horse beside the dressing station for the Stonewall Brigade, he could hardly believe the evidence of his own eyes.

"Lachlan!" he shouted, and went forward to embrace his friend. "Where did you come from?"

"From the West, of course," Lachlan Murrell answered with a typical sardonic smile. "Isn't that where you white men have pushed all of us Indians?"

"What about Araminta and the Rosses? Are they all right?"

"I had a letter from Araminta just before I left

280

Tahlequah, they're living in the Stapler family home in Philadelphia. I'll tell you all about it later, but right now I need to see someone close to General Jackson. On the way here I picked up some news he'll want to hear."

"I'll take you to Major Sandie Pendleton, he's the acting chief of staff since Major Dabney resigned."

They found Pendleton in an upstairs room of the same store building Jackson had once before taken over as his headquarters.

"Haven't I seen you before, Major?" Pendleton asked when David introduced Lachlan.

"I was here about eighteen months ago—with my uncle, John Ross, on the way to Indian Territory."

"I remember now," said Pendleton. "What can I do for you?"

"I have been ordered to join your army on detached duty, Major Pendleton."

"From what unit, Major?"

"Second Cherokee Mounted Rifles." Lachlan placed a sheet of orders before the handsome young chief of staff. "Here are my orders, signed by Colonel Stand Watie."

Pendleton's eyebrows shot up in surprise. "You were at Pea Ridge then, Major?"

"Yes, but I took no scalps." Lachlan grinned. "Three years in the U. S. Army taught me it isn't considered cricket nowadays."

Sandie Pendleton flushed a little, conscious that he had been reprimanded, but didn't take offense. "We'll be glad to have you, Major Murrell. Perhaps Major Preston will help you find a uniform and whatever else you'll need."

"I have a uniform in my saddlebag, Major," said Lachlan. "When I left Richmond, I was warned that the situation was a bit uncertain in southern Maryland, so I judged it the better part of valor to travel in civilian clothing. That's how I happened to learn at Frederick that General McClellan already has a complete plan of General Lee's Pennsylvania Campaign."

Sandie Pendleton dropped the pen he held in his hand. "What did you say, Major Murrell?"

"I almost blundered into Federal headquarters near

281

Frederick a few days ago. While I was hiding in a clump of bushes waiting for night to fall, so I could sneak away under the cover of darkness, I overhead two of McClellan's staff officers talking."

"Just a minute, Major, I want General Jackson to hear this." Pendleton was gone for a few moments, then came back to usher them into an adjoining room. Jackson was sitting before a small desk covered with papers; he stood up to shake hands with Lachlan.

"We meet again, Major Murrell," he said courteously. "And almost on the same spot."

"But under much different circumstances, sir. I'm glad to see the years and many important military engagements have left you unscarred."

Jackson smiled. "The Lord has favored our cause. Major Pendleton tells me you have vital information."

Lachlan recounted quickly his ride from Richmond and the chance encounter with McClellan's officers.

"Do you remember any of the details the Federals described, Major?" Jackson asked.

"I didn't hear very much, sir; they moved on but I couldn't leave my place of concealment. They did say that the orders gave the identity of every unit of our army engaged in this particular venture, and where they are expected to be from day to day."

Jackson went to a window, from which he stood looking down at the scene below. When he turned back, the look of concern on his face showed just how seriously he took the information Lachlan Murrell had brought.

"If General McClellan has a copy of the campaign plan, he knows our forces had to be divided in order to take Harpers Ferry, and is no doubt planning to cut one army off from the other." Jackson's tone became more brisk. "General Lee must have this information as quickly as possible, Major Pendleton. Is Mr. Douglas in the camp?"

"I believe so, sir."

"Find a fresh horse for Major Murrell and send for Mr. Douglas. He was born and grew up in this area, so he will know the shortest and safest route to Sharpsburg."

"Did you hear any more, Major Murrell?" Jackson asked as Sandie Pendleton departed.

"Only a few names—of places. But they weren't familiar."

"Do you remember them."

"There was a reference to South Mountain. And I think they spoke of two gaps."

"What were their names?"

"Turner's was one, I'm sure of that. But the other—"

"Could it have been Crampton's?"

"That's the one, the very one."

"Come with me, please."

Jackson moved to the room where Sandie Pendleton had been working. On one wall was a large-scale map of the area between Harpers Ferry, Frederick, Martinsburg and Hagerstown. In the right lower corner of the map was the name Hotchkiss, from which David knew it had been drawn by Jackson's topographical officer, a skilled surveyor and maker of maps who had been with him almost from the beginning.

"General Lee is already at Sharpsburg but has been forced to halt there while we assailed the Federal forces here at Harpers Ferry." Jackson pointed to the areas as he identified them on the map. "Here is South Mountain, lying between Frederick and Hagerstown and more particularly between Catoctin and Antietam creeks. General McClellan is pushing toward Sharpsburg from Frederick, but to reach a position where he can flank General Lee's troops, he must cross South Mountain either through Turner's Gap on the north or Crampton's Gap on the south. Fortunately, General Longstreet's corps has already reached the Hagerstown area and could defend these points—if he and General Lee are warned in time. That is what I want you and Lieutenant Douglas to accomplish, Major Murrell."

"Are you planning to attack McClellan's rear guard, sir?" David asked.

"We are too heavily outnumbered for that; by last count General McClellan has over eighty thousand troops, while we number only a few thousand, many of them without shoes and some without weapons. But I know

283

him from our former association at West Point and also in the Regular Army. McClellan will move deliberately and in great force, so I am sure General Lee wants me to join him in Sharpsburg, while keeping a weather eye open for a weak spot in the Federal lines."

"Let's hope you find it, sir," said Lachlan.

"I always have, Major Murrell," said Jackson earnestly. "With the help of Almighty God, I always have."

"Does he always talk as if God was his right hand?" Lachlan asked as he and David were walking to the Stonewall Brigade bivouac area for a quick meal before Lachlan started on the ride to Sharpsburg.

"Much of the time. And after a while you begin to believe the partnership is a reality."

"*He* obviously believes it and I suppose that's half the battle."

"You didn't finish telling me about Araminta and John Ross," David reminded Lachlan as he was eating. "Or how they managed to get captured."

"Uncle John never had much enthusiasm for this war, on either side; he only signed a treaty with the Confederacy when it became evident that our people would suffer from trying to remain neutral. I think the main purpose of Colonel Weer's expedition, and certainly Captain Greeno's foray, against Park Hill was to capture John Ross. And personally I'm just as happy that he's out of it. When the war's over—"

"When will that be?"

"Sooner, I think, rather than later. General Ulysses S. Grant, who's running the Union's Mississippi campaign, is a bulldog. Once Vicksburg falls, the Confederacy will have been cut in half as far as the East and the West are concerned and that has to be the beginning of the end."

Lachlan was changing from his civilian clothing into a Confederate uniform, with the insignia of a major on the collar. From the same saddlebag, he produced a pair of high cavalry boots, pulling them on.

"Was anybody hurt in the capture of Chief Ross?" David asked.

"No. The Yankee troops were very considerate and would have let Araminta stay behind. But you know how

284

fond she is of Uncle John, so she elected to stay with him. I suspect the fact that she will now be only a little over a hundred miles from you had something to do with her decision."

"It might as well be a whole world."

"If General Lee is able to carry through his plans to invade Pennsylvania, we could be riding through the streets of Philadelphia a week hence."

David shook his head. "The northern troops are like that mythical story, where the teeth of a dragon were supposed to produce soldiers and every time one was killed ten would appear in his place. The Stonewall Brigade is one of the finest fighting units in history but it's only half the size it was a year ago. And even the best soldier can't fight very long on an empty stomach with his feet cut to pieces by rocks because he can't get any shoes—and often weapons—except what we capture."

"Your commanding officer doesn't seem to share your pessimism."

David smiled. "Like King David in those Bible stories the Moravian missionaries made you study, Jackson believes he's the Anointed One destined to win this war."

"And David did win—don't forget that."

"That must be Kyd Douglas," said David when the sound of hoofbeats sounded outside on the street. "Do you need anything else?"

"I could use a pint of that medicinal whiskey medical officers seem to always have in stock. After riding twenty miles from Frederick since midnight, the prospect of seventeen more makes me thirsty."

"If I know Jackson," said David as he handed his friend the bottle, "we'll be in Sharpsburg about twelve hours behind you and I'll be busy treating blistered feet all the way."

III

"I see you got here as you predicted," Lachlan Murrell told David when the surgeon arrived at the Confederate camp outside the town of Sharpsburg, Maryland, about

285

noon the next day. "No wonder they call your Stonewall Brigade Jackson's 'Foot Cavalry.' "

"Right now half of the brigade are still cooling their feet in the Potomac at Boteler's Ford," David said wearily. "But they'll be ready to fight tomorrow."

"They're liable to have to," said the cavalry officer. "And I guess if we have to fight, this place is about as good as any other."

"I'm sure General Lee never intended to be stopped this far south, but with the river only about two miles to the south and a good ford, in case we need it, maybe you're right. Got any idea what General Lee has in mind?"

"Whipping McClellan's the main event; once that's done he'll be in position for a lightning attack on Baltimore to cut Washington off completely. Or failing that, a drive westward to burn the steel mills around Pittsburgh and maybe go all the way to Lake Erie and isolate the Northeastern Seaboard."

"You're stealing Old Jack's dream," said David, "but it's more likely to turn into a nightmare if A. P. Hill doesn't get here tomorrow with the troops we left behind to clean up at Harpers Ferry."

"McClellan has a reputation for caution; maybe he'll wait. Meanwhile Lee apparently thinks Antietam Creek is as good a barrier as he will be able to find around here and is setting up a line west of it along the Hagerstown Turnpike. Want to know where Jackson will be?"

"In the center, of course, so he can swing in whichever direction the fighting gets the hottest. Does anybody know the odds against us?"

"Lee's headquarters estimate that McClellan has around eighty thousand, or maybe sixty if he holds a fourth in reserve as he usually does."

"Against perhaps thirty-five thousand, or even less if A. P. Hill doesn't get here in time. Not the best odds but we've fought with worst—and won. What will you be doing?"

"I've been assigned to Jeb Stuart's staff," said Lachlan. "We'll be on a hill near what's called Nicodemus Farm, so there might just be a chance to make a flanking movement and prod McClellan in his backside.

"Good hunting," said David. "I'm going to get some sleep while I wait for the rest of the Stonewall Brigade to catch up."

IV

Working under tentage at the southern edge of Sharpsburg, between the town proper and Boteler's Ford, David had no opportunity to learn much about the progress of the battle that began at dawn on September 17. Jackson's corps had been ordered to push northward past a small Dunkard church into the west woods toward where the enemy forces were making a concerted drive to turn the Confederate left. The distant booming of artillery shortly after dawn told him the battle was being fought there, as did the stream of casualties that shortly began to appear.

When Major Hunter McGuire rode into the hospital area several hours after the fighting began, David looked up from a broken leg he was splinting. The foggy mist covering the entire battlefield area until an hour after dawn had now lifted but McGuire was wet to the skin from riding through the woods where Jackson's troops were engaged.

"The Stonewall Brigade is fighting in that cornfield north of the Dunkard church," McGuire reported as he drank a cup of coffee. "Outnumbered as usual about two or three to one."

"What's the shape of the battle now?"

"If Dante were here, he'd say this is more of a hell than the one he described in the Inferno. But General Jackson seems to thrive on it."

"Then he's in the thick of the battle—"

"Where else? The Federals are trying to turn our left flank but they're not having much luck. They're also trying to thrust against our right across that bridge over Antietam Creek south of the Dunkard church; but if A. P. Hill gets here soon with those troops from Harpers

287

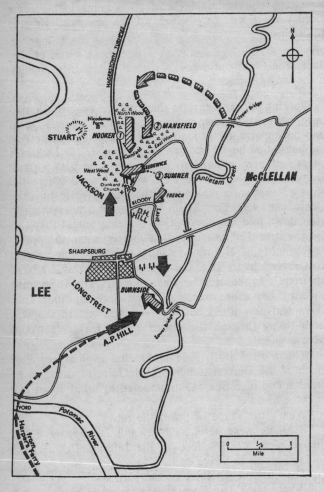

The Battle of Antietam or Sharpsburg, September 17, 1862

Ferry, Jackson still may be able to turn the right flank of McClellan's army."

"Sounds like another Manassas Junction."

"Only worse," said McGuire as he mounted his horse. "By the way, Private Robert E. Lee, Jr., is fighting with the Rockbridge Artillery. I wonder if a son of the General-in-Chief could possibly be a private in the ranks of the Union Army?"

All day long David and the two regimental surgeons assisting him worked at the operating tables. Since the hospital was so near the actual battle lines, the wounded were being brought directly from the battlefield to the hospital. Nor did he need a battle report to know the fighting was furious and that Jackson's forces, particularly the Stonewall Brigade, were bearing the brunt of it; the number of casualties told that story in far more colorful language than any words could have done. At midafternoon, Major McGuire returned on another tour of inspection and this time his expression was a troubled one.

"General Ambrose Burnside and his Union troops have crossed the Lower Bridge southeast of Sharpsburg," he reported. "How long would you need to move the hospital, if it becomes necessary?"

"Where to?"

"Across the Potomac. If this force of Burnside's manages to turn our right flank and swing around Sharpsburg, you'll be caught in a noose."

"Is Jackson retreating?"

"Not so you could notice it." McGuire laughed. "A little while ago I gave him some peaches I'd picked off a tree in the outskirts of Sharpsburg. I told him I was worried about the hospital, too, but he only pointed toward the enemy and said, 'McGuire, God has been kind to us today. They have done their worst.' I left him with his leg thrown over the saddle eating a peach, as if he might be on a picnic."

"When Jackson retreats, I'll move the hospital across the river," said David.

McGuire shrugged. "You're as stubborn as he is, but I'll not order you away. If Burnside does succeed with a flanking swing, try to escape southward behind his forces and somehow manage to get across the river at Boteler's Ford."

McGuire started riding away but a sudden burst of firing to the south made him rein in his horse. "Sounds like the battle has flared up around the bridge Burnside captured," he said.

Just then a courier rode past the hospital and McGuire called to him, asking what had happened.

"General A. P. Hill's division has crossed the Potomac, sir. They're fighting Burnside's troops in the streets of Sharpsburg; I'm taking the news to General Lee and General Jackson."

"Are you certain it's General A. P. Hill?"

"Sure am, Major. He's wearing that bright red battle shirt of his and fightin' like the devil himself."

"Thank God!" said McGuire, but when David suddenly laughed, he looked at him with a frown.

"What's funny?" the other doctor demanded.

"I was thinking God must have told Jackson Hill was almost here. Else how would he have already known when you gave him the peach that McClellan had been stopped?"

"I'll believe that when I see it and it will be a welcome sight," said McGuire. "But all I can see on the battlefield now are rows of dead so thick in some places you could walk across them without the soles of your boots touching the ground. Good luck, David."

Darkness was just beginning to fall and David had ordered Hal Perkins to light the kerosene pressure lamps that illuminated the operating tent, when a chorus of rebel yells sounded to the south. Soon litter bearers coming from that direction reported that A. P. Hill's division had driven Burnside's troops back across the narrow bridge, removing, at least for the time being, the danger that the entire southern part of the Confederate battle line might be turned. At the same time came a report that Jackson had successfully countered a third thrust by Federal forces across the Hagerstown Turnpike between the Dunkard church and Nicodemus Farm.

David continued to work through the night and into the morning. Incredibly, McClellan failed to resume the attack the next day, perhaps because his forces were reported to have suffered 27,000 casualties, almost a third of his army, during that single day at Antietam Creek. Lee's army had also sustained about a third in casualties and the day was already being spoken of as the bloodiest in the history of the War between the Confederacy and the Union, with bodies at one spot along what was called "Bloody Lane" piled as much as fifteen feet high.

Cavalry scouts ranging along the banks of the Potomac to the rear of McClellan's army in late afternoon reported roughtly 12,000 fresh troops joining the Federal force, in addition to some 20,000 McClellan had held uncommitted during the bloody battle, in mortal fear that Stonewall Jackson would somehow once again snatch victory out of defeat with one of his lightning measures. The Confederate army began to retreat across the Potomac shortly after dark and the Stonewall was among the last to cross, its numbers markedly decreased by the single day of fighting.

David was driving one of the hospital wagons with his own horse tethered behind it. And as he splashed through the ford, he saw General Lee sitting on his horse in the stream, watching the crossing with Jackson. Both looked tired and worn but, when the last of the marching men—most of them now wearing shoes, although the rest of their uniforms still left much to be desired—stepped down into the ford and, seeing Lee and Jackson, raised a shout of greeting, General Lee stood up in his stirrups and saluted.

But if Robert E. Lee could thank God that his army had been successfully extricated from what could have been the greatest debacle of the war, the northern press did not. As witness a copy of the New York *Tribune* brought back by Lachlan Murrell, riding with Jeb Stuart's scouts north of the Potomac as they kept watch on the movements of the Union army.

Of Lee's feat in saving his army, the *Tribune* said, in disgust with General George Brinton McClellan, whose star had seemed in full ascendance hardly a year before, only to be shot down by two generals named Lee and Jackson:

He leaves us the debris of his late camps, two disabled pieces of artillery, a few hundred of his stragglers, perhaps two thousand of his wounded, and as many more of his unburied dead. Not a sound field-piece, caisson, ambulance, or wagon; not a tent, box of stores, or a pound of ammunition. He takes with him the supplies gathered in Maryland, and the rich spoils of Harpers Ferry.

V

In bivouac near Martinsburg, David was caring for the wounded from Antietam and arranging shipment of those who could be moved to hospitals farther up the Valley toward Staunton or across the Blue Ridge to Richmond. With Kyd Douglas and Lachlan Murrell, now wearing the plumed hat affected by officers of Jeb Stuart's division, he sat one night over a hot rum punch prepared by Hal Perkins according to an old recipe he had learned from his mother, discussing the recent battle and its possible effect upon the future of the war.

Three days after the Confederate Army retired across the Potomac, President Lincoln had issued a preliminary Proclamation of Emancipation of all slaves belonging to Rebels, the release to take place January 1, 1863. And two days later, Lincoln also suspended the writ of *habeas corpus* for all persons arrested by military authority.

"The North really lost at Antietam," Kyd Douglas maintained. "If McClellan wasn't even able to destroy an army of not much more than a third the size of his own under excellent conditions, knowing in advance the exact plans General Lee intended to follow, that means he's finished."

"The North will certainly be better off if he is." Lachlan lifted his mug and inhaled the fragrance of the punch, then took a long drink before putting it down. "I suppose you know you've got a pearl of great price in Hal Perkins, David. Even in New Orleans they don't make rum punch like this."

"You haven't lived until you've eaten Hal's freshly

caught mountain trout rolled in cornmeal and friend in bacon fat with hush puppies."

"Is that a Virginia dish? I never heard of it."

"A southern one, but worthy of an equally high place with Maryland terrapin, or Chesapeake Bay soft-shell crabs—even your New Orleans bouillabaisse."

"Where do you think the next big battle will take place, Major Murrell?" Kyd Douglas asked.

"Before Richmond."

"By way of the Peninsula?"

"There's only one logical way to attack Richmond— through Fredericksburg, directly against the city."

"It was tried at Manassas—twice," David reminded him.

"The first attack on Manassas was too early in the war," said Lachlan. "The Federal troops weren't trained then and everybody was regarding this as a ninety-days war."

"Sort of a slap on the hand for an erring brother," David agreed. "But they've learned different by now."

"The interesting thing," said Douglas, "is that the North has seen a succession of their best generals throw themselves against the south and each has lost out. Mc-Dowell, Pope and now McClellan—at the rate they're going, Lincoln will run out of generals one of these days."

"You're forgetting one," Lachlan reminded him, "Ulysses S. Grant."

"Grant has been trying to take Vicksburg for almost a year, and hasn't done it yet," Douglas objected.

"True, but he's closing in all the time. Every time Grant gets beaten back, he shakes himself and keeps coming on. When he takes Vicksburg, the whole Mississippi and its tributaries will be in the hands of the Union. Then the next logical assignment for Grant will be right here in Virginia, butting his way like a billy goat or pushing ahead like a bulldog, but never stopping—until he takes Richmond."

"But the Confederacy can fight on," Douglas insisted.

"Not a chance," said the Cherokee officer. "I saw more action that one day at Antietam than in almost a year and a half with Stand Watie's troops in the Deep South.

Make no mistake about it, the war is being fought and decided right here in Virginia and Maryland."

"I hope you're right," said Douglas. "That means I'll have a front seat for the entire performance."

"And with Thomas Jonathan Jackson as the star performer, you can bet it will always be high drama," David added.

"I'd better get back to headquarters." Douglas got to his feet and brushed some pine needles from his uniform. "When General Jackson wants one of his aides, he wants him now."

"And I promised some of the officers I'd take a hand in a little game that's going on," said Lachlan. "Coming, David?"

"Not now. Hal Perkins tells me a few new cases of chicken pox have been reported. I'd better look to them before they give it to everybody else."

"I may be going for a little ride into enemy territory before long," Lachlan said casually. "If you want to send a letter to Araminta, just write it and address it to her. I'll drop it in a Yankee mailbox somewhere north of here."

"I'll write it as soon as I check over these new cases," said David happily. "Don't win too much—good luck."

"I need it," said Lachlan. "Since Farragut took New Orleans, I can make more money playing keno, faro or chuck-a-luck in that little gambling hell about a mile away from camp the boys call Devil's Half Acre than I could shipping cotton through the blockade."

At the bivouac of the 33d Virginia, David had no trouble finding the patients he was looking for; they had all been gathered into one tent by the regimental surgeon in an attempt to keep the disease from spreading to the rest of the camp. And he needed only one look at the virulent-appearing pocks, with their surrounding areas of dark skin, to know this was more than simply an epidemic of chicken pox.

Leaving the area of the 33d, David went immediately in search of Major Hunter McGuire, but the medical director was in Richmond for a conference of division surgeons at the Office of the Surgeon General. As he was discussing the appearance of the dread epidemic with Sandie Pendleton, Stonewall Jackson returned from a visit to the camp of General Richard Ewell's division, where a noted divine, Reverend Joseph Stiles, was holding a revival that had created a great surge of religious interest in camp.

"I don't recall seeing you at the preaching, Major Preston," said Jackson. "It is a glorious thing to be a minister of the Gospel of the Prince of Peace. No position in worldly affairs could possibly equal it."

"I've been busy, sir." David settled for the half-truth. "Checking out some cases of smallpox."

"Don't you mean chicken pox? We have been fortunate in receiving quite a number of recruits lately, according to the latest roster, almost ten thousand since the Battle of Antietam. Childhood diseases always flare up among new young troops."

"These are bona fide cases of smallpox, sir; I just finished examining several of them myself."

"This is serious, Major."

"I have asked Captain Pendleton to issue an order in the morning for all new recruits to be examined at once by the regimental surgeons. Hopefully we can nail down this epidemic before it spreads too far, if every man not vaccinated within the past three years is vaccinated at once, sir."

"I doubt if enough vaccine will be available for that," said Pendleton. "Major McGuire asked me to order more the other day."

"Every recruit must be vaccinated immediately then," said David. "As a rule, only a few have been before they enlisted."

"I'll telegraph Richmond to send us all the vaccine they can by Major McGuire," Pendleton promised.

Jackson went inside his tent and closed the flap, but a candle was burning on a small camp table, silhouetting his shadow against the canvas as he knelt in prayer. And, when David left Sandie Pendleton almost an hour later, the shadow figure was still on its knees, bolt upright and looking upward, as if Jackson were in complete communication with his Maker.

The morning examination of all recruits turned up five more early cases presumed to be smallpox. These, along with those already found to have the disease, were moved to another bivouac area well away from the main camp, where they were supervised by Hal Perkins and the male nurses of the 1st Brigade Field Hospital, all of whom had long ago been successfully vaccinated against the scourge.

The medical supply kits yielded material for only about fifty vaccinations and David immediately went to work immunizing the green troops until the supply was exhausted, except for a few units of vaccine kept in reserve. By nightfall, however, a half dozen more patients had been discovered in the camp with fever, aching bones, severe headache and the toxic symptoms that accompanied the appearance of early smallpox. And by the time Major Hunter McGuire returned two days later with the small supply of vaccine he had been able to obtain in Richmond, the epidemic was in full cry with over fifty cases.

"That's hardly enough vaccine to take care of the extra men we've had to assign to look after the sick," David exploded when McGuire opened the package he had brought.

"The smallpox hospital in Richmond is admitting almost a hundred patients a day," said the medical director. "If anything, their epidemic is worse than ours."

"And I suppose Jefferson Davis isn't likely to let any vaccine be taken out of Richmond until he's sure the city is safe?"

"That's the way it is."

Hal Perkins had been listening; now he spoke. "Couldn't you use crusts from the sores on the men you've vaccinated, sir?" he asked.

"We could, Hal," said David. "But I remember an epidemic two years ago in an army post outside of Washington, when we used some scabs from successful takes for vaccinating others. We kept them from getting smallpox all right, but we gave a lot of men syphilis from the donors. And with the Devil's Half Acre so near and prostitution openly going on, there's enough syphilis in the camp already to infect the whole army."

"I remember reading an article about the transmission of syphilis by vaccination last year," said McGuire. "Somewhere in Georgia three hundred cases of what appeared to be syphilis were traced to crusts of one soldier vaccinated while on furlough by a woman who ran a bawdy house in Augusta. But if the government can't provide us with enough fresh vaccine, David, what are we going to do?"

"The safest thing would be to vaccinate a number of young children and take the material from their sores for use on the soldiers," said David.

McGuire shook his head. "That's not a practical solution. With people even afraid of vaccination, how would you get enough children to use?"

"Negro babies born to slave women have been used against their parents' will," said David. "Nobody would be harmed—certainly not the babies—but you can imagine what Horace Greeley would say about that in the *Tribune*."

"Meanwhile soldiers will be dying," said McGuire. "How many do you think you could vaccinate with the material from one child?"

"You just mentioned a report that three hundred were infected with syphilis from one soldier. With young children, that's one thing we wouldn't have to worry about."

"If we use children and they become sick from the vaccination itself, we could be accused of performing experiments," said McGuire doubtfully.

Hal Perkins spoke.

"My family lives only a little southeast of here below Strasburg, Major Preston," he said. "And my sister has three small children."

"Do you think she'd be willing for them to be vaccinated with some of the good material we saved to immunize the men doing nursing work in the hospital?" David asked.

"Her husband is a prisoner at Johnson's Island in Lake Erie, sir. From what we hear about the treatment of prisoners there, I think my sister would want to do anything she could to hurry up the ending of the war. And as you said about the black babies, sir—vaccinating them is really doing them a favor."

"Take my horse and ride to Strasburg tonight with some vaccine, Hal," said David. "If your sister gives permission, go ahead and vaccinate the children, but be sure she fully understands what we plan to do."

Late that night, after Hal Perkins had left the camp for his home, David sat in his tent writing a letter to Araminta. Lachlan had assured him it would be posted somewhere behind the Union lines during one of Jeb Stuart's raids into enemy territory. And since he had given David the address of John Ross's home in Philadelphia, there seemed a chance that it might go through. He wrote:

> October 8, 1862
> HQ, Valley District
> Army of Northern Virginia
> Near Winchester, Va.

Araminta, dearest,

Lachlan tells me he wrote you recently and posted the letter to you during Jeb Stuart's recent raid into Maryland, so I am taking the chance that this will reach you the same way. Lachlan seems to be enjoying himself here and I believe he has been doing rather well at cards. There is much gambling but they take care that Jackson shall not see them when he passes through the camp. The general attends religious services almost every night and sits—as I have often seen him its in the chapel at the Institute—bold upright and sound asleep. I have actually seen him sleep, standing, for five or ten minutes in the midst of battle, only to awaken ready to order another of his daring maneuvers that have won so many battles.

I trust that you and the Rosses are comfortable in Philadelphia and that the Federal authorities are treating all of you with the consideration you deserve. If you have any difficulty in getting digitalis for Chief Ross, try to contact Dr. Jesse Bayard somewhere in Philadelphia. I hear that he has done well in the army—we were classmates at Jefferson Medical College—and is now a deputy surgeon general in charge of hospitals in that area. Jesse owes me a favor for arranging that he be exchanged following the First Battle of Manassas, when I captured him and the new hospital we have had ever since.

All is lovely here in the Valley. The leaves have turned and the mountainsides are a riot of color, with sumac as red as blood and the sweet gum only a little less so. Did you know climate and vegetation vary by the equivalent of six hundred miles northward for every one thousand feet of elevation? Capt. Jed Hotchkiss, General Jackson's mapping officer, told me that and I have no reason to doubt it.

Our camp near Winchester is roughly two hundred miles from Philadelphia. Today is Wednesday and if I have time on Sunday, I shall ride east to Snicker's Gap in the Blue Ridge and climb about a third of the way up. The elevation at the top of the gap is supposed to be about eleven hundred feet, so I shall be at almost the same climate level as you are in Philadelphia. Then I can at least indulge in the luxury of a daydream that we are together and the terrible war is over.

It is almost midnight and Lachlan says he must have this letter by reveille, so I know he is going with Jeb Stuart on another of those lightning forays behind the enemy lines. He says he has arranged with a lady north of the Potomac— I imagine she is an old flame—to act as a go-between for letters, so I am hoping against hope to hear from you soon. Until then, good night, my darling, and be assured that my love goes with you,

Always,
David

VI

By the time the smallpox epidemic reached its height two weeks later, Hal Perkins brought enough material from the vaccination sores produced on the arms of his sister's children and others, whose parents had offered them as subjects for this experiment in humanity, to vaccinate the remainder of the recruits. And as a result the tide of the disease gradually began to wane and the epidemic was soon under control.

Meanwhile, on October 9, General Jeb Stuart and eighteen hundred cavalry crossed the Potomac at a place called Black Creek. Penetrating into Pennsylvania about thirty miles, they reached Chambersburg and burned military stores there. On the two succeeding days, Stuart's fast-riding cavalry captured a large number of horses before moving east to Cashtown, on the road to Gettysburg and Baltimore. Riding completely around McClellan's army of almost eighty thousand men, Stuart then raced down the Monocacy River Valley to recross the Potomac near Frederick, thumbing his nose at the Union Army and sending shivers of dread throughout Washington and the North.

Only one man was injured in the swift raid, which, like Stuart's first ride around McClellan earlier in the year, accomplished almost nothing in itself except to corral a large number of badly needed horses, but did have a tremendous effect upon the morale of the enemy. Lachlan Murrell was beaming after the raid when he rode over to Stonewall Jackson's camp at Bunker Hill from Stuart's own headquarters at an estate called The Bower about five miles away. In honor of Lachlan's return, Hal Perkins concocted another of his famous rum punches and David sat with his friend by a campfire that night, drinking the punch and talking about the already storied ride through southern Pennsylvania.

"Once or twice I felt like taking a scalp or two," said the irrepressible Cherokee officer. "Just to let those Dutchmen know a real live Indian was part of our raid."

"My ancestors on Mother's side came down the Valley from Germantown, Pennsylvania, in the early seventeen hundreds. They even fought a battle with some Shawnees raiding south along the Philadelphia Way—"

"What was that?"

"The first highroad from Pennsylvania into the Valley. Many of the settlers who came into western Virginia and even western North Carolina followed it. The battle with the Shawnees occurred at a place called Cartmill's Gap not far north of Buchanan, in Botetourt County."

"The Shawnees never were civilized like the Cherokees and the Choctaws," said Lachlan. "But at that they were a lot braver than some of the Dutchmen we sent scooting for shelter when we rode through their barnyards. You should have heard them squawk when we took their best horses—I'll bet they've already sent Secretary Stanton bills for their losses."

"I guess you know that raid you just came back from has egged McClellan on to order another invasion of eastern Virginia?" said David.

"Old Jack and Jeb Stuart planned it that way between 'em," Lachlan assured him. "It takes food and ammunition plus a lot of grain and forage for horses and mules to keep up an army. Jackson figures the Yankees are his best quartermasters, and, if he can goad them into making a move before they're really ready, the chances are he'll catch the enemy off balance. You've been with him long enough to know that's one of the secrets of his success."

"When you've survived a couple of those campaigns to save Richmond, the idea of going back and fighting over the same territory again for the third time, most of it while shaking with malaria, isn't particularly attractive."

"We caught a lot of rolling stock on the Cumberland Valley and the Hanover railroad tracks at Chambersburg and burned much of it," said Lachlan. "But before we cut the telegraph wires, Sergeant Walheim connected up his key and sent a message to Washington, pretending it was from McClellan himself, saying Jackson had crossed the river with fifty thousand troops and was heading for Philadelphia. I'll bet Old Abe wet his pants."

From the pocket of his tunic, Lachlan took a long, slender cigar and lit it from the coals at the end of a stick burning in the campfire. When the fragrant smoke drifted his way, David suddenly stiffened, for the aroma was familiar, even though a year and a half had elapsed since it had first reached his nostrils—in John Ross's suite at Willard's Hotel in Washington.

301

"That cigar," he said in a choked tone. "Where did you get it?"

"Araminta sent me a whole package of 'em, I figured you'd recognize the bouquet. Uncle John always liked the finest Havana wrappers and she can roll 'em better than anyone I know."

"Did you see her?"

"No. But I mailed your letter when I picked up these cigars she sent my friend near Chambersburg—along with some other things." Reaching into the breast pocket of his tunic, Lachlan pulled out an envelope and handed it to David. In spite of the cigar smoke, he easily recognized Araminta's favorite perfume on the thin crinky sheets of onionskin paper. "This is for you."

David took the letter and put it in his pocket, to be read later in private.

"This friend of yours—"

"Maybe the less said about that the better," Lachlan interrupted him. "I suspect there are as many spies in our camp as in the camp of the enemy. The fellow Allan Pinkerton Mr. Stanton has hired is supposed to have them everywhere."

"How soon do you think the Yankees will launch a new offensive?"

"We saw plenty of evidence of preparation on the railroad tracks and roads around Chambersburg and toward Frederick, but my guess would be that we destroyed enough equipment to hold them up for a while. Stuart and Jackson are at work at headquarters now, making up a report to send on to Lee. We heard in Winchester, too, that Jefferson Davis has asked Governor Letcher to draft four or five thousand Negroes to work on the fortifications at Richmond, so he's certain to want us to delay as long as possible before stimulating McClellan into an attack."

Lachlan stood up and stretched himself. "I'd better see whether General Stuart's ready to go back to The Bower. They're having a dance in his honor there tonight."

"Take the rest of the punch with you," said David.

"I've got a half bottle of rum here you might be able to use, too."

When his friend left, David went inside his tent and lit a lantern he kept there against the likelihood of being called to visit some soldier who became ill during the night, or died and needed to be certified so his body could be moved out before reveille. The sight of many men dying from the now decreasing smallpox epidemic and the other illnesses that always took more lives than actual battle often spurred desertions, an ever present problem. By the light of the lantern, he unfolded the sheet Araminta had written and began to read:

708 South Washington Square
Philadelphia, Penn.
October 7, 1862

My darling,

I write this from Philadelphia, where Uncle John, Aunt Mary and I are now interned—I believe that is the word—for "the duration of the conflict between the United States and the Confederate States of America," to quote from the document given us when we were sent to Philadelphia from St. Louis after our capture at Park Hill. I won't go into details about that; Lachlan has written that he is with you, so you know what happened.

We came by boat to Wheeling in the new state of West Virginia Mr. Lincoln is in the process of creating and from there by train to Philadelphia. Fortunately, Aunt Mary's home here on Washington Square had not been damaged by the riot against Confederate sympathizers that took place in the city during the early days of the war. We are very well situated and even have the old nurse who looked after Aunt Mary when she was a girl to help us. Uncle John is doing very well and so far I have been able to get the digitalis he needs, but the news from Tahlequah is not good.

After Uncle John was captured, Capt. John Drew and the Cherokee troops who remain loyal to him stayed at Park Hill to protect the holdings of the Ross and Murrell families. But word has come to us—through a source by which Lachlan is able to communicate both with Park Hill and with us, but which I cannot reveal for the protection of our friends in Pennsylvania—that Stand Watie and his forces have become brigands.

In August, they seized the general store belonging to Daniel Ross and Sam Gunter, both loyal to Uncle John, at Fort Gibson. Watie burned the store and even dumped a hundred hogsheads of sugar on the ground, although many southern soldiers are on less than half rations, and the sugar would have fed Cherokee babies who are almost starving.

On August 21, Stand Watie called a meeting of the Cherokee Council and, at the point of a gun, had himself proclaimed Principal Chief. Watie's men also killed two loyal Cherokees in the orchard of our family's home at Park Hill and, since the Murrells and the Rosses have remained loyal to Uncle John, I don't know what they will destroy next.

On September 15, I went with Uncle John to Washington. He had been invited there by President Lincoln and they had a long conference on September 16. Whatever else you may think of Mr. Lincoln for invading the South, he is very sympathetic to the troubles of Uncle John and the Cherokees who remain loyal to him. And we are daring to hope that, when the war is over, the Union Government will not hold the Cherokee treaty with the South against the Nation.

I try to help, whenever I can, in the hospitals here in Philadelphia. My patients are often prisoners from the South who are sick and wounded, and to a man they are praying, as I am, for this war to end. It must bore you for me to write constantly that I love you. You said once that you would like to be a poet and I only wish I were one of the Brontë sisters or perhaps Elizabeth Barrett Browning, whose poems I read at Mount Holyoke, so I might tell you of my love in poetic phrases. But like you I am no poet and no more words will do, until at last I am with you and can prove my love in your arms.

Please destroy this letter, I'm sure many people would consider me indelicate or forward for saying that, but we Cherokees are taught from birth never to lie. And so, I repeat, I love you.

Always,
Araminta

VII

Late October of 1862 saw the reorganization of the Army of Northern Virginia into two corps, each considerably more effective than the previous group of divisions whose commanders often acted independently of the overall commander. The I Corps, located east of the Blue Ridge, was placed under the command of an experienced warrior, General James Longstreet. The II, with its primary location in the Shenandoah Valley, was under the command of General Thomas J. Jackson.

With the subsiding of the smallpox epidemic, Jackson was now able to proceed with a task he had faced more than once, that of welding new and untried recruits with the proven steel of his veterans in the Stonewall Brigade, making the whole a compact fighting weapon. And as usual David was busy trying to teach the new men the principles of sanitation that kept fevers and dysentery at a minimum, although no southern army—or northern either, judging from newspaper reports—was ever quite without these scourges.

Jeb Stuart's cavalrymen carried out raids across the Potomac almost weekly during late October and early November. Lachlan returned from one of them in November and, seeing David examining a log chapel the troops had just built for General Jackson, stopped on the way to corps headquarters. When the Cherokee officer dismounted, David saw that he was limping.

"Are you wounded?" he asked.

"Just a sprain. I ran into a squad of Dutchmen in Pennsylvania; their horses were almost as fast as mine, so I had to jump a creek to get away. My horse landed a little too close to a sapling and my boot caught in it, twisting my ankle."

"When can you let me have a look at it?"

"Now's as good a time as ever."

The two walked through the portion of the camp occupied by the Stonewall Brigade to where a dressing station had been set up to take care of the cuts, bruises and blistered feet of both the veterans and the new recruits who had brought the brigade almost up to its usual strength for the past year, although still a considerably lower figure than at the time of First Manassas.

Careful examination revealed an angry-looking bruise on the calf of Lachlan's left leg and some swelling of his ankle, but the thigh-high boots he wore had protected him somewhat and possibly prevented a fracture. There was another bruise over his lower ribs on the same side, but the skin was not broken anywhere, so no treatment was needed. The examination finished, Lachlan dressed and went on to headquarters.

As David was leaving, he noticed a small packet of cigars like the ones Lachlan smoked lying where the cavalry officer had put his tunic while he'd examined him. Recognizing the skilled touch of Araminta in rolling the fragrant cigars, he picked up the small packet. The thread holding them together broke, however, and the packet fell apart in his hands, revealing a sheet of the familiar onionskin paper Araminta used in her letters to him hidden inside. A glance at the writing identified that, too, as hers, and the brief message written there sent him hurrying after Lachlan, whom he could still see moving through the camp toward headquarters in the light of several campfires. When the physician caught up with the Cherokee officer and handed over the packet of cigars, Lachlan took them and put them in his pocket.

"Must have fallen out when I took off my uniform," he said. "Araminta sent them to me."

"She sent this, too." David handed him the sheet that had been inside the packet.

"Did you read it?" Lachlan asked quickly.

"When I saw her writing, I thought it was for me—until I read the message."

"We'd better find some place where we can talk without being overheard." There was no levity now in Lachlan's tone.

"The chapel—nobody will be there this time of night."

The moon was shining through the windows of the small log building, making it possible for them to see without needing a light, which might have attracted attention from the rest of the camp.

"Araminta has been in Washington recently with

306

Uncle John," Lachlan explained. "She learned from a clerk in Secretary Stanton's office that the order will shortly be issued relieving McClellan and placing General Ambrose E. Burnside in command of the Army of the Potomac. She thought this news would be of help to General Stuart and General Jackson, and, of course, to General Lee."

"Why wouldn't the order be issued right away?"

"With state and congressional elections coming tomorrow, I suppose Lincoln thinks it best not to announce any radical change in the makeup of the military forces until the voting is over. Much of the North isn't happy with the progress of the war and any sudden change could make the people think Lincoln doesn't know his own mind and with the Democrats expected to increase their hold on Congress, something like this could give them even more seats."

"If Araminta is sending information she acquired in Washington or Philadelphia across the lines, that makes her a spy. How could you let her take that risk, Lachlan?"

"You know my sister! If she thinks it's her duty to help the South, she's going to do it. And there have been other women spies—Rose Greenhow and Belle Boyd, for example."

"Both had affairs with Federal officers," David snapped. "Would you want your sister to do the same?"

"Of course not. But if she insists on sending information to me, the best protection I can give her is keep it from falling into enemy hands. This particular message could be very important."

"How?"

"You know how Burnside operates; we saw a sample of it at Antietam, when he bulled his way across that bridge and then had to retreat after A. P. Hill's division arrived. Once he gets in command he'll be sure to try another drive southward against Richmond. In fact, he's already building pontoon bridges farther down the Potomac in order to cross the Rappahannock."

"How did you learn that?"

"From Araminta. She sent another message—one I didn't lose."

"See that you don't lose any more either," said David angrily. "Is the sort of business Belle Boyd's involved in what you're encouraging Araminta to get into?"

"Careful, friend—even though you're going to be my brother-in-law. Belle Boyd's a trollop, though an uncommonly cute one; I met her once in Washington. But the finest blood of Scotland and the Cherokee Nation flows in Araminta's veins, so you don't have to worry about her being true to you."

"I'm not worrying about her being true, I'm concerned for her life. I can't write anything like that to her because my letter might fall into enemy hands, but when you communicate with her again, tell her I forbid any more spying."

"A lot of good your ordering my sister will do, my friend, but I'll send her your message by word of mouth. Now I'd better get this information to Sandie Pendleton so he can tell Old Jack."

"That means we'll be crossing the Blue Ridge again soon," said David. "I wonder what route we'll take this time."

VIII

On November 4, 1862, as expected, the Democrats made considerable gains in the off-year Union congressional and state elections, a stern warning to President Lincoln that the people were not happy with the prosecution of the war since his election just two years before. And on November 5, the following order was printed in all major newspapers, as usual finding its way the next day to Jackson's headquarters just north of Winchester:

By direction of the President, it is ordered that Major General George B. McClellan be relieved from command of the Army of the Potomac; and that Major General Ambrose E. Burnside take command of that Army.

Two days later, General Fitz-John Porter, a corps commander under McClellan, who had been charged with willful disobedience at Second Manassas, was replaced by General Joseph Hooker. And on November 7, an officer from Washington bore the order to McClelland at Rectortown, Virginia, bringing the military career of one of the most colorful, if cautious, military figures in the North summarily to a halt.

On the same day, General Braxton Bragg once again took command of the Army of the Mississippi for the Confederates and placed one corps under a former bishop of the Episcopal Church, General Leonidas Pope, the other under General William Hardee. At about the same time another Federal military figure, General William Starke Rosecrans, began to move the Federal Army of the Cumberland to Nashville, Tennessee, from Kentucky.

Once again the giant claws devised by Ulpsses S. Grant, closing ever so slowly but never relenting, began to menace both the political heart of the Confederacy at Richmond and its fertile breadbasket in Mississippi and Louisiana, far to the south. Meanwhile other Federal forces moved by land and water in an attempt to join at Vicksburg and cut the western group of rebellious Confederate states off completely from those in the East. And this ambition Abraham Lincoln made perfectly clear in the orders making General Nathaniel P. Banks, Stonewall Jackson's old enemy in the Valley of Virginia, a supreme commander of the Union Department of the Gulf, replacing General Ben Butler, now in disgrace because of excesses during his military rule of New Orleans.

"The President," Lincoln wrote Banks, "regards the opening of the Mississippi River as the first and most important of our military and naval operations." And so, it was apparent, did a whiskey-drinking, cigar-smoking, hard-driving general named Ulysses S. Grant.

On Sunday, November 8, while General Burnside was wanting for McClellan to make an emotional farewell address to his troops, Federal cavalry carried out a spectacular raid into Fredericksburg, just over fifty miles north of Richmond. And the next day Federal skirmishers attacked Charles Town, no more than fifteen miles from Winchester.

Other northern forces carried out operations along the Orange and Alexandria Railroad in the northern part of Virginia east of the Blue Ridge and, four days after McClellan's departure, Abraham Lincoln approved the reorganization by General Burnside of the Federal Army of the Potomac into the Right Grand Division under General Edwin Vose Sumner, the Central Grand Division under Joseph Hooker and the Left Grand Division under General William B. Franklin. The next day the Federal Army of the Potomac began moving from Warrenton, Virginia, toward Fredericksburg in a drive pointed southward toward Richmond.

On November 17, Sumner's Right Grand Division reached the bluffs across the Rappahannock River from Fredericksburg as both Federal and Confederate armies began to converge toward that vital water artery across the direct road between Washington and Richmond. On November 19, Longstreet's Confederate corps took up a position on the heights above Fredericksburg, and on the twentieth General Robert E. Lee arrived to take full command of all forces there.

Jackson was still in the neighborhood of Winchester, waiting to see whether the Federals would also launch a foray toward the northern part of the Valley, designed to keep him in place there and thus reduce the forces defending Fredericksburg. Meanwhile the religious revival that had stirred the camp of the II Corps, as nothing had done before, had come to a peak at the middle of November with the completion of the small chapel.

When Jackson declared an impromptu prayer meeting late one afternoon to dedicate the house of worship, there was a great stir in the camp. Soldiers by the thousands hid the cards and dice with which they whiled away much of their time, when not fighting the enemy or each other, and left their tents to fall in behind Jackson and the headquarters party.

David Preston was writing to Araminta but, when Hal Perkins told him Jackson was on the way, he put down pen and paper and joined the others. The chapel could

310

have held only a small fraction of the hundreds of men who followed Jackson, so he climbed the two steps to the small porch in front of the door and turned to the sea of faces uplifted toward him. They were still a motley crew by most military standards; uniforms were ragged and since at least half of their equipment had been captured by the enemy, many wore blue that had been bleached in limewater to give a faint resemblance of Confederate gray.

Beards were prevalent, too, and long hair, sometimes tied in the back with a greasy piece of cloth in a pattern similar to a Colonial hairdress. The Stonewall Brigade in particular were a wild-looking crew of diverse lineage, character and speech, but all united in the worship of the man who had made their name a badge of honor throughout the world in the eighteen months he had been their leader.

The Stonewall Jackson who knelt on the porch of the small chapel to lead his men in prayer was not much different in appearance from the Tom Fool and Old Jack of VMI days, David thought. His beard was tinged somewhat more heavily with gray and blue eyes burned with a slightly more intense fire, but the uniform was as dingy as ever, for, even though Jeb Stuart had presented Jackson with a fine new dress coat, he wore it only on the most formal military occasions.

There *was* a difference, however, but only one who had known the Jackson of old could detect it. In those days, Jackson's speech had often been diffident and halting, particularly when he lectured in class or led the congregation of the First Presbyterian Church at Lexington in prayer. So boring had been his teaching, in fact, that at one point the student body at VMI had petitioned alumni to intercede with the administration for a more accomplished teacher to be appointed to take Jackson's classes.

But when Jackson conversed with his God, as he did now, his voice took on a new assurance, a vibrant timbre that had never been in it during those years at the Institute. To the listeners, as Jackson prayed for their lives to be spared in the forthcoming trial at arms and for victory over the enemy, for their physical welfare, but above all for their spiritual health, it seemed as if he were talking to a respected partner, a Heavenly Father who recognized the justice of their Cause and would give them the victory.

Walking back through camp after the meeting with Jackson's party, David found himself with Major Hunter McGuire, who was now medical director of the II Corps, a position that kept him busy with administration and the reports General Lee insisted the commanders of the several corps and subsidiary organizations deliver to him regularly.

"General Jackson seems to be happy these days," David observed.

"Wouldn't you be if you were expecting hourly to become a father?"

"I'm so far from even being married the idea hardly has any meaning yet."

"Is your fiancée being treated well as a prisoner?"

"They're not exactly prisoners; it's more a case of being interned until the war is ended. Actually John Ross spends part of the time in Washington at the invitation of President Lincoln and Araminta says he and the President have become quite close friends."

"That's an odd relationship—a Cherokee chieftain and the President of the United States."

"John Ross—and Araminta, for that matter—is as proud of being Cherokee as you and I are of being Virginians."

"Which is saying a lot." McGuire smiled. "Preacher Stiles said in one of his sermons the other night that the hardships of this war are in some ways a punishment from God upon Southerners for having such an over-weening pride in the states they come from and their lineage."

"We Virginians are doubly guilty," David agreed. "Have you decided where you'll practice after the war?"

"In Richmond, if there's anything left of it; I hope to teach there at the medical college. How about you?"

"Teaching could be a challenge, but I think I'll stick

to the pratice of medicine. Still, even if you do that, Richmond will be a good place."

"Reverend Stiles likened the city to the field of Armageddon in the Book of Revelations. The final battles of this war will almost certainly be fought there and, if Burnside is still in command then, Richmond will probably be destroyed. He's already issued an ultimatum to the mayor of Fredericksburg, ordering him to surrender the city or see it bombarded with heavy cannon."

"No Union general has threatened a southern city with destruction before. That would be criminal."

"Burnside offered the mayor sixteen hours in which to evacuate the sick, wounded, women, children, aged and infirm. But the mayor has requested more time."

"What did Jackson say when he heard of the ultimatum?"

"I've never seen him so angry. You heard him just now praying for victory, and I'm sure part of the intensity he put into the prayer came from a wish to defeat Burnside. I understand, too, that Burnside is using Jeb Stuart's attack upon the rail yards at Chambersburg in October as a reason for the ultimatum to Fredericksburg."

"But Stuart didn't attack the town. Lachlan Murrell was there and he specifically told me all they did was burn as much of the railroad yards as they could and destroy the supplies on the cars."

"Your brother-in-law-to-be likes riding with Stuart, doesn't he?"

David smiled. "Lachlan's a romantic, something of a throwback, I suppose. He looks like an Indian but in many ways he thinks less like one than John Ross and Araminta."

"I know Jeb Stuart is very fond of him, but then the makeup of Stuart's cavalry is certainly varied enough. He never goes anywhere without that banjo picker of his practically riding behind him. And Major Von Borcke can hardly speak English—"

"I remember reading somewhere that Baron von Steuben knew only two words of English when he came to Valley Forge to train Washington's troops there. The

313

words were 'God damn,' but they didn't seem to hinder him from turning out a fighting army."

"I hear that when Major Murrell goes into battle, he shouts what he calls an Indian war cry. Captain Pelham says its the only sound in the world that's more chilling than the rebel yell of the Stonewall Brigade."

They had come to David Preston's tent. "Would you care to come in?" he asked McGuire. "I can offer you some passable brandy."

"No, thanks. The general's waiting for orders to move across the Blue Ridge toward the Rappahannock. When they come, we'll probably start marching in the middle of the night, so I'm going to get some sleep. Good night."

Darkness had fallen and shortly it was time for "tatoo," the rolling of the drums from unit to unit, starting with the Stonewall Brigade, that signaled "lights out." It was a moment David had come to love and, when the first drum sounded, he went outside to listen. One by one in rapid succession, others took it up until the entire camp was swept by the thundering rhythmic sound that seemed to make the very air vibrate and stiffened the hairs along the back of his neck with the thrill of the percussive beat.

The last drum had not quite died away when David heard the first keening rebel yell. Then gradually, in the wake of the drums, human voices began to swell in a chorus of driving sound. From tent after tent men poured out, moving toward the parade ground before Stonewall Jackson's tent. Many carried candles held in the rings of bayonets, when the blade was stuck in the ground, the shaft formed a candle holder to furnish light for gambling.

A veritable sea of tiny lights bobbed through the camp as the chorus of yells swept it again and again, not ceasing until Jackson came out of his tent and walked to the rail fence that served to isolate the headquarters area somewhat from the central parade ground itself. With his chin resting upon his hand in a gesture quite familiar to all these men, he waited until the cheering finally died away amidst cries of "Stonewall! Speech! Old Jack!"

When the sound finally ceased Jackson lifted his clenched fists in the sign of victory as he acknowledged the accolade of these men, most of whom he had personally led into the very jaws of death again and again—and safely out again. As the chorus of yells rose once again, he moved back to his tent, pausing in the open flap to say in a voice filled more deeply with emotion than David had ever heard him use:

"That was the sweetest music I ever heard."

IX

On November 25, Stuart's cavalry made another dash across the Potomac to seize the government telegraph office at Poolsville, Maryland. There Sergeant Walheim was able to intercept enough messages to reveal that, as had been rumored, General Burnside intended to concentrate the entire main Federal force of about 120,000 men in Virginia against Fredericksburg and the Rappahannock River.

Jackson and much of his army had left several days before, moving down the Valley to Strasburg and New Market, from where he turned east of the Massanutten Range into Luray Valley. The news brought from Poolsville by courier was all that was needed to free him from any need to remain in the Valley, against a possible thrust in that direction by Federal troops, and send the long lines of gray-clad men on yet another journey into Piedmont Virginia.

Moving eastward from Luray Valley, Jackson's troops began to climb the Blue Ridge toward Fisher's Gap, lying almost due west of Culpeper, Virginia. The going was not easy for the roads were sometimes icy in the morning, but they had been able to cross the Shenandoah River on bridges this time instead of being forced to wade, as on another occasion when they had moved east to relieve Richmond. In spite of the stores captured at Harpers Ferry, many in the Stonewall Brigade were still without shoes, but their ranks had been swelled somewhat by conscription and a few volunteers.

Promptly after Jackson's II Corps moved out of their

camp near Wincnester, word came that a small Federal force had moved south from Bolivar Heights at Harpers Ferry to captured the undefended city. But the main threat to the South in Virginia was now on the Rappahannock River and no attempt was made to hold the northern part of the Shenandoah Valley.

Marching down the eastern slope of the Blue Ridge toward the foothills and the rich farmlands of the Virginia Piedmont, David could hear the ragged, bearded and often shoeless men of the Stonewall Brigade shouting their favorite refrain in praise of their commander. The words, anonymous in authorship, had been found on the dead body of a sergeant in the Stonewall Brigade.

> Come, stack arms, men; pile on the rails,
>   Stir up the camp fire bright;
> No matter if the canteen fails,
>   We'll make a roaring night.
> Here Shenandoah brawls along,
>   There burly Blue Ridge echoes strong,
> To swell the brigade's rousing song
>   Of "Stonewall Jackson's way."

> We see him now—the old slouch hat
>   Cocked o'er his eyes askew—
> The shrewd, dry smile—the speech so pat—
>   So calm, so blunt, so true.
> The "Blue-Light Elder" knows 'em well—
>   Says he, "That's Banks; he's fond of shell—
> Lord save his soul! We'll give him—" Well,
>   That's "Stonewall Jackson's way."

> Silence! Ground arms! Kneel all! Caps off!
>   Old Blue-Light's going to pray.
> Strangle the fool that dares to scoff.
>   Attention! It's his way.
> Appealing from his native sod,
>   In forma pauperis to God—
> "Lay bare thine arm, stretch forth thy rod."
>   Amen! That's "Stonewall Jackson's way."

316

He's in the saddle now! Fall in!
　　Steady, the whole Brigade!
Hill's at the ford, cut off! We'll win.
　　His way out, ball and blade.
What matter if our shoes are worn!
　　What matter if our feet are torn!
Quick step! We're with him before dawn!
　　That's "Stonewall Jackson's way."

The sun's bright lances rout the mists
　　Of morning and, by George!
There's Longstreet struggling in the lists,
　　Hemmed in an ugly gorge—
Pope and his Yankees, whipped before—
　　"Bayonet and grape," hear Stonewall roar.
Charge, Stuart! Pay off Ashby's score!
　　In "Stonewall Jackson's way!"

Ah, maiden! Wait and watch and yearn
　　For news of Stonewall's band!
Ah, widow! Read with eyes that burn
　　That ring upon thy hand;
Ah, wife! Sew on, pray on, hope on,
　　Thy life shall not be all forlorn—
The foe had better ne'er been born,
　　Than get in "Stonewall's way!"

BOOK SIX

Chancellorsville

I

December 25, 1862
Near Moss Neck, Virginia

Dearest Araminta:

I write this in winter quarters near Guiney's Station, a stop on the Richmond, Fredericksburg and Potomac Railroad. We came here about two weeks ago after the battle of Fredericksburg and are fairly well situated—for winter quarters, which are never very pleasant. The men have built log huts and I share one with Lachlan, who is with us again.

You have probably read about General Burnside's disastrous decision to make a direct assault across the Rappahannock River at Fredericksburg against our forces, who were in a considerably superior position, occupying heights on the south bank. We won a great victory but, unfortunately, each time we win seems to bring us nearer to the point of not being able to go on much longer.

The Stonewall Brigade fought only in the latter part of the battle, but its losses were very heavy and at the end the roster was down to four hundred and eleven. By actual count we have lost about a third of the Brigade since crossing the Blue Ridge a month ago and eleven out of fifteen field officers were killed or wounded and out of action following the battle of Fredericksburg.

General Jackson is in good spirits at the moment, perhaps because Mrs. Jackson gave birth in North Carolina to a baby girl named Julia, just before the battle. Unfortunately, however, there is a great deal of dissension among the officers in the camp, even at the highest level. However much we admire Jackson, no one can deny that he grows more fractious as the war wears on and more intolerant of things others would overlook as the ordinary foibles of mankind. He is carrying on a running battle with Gen. A. P. Hill, too, so charges and counter charges fly all the time. General Lee tries his best to pour oil on the troubled waters, but even his special genius is hard put to keep things on something like an even keel.

Yesterday, we had our first snowfall and there was much merriment in the camp by those who weren't able to go home for Christmas. Hunter McGuire and I tossed coins to see who would get leave and he won, so here I am, serving as family physician to a bunch of boys of all ages. Strangely enough, even though many have had to do with makeshift sandals instead of shoes, or buskins of blanket strips to protect their feet from freezing, as well as tattered uniforms, the spirits of the Stonewall Brigade are excellent.

As to what the future holds for us, no one can really predict—except that in the spring there will undoubtedly be another grand assault toward Richmond by the North and the Stonewall Brigade will be in the forefront, as always, when it is repelled. My own work becomes more difficult daily as our supplies of medicine diminish. Quinine is almost unobtainable now and I am thankful that we need little of it in winter, when malaria is on the wane. I had another attack last fall before cold weather set in and can expect more chills and fever, as can hundreds of our troops, when the weather turns warm again.

At night I often think of you and thank God that you are safe in Philadelphia, where at least there must be enough nutritious food for the three of you and medicines if you become ill, which God forbid. It is terrible for a country to be torn apart as this one is now and for people to be separated from their loved ones.

Lachlan thinks the war was lost in the summer of 1861, when Jackson was not allowed to pursue the Union Army into Washington after First Manassas. And again when we stopped during the invasion of the North at Sharpsburg and Antietam. He may be right, for certainly the outlook, as far as a Confederate victory is concerned, grows dimmer each day. Only the sort of dramatic turn to the war a man like Jackson might be able to give it would afford any hope whatsoever. He may still pull something off—I'm sure he's working on it all the time—but time and supplies are growing shorter every day, while desertion and disease thin the ranks of the southern armies.

As for me, I can only pray that another Christmas will find the fighting ended and us together. Please bid the Rosses Merry Christmas for me. Unfortunately, all I can send you is my love, which, I am pleased to say, gains in strength as the months pass. Which is more than I can say for my own spirits on this Christmas Day, even though, for a change, the weather here has turned warm and sunny.

> Merry Christmas, my darling,
> David

II

Washington Square
Philadelphia, Pa.
March 15, 1863

Dearest Heart:

We have just returned from Washington, where President Lincoln gave Uncle John his assurance that, when this horrible war is over, a new treaty will be negotiated with the Cherokee Nation and our people will be allowed to hold their lands in peace, without retribution. Uncle John is naturally very happy and has seen to it that the terms of his agreement with Mr. Lincoln are published throughout the Nation and among the other four Civilized Tribes. This was a great victory for Uncle John and will do much to pull the fangs of those who sought through deceit to destroy all he has done for our people through the years.

Since returning to Philadelphia, I have renewed my work in the prison hospital. Prisoners from General Grant's operations against Vicksburg and those of General Sherman, who seems to be as dogged and determined as Grant, say that, once Grant holds Vicksburg, the war will be virtually over. Many of our boys were in terrible physical condition when captured and say that, during the winter, thousands died from sickness and exposure because there was never enough food or equipment to keep the troops in fighting condition.

Here in the North, I believe some of your southern generals are admired perhaps even more than the Union generals, particularly General Pope, who, everyone admits, failed dismally, as did Burnside. Jackson is a hero to all, but Gen. Jeb Stuart is not far behind him and neither is Longstreet. I must be careful now about what I write because I am sure the agents of Mr. Allan Pinkerton, who spied on us all the time we were in Washington, are also watching us here. If someone paid him enough, I have no doubt that Pinkerton would manufacture evidence against us, as he has against others, since it is no secret that he tailors his reports to suit the desires of those who pay him.

Darling, now that spring is coming, I am more lonesome for you than ever before. I remember as if it were yesterday, those days in Washington and I long to see your home in the Valley that you love so much. I have come to love it, too, just from your descriptions of the flowers, the dogwoods, laurel and rhododendron which will soon be blooming again.

Here in the North, it is still cold and damp, and with so much coal being used by factories and ships of the blockading fleet, it is difficult to buy enough to keep the house warm and prevent Uncle John from getting a chest cold, which you warned me might be serious for him. Fortunately, we have been able so far to obtain enough digitalis for him and to import enough tobacco from Cuba for his cigars.

The people of Philadelphia are very good to us, largely, I suspect, because of Aunt Mary, whose family has deep roots here, particularly among the Quaker community. But I shall certainly have no regrets when, at last, we are able to return to the South, particularly because it means I will be coming to you.

With all my love, always,
Araminta

321

III

With the coming of spring General Stonewall Jackson moved from his relatively luxurious quarters at Corbin Hall near Moss Neck to a tent at Hamilton's Crossing, about ten miles nearer Fredericksburg. When he sent for David Preston one day in early April, the surgeon reported to Jackson's tent and waited until the II Corps commander finished signing some papers. Finally, he pushed them aside with a sigh.

"You find me immersed in an exceedingly unpleasant task, Dr. Preston. Six deserters were captured last month and tried by court-martial. Now it has become my duty to approve or disapprove the verdicts of the court."

As David very well knew, the courts-martial of the II Corps largely reflected the will of the commanding officer, since nothing was added to the stature of a court or its members by having a verdict overturned by higher authority.

"The verdicts in these six cases were severe, but fair, Doctor. One man is to serve six months at hard labor with ball and chain. Two are to be publicly flogged. Three are to be shot." Jackson sighed. "It has just been my unpleasant duty to write their death warrants."

"I am concerned with maintaining life, not destroying it, sir. Which is why I hope never to be given a major command."

"I can understand that all your training would stand against such a drastic measure, Major." Jackson was combing his beard with his fingers. "And yet, unless desertions are punished, we may well be in the position of Poor Richard's Almanac that says, 'For want of a nail, the shoe was lost, for want of a shoe the horse was lost, for want of a horse the rider was lost.'"

"I can't argue with you there, sir."

"We are engaged in a great Cause, Doctor; if that were not true, God would not have favored our arms as He has done. So nothing must be allowed to interfere with the successful prosecution of the War and the defeat of our enemies."

"Some people find it hard to believe God favors slavery, sir."

"Not if they read Scripture! Paul expressly orders servants to be obedient to their masters."

Knowing Jackson's rigidity where matters of religion were concerned, and his irritation toward those who dared to argue with him, once a decision was made, David said nothing.

"We have it upon good authority," Jackson continued, "that General Hooker is about to launch another offensive against Richmond. Did you know him when you were in the United States Army?"

"No sir. I believe he had left the service before then."

"Hooker is a very handsome man and quite vain about his nickname of 'Fighting Joe,' so we can expect action from him."

"In the Valley, sir? Or here in northern Virginia?"

"Not in the Valley certainly. We've beaten the enemy there too often and Hooker is too good a soldier to split his forces that much. But large armies have one inherent weakness, Major Preston. They are difficult to move effectively which is why I have always preferred a smaller unit capable to moving swiftly."

"In that respect, you wrote the book, sir. Military experts believe you have outdone Napoleon."

Jackson smiled, obviously pleased by the compliment. "The student should always strive to outperform the master. I have studied the career of Napoleon as I have studied my Bible, but it appears now that the days of rapid movement in this war—at least here in Virginia— may soon be over. Neither Mr. Lincoln nor President Davis is willing to risk placing his capital in danger of capture, so we have almost approached a stalemate. And stalemate is not really my kind of war."

"Perhaps you should be in charge of the Mississippi campaign, General. The Stonewall Brigade and much of the Second Corps are Virginians, but they would follow you wherever you led them."

"I'm sure of that." Jackson's voice was warm with pride and affection for the troops who had made him their hero, however improbable the dingy-uniformed figure

323

might have appeared to a casual observer as being tailored for the hero role.

"Fate has cast me for this task," Jackson continued. "And since it lets me serve our Cause while still seeing my wife and baby occasionally, I shall not complain. Especially since I am convinced that it is also the will of God."

Jackson paused for a moment and when he spoke again, it was almost as if he were musing to himself. "Besides, we may just be able to show General 'Fighting Joe' Hooker a thing or two, when he decides to make his move. The area I expect him to choose for the next battle is called the Wilderness."

Moving to a small camp table, Jackson took a Bible from it. As he leafed through the pages, seeking a passage to read, David saw that the only other book on the table was *Napoleon's Memoirs*.

"Here it is." Jackson brought the Bible over to the lantern which hung from the ridgepole of the tent. "Listen to the words of Moses, when the Children of Israel were on the way from Egypt to the Promised Land, Dr. Preston: 'For if ye turn away from after Him, he will yet again leave them in the wilderness; and ye shall destroy all this people.' Our brethren of the North have turned from the way of the Lord by attacking us and God will surely punish them by delivering them into our hands."

Again Jackson ruffled the pages and quickly found another passage, obviously one with which he was quite familiar.

"And here in Ezekiel, the Lord says through the mouth of the Prophet:

"I will leave thee thrown into the wilderness, thee and all the fish of thy rivers; thou shalt fall upon the open fields; thou shalt not be brought together, nor gathered; I have given thee for meat to the beasts of the field and to the fowls of the heaven."

Jackson closed the Bible with a snap and put it back on the table. "There's our strategy, Major, set down thousands of years ago in the Holy Bible. With God's help we will divide General Hooker's army, as we have divided others the enemy has sent against us. Then we will destroy his men and leave their bodies to rot in the wilderness."

IV

Two mornings later, allowing time for General Lee to approve Jackson's death sentences for three of the deserters, the entire II Corps of the Army of Northern Virginia was ordered to form in a field near Harrison's Landing. As he joined the small detachment of medical troops that served the 1st Field Hospital of the II Corps, David could see three graves already dug at the edge, near the woods before which the troops were formed, and the three men standing before the graves, their eyes covered with blindfolds.

Hal Perkins, in a freshly pressed uniform with the stripes of a master sergeant on the sleeve, came rigidly to attention when the order was given for the entire II Corps. Silence gripped the thousands of watchers, broken only by the prayers of one of the condemned.

From the woods came the rhythmic beat of a drum and the fiiring squad, twelve grim-faced soldiers under an equally grim lieutenant, filed upon the field between the condemned men and the woods.

"Detail, halt!"

At the command, the men of the squad came to a stop.

"R-i-g-h-t f-a-c-e!"

The squad turned as one man to face the blindfolded three, and the lieutenant in command glanced quickly at the spare figure in rusty gray sitting bolt upright in the saddle of Little Sorrel no more than a dozen paces away. Jackson's head was held unusually high so he could see beneath the visor of the inevitable rumpled cap and his eyes were fixed unwaveringly on the three men kneeling before their graves. When the lieutenant in charge of the firing squad saw no sign of relenting on the part of the stiff figure of the commanding general, his head snapped back to the front.

"Pre-s-e-n-t arms!"

Lanyards snapped smartly as twelve highly polished Sharps rifles were lifted into position.

"Prepare to fire!"

Twelve instruments of death were raised to firing position.

"Read-y-y! Aim!"

Twelve eyes looked down polished rifle barrels, centering the sights on the breasts of the condemned men. Two of them had straightened up at the last command but the third began to slump forward.

"Fire!"

As the crack of twelve rifles echoed back from the woods, two bodies tumbled forward into the open graves, killed instantly. The third, who had been slumping to the ground, perhaps in a faint, jerked spasmodically, where the minié balls intended for the heart had torn into shoulder and neck, and blood gushed from several wounds. A half dozen recruits toppled to the ground here and there, while from the massed ranks came the sound of retching. The lieutenant drew his pistol and, moving around the center grave, put the muzzle to the head of the wounded deserter and pulled the trigger. The final shot rang out and, with the barrel of the pistol, the officer nudged the body forward so it would tumble into the grave.

"Major Pendleton, take command," Jackson ordered, and turned his horse to ride from the field, a strangely ungainly figure to have been given life or death control over nearly twenty thousand men.

V

Mrs. Jackson arrived from North Carolina with the baby daughter, Julia, on April 20, and for a week the general was busy playing the roles of husband and father, with evident relish. Then on April 27, a courier came from General Jeb Stuart—keeping watch with his troops on the headwaters of the Rappahannock around Culpeper Court House and Brandy Station on the Orange and

326

Alexandria Railroad—with word of suspicious activity in the enemy lines. Jackson immediately sent his wife and baby southward to North Carolina and began to make preparations for countering whatever mischief General Hooker was trying to put into effect.

When David Preston received an order late that afternoon to join a headquarters party at dawn the next morning for an examination of the military situation, he knew from experience that Jackson expected action and that his own task was to choose possible locations for the field hospital, once the actual fighting began.

A heavy fog had settled over the countryside around Hamilton's Crossing during the night, making the visibility very poor, when David joined General Jackson and a half dozen officers of his staff shortly after dawn. With them were four couriers whose duty it would be to carry messages back to individual commanders as the situation was evaluated. A little farther along, they were joined by General Robert E. Lee with several other officers. Once again, David was struck by the quiet dignity of the courtly officer, who had turned down the position of General-in-Chief of the Union and only recently—almost two years later—had finally been entrusted with the most important—if most difficult—position in the Confederate military forces, that of defending Richmond against repeated assaults by the far more numerous armies of the Union.

When the party came out on a clearing overlooking Fredericksburg, the horses were halted. While the couriers held the reins of their mounts, the officers moved to a rocky outcrop from which the river and the bottomlands below were visible, as well as the farther shore. Unslinging his binoculars, David chose a spot a little distant from the others but near enough so he could hear the discussion.

The scene before him was one of feverish activity, as Federal troops on the opposite bank worked to float a pontoon bridge across the breadth of the Rappahannock River. Two rows of flat-bottomed boats stretched halfway across the river from the northern shore, and a long line of blue-clad men were carrying planks and securing

327

them to the gunwales to make a floating road. At regular intervals, big guns on the hill across the river belched clouds of smoke and huge cannonballs arched across to fall in the bottomland where any attack on the river crossing operation by Confederate forces must occur. A fine drizzle was falling but the men on the boats worked on.

"I will give the order, if you think an assault upon the crossing is feasible," David heard Lee say, but Jackson shook his head.

"This is obviously a feint," he said. "I'm sure General Hooker knows we can bring Captain Poague's artillery unit up here with a few Parrott guns and sink those pontoons any time we wish."

"Shouldn't we do it anyway, sir?" Sandie Pendleton asked.

"We'll let General Hooker think he's fooling us a while longer," said Jackson. "The main Federal attack will come west of here, probably around Chancellorsville. And with some of Longstreet's corps sent on a fool's errand around Suffolk by President Davis in search of forage, we can't afford to let the enemy flank us." Jackson turned to Lee. "Do you agree, General?"

"Quite." Lee unfolded a map handed him by an aide. "Chancellorsville has to be the key, with River Road and the Orange Plank Road converging on the Fredericksburg Turnpike there. I just hope we can hold things off a few days until Longstreet gets back."

The two generals bent over the map while the aide protected them as best he could from the rain by holding over their heads one of the waterproof sheets in which soldiers and officers alike wrapped their blanket rolls.

"General Jubal Early can contain this crossing with the help of a Mississippi brigade and a few guns," said Lee.

"Early backed up the Stonewall Brigade well at First Manassas," Jackson agreed. "While he holds the heights overlooking Fredericksburg, General McLaws can march his division with the remaining troops of Longstreet's corps toward Chancellor House along the Orange Turnpike."

"It's settled then," said Lee.

328

On April 28, Federal troops were reported by Jeb Stuart's cavalry scouts to be crossing the headwaters of the Rappahannock in strength at Kelly's Ford, about twenty miles northwest of Fredericksburg and Hamilton's Crossing, where Jackson and the II Corps waited to see what Hooker's plan of battle would be. Obviously, "Fighting Joe" had torn a leaf from Jackson's own book with a wide flanking movement.

The following day, however, Hooker divided his forces to send the Federal troops of General Oliver O. Howard and General H. W. Slocum eastward across the Rapidan River, a major tributary of the Rappahannock, at Germanna Ford, while those of General George G. Meade crossed the same stream about five miles to the east at Ely's Ford. Both were obviously heading for Wilderness Tavern and Chancellor House—often called Chancellorsville, although one large brick house and outbuildings composed the settlement—intending to flank the Confederate position and entrenchments being held by Jackson south of the turnpike and Plank Road.

When that same day the Federal III Corps, under General D. E. Sickles, and the II, under General D. N. Couch, appeared at U.S. Ford, threatening to drive directly south on Chancellorsville, a time of decision for Lee and Jackson had been reached. The Confederate Army must either stand and fight against a flanking force of much greater strength, or it must retreat toward Richmond and a less favorable position for defending the southern capital, probably at the North Anna River, while they waited for Longstreet to return from futile expedition toward Suffolk in search of forage. That Hooker had no doubt what the decision would be was volunteered by a Federal staff officer captured by Jeb Stuart's troopers while on a tour of inspection.

"I have Lee in one hand and Richmond in another," Hooker was reported to have boasted—and with considerable reason, since in three days he had carried out a largely unopposed flanking movement around Lee's entire force.

Hooker apparently hadn't considered, however, that his army of roughly 135,000—more than twice the 60,-000 Lee could throw into battle—was now divided into three parts. Largest was the two-pronged advance on Wilderness Tavern and the heavily overgrown area called "The Wilderness" from the northwest. Second was the threat of Sickles at U.S. Ford. And third was the force at Fredericksburg and the pontoon bridge being watched by General Jubal Early's division, with Captain W. T. Poague's unit from the Rockbridge Artillery and its captured Parrott guns pinpointed on the pontoons at the center of the bridge, should the Federal forces decide to cross the river and attack.

Watching Jackson at his headquarters several miles from Chancellor House, David could see his commander's impatience growing steadily as reports on the progress of Hooker's flanking march poured in from the cavalry scouts of Stuart's command, who were infiltrating the Wilderness area and the roads approaching it from the west, down which the enemy troops were marching.

On May 1, Jackson's main body moved nearer to Chancellorsville. The 1st Field Hospital had no orders to follow, by which David understood that Jackson had not yet made up his mind about the immediate future.

David himself rode with the members of Jackson's staff and about ten-thirty a courier, his wide hat and high boots identifying him as belonging to Jeb Stuart's cavalry, brought his horse to a hoof-sliding stop near Jackson and handed a message to Sandie Pendleton, who opened it and read it aloud.

"General Stuart says he is on the road from Spotsylvania Court House and will close on the flank and hold all he can when the brawl opens."

"Trust Stuart to think of the battle as a brawl. With luck, and God's help, we'll have General Hooker dancing to our pipers before another day passes." Taking a short pencil from his pocket, Jackson scribbled a brief answer in his crabbed hand and gave it to the courier. "Tell General Stuart I trust that God will give us a great victory and to keep closed on Chancellorsville," he said.

A short time later General Lee rode up, surrounded

by a small staff. He and Jackson conferred for a few minutes alone, then Lee rode away to the southwest. Shortly afterward Jackson, with his staff, started along the right-of-way of an unfinished railway section toward Catherine Furnace, an abandoned iron mine about seven miles away, where, a road led northwestward toward both the Plank Road and the Turnpike.

A South Carolina regiment was holding a hill nearby and the Jackson party rode to its summit with the unit commander, Captain Alex Haskell, a handsome young officer. As they came to a stop on the summit of a hill, David saw lying before them like one of Jed Hotchkiss' superb maps, the massive forces of Hooker's army, in triple lines protected by earthworks that would make a frontal attack nothing less than suicide.

Jackson studied the situation of the enemy absentmindedly for about five minutes, but nobody spoke. Accustomed to such periods of deep thought on the part of their commander, they knew the military genius housed in Jackson's brain was busy at work. Finally he shook his shoulders, as if to throw off some invisible weight, and turned to the South Carolinian.

"Hold this ground, Captain Haskell," he said. "You will be relieved at nine o'clock." Turning to the others, he added briskly, "Let's find General Lee, gentlemen, and make some plans for tomorrow."

Lee wasn't far away, sitting on a log in a protected wooded area between the turnpike leading to Fredericksburg and the Plank Road from Chancellorsville southeastward. He was deep in thought while he studied the inevitable map, unfolded and spread out on his knee. When Lee beckoned to Jackson, the II Corps commander dismounted and, leaving his horse for a courier to hold, walked over and sat down beside the commanding general of the Army of Northern Virginia.

"General Hooker is trying to hold us along this front, while he carries out some kind of trick," said Jackson without preamble. "Why else would he keep a force of that size in breastworks when they could be attacking?"

"It's not like 'Fighting Joe' to delay long," Lee answered. "I believe he will attack tomorrow, most likely directly south of Chancellorsville, and we must somehow outwit him."

"Hooker is overcautious," said Jackson. "If we can strike him briskly in a weak spot tomorrow, his troops will be back across the Rappahannock River by nightfall."

"I wish I had your optimism." Lee pointed to the map. "The Wilderness around Chancellorsville is so thick the enemy can hardly attack through the trees on the right, so we should be safe in that area. And Early reports he is still holding the forces trying to cross the Rappahannock."

"Which means that particular threat is merely a feint, and Hooker is actually concentrating on flanking our left."

"But how do we discover that?" Lee asked.

"Why not send out some engineers to study the situation?"

Lee agreed and two engineers were sent to scout the Federal positions a short distance away. While they waited for a report, the two generals and their staffs ate cold rations, washing them down with fresh water from a spring branch draining into Lewis Creek, which ran almost directly through the Wilderness.

While they were eating, a flamboyant figure appeared and dismounted, the plume in a broadbrimmed hat intact though the wearer had been riding through the trees at the edge of the Wilderness area, identifying General Jeb Stuart wherever he went.

"Fitzhugh Lee and some troopers have flushed out the Yankees' right flank among the woods toward Wilderness Tavern," Stuart reported as he wolfed down his bread and meat. "It's hanging in the air, waiting to be cut off by a strong enough force."

"Yours?" General Lee asked.

Stuart shook his head. "It will take more men than I have. But if Hooker's right flank is turned, we can move east along the turnpike and cut him up between Wilderness Tavern and the Chancellor House. The Federal cannon will all be pointing southward and, before Hooker knows what happened, we can storm those elevations along the creek and put a lot of his artillery out of action."

"How far would it be?" Jackson asked.

"Once you get to Wilderness Tavern and start back east, four miles or so along the Plank or the Turnpike should bring you right into Chancellorsville. But it has to be done in secret—and soon."

Jackson leaned forward and studied the map for several moments before he spoke.

"If we cut the Plank Road west of the Wilderness, the Stonewall Brigade can hold that position while the main body continues north and swings back along the turnpike," he said. "With the Stonewall Brigade already attacking, the enemy could hardly be expecting another force as far north as Wilderness Tavern."

"That's a job for the brigade." Stuart agreed. "Hooker will be sure the devil himself has lifted the entire Stonewall Brigade over the Wilderness and dropped it down on his flank."

"Not the devil," Jackson objected quietly. "But the Almighty."

While they were talking, the engineer officers who had been sent out to reconnoiter returned. Their report was terse; the enemy was in too much strength between Chancellorsville and the spot where the three generals were conferring to permit a frontal assault, particularly because of heavy concentration of Federal cavalry along the ridges on the east bank of Lewis Creek. The only chance of success appeared to be the wide swing to the west Jackson had recommended.

"The cavalry will cover the Stonewall Brigade when it makes the attack along the Plank Road," said Lee. "But your whole movement, General Jackson, must be kept well south of Catherine Furnace because of the Federal artillery on those heights Stuart spoke of."

"We'll be there," said Jackson confidently. "But someone will have to hold here and give Hooker the impression we are still waiting for an attack."

"General Archer and General Thomas will carry out the holding operation around Catherine Furnace, while

333

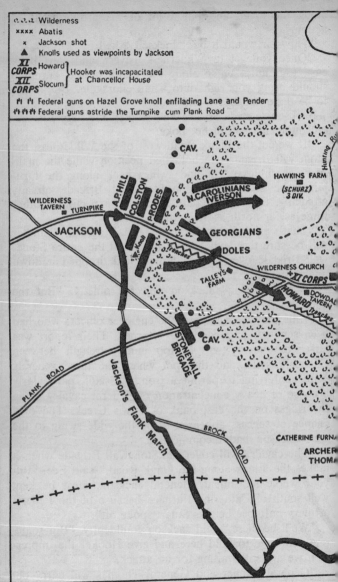

Legend:
- Wilderness
- Abatis
- x Jackson shot
- ▲ Knolls used as viewpoints by Jackson
- XI CORPS — Howard } Hooker was incapacitated
- XII CORPS — Slocum } at Chancellor House
- Federal guns on Hazel Grove knoll enfilading Lane and Pender
- Federal guns astride the Turnpike cum Plank Road

CAV.

A.P. HILL
COLSTON
RODES

N. CAROLINIANS
IVERSON

HAWKINS FARM
(SCHURZ)
3 DIV.

WILDERNESS
TAVERN — TURNPIKE

JACKSON

GEORGIANS

Knoll

trenches

DOLES

WILDERNESS CHURCH — XI CORPS

TALLEY'S FARM

DOWDALL
TAVERN

HOWARD

CAV.

STONEWALL
BRIGADE

PLANK ROAD

Jackson's Flank March

BROCK ROAD

CATHERINE FURNACE

ARCHER
THOMAS

Jackson's Flank March at the Battle

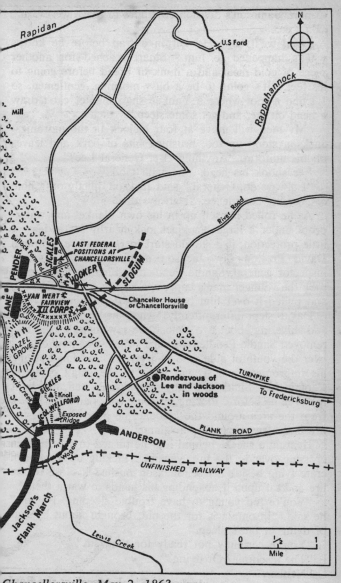

Chancellorsville, May 2, 1863

General Jameson's division continues to move westward," said Lee.

"And we'll have Hooker in a trap before he knows what's happened to him." Stuart reached for another piece of cold meat and a hunk of bread before going to his feet. "It's going to be a busy morning, gentlemen, so I'll find a spot where a Yankee sharpshooter can't draw a bead on me, and get some sleep."

"My men will move at four o'clock in the morning." Jackson stood up too, brushing bits of bark and leaves off his uniform. "Anything else, General Lee?"

Lee shook his head. "Go with God."

"I always do, General," said Jackson quietly on a note of absolute confidence. "I always do."

As he rolled himself up in his own blanket and waterproof under a large blackjack oak nearby for at least a little protection, if it should start to rain before morning, David Preston saw Jackson arguing with his young inspector general, Sandie Pendleton. Finally, the general took the younger man's cape, not having one of his own, and pulled it over him before lying down himself.

David slept intermittently; when he awakened, cold and shivering about two o'clock, he saw that Jackson had removed Sandie Pendleton's cape, which was now draped over the youthful aide who had given it to him. Leaving his impromptu bed, David went to the small campfire Captain J. P. Smith, the baby of Jackson's staff, had built the evening before. Picking up some sticks and dry leaves from the area around the bivouac, he piled them on the fire and blew the coals into flame.

Hearing a sneeze behind him he turned to see Jackson crossing over to the fire, yawning. Picking up a wooden crate lying beside a tree, Jackson pushed it close to the fire and sat upon it, extending his hands to warm them.

"You're too young to have trouble sleeping, Doctor," he said. "Insomnia is for the old, brought about by fear of dying in one's sleep."

"You're certainly not ready for that, sir."

"The insomnia? Or dying?"

"Neither."

"Your purpose in life is to combat death, so naturally
336

you can see nothing of good in it; but to one who trusts God and His Son, death holds no threat. If you are saved, you may welcome the privilege of crossing over the river and being with Him." Then Jackson added, almost it appeared, to himself, "Although I would like to watch my little girl grow up to be the lovely and gracious woman her mother is."

A sudden clatter of metal broke the stillness of the night. Startled by the sound, David saw that Jackson's saber, which had been propped against a nearby tree, had fallen and struck a rock. He shivered again, half convinced the falling of the saber was some sort of omen.

Sandie Pendleton, too, had awakened and, realizing the cape he'd given Jackson earlier now covered him, was protesting to the commander.

"You were shivering in your sleep, Major Pendleton, and you are too good a staff officer for me to risk losing you," Jackson soothed the younger officer like a father. "You can be helpful, though, by finding a coffeepot and making some coffee for us."

Pendleton departed, wrapped in his cape, just as a slight figure dressed in civilian clothes moved into the circle of light by the fire, David recognized Reverend Beverly T. Lacy, a Richmond minister who had become Jackson's chief chaplain after the departure of Major Dabney. Lacy owned property in the area and had ridden in to the camp late the night before.

"Have a seat, Dr. Lacy. Pendleton has gone for some coffee to wake us up," said Jackson. "But I hope you are already awake enough to tell me whether there's a road in the vicinity by which I might reach the Plank Road for a flanking movement between the Wilderness Tavern area and Talley's Farm?"

"One or two country roads cut across the turnpike west of Chancellorsville," said Lacy. "If I may look at your map I might be able to locate them for you."

Jackson handed him the map and produced the inevitable stubby pencil from his pocket.

"Mark them, please, Dr. Lacy." He watched closely while the Richmond divine penciled in the routes before handing it back, but Jackson studied the map only briefly.

337

"They're both too close to the enemy," he said. "We must avoid his artillery on the ridge north of where the unfinished railway crosses Lewis Creek. Wasn't there another way ore was brought to the smelter at Catherine Furnace?"

"I'm not sure, General, but Colonel Wellford at Catherine Furnace should know. I believe he's there now."

The smell of the coffee Sandie Pendleton had been boiling over the campfire had wakened the rest of Jackson's staff and Major Jed Hotchkiss was sent to bring Colonel Wellford. He came back in an hour, without Wellford, but with a map he had sketched out from the information given him. It showed a circular road well to the west and clear of Federal shelling, except where it crossed an exposed ridge beside Lewis Creek.

VII

At 8 A.M. on the morning of May 2, the entire II Corps started southwestward in a wide flanking march around the Wilderness. To avoid shelling by Federal batteries, the wagons, including those of the 1st Field Hospital, made an even wider swing out of the range but, as usual, David Preston rode with the staff to locate the position where the hospital would be set up on the eve of the battle.

On Jackson's instructions, the men marched in a loose formation, a not unusual military technique for the Stonewall Brigade. David didn't need to be told the reason when he saw the Federal observation balloons floating in the air above the heights some distance to the east, near Fredericksburg.

At midmorning and the southernmost point of their route from Chancellor House, the supply train was attacked briefly by a band of Federal cavalry skirmishers. And when some of the attackers were wounded, they revealed that observers in the balloons had been studying the movement of the Confederate troops through their glasses in the haze of early morning, and had reported them to be in full retreat. Informed of General Hooker's assumption that he had already beaten his opponents, Jackson was quite pleased.

"Those balloons are filled with hot air," he observed. "How could they possibly reveal the truth to the enemy?"

In the original plan, the main attack was to have been sent along the so-called Plank Road, as soon as Jackson's flanking force reached it at the end of a quarter circle of movement around the western edge of the Wilderness. But just south of Plank Road, they were joined by General Fitzhugh Lee's 2d Brigade from Stuart's cavalry. At Fitz Lee's suggestion, Jackson and his staff rode near the enemy lines to observe; David Preston rode with them and the sight that met his eyes was startling.

Triple rows of trenches, breastworks and artillery positions were located along the turnpike in the neighborhood of Talley's Farm, about a mile west of where they stood—all pointing south. Apparently not even considering the possibility of an attack from the northwest, the Federals obviously thought themselves secure in their own breastworks—facing south. The Confederate observers could see even butchers engaged in preparing steak to be cooked over campfires that night for the evening meal.

Jackson didn't quibble over Fitz Lee's suggestion that he continue northward across the Plank Road about a mile to the turnpike just east of Wilderness Tavern and attack from both points. Leaving the Stonewall Brigade to hold the more southern road until the signal to attack was given by the artillery, Jackson moved on with the rest of the II Corps, plus several brigades from Longstreet's I Corps which had not gone on the foraging expedition to the Tidewater region.

Here, David Preston had to leave the headquarters group, since he and Major Hunter McGuire had decided the hospital should be located beside the Plank Road. There facilities for evacuating the wounded to the rear once the battle began or, if the necessity should arrive, westward toward the foothills of the Blue Ridge, were easily available. Working with Hal Perkins, David and the members of the hospital unit quickly set up the tents among the protecting trees just off the road where a brook at the edge of the Wilderness afforded an ample supply of water.

It was five o'clock on the afternoon of May 2 before Jackson's troops were in position to start the final phase of the battle for Chancellorsville. To the Stonewall Brigade, hidden at the edge of the dense forest of scrub oak and blackjacks, along with a few pines, known as the Wilderness, it was a time of suspense. Once the battle began, the brigade had orders to move forward toward the trenches the Federals had dug along the farther bank of Louis Creek and a junction with the rest of the II Corps, moving eastward along the Fredericksburg Turnpike. Meanwhile, the cavalry screen was supposed to skirmish ahead of the brigade to feel out the enemy, but so far no contact had been made.

The sudden boom of cannon to the north signaled the start of the battle and minutes later the Stonewall Brigade began to press forward along the Plank Road toward Wilderness Tavern and Chancellorsville, where General Hooker waited, quite unaware, they hoped, of Jackson's "Grand Flank March," as it was to be called later. As yet there were few casualties and for about a half hour the unit encountered only the advance guard of the enemy, mostly an occasional picket. These were cut down and killed before they were able to send any information back to the commander of the Federal XI Corps defending the junction of Plank Road and the turnpike near Wilderness Church and a place called Dowdall's Tavern between it and Chancellorsville. The few casualties brought back were enough to keep David busy, but nothing like the steady stream that usually came with a frontal assault. By which he knew Jackson's strategy of outflanking the flankers was apparently working exactly as planned.

Darkness had begun to fall when David received an order to move the hospital along the Plank Road to its junction with the Fredericksburg Turnpike at Wilderness Church. It was quite dark by the time they put up the hospital tents and the first casualty soon appeared. Not long after the heavy fighting began, a burly sergeant walked in holding a shattered arm in which a spurting artery had been secured by a tourniquet.

"The battle's won, Major," he reported. "I guess you'll have to take off my arm but I can still whip more Yankees with one arm than two of 'em can do to us."

"What about General Jackson?"

"He don't know the meaning of fear, sir. I saw him ride out at the head of the brigade and sweep the Yankees right back into Hunting Run. General Lane's and General Pender's brigades are a half mile from Chancellor House and somebody said Hooker's runnin' for his life."

"I wish General Jackson wouldn't take so many chances."

"Major Pendleton's always telling him that, but the Lord's with 'Old Jack,' Major. The only trouble is, since we got into the woods and it started getting dark, you can't tell one person from another, so the only sure thing to do is shoot at anything that moves."

The chloroform cone with cotton stuffed into it was dropped over the sergeant's mouth and nose by Hal Perkins' expert hands and with three breaths he was out. David began the amputation, but no matter how many thousands of times he'd been forced to perform the operation during the war, he still hated it, as the fleshing scalpel outlined the longer front flap of skin and muscle in two swift strokes, then turned to the back to outline a shorter one below. The bone saw, sharpened before every battle by Hal Perkins, grated briefly and another useless arm dropped into the tub beside the table. Whipcord ligatures closed the vessels, the ends left long so they could be pulled out of the stump after the arteries had been closed by blood clots several weeks later.

Darkness brought no slackening in the flow of casualties from the intense fighting now going on between the hospital and Chancellor House, roughly a mile away. It had been a hot, muggy day and David worked with two assistant surgeons, stripped to the waist. Their bodies and garments were bloodstained like butchers' and, as the hours wore on the pile of amputated arms and legs tossed under a blackjack oak just outside the surgical tent grew steadily higher. At the same time, the sickly sweet smell of blood and lacerated human flesh mixed with the pungent aroma of chloroform to create a miasma that always hung over a forward military hospital during a crucial engagement.

The wounded filtering back from the scene of the most intense fighting reported that Jackson was still in the forefront, refusing to let anything stop the forward movement that was pushing the enemy back toward Fredericksburg and the river. General Hooker himself, they reported, had almost been captured when the victory-scenting troops of General A. P. Hill's corps pushed on at Jackson's command to the immediate neighborhood of Chancellorsville. The abatis fortifications of felled trees with the branches facing the direction of a possible attack protecting the Federal command headquarters at Chancellor House had been penetrated, too, and the enemy was reported to be in rout all along the line.

Shortly after nine o'clock, a courier riding past the hospital in search of General Jeb Stuart, paused long enough to shout the startling news that Stonewall Jackson had been shot. David was in the midst of an amputation when Hal brought him the word.

"Are you going forward to help look after General Jackson, sir?" Hal asked while he completed the operation.

"Major McGuire is with the general, there's too much to be done here."

"I guess you're right, sir." Hal looked around the busy hospital. "But I'd sure feel a lot better about General Jackson if you were with him."

During the next hour, as bits and pieces of information about Jackson's injuries filtered back with the wounded brought to the II Corps Field Hospital, something resembling a pattern began to take form. As with any rapid advance carried out in one of Jackson's lightninglike attacks upon an unsuspecting enemy, there had been much confusion. Regiments and smaller units moving forward more rapidly than others were sometimes cut off, at least temporarily, forcing them to fight their way out or be captured. Others faltered in the heat of battle, As David

342

had seen even the tough veterans of the Stonewall Brigade do occasionally, though not very often.

Knowing Jackson, David was sure he had been in the forefront of the activity, urging troops on here, directing the placing of artillery there, always alert to the many small details that made him the great military leader that he was. And so he was not really surprised to hear that in the darkness and the confusion of the battlefront, "Old Jack" had actually been shot by Confederate troops, some said from the 18th North Carolina.

All reports agreed that Jackson was seriously wounded, that Dr. McGuire was with him, and that an attempt was being made to evacuate him by ambulance, which was being slowed by enemy fire. When one soldier with a superficial scalp wound, where a bullet had creased his skull, walked in with the news that the ambulance bearing General Jackson and Colonel Stapleton Crutchfield, chief of the II Corps Artillery, was not far behind, David sent Hal Perkins to clear out his own tent for the general's use and ordered warm blankets made ready to be placed over the wounded man as soon as he arrived.

It was about eleven o'clock when a canvas-covered, horse-drawn ambulance appeared, surrounded by riders, most of whom David recognized as members of Jackson's own personal staff. About that time, too, Dr. Harvey Black, the troop surgeon with Jeb Stuart on the left front, rode up with several other medical officers. When David pulled aside the canvas at the rear of the ambulance, he saw Hunter McGuire sitting inside, holding a dressing against Jackson's upper arm.

"His pulse is weak," said McGuire. "He needs stimulants."

David nodded and personally took one end of a litter pole to help lift Jackson from the ambulance. While others carried Colonel Crutchfield, who was more concerned about Jackson than about himself, to the large hospital tent and a waiting cot, the general was transferred to David's own tent, where he was wrapped in the warm blankets Hal Perkins had prepared.

When David poured a liberal drink of whiskey and

held it to Jackson's lips, the wounded man opened his eyes and even managed to smile as he drank gratefully.

"You'll think me a drunkard, Doctor," said Jackson. "But whiskey seems to stop the pain more effectively than the injection Dr. McGuire gave me."

"Morphia," said McGuire in a low voice. "He was in much pain at first."

"We must allow the general to rest, gentlemen." McGuire spoke quietly to the other surgeons who were crowding into the tent. "The bleeding has stopped, so heat and stimulants will do him more good than an examination at this time."

"I agree," said David.

"I'll sit with him," Captain James P. Smith, the youngest aide, offered from the door of the tent, and the medical contingent filed out to gather around a campfire outside. It was damp and already the temperature was beginning to drop sharply with the fall of night. When David passed around a bottle of whiskey from the medical stores, hardly anyone refused a drink.

"Can you tell us what happened, Dr. McGuire?" asked Dr. Black.

"General Jackson was rallying the troops moving against Chancellor House," said McGuire, "but it was dark and the woods were so thick the men were hardly able to see each other. I was not with him but Captain Wilbourn, Lieutenant Morrison—and I believe Lieutenant Wynn were."

Morrison, David knew, was Mrs. Jackson's younger brother, now an aide to Jackson and a highly respected officer.

"I understand that General Jackson was riding in search of General A. P. Hill, to tell him the enemy was routed and he must push on before the Yankees had a chance to re-form," McGuire continued. "Confusion was everywhere and I suppose the general and his party must have been mistaken for Yankee cavalry by pickets of the 18th North Carolina. Anyway, as they were riding past, a volley was fired at them. General Jackson wasn't hit in the first round but Sorrel reared and he was almost unseated by an overhanging branch, according to Lieutenant Wynn. As the horse rushed away, a second volley struck General Jackson and Sorrel plunged into the underbrush, almost knocking him from the saddle."

"I always dread fighting after dark for just that reason," said Black.

"Lieutenant Wynn was close by and managed to stop the horse," said McGuire. "Captain Wilbourn rode up about that time, and the two of them managed to carry the general to the shelter of a tree. General Hill, I am told, arrived while Captain Wilbourn was looking for an ambulance and brought Dr. Barr, who was at a regimental dressing station nearby. Dr. Barr was with General Jackson when I arrived a few minutes later. He told me there are three wounds, one in the left shoulder that required a tourniquet, another in the left forearm and one in the right palm."

"None of those should be fatal," Dr. Black observed.

"In themselves, no," McGuire agreed. "But as they were carrying General Jackson on a litter to an ambulance, the party was fired upon again and one litter bearer dropped a pole, letting him fall to the ground. His side, I am told, struck a rock and he complained immediately of severe pain, so there's some possibility of broken ribs."

"He seemed to be catching a cold last night," David volunteered. "He slept out in the damp without a blanket or waterproof."

"Protecting me," said Sandie Pendleton bitterly "It was always his way to think of others before himself."

David was sure only he noticed the unconscious use of the past tense when the young officer spoke of his commander, but the word "was" still had an ominous ring.

"I got to him just after the litter had been dropped and found him in severe pain," McGuire added. " 'I'm badly injured, Doctor,' he told me, 'and fear I am dying.' "

"As soon as the general becomes conscious again he'll want to know what's happened in the battle." Sandie Pendleton got to his feet and drew his waterproof about his shoulders. "I'd better go and find General Stuart.

345

General Hill was wounded shortly after General Jackson was shot, and Stuart is the man to take over now."

Two hours after Jackson arrived at the field hospital, David and Dr. Hunter McGuire decided his condition had improved to the point where an examination could be carried out under anesthesia, since probing for fragments of the bullets that had struck Jackson's body was certain to be painful. Dr. R. T. Coleman, now surgeon of Jackson's old division, administered the chloroform and David, since he was commanding officer of the field hospital, assisted McGuire.

The bullet in Jackson's right hand could be felt under the skin on the backside; it had entered the palm, fracturing two of the metacarpal bones before lodging beneath the skin. When McGuire incised the skin over the lump, the bullet popped out and he held it up to the light.

"That's a small-bore Springfield—ours," one of the other men said.

"CSA troops fired on him," McGuire agreed. "The North stopped using those old-fashioned muskets a long time ago."

The bullet that had struck Jackson's shoulder had torn the muscles badly and fractured the long bone known as the humerus in the upper arm, damaging the main arterial supply to the arm itself in its passage through the flesh. Further down, below the elbow, still another bullet had torn its way through the arm, to emerge on the inner side near the wrist. Seeing the wounds, McGuire looked up at David Preston questioningly.

"Could you save it with an excision under antiseptic conditions?" he asked.

"Perhaps, if the artery wasn't torn. But with the danger of gangrene below the shoulder, if we tie off the artery in the upper part of the arm, it's a forlorn hope."

"And certainly not a risk worth taking," McGuire agreed. "We'll go ahead then."

Working swiftly, the corps medical director amputated the arm about two inches below the shoulder, making no attempt to create flaps. This could be done later, after the general's condition had improved. The entire operation covered less than half an hour.

When Sandie Pendleton arrived several hours later, Jackson was asleep, but awakened when the younger officer, who had been almost like a son, entered the tent.

"Well, Major," Jackson greeted Pendleton. "I'm glad to see you. I thought you were killed."

Pendleton explained that General A. P. Hill had been wounded and that Jeb Stuart was now in command. Stuart had asked for any suggestions Jackson might have for the prosecution of the attack and, for a few moments, the general seemed to have some of his old enthusiasm. But it quickly faded away and he sent instructions to Stuart to do whatever seemed best to him.

The following morning, Sunday, May 3, Jackson appeared to be considerably better and asked for news about the battle, which was still raging. When informed that General Hooker was in retreat and already crossing the Rappahannock toward Washington, he was very pleased.

"You see me severely wounded, but not depressed; not unhappy," Jackson assured his chaplain when Lacy arrived later. "I believe it has been done according to God's holy will, and I acquiesce entirely in it. You may think it's strange, but you never saw me more perfectly contented than I am today; for I am sure that my Heavenly Father designed this affliction for my good. I am perfectly satisfied that either in this life or in that which is to come, I shall discover that what is now regarded as a calamity is a blessing. I can wait until God, in His own time, shall make known to me the object He has in thus afflicting me. If it were in my power to replace my arm, I would not dare to do it, unless I could know it was the will of my Heavenly Father."

"You have great faith, General," the chaplain said on a note of awe. "I can only wish mine were the equal of it."

"It has been a precious experience to me that I was brought face to face with death and found that all was well," said Jackson. "I then learned that one who has been the subject of converting grace and is the child of

God can, in the midst of severest suffering, fix the thoughts upon God and heavenly things and derive great comfort and peace."

Reports from the front during the morning of May 3 told of the gallant charge by the Stonewall Brigade, shouting Jackson's name, that had been the final stroke in driving General Hooker's forces from the battlefield.

"It was just like them to do so, just like them," Jackson said proudly when informed of the brigade's action. "The men of that brigade will, some day, be proud to say to their children, 'I was one of the Stonewall Brigade.' They are a noble body of men."

"It belongs to the brigade and not to me," he insisted when someone claimed the honor for him because of the name Stonewall. "For it was their steadfast heroism which earned it at First Manassas."

That morning, Jackson received a note from General Lee expressing his regret at the accident. In order for Major Hunter McGuire to remain at Jackson's bedside, David Preston was appointed temporarily to the position of corps medical director and therefore had to be away from the field hospital. But little was going on now, the battle consisting only of a few skirmishes by Stuart's cavalry against the retreating elements of Hooker's army.

It was the afternoon of May 4 before David got back to the hospital and learned that Jackson was complaining of some pain in the side where he had been dropped and his chest had struck a rock.

"What about the temperature?" David had left his thermometer at the hospital since there was little use for it in the field.

"It has been rising steadily all day," McGuire reported soberly. "I would appreciate it if you would examine him with me."

Working carefully because Jackson was drowsy, except for being roused up by pain whenever a spasm of coughing occurred, David listened with his stethoscope over the lower ribs where the pain seemed to be centered. Jackson's breathing was somewhat shallow and occasionally quite painful, whenever he was seized by a spasm

348

of coughing. His color had improved considerably but David knew that could well be due to the rising fever.

Nor was he surprised by what he heard in the stethoscope as he moved the funnel-shaped bell about over Jackson's chest. The fairly loud rushing sound with both inspiration and expiration unquestionably came from the rubbing together of the two layers of pleura, one forming the inner lining of the chest cavity, the other covering the lung itself.

Pleuritis, or pleurisy, was a common enough finding where a severe blow had been struck to the lower rib cage, bruising tissues and the organs beneath, whether or not accompanied by fracture of the ribs. As far as they could tell in Jackson's case, there were no fractures and the inflammation in the pleura appeared to be a protective reaction, designed by the body to produce fluid and separate the inflamed layers, thus lessening the pain. But the spattering of sound in the stethoscope when Jackson took a breath, like shot being shaken up in a container, had deeper significance to David's trained ear, indicating an inflammation of the lung substance itself.

Nodding for McGuire to listen, David held the bell of the stethoscope in place against Jackson's skin, and when McGuire raised his head to meet David's eyes, his expression was grave.

"You heard the congestion?" David asked as the two doctors discussed Jackson's condition outside the tent.

McGuire nodded. "Could you tell how much lung is involved?"

"I heard rales over an area larger than my hand, which probably means most if not all of the lower lobe is inflamed."

"It's pleuropneumonia, all right. Do you think the blow caused it?"

"Who can say? He was severely chilled the night before the battle began, when he gave up a woolen cape so Sandie Pendleton would be covered."

"That's like him," said McGuire. "In the ambulance the general was more concerned about Colonel Crutchfield than he was about himself, though his wounds were

349

far more serious than Crutchfield's. General Lee is very anxious for Jackson to be moved as quickly as possible; many Federal troops were never committed to the battle and if General Hooker organizes a counterattack, the hospital could be captured."

"How about taking him to Guiney's Station? It's accessible by ambulance."

"That would be an excellent place," McGuire agreed. "It's getting damp and cool outside, but we can move him first thing in the morning."

When David looked into Jackson's tent at dawn on May 5, the general was feeling better. His pain appeared to have lessened somewhat and his temperature had not risen any higher during the night. While David was there, Hunter McGuire came into the tent, holding a message.

"I have a note here from General Lee, sir," he said. "Shall I read it to you?"

The message was brief, wishing the stricken Jackson a speedy recovery and return to duty.

"General Lee is very kind, but he should give the glory to God," said Jackson when Lee commented glowingly upon Jackson's victory. "Our movement here was a great success, I think the most successful military movement of my life, but I expect to receive far more credit for it than I deserve.

"Most men would think that I had planned it all from the first; but it was not so," he added. "I simply took advantage of circumstances as they were presented to me in the providence of God. I feel that His hand led me, let us give Him all the glory."

"General Lee is anxious for you to be moved to a safer place, sir," said McGuire. "He fears the hospital here might be captured."

"If the enemy does come, I'm not afraid of them. I have always been kind to their wounded, and I am sure they will be kind to me. However, Lee is my superior and I will do as he commands."

"An ambulance will be here about eight o'clock tomorrow morning," McGuire told him.

"Is there any news from the field, Dr. Preston?" Jackson asked.

"Only that the enemy is being pursued as far as the Rappahannock."

"General Hooker's plan of campaign was in the main a good conception, an excellent plan. But he should not have sent away his cavalry, there was his great blunder. Had he kept his cavalry with him, his plan would have been a very good one."

On the evening of the day Jackson was moved to a house adjoining Guiney's Station, David met Lachlan Murrell and he and several others of Stuart's officers devoured a meal of rabbits Hal Perkins had shot, skinned and broiled over the coals of a campfire.

"Any news from General Jackson?" Lachlan inquired, handing David a rabbit leg.

"Not since morning."

"What do you think of his chances?"

"The amputation is healing well, but I don't like the pneumonia. How about the situation in the field?"

"Stoneman's Federal cavalry is still doing some skirmishing along the south bank of the Rappahannock, but Hooker's main body is crossing the river to the protection of the north bank and that means the fighting is pretty well over. Actually, Stoneman's operation is mainly designed to cover Hooker's retreat."

"Stonewall Jackson won another battle," said David. "But this time the Stonewall Brigade had more casualties than they've ever had before—493 men, including all of its principal officers. The entire brigade isn't as big as a full-sized regiment now."

"Will they stay together if Jackson isn't able to take command again?"

"If General Lee will let them."

"That organization's too famous and has too much spunk for anyone to destroy it, even if Jackson is out of action for the duration," said Lachlan. "They're behind those earthworks at Chancellor House now and, if the Federals can muster enough men for a counterattack, the Stonewall Brigade is going to be right in the forefront of the action again."

Lachlan got to his feet wearily and tossed away the

bone from which he had been gnawing the last bits of boiled meat. "I'd better be moving. The way this thing is going, I should be able to cross over into Pennsylvania in a few more days and by the time Araminta will probably have some information for us on what's happening among the enemy since 'Fighting Joe' got himself slapped down."

"I still wish she didn't take such chances."

"She's a Cherokee, and Cherokee women have always followed their men into battle, even fighting beside them when the going got rough."

"Let me know if you hear anything from her."

"I'll do that. Where will you be?"

"Up front with the troops, until Hunter McGuire is able to leave General Jackson. Take care of yourself, Lachlan."

"I'm an Indian, remember? We can run rings around you white men without your even knowing we're there."

On May 7, with Hooker's shattered army now safely across the Rappahannock, the much shrunken Stonewall Brigade was pulled back to its old campground at Hamilton's Crossing. Only vague reports had reached him lately about Jackson's condition, so David decided to ride to Guiney's Station and find out for himself. One look at Dr. Hunter McGuire's face when he came into the small building which had been taken over as a private hospital for Jackson, told him all was not well.

"I was hoping he would pass a crisis but this doesn't behave like classical lobar pneumonia," said the other doctor. "It's already spread to another part of the right lung."

Jackson was conscious and recognized David, but the burning light in his eyes indicated that the fever in his body was busy destroying his reserves of strength. At times, too, his mind wandered and he would suddenly become excited, as he relived in delirium some of the climactic moments of his major battles.

David's examination confirmed McGuire's belief that the inflammation in Jackson's lung had spread to another lobe. All over one side of the chest now, the breath sounds had the whistling in-and-out character that told of an organ almost solidified by inflammation. Rarely, in David's experience, had a patient recovered from such extensive involvement of the lung, even if he had not already undergone the blood loss and shock that went with the wound and the amputation.

That afternoon, a strong mustard plaster was applied to the right side of Jackson's chest, at the suggestion of one of a half dozen civilian doctors who had been called into consultation. It was hoped to achieve the counter irritation of a blister that was considered a benefit in cases where internal organs were inflamed and it did seem to help awhile. But on the morning of May 9, Jackson opened his eyes during the rather lengthy examination by several of the consultants and spoke rationally for the first time in several hours.

"I see from the number of physicians that my condition is dangerous," he said. "But I thank God, if it is His will, that I am ready to go."

David had to return to his post with the troops that afternoon to report on Jackson's condition to General Jeb Stuart, now in command of the II Corps. He rode by General Lee's headquarters, accompanied by Jackson's personal chaplain, Reverend Lacy. They found Lee much concerned at their report that Jackson appeared to be dying.

"God will not take him from us now that we need him so much," said Lee brokenly. "When you return, Mr. Lacy, I trust you will find him better. And when a suitable occasion offers, please give him my love and tell him that I wrestled in prayer for him last night, as I never prayed, I believe, for myself."

Lee turned his head quickly, but not before they saw the tears in his eyes. And when he spoke again, it was to order a religious service held throughout the army the next day and Sunday to pray for Jackson's recovery.

"I will hold the service myself, General," Lacy promised. "And we will all pray for our friend."

By Sunday afternoon, however, word came to the Stonewall Brigade, in camp at Hamilton's Crossing, that their beloved commander was dead.

353

"Let us cross over the river and rest under the shade of the trees," had been Jackson's last words, it was announced.

The men of the brigade had crossed many a river at Jackson's orders and many had crossed that same last river before him while obeying his commands. But until the time came for another battle, the all but shattered remains of the noble company of tattered and weary veterans who had borne the name of Stonewall with their commander, must go on fighting.

Jackson was buried at his beloved Lexington with full military honors, after lying in state overnight in the lecture room where so many young officers-to-be had laughed at him behind his back, calling him "Old Jack" or "Tom Fool." No one laughed that day.

Standing bareheaded in the cemetery at Lexington, David and Lachlan—as former cadets under Jackson they had been allowed to accompany the body, although the rest of the Stonewall Brigade, over their considerable objection, had been held at the battlefront against an attempt by Federal forces to recoup some of their staggering losses by a fresh attack—watched the cadet regiment march with the coffin in the formal military parade. The crash of rifles from the Guard of Honor and the high sweet notes of the bugler blowing the final requiem for the Confederacy's then most famous general were something they knew they would never forget.

"What do you suppose comes next?" David asked Lachlan as they were riding back to Richmond on the train that had brought Jackson's body to Lexington.

"Old Jack always wanted to lead an invasion deep into Pennsylvania," said the Cherokee officer. "He and Lee tried once and failed—at Antietam. But with Hooker's forces cut up the way they were at Chancellorsville, this might be the time. I wonder if Lee will dare to try it."

"Now, if ever, is the time," said David. "We should know soon."

The final tribute to the memory of General Stonewall Jackson came in a Special Order for the 1st Brigade of his old division, also called the Stonewall, in the Army of Northern Virginia, which read:

Special Orders
No. 129
XVIII

The following resolution has been submitted to the Secretary of War from the officers and soldiers of the brigade formerly commanded by Lieutenant General Thomas J. Jackson:

> Resolved, that in accordance with General Jackson's wish, and the desire to honor its first great commander, the Secretary of War is requested to order that it be known and designated as the "Stonewall Brigade" and that in thus formally adopting a title which is inseparably connected with his name and fame, we will strive to render ourselves more worthy of it by emulating his virtues and, like him, devote all our energies to the great work before us of securing to our beloved Country the blessing of peace and independence.

The Department cheerfully acquiesces in the wish thus expressed, and directs that the brigade referred to be hereafter designated the "Stonewall Brigade." It commends the spirit which prompts the request, and trusts that the zeal and devotion, the patience and the courage of the fallen hero, whose name and title his earlier companions in arms desire so appropriately to honor and preserve, may attend and animate not only the "Stonewall Brigade," but each brigade and every soldier in the armies of the South, now struggling to drive back from their border an implacable and barbarous invader.

By Command of the Secretary of War

John O. Rivers
Assistant Adjt.-General, C.S.A.

BOOK SEVEN

Gettysburg

I

On June 11, 1863, David Preston stood beside the wagons of the 1st Field Hospital of the II Corps, Army of Northern Virginia, and watched the men of the Stonewall Brigade file through Chester Gap in the Blue Ridge Mountains. About twenty-five miles southeast of Winchester, Virginia, the gap was at an elevation of slightly over two thousand feet and familiar ground to both David and the brigade.

Some fourteen hundred strong, the famous unit was part of what was known as the Stonewall Division, under the command of General Edward "Old Allegheny" Johnson, whose wound David had treated a year before at the Battle of McDowell. Some ten miles away, almost directly westward, was Front Royal and a little beyond it, the Valley Turnpike, over which the Stonewall Brigade had traveled so many times during the climactic summer of 1862 in Jackson's whirlwind series of campaigns.

The men making up the brigade were a breed unto themselves and already a legend in their own time; lanky, sunburned, jaws distended almost to a man by cuds of chewing tobacco, largely filched from tobacco packhouses along the road or captured from the enemy; their uniforms consisted for the most part of bleached blue trousers stripped from Yankee dead on the battlefields and

356

butternut shirts cut, sewed and dyed by loving hands at home.

Roughly half carried Enfield rifles, also captured from the enemy, along with a large supply of ammunition, while the others bore the less efficient Springfields, or the long-barreled muzzle-loaders with which a mountain man could "bark" a squirrel and tumble it dead from a limb without singeing its fur. Many were barefooted too, from the ever present lack of shoes.

Since the death of Stonewall Jackson a month ago, something of a lull had settled over the battlefields in northern Virginia blocking the important routes between the two capitals, Richmond and Washington. The lull could almost have seemed a tribute to the daring leader who had been cut down at Chancellorsville by his own men, but now the hiatus in active fighting was over, as Jackson would have wished.

Jackson's old II Corps was commanded by General Richard S. Ewell now, lately returned to active duty after a knee shattered by a minié at Second Manassas the year before cost him a lower leg. The corps, too, was glad to be returning to the Valley they loved, but it also had another distinction now, though not an advantage— of being the only unit in the army commanded by a general who had to be strapped to his saddle in order to ride a horse, usually traveled in a buggy, and was called Old Baldy.

A cheer came from the ragged line of men when they saw the fertile Shenandoah Valley before them, once again ripe with proof that, although the area had known little but death, pain and destruction these past two years, it still possessed the ability to renew itself each year with the coming of springtime.

"Hey, doc!" A tall man shouted from the line of marchers and David recognized Jed Burnet, the deserter who had taken his horse almost two years ago between Martinsburg and Harpers Ferry. "My foot's bleedin'. How 'bout findin' me some shoes?"

"General Milroy has eight thousand well-shod Yankees at Winchester, Jed. I'm sure you'll have a chance to get your own."

"Hope some of 'em's my size." Burnet's voice floated back as he marched on downhill. "I sure need 'em."

"There goes an example of the spirit of the South, Hal," David told the senior noncommissioned officer of the hospital unit, who was standing beside him. "That fellow deserted at Harpers Ferry two years ago and took my horse. Now he's back to help finish the war."

"And riding shank's mare like the rest of 'em, sir. If that Federal column at Winchester doesn't have plenty of medical supplies we're going to be in much the same fix."

Hal Perkins was only two years older than he'd been that day at Falling Waters, David thought, but at twenty-one, he was a soldier in every way. Even as the Stonewall Brigade had become a unit of veterans in the same period and heroes of the Confederacy twice over. Like theirs, too, Hal's body was strong, his jaw firm, his eyes direct and confident with the conviction of knowing his job and doing it well.

"One thing worries me, Major." Hal's voice broke into his thoughts. "It's five days already since we left the Rappahannock; but when General Jackson was leading us, we sometimes crossed a couple of mountains and fought two battles in less time."

"Winchester has to be taken again and General Ewell can't afford to go blundering in against it. Besides General Milroy is a capable officer."

"But one who learned to retreat at McDowell."

David nodded, remembering the night he and Lieutenant—now Captain—Kyd Douglas had stood on the hill and watched the campfires of the enemy in the valley below, only to find it empty of northern troops when the sun rose. His musing was interrupted when a tall man in dusty black civilian clothes pulled the mule he was riding to a stop and dismounted gingerly.

"Ed Mattox!" David cried. "What are you doing here?"

"I asked myself that question at the foot of the mountain and halfway up I asked the mule, but neither of us had the answer." Mattox shook hands with David and Hal, then started beating dust out of his clothing.

"Doing some more battlefield reporting?" David asked.

358

"I'm a full accredited war correspondent to the Second Corps, with credentials signed by Dick Ewell himself. Mind if I tag along with you the way I did before?"

"We're glad to have you," David assured him. "Maybe you know where we're going—after Winchester, of course."

From the pocket of his coat, Mattox took a rolled-up section of newspaper and gave it to David.

"Yesterday morning's Washington *National Intelligencer* says Lee is launching a lightning thrust into Maryland to scare Washington and take the pressure off Richmond."

"That makes sense."

"If it lulls Lincoln and Secretary of War Stanton into thinking so, yes. But if they had any idea how the defenses of Richmond were weakened to provide troops for this campaign, they'd think differently—and so, I suspect, would Jefferson Davis."

"Then this campaign really is more than a diversion to relieve Richmond?"

"The other two corps of the Army of Northern Virginia will be moving north, one after the other, in the next few days," said Mattox. "And Jeb Stuart's job is to guard the right flank and keep Lee informed as to the strength and location of the Yankee army that will be chasing us hell-for-leather, as soon as Joe Hooker realizes there's practically no army left between him and Richmond."

Hal Perkins whistled softly. "Somehow you don't think of General Robert E. Lee as a gambling man."

"Especially with such high stakes," said David. "But suppose Hooker decides to take Richmond?"

"It won't do him much good, with Lee holding Washington, Baltimore and Philadelphia by then, to say nothing of Harrisburg," said Mattox. "That's why I couldn't afford to let this one go by and not be with it."

"What's between us and Harrisburg right now besides Milroy and eight thousand men?" David asked.

"That about says it. If Hooker is fooled badly enough to go for Richmond, Jefferson Davis can skedaddle for Danville or Lynchburg, tearing up railroad tracks behind

359

him. And by the time Hooker discovers he's been fooled and turns around, Horace Greeley and the Peace Party will be raising such a stink, along with Congress, that Lincoln will have no choice except to give the South the negotiated peace that's all we ever wanted anyway, just to get Washington back."

"It's a daring plan," David agreed. "But then it was all that when Stonewall Jackson first described it to me one night in the Valley last year."

"It does have all the earmarks of a Jackson inspiration," Mattox conceded. "But I'd feel a lot better if Old Jack himself were up ahead there directing this campaign to seize Winchester."

II

And seize Winchester they did, just three days later.

On the second day of the attack the Stonewall Division found itself facing Federal General Robert H. Milroy's entire division retiring from Winchester toward Charles Town and Harpers Ferry. With the Stonewall Brigade in the van, shouting the rebel yell as they had with Jackson, the southern troops came upon Federal pickets and, engaging the enemy almost hand to hand, itself delivered the *coup de grâce*, so to speak, to an entire Federal division. Only General Milroy and about three hundred cavalry managed to escape the trap, leaving more than three thousand of the enemy as prisoners or casualties, along with large mounts of badly needed supplies.

As the jubilant Confederate column swung into the main street of Winchester, they were greeted by a large portion of the population singing the "Bonnie Blue Flag," to which the Stonewall Brigade happily added the words of an old Negro spiritual, "All God's Chillun Got Shoes."

The next morning the II Corps, with one-legged General Richard Ewell riding in a buggy at its head, moved northward along the pike to cross the Potomac at Shepherdstown and march on to Hagerstown the next day. There they met a mixed reception, but one burly Irishman in the 33d Virginia expressed the feelings of the marching soldiers in answer to a remark about their uniforms from a woman observer along the way.

"Bejabbers, lady!" he shouted. "We always put on our dirty clothes when we go hog killing."

Plodding onward in the June heat through fertile farmlands where cherry trees were heavy with ripe fruit —but only for a few moments after the lead columns reached them—the long gray lines camped overnight on their old battlefield at Antietam. Crossing the border into Pennsylvania the next day, they pushed on toward Chambersburg through the fertile Cumberland Valley, farther west and north than any major southern army had yet infiltrated.

On strict orders from General Lee, the invaders refrained from pillaging the farms where grain and potatoes were stored, hoping to strengthen the pro-Confederate sentiment supposed to be rife here in Maryland and Pennsylvania. Whatever rations they needed were scrupulously purchased by supply officers with Confederate money, which the thrifty Pennsylvania Dutch farmers accepted, although with open contempt for its value.

On June 27, General Robert E. Rodes's division of Ewell's II Corps, including the Stonewall Brigade, reached Carlisle Barracks, some thirty miles north of Gettysburg. About the same time General Jubal A. "Old Jube" Early seized the city of York, thirty-five miles to the west, in an attempt to capture the vital bridge over the Susquehanna River between Wrightsville and Columbia. Always eager to be moving, Early was hoping to cross the river and, moving along the east bank for another thirty-odd miles, seize Harrisburg, the capital of Pennsylvania.

Meanwhile General Robert E. Lee had set up temporary headquarters at Chambersburg, about twenty-five miles west of Gettysburg. Although he could easily have taken Gettysburg, when a portion of Early's command passed through it on the way to York, Lee chose to concentrate his forces nearer the low foothills of the Appalachian Range and the passes through South Mountain, its eastern wall. There the advantage of the terrain was his in the major battle now beginning to shape up with General Joe Hooker and part of the Federal Army of

361

the Potomac reported to have crossed that river on June 26 in pursuit of the rapidly moving Army of Northern Virginia.

Plodding northward toward Chambersburg a few days behind Ewell's swift advance was the I Corps, under General James Longstreet, still rankling because Lee had selected the strategy of invading Pennsylvania instead of Longstreet's own preference, an expedition to aid General Braxton Bragg in the South and, hopefully, pull the teeth of Grant's several-pronged grasp on Vicksburg. Behind Longstreet was the III Corps, led by General A. P. Hill.

With the stage thus set and little resistance so far, Lee waited near the ramparts of South Mountain for news of Federal pursuit from the man whose task it was to guard the right flank of the two advancing Confederate columns and keep him informed of any threat. General J. E. B. Stuart, however, seemed to have vanished with his entire command and at that very moment seventeen days after Ewell's II Corps had started the march northward from Chester Gap on the crest of the Blue Ridge, the cavalrymen of Stuart's command were gorging themselves on the contents of a Yankee supply train of a hundred and twenty-five wagons captured almost without a shot at Rockville, Maryland, nearly a hundred miles to the southeast. And completely out of touch with either Lee or a pursuing Federal force quickly thrown across the Potomac to counter the southern advance.

During those seventeen crucial days, Stuart had fought one bloody, but largely indecisive, battle at Brandy Station on the Orange and Alexandria Railroad near Culpeper on June 9, when his troops, resting after a flamboyant parade, review and formal ball, had been caught napping. Expected by Lee to be on the right flank of Ewell's II corps by June 21 or 25, Stuart had allowed a large Federal army to be put together with frantic haste during those crucial seventeen days at the insistence of President Lincoln and Secretary Edwin M. Stanton, to protect Washington.

News of the pursuing Federal force under command of General George G. Meade—"Fighting Joe" Hooker having asked to be relieved after a quarrel over strategy —finally reached Lee from a spy named Harrison who had been sent into Washington to discover the Union plans. On the night of June 28, Harrison reported that the large Federal Army of the Potomac had now crossed that river and was in the neighborhood of Frederick, Maryland.

Since the new commanding general of the Federal Army of the Potomac appeared to be following a predictable course, Lee decided to take measures to keep the enemy at the maximum distance from his own lines of supply from the west and the south by way of the Cumberland and Shenandoah valleys. General A. P. Hill was therefore directed to take his corps east of the Appalachians with Longstreet to follow, while General George E. Pickett's division remained on guard at Chambersburg.

The final days of June were a period of considerable tension for Robert E. Lee, still anxiously awaiting some word from Stuart's usually reliable cavalry. But having gorged themselves on the captured supplies, Stuart's troopers were now moving slowly northward, followed by about four hundred prisoners, who had to be guarded.

On June 30 Stuart's cavalry finally crossed over into Pennsylvania, heading toward Hanover and the Baltimore-Gettysburg Turnpike. But more than a week had been wasted during which a massive Federal army had been allowed to progress toward an ultimate confrontation, largely unimpeded by the sort of slashing attack for which Jeb Stuart had become famous.

III

The Stonewall Division, with the Stonewall Brigade and the 1st Field Hospital, was in bivouac at Carlisle Barracks at the end of June, awaiting orders to join General Jubal Early's division in an attack on Harrisburg. Food was plentiful, thanks to cattle driven along behind them in the advance northward through southern Pennsylvania. But once started on a campaign, the brigade liked to fight and nobody was doing any of that at the moment.

Roughly 150 miles north of their old quarters on the south bank of the Rappahannock at Harrison's Landing, deep in enemy territory and a day's march from Lee's main forces, the brigade felt alone and uncertain. Past experience told them the enemy would soon strike in force, however, and orders finally came on July 1 for the Stonewall Division to start southeastward, apparently presaging a junction with Early for the expected attack on Harrisburg.

The line of march soon turned in a more southerly direction, however, and shortly they were passed by part of Early's force escorting a batch of Federal prisoners southward. Realizing now that Harrisburg was not to be attacked, the mood of the brigade quickly changed and with it the inevitable increase in stragglers, though, since they were deep in enemy territory, there was not much desertion.

One of those falling out along the march turned out to be Jed Burnet. The mountaineer had gotten himself a new pair of shoes but they hung around his neck by the strings now and he was limping. The cause, too, was easy to see, a blister the size of a silver dollar on his heel.

"Reckon I'd sure been better off if I'd stayed barefoot, doc," he said. "Kin you do anything for me?"

"I'll let the water out." David pricked the blister with a needle and extracted the fluid before binding a soothing salve over it.

"Sergeant Perkins will give you some alum to put in water tonight and soak your foot," he told Burnet.

"I guess it's my haid that needs to be soaked," said the mountaineer ruefully. "Times got real hard at home an', when I heered how our soldiers wuz eatin' high on the hog with what they took from the Yankees, I figgered I'd be better off in the army."

"Did you have any trouble getting back in?"

"Not a bit. Just spelled my name with two t's, high-falutin' like, and used Jim as a front handle."

"Didn't anybody in the Stonewall Brigade recognize you?"

"Shucks, doc! I guess you'n me'n the sergeant here are pretty near the only ones left of the old bunch, 'cept Colonel Stannard. An' he wouldn't rat on nobody from Botetourt or Rockbridge County."

"Are you going to stay in this time, Jed?"

"Guess so. The way people're talking these days, if the Yankees win, they're a'goin' to give all the land to the niggers and make white folks work for 'em. 'Tween that an' gettin' shot, I guess there ain't no difference."

"You don't really believe that, do you?"

"It's what's bein' told everywhere," said the mountaineer as he limped off, still carrying his shoes.

Watching the last members of the Stonewall Brigade swing by, David couldn't suppress a thrill of pride. They were ragged, their hair and beards were unkempt, they were dirty and their mustaches were stained with tobacco juice. Here and there a man clumped along, his tight or too loose shoes—it was as bad one way as the other—hanging by the strings from his neck or his shoulder as Jed Burnet's had been, while others trailed their rifles. But there was still a certain undefinable pride about them, a distinctive élan that had always marked Stonewall Jackson's men. And somewhere in the heaven he'd been so confident was his home, David was sure Old Jack himself was watching and approving.

Just before dark the Stonewall Division marched through Gettysburg, and went into bivouac about a mile southeast of the center of town at the foot of a commanding elevation called Culp's Hill. It was July 1, and Stuart's cavalry was reported to be still far to the southeast, completely out of touch with both the enemy and with General Robert E. Lee, who was trying to make the best of the situation, though blind to any knowledge of just what the Federal forces, thought to be near Taneytown, Maryland, about fourteen miles to the south —were doing.

The small college town of Gettysburg was said to number about twenty-four hundred people; its dingy white four-storied buildings, their rounded cupolas, and rows of chimney pots were set here in the hills a few miles east of the low mountain ranges of the Appalachian chain. Just beyond the southern edge of the town was a sharply rising elevation called Cemetery Hill. Site of the public cemetery for the town, it continued southward for about two miles as a rolling area called Cemetery Ridge, ending in two higher elevations called Little Round Top and Big Round Top, the latter being the highest elevation in the area. A short distance east of Cemetery Hill was the rolling wooded elevation called Culp's Hill, at the foot of which the Stonewall Division had made their camp for the night.

IV

"Where the hell have you been?" Joe Stannard asked when he limped into the bivouac area of the 1st Field Hospital shortly after they made camp. The former Lexington lawyer's uniform was dusty and his face was streaked with sweat.

"Coming to your rescue, like always," David told him. "Are you wounded?"

"Sprained my ankle climbing a hill north of town, at a place called Oak Ridge. We had a right smart little scrap up there this afternoon."

"I could still hear the firing when we came through Gettysburg," said David. "Let me take your shoe off so I can get a look at that ankle."

The sprain was rather severe and the ankle was already badly swollen and discolored. "We'll bed you down here and keep a wet dressing of Epsom salt solution on the ankle tonight to reduce the swelling," David told Stannard. "Want me to list you as a casualty and unfit for action?"

"Hell no! The real fighting will come tomorrow; this afternoon was what the Italians call antipasto."

"What happened?"

"The Yankees occupied a position on McPherson's

Ridge just northwest of the town. Part of Rodes's division from our forces got here from Carlisle about one o'clock—"

"They left during the night and the rest of us followed later."

"Rodes deployed his men along Oak Ridge, just northwest of Gettysburg, opposing General Abner Doubleday's Yankees. There was some pretty sharp fighting on Oak Ridge, but the Federals were reinforced from Meade's main body moving north from Taneytown, and Rodes was being pushed back. When the rest of us arrived from York, Old Jube used his artillery, threw his infantry in at the same time, and we rolled up that Federal force the way Old Jack did Banks in the Valley last spring. They broke and ran through Gettysburg to Cemetery Hill and for a little while it looked like a rout, but they managed to regroup. About that time, Old Baldy Ewell got shot in the leg—the wooden one."

"Thank God for that."

" 'You see how much better fixed for a fight I am than you are?' he told General John B. Gordon, who was riding with him. 'It don't hurt at all to be shot in a wooden leg!' "

"Unless you get some splinters in the other one—or in your tail."

"I guess it must have shaken Ewell up a little at that," said Stannard. "Sandie Pendleton told me just now that Lee sent an order to Ewell about three o'clock this afternoon to press on and take Cemetery Hill. But if Old Baldy got the order, he didn't put it into effect; the Federals are occupying that point now along with part of Cemetery Ridge and Culp's Hill right over your head. What it amounts to, according to Sandie Pendleton, is that the Yankees now hold a line about three miles long, shaped like a fishhook. Most of it's on high ground, too, which puts them in an excellent position."

"And us in a bad one."

"The worst." Joe Stannard took a small map from his pocket and spread it out so they could study it in the flickering light of Hal's cooking fire. "The Union right flank is anchored on Culp's Hill here and the left flank

367

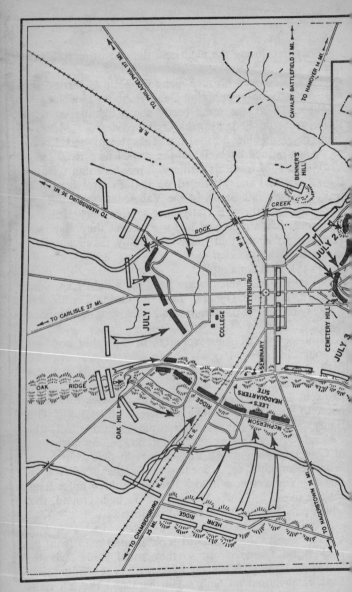

TO PHILADELPHIA 117 MI.

TO HARRISBURG 36 MI.

CAVALRY BATTLEFIELD 3 MI.

TO HANOVER 14 MI.

R. R.

BENNER'S HILL

CREEK

ROCK

W. M.

JULY 2

TO CARLISLE 27 MI.

JULY 1

COLLEGE

GETTYSBURG

CEMETERY HILL

JULY 3

OAK RIDGE

SEMINARY

OAK HILL

RIDGE

LEE'S HEADQUARTERS SITE

McPHERSON

R. R.

W. M.

TO CHAMBERSBURG 23 MI.

HERR RIDGE

TO HAGERSTOWN 36 MI.

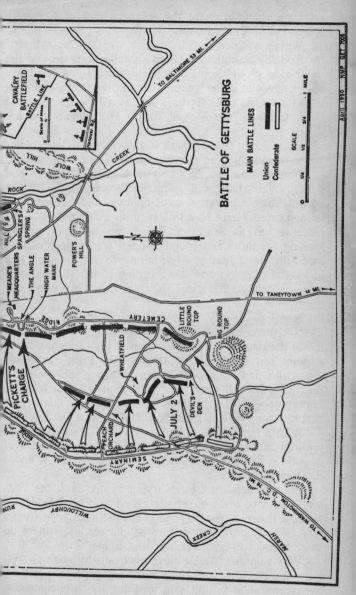

BATTLE OF GETTYSBURG

MAIN BATTLE LINES

Union
Confederate

SCALE

0   1/4   1/2   3/4   1   MILE

CAVALRY
BATTLEFIELD
BATTLE LINE

Scale of miles
0   W

Hanover Rd.

TO BALTIMORE 53 MI.

CREEK

WOLF
HILL

ROCK

HILL

SPANGLER'S
SPRING

POWER'S
HILL

N

TO TANEYTOWN 14 MI.

MEADE'S
HEADQUARTERS

THE ANGLE

HIGH WATER
MARK

RIDGE

CEMETERY

LITTLE ROUND
TOP

BIG ROUND
TOP

PICKETT'S
CHARGE

WHEATFIELD

RIDGE

SEMINARY

PEACH
ORCHARD

JULY 2

DEVIL'S
DEN

TO WASHINGTON, D.C. 76 MI.

WILLOUGHBY

RUN

MARSH

CREEK

APRIL 1956   N.M.P.   G.N.M.P.

on another elevation at the southern end of Cemetery Ridge called Little Round Top."

"What's our position?"

"Roughly a semicircle about six miles long around the outer side of the hook. Our right flank is on Seminary Ridge opposite Little Round Top and the left is deployed in the outskirts of Gettysburg and along the east bank of Rock Creek at the foot of Culp's Hill, where you are now."

"What I don't understand is how General Lee let his army get into such an unfavorable situation," said David.

"Don't blame Lee, he's only making the best of a bad bargain. Jeb Stuart still seems to be somewhere east of here fighting a private war of his own and Lee couldn't even be sure where Meade was, until Pettigrew's brigade came as far as Seminary Ridge day before yesterday looking for shoes and found Federal troops approaching from the east. Pettigrew withdrew to let General Lee know the situation and this morning Heth's division was sent to occupy Oak Ridge, just northwest of Gettysburg itself."

"Had Lee already decided to fight here?"

"Not then. But when Heth tangled with the Yankees it was decided for him, so Lee moved his headquarters to a point just north of the Hagerstown Pike." Stannard moved his finger across the map following the course of the ridge marked upon it. "What makes Gettysburg so important is it's a junction town with ten converging roads; I suppose you could call it a natural battlefield."

"With a lot of hills to be stormed and the Federals on top of most of them from the look of things," said David doubtfully. "What do you think Old Jack would do under these circumstances?"

"Pretty much what Lee's trying to do, flank the Federals north of town on what's called McPherson's Ridge and cut them to pieces. Then catch the enemy on Cemetery Hill and crush him before he can get his artillery up there to rake us with canister and grape."

"Why wouldn't Meade move his troops through Gettysburg and out on the Carlisle Road to counterattack?"

"He could, if he felt safe in doing it," said Stannard.

"But with Culp's Hill in our possession, our artillery could keep Meade's batteries pinned down on Cemetery Hill."

"Then why aren't we on top of this elevation instead of down here at the bottom?"

Stannard shrugged. "Lee usually leaves details like that to his generals and Old Baldy Ewell's stump is paining him again. Maybe Lee wants this position held until A. P. Hill and Longstreet can get here with more strength tomorrow. Or again, he could be waiting for Jeb Stuart—who knows?"

"Have you had time to find out what happened today?"

"A lot of stories are going around, as usual. The gist of it all seems to be that both armies sort of stumbled into each other at Gettysburg. The Federals got here first, though, and chose the best spots, which gives Meade the advantage. And the worst part is, if Jeb Stuart had done what he was supposed to do, and if Longstreet wasn't miffed because Lee turned down his plan to strengthen our forces in eastern Tennessee so Grant couldn't tighten the screws on Vicksburg, we might have already won the battle for Pennsylvania."

"And maybe the war?"

"Who can tell? But at least we'd have had some chance. As it was, the Federal cavalry moving ahead of Meade's main force ran into General Heth's division advancing eastward from Cashtown early this morning. Instead of holding their ground and waiting for Lee to decide where he wanted the battle to be fought, our boys started fighting. And the result was that the Union commander grabbed as many of the heights as he could for his artillery. Now we'll have to fight it out with most of the advantages—besides numbers—with the Yankees."

"So what's the battle plan?"

"Longstreet's supposed to lead the main attack on the Yankee left flank tomorrow morning, hoping to turn it and move northward along the Taneytown Road or the Baltimore Pike to cut the enemy off. Ewell and Early, which means us, are supposed to take care of the Federal

371

right and center to keep Meade from shifting troops toward his left flank to help stop Longstreet."

"It sounds like good strategy—at least on paper."

"I guess it is. But if Longstreet were Jackson, I'd expect part of his forces to engage in a holding operation somewhere in the neighborhood of Little Round Top, while he makes a wide flank march to the northeast to cut the Hanover Road and then head south."

"Like the Grand Flank March Old Jack made at Chancellorsville, when he tore through the Wilderness that afternoon and caught Hooker with his pants down?"

"Exactly."

"The last we heard, he was lobbing shells into Carlisle Barracks trying to scare the hell out of a few Federal militia."

"More than a few—and with some cannon, too." Both men jumped to their feet as a voice from the shadows just outside the flickering flame cast by the burning pine knot. Stannard's hand reached for the pistol at his waist, but dropped when a familiar figure, saber and spurs jingling, broadbrimmed hat covered with dust, strode into the circle of light.

"Lachlan!" David cried. "Lachlan Murrell!"

"A helluva fine pair of soldiers you two are," said the Cherokee officer. "If I were still just a redskin, instead of an officer and a gentleman by act of Congress, I could have scalped you both."

Lachlan had never looked more completely exhausted or less immaculate. Lines of weariness were etched in the dark skin of his face, which was gaunt almost to emaciation, the cheekbones even more prominent than usual. And as he sank to a rock by the fire the only thing resembling Lachlan's normal mien was the merry light in the dark eyes.

"Speak of the devil!" Joe Stannard exclaimed. "Where did you come from, Major?"

"Carlisle Barracks—and riding like the devil himself was on my tail. Got any medicinal spirits around here, David? And a hunk of bread if nothing else? I haven't taken time to eat since early morning."

David called to Hal Perkins, who brought a fresh bottle of whiskey and a slab of bread and cold meat.

"I'd be happy to cook you some supper, Major Murrell," said Hal. "But we don't have anything else."

"What I need is whiskey, food and sleep—in that order," said the cavalry officer. "So if you want any questions answered before I start sleeping, gentlemen, you'd better ask them now."

"When is Stuart going to get here with his cavalry?" Joe Stannard asked.

"Tomorrow—with luck. That's what I rode from Carlisle to tell General Lee."

"What were you doing at Carlisle?" David asked. "We captured that whiskey you're drinking there several days ago."

Lachlan upended the bottle and drained it. "No wonder there wasn't any left for us."

"You still haven't answered my question," David reminded him.

"Or mine," said Stannard.

"I guess you could say Jeb made a little mistake of judgment," Lachlan admitted. "He figured if he could make enough noise nearer Washington and Baltimore, the Federals might split their forces."

"Makes sense," Stannard admitted. "But I hope Washington and Baltimore knew more about it than we did out here in Pennsylvania."

"They did. Newspapers in both towns were screaming for Hooker—"

"Meade's in charge now."

"I know—and not wanting to keep moving farther away from Washington into Pennsylvania may have been why Fighting Joe asked to be relieved of his command."

"He didn't do us any favor there," said Stannard. "From what I hear, Meade is as stubborn as Grant."

"Maybe." Lachlan stood up and stretched, yawning. "A couple of days ago Sergeant Walheim managed to tap in on the telegraph line between Gettysburg and Baltimore and we learned that elements of the Army of Northern Virginia were already at Carlisle and York, so Stuart figured that Lee had decided to flank Meade at

Gettysburg and cross the Susquehanna at Wrightsville."

"We'd have done it, too," said Stannard. "But the Yankees damaged the bridge as they retreated and there wasn't time to repair it before we were ordered back here to Gettysburg."

"We learned that at York and moved on to Carlisle," said Lachlan. "Stuart figured the thrust at Harrisburg might still be made through Carlisle, so we headed along the west bank of the Susquehanna, hoping to find a bridge we could hold until Lee's main body came up. Then when we got to Carlisle, it was obvious that Gettysburg is where the fighting's going to be, so I was sent to tell Lee Jeb will be here tomorrow."

"In time to turn the tide, do you think?" David asked.

"Who knows?" Lachlan said. "But if Old Jack were running this show, he'd be sneaking around between Big Round Top and a place called Devil's Den without Meade knowing he was there, until he could attack in both directions at the same time. Then he'd come charging up through the wheat fields and the peach orchard between Seminary and Cemetery ridges to clean the Yankees out before Meade's main force gets here from the south."

"Jackson wanted for so long to make this sort of an invasion into the heart of the North," said David. "Maybe his spirit will be looking over General Lee's shoulder."

V

When David woke up just before dawn, bacon was already frying over a small campfire and six eggs lay on a flat stone not far away, proving again Hal Perkin's ability to produce luxuries in the field, seemingly by magic. But when he glanced toward the cot where Lachlan Murrell had been sleeping, he found it deserted.

"Where's Major Murrell, Hal?"

"A courier from General Lee's headquarters stopped by about an hour ago on the way to deliver some orders to General Ewell, sir. When he said General Stuart was reported to be about five miles east of here, Major Murrell rode that way."

"Did the courier tell you anything else?"

"A little, sir." Hal brought David a tin plate with bacon, eggs, bread taken from a baker's shop in Gettysburg and a cup of strong coffee. "He was a master sergeant and pretty thirsty."

"So that's how you manage to know more about what's being discussed at the top than even division commanders do? No wonder this hospital uses more whiskey than any other one in the Army of Northern Virginia."

"Spirits have their uses, sir—sometimes more important ones than their medicinal value," said Hal with a smile. "The courier said General Ewell was supposed to seize Cemetery Hill and Culp's Hill yesterday afternoon right after General Rodes's and General Early's troops got to Gettysburg to support him. But General Ewell decided to wait for General Johnson to bring up the Stonewall Division, and, by the time we got there, he decided it was too late to take the hill."

"That isn't like Ewell."

"The latest word is that General Lee has ordered General Ewell to occupy Culp's Hill and Cemetery Hill the first thing this morning, when the main attack starts from the right side of our line. But General Ewell must be hesitating again, because the order to storm Culp's Hill hasn't come down from his headquarters yet."

Hal poured David another cup of coffee from the battered pot bubbling over the coals. "Last night you said you hoped General Jackson's spirit was watching over this invasion, sir. But from what I heard, that doesn't seem very likely."

"He certainly doesn't seem to be guiding Ewell."

"Or General Longstreet either. They say he's been against this invasion from the start."

"How did you learn that, Hal?"

"The courier said General Lee and General Longstreet were arguing last night. General Lee said if the enemy is on Seminary Hill this morning they must be attacked, but General Longstreet insisted that if the Yankees are here, it's most likely because they want us to attack— which he claims would be reason enough not to do it."

David suddenly discovered that he had lost most of his

375

appetite for breakfast. It was no secret that, following the death of Jackson, Longstreet had come to consider himself the equal of Lee—and with some reason, it could be admitted. While Longstreet had been very busy fighting the first two years of the war, Lee had been largely a bystander, as military adviser to Jefferson Davis in Richmond or even farther away, in Western Virginia. Only with the Seven Days Battle around Richmond and the subsequent clash at Chancellorsville had Lee taken full command in northern Virginia.

And now, with Longstreet sulking and objecting to Lee's strategy, there was every chance that in the final contest the volatile South Carolinian might not attack with the boldness and dash needed to drive the Federals from the commanding positions they had occupied late the afternoon before, after almost being routed earlier by the Confederate forces.

"The courier said General Longstreet wants to wait 'til General Pickett's division gets here, so it looks like the Virginians may still have to settle this battle like we usually do." Hal took David's only partially emptied plate. "Come to think of it, sir, Jed Burnet may have been right about something he said at Chancellorsville."

"What was that?"

"The Yankees were giving us a bad time and one of the men in the Thirty-third said he'd like to send them to hell. But Jed said if the Yankees started to hell, Old Jack would be sure to outflank 'em and get there first with the Stonewall Brigade right behind him. But I guess they were both wrong, because, if I'm sure of anything, it's that the general is in heaven."

"Let's hope so," said David.

He couldn't keep a vivid picture from forming in his memory, however: three men blindfolded and standing before their own graves, while a stern figure in dingy gray sat ramrod-straight on Little Sorrel and watched the firing squad pull the triggers, sending them to their deaths, although the same voice that had condemned the men could have saved them. And now, with two generals quarreling over how a crucial battle would be fought, and another so unsure of himself that he seemed to have lost all of his effectiveness, many soldiers could die tomorrow because the men who led them failed to function with full efficiency.

VI

At the headquarters of the II Corps when he went there that morning for orders, David found a sulking Ewell and a fuming Early. The former was obviously not yet convinced that he should have attacked Culp's Hill the night before and still undecided about whether to order an assault this morning, probably, David surmised, from fear that the enemy was now on the height in force. Having saved the day yesterday afternoon with a slashing attack immediately upon his arrival from York, Early was eager to get on with storming the hill. But since neither general seemed able to convince the other, the situation was very much of a standoff. While they debated, a tremendous cannonading broke out to the north.

"That would be Latimer's batteries on Benner's Hill," said Early. "Give him a half hour to silence the Federal cannon on Cemetery Hill and Culp's Hill and we should be able to attack and turn the Yankee right before all of Meade's forces get here from Taneytown."

Ewell made no comment but stalked off, limping on his wooden leg.

"I'd better get back to my hospital," David told Early. "Where would you suggest that I set up, sir?"

"On the bank of Rock Creek between Benner's Hill and Culp's Hill is probably the best place." Old Jube laughed. "Dick Ewell's only got one leg to worry about, but I've got two. And if a Yankee minié hits me, I want somebody I can trust using the scalpel."

By the time David got to where Hal and the hospital unit were waiting, the cannonading to the north had reached a peak, obviously because Union batteries on Culp's and Cemetery Hill had answered. And when, several miles to the southwest, judging from the sound, the deep-throated muttering of additional cannon fire

377

began shortly, it appeared that Longstreet had finally launched the scheduled attack on the Union left in the area of the Round Tops.

The hospital had barely been set up on the bank of Rock Creek, under the protection of the Confederate battery on Benner's Hill and near a side road off the Baltimore Turnpike, when the first casualties began to arrive. They were largely limited to skirmishers wounded while feeling out the enemy, however, and later in the morning the firing from Benner's Hill died away, too, a sure sign that its batteries had been silenced by enemy fire.

All through the day and until late afternoon, David and his unit waited, but could learn almost nothing about what was happening except from the couriers who passed back and forth between the two widely separated flanks of the Confederate line south of Gettysburg. Then shortly before darkness fell, the sudden crackle of rifle fire from the slope of Culp's Hill warned that the attack in this area had finally gotten underway—almost twelve hours late.

Soon couriers reported fierce fighting to the southwest, where the Union main body, driving northward from Taneytown, had collided in force with Longstreet's troops. Which could only mean that a concerted attack by the southern army, scheduled to have been delivered in the morning, had been delayed until almost four o'clock in the afternoon, probably by Longstreet's hesitation at one end of the battle line plus Ewell's indecision at the other.

Shortly after the fighting began, casualties started arriving at the 1st Field Hospital and from then on David was able to follow the progress of the battle here on the left flank fairly closely. But by now it was a familiar tale of missed opportunities that had seemed to characterize the Gettysburg Campaign so far where the South was concerned.

When Ewell finally loosed the Stonewall Brigade and Stonewall Division under General Edward Johnson, with Jubal Early's division, against the heights above them, the southern troops fought as usual with great bravery. Johnson's forces occupied the crest of Culp's Hill after

378

considerable fighting but paused there, not realizing until hours later, when the opportunity had passed, that Union supply trains were clogging the Baltimore Turnpike, only a few hundred yards away in easy cannon range.

Attacking the eastern slope of Cemetery Hill, Early's men met very heavy resistance but, carrying out a slashing charge—in true Stonewall Jackson fashion—managed to reach the crest of the hill. Rodes's division was in Gettysburg itself within easy reach, but made no attempt whatever to buttress Early's attack by launching a thrust from the west. Thus the opportunity to turn the extreme right flank of Meade's army was lost and, hard pressed on Culp's Hill, the now thoroughly disgusted Old Jube finally retired from his original position around ten o'clock, leaving the vital position still in Federal hands. In the end, it was quite apparent that some six hours of heavy fighting and hundreds of casualties had actually accomplished nothing of any importance on the Confederate left.

Meanwhile, at the other end of the fishhook, on the Confederate right, Longstreet had failed to take Little Round Top or dislodge the Federals from their commanding position at the southern end of Cemetery Ridge. And thus the second day of heavy fighting at Gettysburg ended long after dark on a battlefield littered with dead, both gray and blue, but with all the important positions still held by the Federal army. Jeb Stuart's cavalry had arrived by noonday but too late, and too tired after a forced march from Carlisle Barracks, to change the outcome of the battle.

During the lull in the fighting on Culp's Hill after the Stonewall Division reached the top, David was able to pause long enough for a hunk of bread and a cup of coffee in the clearing beside Rock Creek where the hospital had been established. The lull was brief, however, and he'd barely finished the hasty meal when more litter bearers appeared. The third casualty was Jed Burnet.

"Guess I should've kept your horse and stayed in Botetourt, Dr. Preston," said Burnet as he was being shifted to the operating table in the hospital.

David didn't need to listen to the bubbling of air in and

out of the large wound in Burnet's chest wall to know the diagnosis—and the probable prognosis as well.

"Don't try to talk," he advised Jed. "I'm going to close that wound and I can't risk giving you chloroform."

"Don't have much feeling left anyway, but I could use another shot of whiskey."

Hal Perkins handed the mountaineer a half glass of straight whiskey and Burnet drank it. A spasm of coughing followed that left him gasping and the trickle of blood from the corner of his mouth told the surgeon without further examination that the lung itself had also been perforated. Working swiftly, David strapped a dressing of scorched linen tightly over the jagged wound where the projectile had passed between two ribs, tearing a hole in the muscles of the chest wall, the pleura lining the chest cavity, and the lung itself.

The sucking stopped when air was prevented from entering the chest through the wound, but there was no way of keeping it, or blood, from escaping through the torn lung into the chest cavity. And as pressure built up in Jed's chest, it would squeeze the spongy organ, decreasing the amount of lung tissue left for breathing.

The only chance—and it was almost infinitesimal—was that Burnet might be able to live with one lung. And even then, only if the blood loss and the shock occurring before the wounded man reached the hospital weren't too much for his tough, wiry body to withstand and sepsis did not follow. But here statistics were all against survival.

"I've always said you brought me good luck, ever since the day I took your horse 'tween Harpers Ferry and Martinsburg, Major Preston|" Jed was able to speak more easily with the air no longer whistling in and out through the opening in his chest wall. "You saved me many a mile afoot on the way home that time; and now I find you here when I'm in trouble from a Yankee bullet."

"Better not waste your breath talking, Jed. Sergeant Perkins is going to give you a hypodermic injection to ease the pain and I want you to sleep."

"Whatever you say, doc. But I can't help thinkin', if we'd've took that hill last night afore the Yankees got

380

them cannon up there, none of this would've happened."

"You could be right." David turned toward another cot, but Jed Burnet's voice stopped him.

"Bein' as how you've allus been good luck for me, doc, I'd appreciate it if you wouldn't have me sent back to a hospital where some doctor that's not as smart as you is in charge. Long as you're close by, I feel a lot safer."

"I'm not planning on going anywhere, Jed."

"An', Major?"

"Yes."

"If I don't come through, promise that you'll see me planted proper. After all, us Botetourt men ought to stick together."

"I promise." The sudden lump in David's throat kept him from saying more.

Hal Perkins gave the wounded man an injection from their dwindling supply of morphine and David moved on to another cot to control a bleeding artery. But he couldn't help admitting to himself that Jed had spoken the truth about their position. And admitting it, he knew something of what fiery Jubal A. Early must have felt when a suddenly timid general named Ewell had failed to seize and hold the elevation of Culp's Hill the night before.

Ed Mattox had been helping out in the hospital part of the day but had climbed Culp's Hill with the attack that afternoon. The newspaperman returned to the hospital area as Jed Burnet was being brought in and heard the conversation between David and the wounded mountaineer.

"A friend?" he asked.

"You could say that. He took my horse when he deserted from Harpers Ferry a little over two years ago and I had to walk ten miles." David moved on to start splinting a broken leg, but Mattox followed.

"Doesn't sound like much of a friend," he observed.

"Jed Burnet's a Botetourt County man and proud of it, Ed. The same way the Stonewall Brigade has always been proud of being southwest Virginians. In a way you could say he represents the brigade," he added, handing Mattox one end of the splint to hold.

381

"Not what's going to happen to it, I hope," said Mattox soberly.

"It's already happened several times. In the spring of 1861 at Harpers Ferry the First Brigade numbered over four thousand, the largest it's ever been. In every battle they've fought—and that's been practically all the major ones since the war began, from Manassas to Gettysburg—the Stonewall Brigade was in the forefront. It has lost more men per capita than any other unit."

"No argument about that."

"That's what the North has never been able to understand—how people who know by now they can't win keep on fighting and dying." David expertly finished bandaging the splint in place.

"You could say the whole South is one large Stonewall Brigade that doesn't know when it's licked," Mattox agreed. "After every engagement only a few are left, but each time a large percentage of volunteers, even conscripts, choose the brigade over any other unit, so the strength gets built up again."

"But with the final total always less than the time before. I guess that's the way the whole war will go, until hardly anybody's left. Did you get to General Lee's headquarters tonight?"

"For what it's worth, Lee's trying to decide whether to take the big gamble tomorrow and see if he can split Meade's army right down the middle."

"Any idea what the decision will be?"

Mattox shook his head. "I suspect only General Lee knows that, so let's get some sleep."

David was sure *he* knew, however, when just after dawn the next morning a courier arrived from Lee's headquarters instructing him to move the 1st Field Hospital to a position near Lee's new headquarters almost in the shadow of the Lutheran Seminary on Seminary Hill.

VII

At midmorning the 1st Field Hospital unit, carrying their wounded, including the steadily weakening Jed

Burnet, passed through the town of Gettysburg, and reached the position to which David had been directed. A little over a mile to the rear of Lee's headquarters at a point where the Hagerstown Turnpike crossed a narrow stream called Willoughby Run, it was in an ideal location for casualties to reach it from any part of the Confederate right, with a clear route for evacuation by way of Hagerstown, if that became necessary.

In Gettysburg David had learned that Jeb Stuart's cavalry had ridden through earlier in the day, going east with the probable intention of trying to turn the Federal right flank and thus take some of the pressure off the Confederate troops on the left, where the fighting had developed into a stalemate the previous day.

All about him now brigade after brigade was moving into position along Seminary Ridge. Their bayonets gleaming, the grim-faced men were ready for what was obviously going to be the last-ditch attack at the center of the Federal line from a half to two thirds of a mile away on the heights of Cemetery Ridge. Leaving Hal and the medical troops to set up the hospital tentage, David ate a hasty noonday meal, then crossed the rolling terrain between Willoughby Run and the top of Seminary Ridge, from which vantage point, the whole battlefield lay in a panorama before him.

As Joe Stannard had said, the Union position was indeed that of a fishhook, with the shank reaching southward along Cemetery Ridge as far as Little Round Top, where Longstreet's forces had been repulsed the afternoon before. The curve of the hook extended just south of Gettysburg itself to Cemetery Hill, while the barb was represented by Culp's Hill, scene of yesterday's fruitless attack by Old Allegheny Johnson with the Stonewall Division and the Stonewall Brigade.

Seeing an officer standing on a higher level studying with his glasses the effects of the artillery duel that continued between Confederate batteries on Seminary Ridge and Union guns on the heights of Cemetery Ridge to the east, David climbed up to where he stood. He was surprised to recognize former Captain—now Colonel—E. P. Alexander, the companion with whom he had shared the much higher elevation of a signal tower, not needed now, a little more than two years earlier at the start of the Battle of Bull Run, also often called First Manassas.

"This is indeed a surprise, Major Preston," said the other officer as they shook hands. "I thought the Second Corps was at the left end of the line."

"My hospital unit was there until a few hours ago. General Lee ordered us to set up near where the Hagerstown Pike crosses Willoughby Run."

"An excellent location. You're sure to be needed, too, once the main attack is launched north of that peach orchard you can see over there."

"Surely not a charge across the lowlands—right into the face of the enemy?" David exclaimed.

"Longstreet asked the same question a few hours ago. But General Lee believes only a direct charge has any chance of breaking the enemy lines and throwing them out of the strong positions they now hold east of here." Alexander raised his glasses and studied the area for a moment, then lowered them. "You were with Stonewall Jackson for quite a while, weren't you?"

"Two years—until his death."

"Isn't this the sort of a forthright attack Jackson would launch?"

"Against a commanding position with artillery?" David shook his head. "Jackson's way would have been to swing around the enemy's left flank yesterday or the day before and attack while Meade's main force was still moving north from Taneytown."

"General Lee expected just that to be done yesterday, but, when you look back over the past few days, it's apparent that not many things have been done the way Lee planned them. That's water down the drain, though; the way he sees it now, his only chance to win at Gettysburg is to split the enemy down the middle by cutting the long shank of the fishhook in two."

"It's still a gamble," David insisted. "And a long shot at that."

"Their fire seems to be slackening." Alexander suddenly lifted his binoculars and swung them toward the opposite ridge, from which the enemy artillery barrage had been coming, but lowered the glasses after only a brief study.

"I'm going to send a message to General Pickett," he said, his voice suddenly taut, as he picked up his signal flags.

Listening to the enemy artillery, David was not at all certain their fire had actually begun to wane, but knowing Alexander was an artilleryman, he didn't voice his doubts. Seconds later a signal flag appeared at a point where Seminary Ridge angled slightly eastward.

"Message received," said Alexander. "I hope that charge begins soon: my battery is getting low on ammunition. If you'll excuse me, Major, I'll check the elevation of my guns."

"I'll stay here awhile," said David. "The hospital won't start receiving casualties until after the engagement really begins."

For almost half an hour there was no change in the situation, the artillery barrage continuing intermittently on both sides. Then the cloud of smoke from bursting shells floating over the area between the two ridges was momentarily pushed aside by a wayward breeze.

David was able to distinguish long lines of men in gray moving forward now, bayonets gleaming whenever the sun broke through the haze of smoke to reach them. At that distance, the advancing troops looked like toy soldiers but, when he focused his glasses upon them, he could distinguish the tense faces of the men at the front of the charge. One minute the gray waves flowed over the fields like the rising tide surging across a beach, then the thunder of artillery reached David's ears and he suddenly understood the reason for what Colonel Alexander had taken to be a lessening of enemy fire.

Some of the Union artillerymen had apparently stopped firing briefly in order to swing their pieces to enfilade across the open field from Little Round Top to the south and Cemetery Ridge on the north. A withering cannon fire now poured across the flanks of the advancing Confederates and, like wheat before the blade of the reaper's scythe, the gray lines began to go down.

David's thrill of pride at seeing the gallant charge

across the largely open land changed suddenly to horror as a hail of death swept the field. For a moment the gray wave appeared to be smothered by the barrage of grape and shrapnel raining upon them. Then it's faltering elements rallied and joined to form a new, but much thinner, line had moved on into the very teeth of death.

So far the firing had mainly been from the Union artillery, but, as the attackers approached a stone wall buttressing the Union position, the enemy infantry behind it loosed volley after volley literally into their faces. Against such a wall of lead even the bravest human flesh could not hope to stand, yet a few men did reach the stone wall and even crossed it.

With his glasses, David saw the Confederate commander, cap borne high on the point of his sword as an impromptu battle flag, leap the barrier. He even fancied that he could read the officer's lips shouting, "Follow me," in the instant before he was cut down. Then, engulfed by a wave of Union infantry counterattacking, the remnant of the Confederate charge that had reached the stone wall was swallowed up.

Dead men, battle flags, weapons, all kinds of equipment littered the open field, where moments before brave men had launched an attack that was doomed even before it began by the human frailties of the leaders who had ordered it. And realizing that he had just witnessed one of the greatest human tragedies of the age, David turned and stumbled down the hillside toward the hospital, where shortly his own work would begin.

Laboring to repair the effects of the carnage of the afternoon, David Preston could think only of the welfare of the wounded men who poured into the hospital area from the battlefield. Casualties from General Jeb Stuart's troopers started arriving at the hospital shortly after dark, bringing word that a desperate attempt had been made by Stuart to turn the Union right and reduce the enemy force opposing Lee's gamble to break the Federal line. In an unsuccessful battle with opposing cavalry about three miles east of Gettysburg, however, Stuart's troopers had been forced to withdraw. But when David asked about Lachlan Murrell, none of the wounded men remembered seeing him during the fight.

The flow of casualties continued most of the night and David got no sleep. Working at the hospital throughout the next morning with his ears assailed by the moans of the wounded, for whom there was no more morphine and little whiskey left, he realized that a strange quiet had fallen over the battlefield apparently while both sides paused to lick their wounds and bury their dead. Jed Burnet had been losing ground steadily through the night but, to David's surprise, when he moved through the hospital area during the morning, Jed was still alive.

Shortly after noon John Imboden, now a brigadier general of cavalry in command of the considerably irregular band of horsemen recruited from the upper Valley around Lexington, rode into the hospital area and dismounted.

"You look like hell, David," he said. "How long has it been since you slept?"

"Who keeps track at a time like this? You work till you drop or your job is finished."

"Yours is about over, for the time being. General Lee has ordered a retreat and my job is to guard the hospital and supply trains. When can your wagons be ready to move?"

"Hal will get them loaded and lined up in an hour."

"He'd better start right away then, I hope to get the train as far south as Fairfield by dark."

"What about those too sick to be moved?"

"They'll have to be left behind." Imboden gave him a probing look. "Something wrong. What is it?"

"Remember Jed Burnet?"

"Can't say that I—Wait a minute. Wasn't that the name of the deserter who took your horse while we were still at Harpers Ferry two years ago?"

"Yes. He's dying—from a chest wound."

"Leave him behind then—for the Yankees to bury."

"Jed was wounded day before yesterday and I was sure he wouldn't last twenty-four hours. But he's still alive."

"The Yankees will take care of him. They're not exactly savages."

"I promised to stay with him, John—until he's properly buried."

"A promise like that to a dying man means noth——" Imboden stopped suddenly. "But it does to you, doesn't it?"

David nodded without speaking.

"Mind telling me why?"

"Jed said it: We Botetourt men have got to stay together."

"Of all the quixotic—" Imboden shook his head. "But if I were in Burnet's place—and I may be before this is over—I'd want you to do the same. You know the exchange of prisoners has practically stopped, don't you?"

"Yes. But Jed would do the same for me. And so would you, John."

"It's good-by then. If Old Jack were here, he'd know just the verse of Scripture to fit the occasion but only one comes to mind right now—I hope I can get it right: 'Greater love hath no man than this, that a man lay down his life for his friends.' "

"I'm not figuring on getting shot, John." David managed a smile. "After all I *am* a doctor."

"And a damn good one," said Imboden huskily. "Take care of yourself; I'm counting on your being back in God's country when the war's over. After four years of this, I want to be sure of having a good doctor looking after me in my old age."

As he was gathering the reins of his horse preparatory to mounting, Imboden turned back to David. "By the way, I've got a new second-in-command. Your friend Lachlan Murrell had a hell of a row with Jeb Stuart over the mess Stuart's made of this campaign and, instead of having him court-martialed, Stuart transferred him to my command."

"Thank God for that," said David fervently. "I was afraid that crazy redskin might have gone and gotten himself killed."

The silence that had enveloped the battlefield since the firing stopped the afternoon before was like a funeral pall now. David felt very much alone as he moved about attending to the gravely wounded, both blue and gray, who had been left in his care. An hour ago Hal Perkins, objecting strongly to leaving him, had been ordered to join the retreating army with the rest of the hospital complement. The road to Hagerstown was the shortest and most direct way to the Potomac River crossing, and General Robert E. Lee must soon negotiate it or find his army destroyed.

Not much more than an hour later Jed Burnet was aroused from sleep by pain. "The fighting's over, ain't it, Major?" he asked.

"Yes, Jed. It ended yesterday afternoon."

"And we lost again?"

David nodded. "But the enemy lost, too—heavily."

The dying man managed a wry smile. "Looks like us Virginians ought to stay south of the Potomac; Yankee country ain't good for us."

Jed grimaced suddenly with pain.

"I'm sorry I don't have any more morphine or whiskey," David told him.

"Never mind, doc; my time's 'bout up anyway." His voice was little more than a whisper now. "When you get back to Botetourt, wish you'd tell my ole lady I fit a good fight."

"I'll do that."

"I've allus been proud of belongin' to the Stonewall Brigade. When they're plantin' me, could you ask 'em to fire a salute—even if it's only one gun?"

"I'll do my best," David assured the dying man.

"I kilt me a bunch of Yankees, but somehow it ain't as satisfying as I thought it'd be. I guess killing ain't the answer after all." The whisper trailed off and for a moment David thought the end for Jed Burnet had already come.

Then the faint whisper reached his ears again. "When I see Old Jack in heaven, I'll tell him he'd still be proud of the Stonewall Brigade. Good—" The whisper ended the faint movement of breathing and, when David picked up Jed Burnet's wrist, the fluttering beat of his pulse could be felt no more.

VIII

The sun was still an hour or more high over South Mountain when David reached the top of the low elevation from which he'd watched the gallant, but sadly futile charge of Pickett's division, it seemed now ages ago. The bodies of the fallen, most of them still unburied, lay almost in windrows, forming an oddly geometric pattern that somehow had a look of peace about it. He was carrying the body of Jed Burnet on his shoulder for, remembering the view of the battlefield from there as he had watched the final charge, it seemed a logical resting place for a veteran of the Stonewall Brigade.

The sight of a flock of buzzards soaring in the sky above yesterday's battlefield lent additional urgency to David's task as he deposited Jed's body, wrapped in a hospital sheet, on the ground beneath a tall pine and began to dig in a spot at the edge of the clearing overlooking the battlefield. The satisfaction of having found a place where he was certain a veteran of the Stonewall Brigade would be content to rest erased some of the exhaustion resulting from the climb to the top of the ridge bearing the weight of Jed Burnet's body. But he still had to stop and lean upon the shovel when an attack of vertigo from the sheer weariness of the past forty-eight hours seized him.

Half staggering as he threw out each shovelful of dirt, he wasn't conscious of the sound of horses' hooves and the creak of saddle leather until he looked up to see a beefy man in the uniform of a Union cavalry major sitting his mount a few yards away, with a cavalry pistol in his hand. Behind him were a sergeant and a trooper, both likewise mounted.

"You there, Johnny Reb!" the officer called. "What the hell do you think you're doing?"

"Burying a friend."

"Leave the carcass be; those buzzards up there will take care of him."

David did not stop digging, even when he heard the click of the pistol being cocked.

"Did you hear me, Rebel?" The officer shouted

angrily. "Drop that shovel or I'll put a bullet through you."

David leaned upon the shovel and looked up at the the redfaced officer. "I served under General Meade when I was a captain in the U. S. Army Medical Corps, Major," he said evenly. "I hardly believe he would approve of murdering an unarmed doctor."

"Is that your hospital we passed down beside the creek, Major?" The speaker was the Union sergeant.

"First Field Hospital, Second Corps, Army of Northern Virginia."

"What the hell difference does that make?" the cavalry major demanded, but his voice was losing some of its bluster.

"That's Stonewall Jackson's old outfit, Major Kirby," said the sergeant. "Jackson always ordered Confederate medical officers to give Federal casualties the same treatment as his own."

"If you looked, you saw some of your men in my hospital." David took up the shovel again but staggered, and the sergeant dismounted quickly.

"Sit over there under the tree and rest, Major," he said, taking the shovel. "You look like you need it."

David turned the shovel loose, conscious that, if he'd tried to dig another stroke, he would probably have fallen into the shallow grave.

"Why didn't you say you were a doctor?" The Union major's tone was less unpleasant now. "Who is it you're burying?"

"Private Jed Burnet, Stonewall Brigade."

"A private?" Kirby's tone echoed his disbelief.

"We came from the same county in southwest Virginia," David explained wearily.

Dismounting, the Union major walked over to where David was now slumped against the tree, pulled a flask from his hip pocket and handed it to him. "Take a swig of this, you look like you need it," he said. "My apologies for being rough with you just now, Major but your Jeb Stuart caught my squadron in a cross fire about three miles east of here yesterday and I lost half my men."

"I guess everybody lost." David accepted the flask and

391

took a long drink of the bottled-in-bond whiskey, a far cry from the sort of brew the southern forces were usually able to purchase for medicinal spirits.

The second trooper had dismounted now and was helping to dig the grave. This done, they deposited Jed Burnet's body in it.

"Could you grant me a request, Major Kirby?" David asked. "I promised Private Burnet to have a volley fired over his grave."

The Union sergeant didn't wait for the officer to answer.

"Seeing as how he was your friend, Major, maybe you'd like to say a few words, too, and throw in the first shovelful of dirt?"

"Just a volley would do. Jed would be mighty proud."

Silently the sergeant unholstered his pistol and handed it to David butt first. Getting to his feet he stood beside the grave and, lifting the weapon, fired once into the air. Then handing back the pistol, he pitched the first shovelful of dirt into the shallow grave.

"Would you like to leave some sort of a marker so he can be moved later on?" the Union officer asked while the two enlisted men were filling in the grave, but David shook his head.

"Jed Burnet was a mountain man, Major. I think he would rather remain here among the trees without being disturbed."

They watched while the enlisted men finished the burial and put a crude cross cut from pine boughs at its head.

"My thanks—and Jed's to all of you," said David when the task was finished. "Major Kirby, I am your pris——"

"Not quite." The voice was that of Lachlan Murrell, and David turned quickly to see his friend step from the underbrush around the burial site, a cocked cavalry pistol in his hand. At the same moment four gray-uniformed troopers from John Imboden's cavalry unit also appeared.

"It's time to go, David," said Lachlan.

"What the hell?" Major Kirby started to bluster but Lachlan waved his pistol at him and the objection died in the Union officer's throat.

"If you gentlemen will just drop your weapons, nobody will be harmed," he said. "We'll have to take your horses, too, I'm afraid. Dr. Preston needs a mount and we're somewhat short of remounts ourselves."

Lachlan nodded toward one of the Confederate troopers. "Get their weapons, corporal, and take the other two horses. Major Preston can ride the major's mount."

"How in the world—?" David found his voice at last but Lachlan shook his head.

"Explanations later, David," he said. "The road down there is swarming with Yankees."

"What are you going to do with us?" Kirby asked.

"I only came back for Major Preston," Lachlan assured him. "The rest of you can go as soon as we're out of range."

David mounted Major Kirby's horse and the Confederate party left immediately. When he started to speak, however, Lachlan put his finger to his lips and shook his head. By which he understood that, with the enemy all around them, it was best to be silent. Only a half hour later, when they had made a wide swing and finally reached the Hagerstown Turnpike, did his friend break the silence.

"You didn't think I was going to let you be captured, did you?" Lachlan demanded.

"But—"

"Just because you made an ill-advised promise to a man who once stole your horse didn't mean the South had to lose its finest surgeon. I was leading a troop of skirmishers watching for any sign that the Yankees are going to try blocking the passes into the Cumberland Valley and only saw John Imboden about an hour ago. When he told me you were staying behind, I called for volunteers to come back and get you—in bonds if necessary."

"Practically everybody volunteered, Major Preston," said the corporal who was leading the extra mounts. "So Major Murrell took four of us that were wounded back in Virginia and would've died 'cept for you."

"Thank you all," said David gratefully. "How is the retreat going?"

"Either Meade's afraid General Lee's got something up his sleeve or the Yankees took a lot more punishment in those days of fighting than we realized," said Lachlan. "So far, there's been almost no pursuit."

Darkness found David reunited with Hal Perkins and the rest of the complement of the 1st Field Hospital on the Fairfield Road southwest of Gettysburg, part of a seventeen-mile-long wagon train guarded by Imboden's cavalry. It was a joyous reunion but darkened by the knowledge that a perilous retreat to Virginia still lay ahead and that the most serious thrust yet made into the North itself had ended in defeat.

Still another old enemy, rain, harassed the long train as it crept southward, but with its customary tenacity, the southern army kept going. On July 6, the hospital and wagon train reached Williamsport on the Potomac, only to find the river swollen beyond fording. And, as if that were not bad enough, they found a copy of the New York *Times* for July 5, with the black banner headline: "GRANT TAKES VICKSBURG. TWENTY-NINE THOUSAND REBELS SUR-RENDER."

BOOK EIGHT

New Market

I

Only a highly optimistic people could have absorbed the twin disasters of Vicksburg's fall and the failure of the Gettysburg Campaign, almost on the same day, without considerable pain and despair—and the citizens of the Confederate States of America were far from optimistic in summer of 1863.

Both North and South alike had acclaimed the feat of General Robert E. Lee in executing a masterful retreat after the Gettysburg defeat. Union forces under Genaral George G. Meade had also been badly hurt in the battle. As a result, the Federal army was slow to pursue the Army of Northern Virginia in its crossing of the rain-swollen Potomac, protected by heroic work on the part of General John Imboden's cavalry and General Jeb Stuart's troopers, thereby softening somewhat the sting of Stuart's failures in the earlier part of the Gettysburg Campaign.

Briefly, following the return of the Confederate army to its old haunts in the northern part of the Shenandoah Valley, it had appeared that Meade would be able to deny Lee the passes through the Blue Ridge into the eastern Piedmont area. There massive Union forces were once again being concentrated on the old battlegrounds around Manassas, Chancellorsville and the Wilderness.

But a combination of errors by Meade's corps commanders finally let Lee slip through and form a new line along the Rapidan River at the headwater of the Rappahannock, re-establishing to a large degree the stalemate, as far as the North was concerned, in the intricate and prolonged contest for the southern capital.

In the South, Grant followed up the capture of Vicksburg with an attack on Chattanooga, Tennessee, late in September, only to suffer a rather humiliating defeat at Chickamauga Creek, a few miles southeast of that city. And, in yet another of many instances where families were split by conflicting loyalties, Abraham Lincoln mourned the death of his brother-in-law, Ben Hardin Helm, a Confederate brigadier general, in the same battle.

The last week of November, with General William Tecumseh Sherman as his strong right arm, Grant avenged the Federal defeat at Chickamauga, however, by trouncing General Braxton Bragg's Confederate army at Lookout Mountain and Missionary Ridge. Neutralizing Chattanooga allowed the Union armies to begin the advance toward Atlanta, Grant's next goal in his campaign to destroy the southern part of the Confederacy piecemeal.

Supplies of all kinds had been growing shorter and shorter in the Confederacy, particularly after England finally took a forthright stand in favor of neutrality. As a result, loans from that source, though often flowing promptly back to English merchants in trade through the daring of blockade runners, had largely dried up. Earlier in the war, the South had been able to obtain a considerable amount of supplies from thrifty Yankee merchants who sold to brokers in the neutral Mexican port of Matamoros, just south of the Texas line on the Gulf of Mexico. The sympathies of the Mexican government were with the Confederacy, so purchasing agents from the Confederate Army had been able to buy much of what they needed in Mexico, paying in southern cotton that shortly found its way to the looms of England, both Old and New. But now that traffic, too, had almost dried up because the Confederacy was desperately short of funds.

Although there was almost no lack of anything north

of the Mason-Dixon line because of the war, and despite the fact that the Union was obviously the winning side, all was not rosy there either. Conscription lists were growing longer as larger armies were needed for the expanding Federal campaigns. The resentment of men subject to conscription grew hotter all the while, too—and rightly so. The law had been so written that anyone could probably escape if he had money enough to hire a substitute— or pay $300 to be deferred until the next conscription, when the war might well be ended.

Because of inequities in the draft, riots occurred in almost every major northern city, the worst being in New York, where a group of angry men attacked a conscription office during a drawing, sacking it and then going on to hang a number of Negroes from lampposts along Fifth Avenue, on the theory that, slavery being the main issue, the blacks were to blame. Many people, too, resented President Lincoln's dictatorial suspension of the writ of *habeas corpus,* as well as the use of censorship by Secretary Stanton, to whom the President had given powers never before granted to a Secretary of War.

On November 19, a military cemetery was dedicated at Gettysburg with considerable ceremony, featuring an hour-long address by the most famous orator of the day Edward Everett. Almost as an afterthought, President Lincoln was invited to say a few words and gave a brief speech, which most of the hearers considered to be a feeble effort compared to the fluid oratory of Everett.

Weary of war and the heavy losses that seemed to turn every so-called victory into defeat, the people of the North could find little to praise in Lincoln's policies. And nowhere was this more true than in his insistence that black and white should be considered equal, even at the ballot box. Lincoln's political enemies confidently predicted that this one factor, more than anything else, would be responsible for his expected defeat in the 1864 election. And in a time of turmoil and despair, moderates on both sides were clamoring for a negotiated peace, with radicals of either extreme denouncing those wishing to end the war as traitors, while newspaper editorials in both the North and the South were busy attacking their Presidents.

With General George B. McClellan, nursing a bitter hatred of Lincoln because of his own failures, practically certain to be their nominee for President in 1864, the Democratic Party was already on the campaign trail. Leading the pack was former Congressman Clement L. Vallandigham, who had been convicted by a military court of opposing the war to "suppress an unlawful rebellion," preventing his possible election as governor of Ohio. Hating Lincoln even more than McClellan, Vallandigham expressed the sentiments of the anti-war party in the North in a ringing abjuration to:

Stop fighting. Make an armistice—no formal treaty. Withdraw your army from the seceded states. Reduce both armies to a fair and sufficient peace establishment. Declare absolute free trade between North and South. Buy and sell—Recall your fleets. Break up your blockade. Reduce your navy. Restore travel. Open up railroads. Re-establish the telegraph. Reunite your express companies. No more *Monitors* and ironclads, but set your friendly steamers and steamships once again in motion. Visit the North and West. Visit the South. Exchange newspapers. Migrate. Intermarry. Let slavery alone. Hold elections at the appointed times. Let us choose a new President in sixty-four.

No one, North or South, was more thoroughly sick of war than the Stonewall Brigade. Encamped on the Plank Road near Orange Court House, they were roughtly fifty miles east of their old stomping grounds in Elk Run Valley, and seventy-five miles north of Richmond. Tired of fighting and seeing their comrades die, sick at heart because of separation from their loved ones, most of the Stonewall Brigade endorsed the sentiments of one veteran soldier who wrote to his wife: "I think, if fighting will settle the matter, there has been enough now, and if fighting wouldn't settle it, there is no use of any more blood shed, for it is the general belief among the soldiers and in foreign countries that fighting can't settle it."

Caring for the troops, largely engaged in picket duty in

an area where they had fought even more times than in their beloved Shenandoah Valley, David Preston was once again stricken, as he had been each summer, with a severe attack of malaria. Delirious from the bone-wracking scourge and with quinine supplies nonexistent, as far as regular issue by Richmond was concerned, he might well have died had not Hal Perkins taken it upon himself to seek at least enough of the vital drug to save his patient.

With money furnished by Lachlan Murrell, who still managed to get funds from the sale of Cherokee cotton at Matamoros, Hal contacted a Marylander with whom he had dealt before. This thriving entrepreneur had built up a very lucrative trade buying various supplies sold to him at Baltimore by Union supply sergeants and transported on Chesapeake Bay oyster boats to the many landings downstream from Fredericksburg on the Rappahannock. From thence they were hauled overland to be sold to those in the southern armies fortunate enough to be able to afford them.

Treated with heroic doses of quinine, David recovered to where he was able to take the 1st Field Hospital with the Stonewall Brigade when Meade tried to turn the flank of the Army of Northern Virginia at Mine Run, a small tributary of the Rapidan River. In an engagement on November 26, 27 and 28, the hardy veterans of the South sent Meade's forces reeling back, ending the threat from the North for the winter.

As usual in the forefront of the fighting, where Lee mustered only 48,500 to Meade's 85,000, the Stonewall Brigade lost twenty killed, 124 wounded and ten missing. Any jubilation Lee's army might have felt at once again repelling a Union attack in their old battlegrounds northwest of Richmond in the eastern foothills of the Blue Ridge was immediately countered, however, by news from the South.

At almost the same moment when the Stonewall Brigade had been moving into the Rapidan breastworks preparatory to opposing the expected Federal attack at Mine Run, Federal forces under Grant and a leader whose star was rapidly rising in the North, General William Tecumseh Sherman, were seizing Lookout Mountain and Missionary Ridge. By outflanking Chattanooga, Sherman neutralized the effects of the Confederate victory at Chickamauga Creek, just south of that city, two months earlier. And by the time the weary Stonewall Brigade, badly battered, went into winter quarters once again near the Rapidan headwaters, Sherman was already moving southeast toward Atlanta, in the obvious hope of taking that vital city and cutting a major rail lifeline of the Confederacy.

Meanwhile, General James Longstreet, in a desperate attempt to foil Sherman and aid the embattled Braxton Bragg, had moved his corps southward to eastern Tennessee in one of the classic military movements by rail until that time. It was a maneuver Longstreet had been advocating since before the Gettysburg Campaign, but he failed to accomplish his purpose and was now under siege at Knoxville by a superior Federal force in Grant's campaign to clean the Confederate forces out of Tennessee and prepare for the major advance against Atlanta.

II

Christmas 1863, was a depressing season for David Preston, as it was for most of the Stonewall Brigade, tied down in winter quarters almost in sight of the enemy. He had not written to Araminta since the previous Christmas, when she had mentioned in a letter that she was being watched by the Pinkerton agents who served as Lincoln's Secret Service. But Lachlan was in occasional communication with her through their agent in Chambersburg, a Mrs. Ellen Porterfield, and had assured David that Araminta understood his not writing was prompted by the fear of his letters being captured and leading the Pinkertons even closer to making a charge of spying against her.

Letters from Araminta still came occasionally through Lachlan, however, since one of the tasks given Imboden's cavalry was that of watching the northern end of the Shenandoah Valley for any sign that a new campaign was getting underway to press up the Valley and divert some of the troops now opposing the annual southward thrust of the Federal Army of the Potomac toward Richmond.

It was Christmas Eve when Lachlan rode into the camp on the Rapidan and dismounted, turning his horse over to one of the hospital orderlies.

"I figured if anybody was magician enough to pull a Christmas dinner out of the hat, it would be Hal Perkins," he said. "Don't tell me I'm wrong."

"You're just in time, Major," said Hal. "My folks across the mountain sent me a wild turkey, along with some of the fixings. Sorry we won't have any cranberries; they only grow up North."

"I wish you'd told me; I'd have organized a little raid into some cranberry bogs." From his saddlebags the Cherokee officer took a carefully wrapped bottle. "But I took care of the spirits, anyway. That's fine French brandy, intended for the table of a Federal corps commander with the improbable American name of General Franz Sigel."

"How did you get it?" David asked.

"We made a little raid on Sigel's headquarters last week in the middle of the night. There's no funnier sight than a German general trying to buckle on his sword over his nightshirt."

"Does that mean more action in the Valley?" David asked as he ushered Lachlan into the log hut that had served him as winter quarters since the Battle of Mine Run a month before.

"We ride through the area about once a month," said Lachlan. "Haven't seen any concentration of the enemy yet, but it's bound to come when the weather warms up in the spring and Meade figures the odds are enough in his favor to make another move toward Richmond."

"Maybe we'll be going back to the Valley then."

"I doubt it. Grant's the only Yankee general who's having much success these days, so I think you're going to see more and more of the action confined to masses of troops aimed at one spot in the hope of overrunning inferior numbers."

401

"At whatever cost?"

"They've got the soldiers and the supplies for it. Any facilities for taking a bath around here?"

"The officers have taken over a tobacco barn down by the creek and put an open boiler over one of the flues so it can be fired from outside. We keep a fire going and the boiler filled but you'll have to carry in your own cold water from the creek."

"Sounds like heaven." Lachlan reached into the breast of his uniform tunic and took out a letter. "You can read this while I get my bath. Then we'll have some brandy before we sample Hal's cooking."

David didn't need to be told the source of the letter, just the sight of Araminta's familiar handwriting had been enough to set his pulse racing. When he opened the pages he could even fancy that a touch of her familiar scent still lingered upon them:

Philadelphia,
Dec. 15, 1863

My Own Dearest One,

I know you haven't written for fear of leading the Pinkerton agents who constantly watch us to me. But I couldn't let another Christmas go by without risking at least a brief note to tell you how much I love you and that I am only waiting for this terrible and senseless war to end to become your wife. Do I shock you by saying that? I know many in the South would consider me a traitor, but it should be apparent by now to everyone that all we can hope for is to make the cost to the Union so high that they will at last allow the South to go in peace.

Here in the North there is great dissatisfaction with Mr. Lincoln and his policies but I believe President Davis is just as stubborn in the South. Still, if Mr. Lincoln is defeated ten months from now, as many think he will be, something may be worked out to end the war. I hate not being able to tell you any good news but Uncle John is not doing well at all. The doctor we have now—he seems capable and was recommended by your friend Dr. Jesse Bayard—is following the treatment you prescribed for Uncle John. He has increased the dosage of the powdered leaves of digitalis and draws blood once a month to decrease the plethora. Did you know that Dr. Bayard is now an assistant surgeon general stationed in Washington? I met him only once, but he seems to be a kindly man and he is certainly grateful to you for sending him directly to Dr. McGuire after you captured him and his hospital at Manassas, so he could be exchanged promptly.

We will be going to Washington again, perhaps at the end of February. At least it will be a welcome change, even though whenever we are there, we're watched closely all the time. I write ahead for reservations each time we go and so far the manager of the National Hotel has been able to give us the same suite we occcupied when I first met you. It is not only comfortable, but just being there reminds me of the precious days we had together in Washington.

At least once each time we are in Washington I dine at Monsieur Cruchet's and he never fails to ask about you. Although I pretend complete ignorance each time of your whereabouts, I am sure Monsieur Cruchet, being a Frenchmand and romantic, can tell from the tone of my voice and the heightened color in my cheeks when you are mentioned, what it means to me even to hear your name spoken. With all of Mr. Lincoln's troubles these days, Uncle John plans to spend at least a month in Washington, perhaps longer, in order to remind the President of his promise that the Cherokee Nation will not be penalized after the war for their brief alliance with the Confederacy.

Darling, I could write all night but you would become tired of reading simply "I love you" over and over, so I had better close before I weary you. I know I am utterly shameless in thus revealing my feelings, when a young woman is supposed to keep even her betrothed in suspense about the degree of her affections. But I cannot where you are concerned; we have always been truthful with each other and I know we always will. You may not hear from me before another Christmas but each night I pray that, long before that time, I shall be in your arms.

Always your beloved,
Araminta

III

Ed Mattox, the reporter for the Richmond *Enquirer* who was now a full-time war correspondent and unofficial historian for the Stonewall Brigade, since his reporting of Jackson's whirlwind campaign in the summer of 1862 had helped make them famous, also appeared at the camp on Christmas Day. The lanky reporter claimed to be on a special assignment to write a story about the privations of the troops in the Rapidan earthworks. David suspected, however, that with Mattox being a bachelor the visit was mainly to enjoy the hospitality and companionship of his old battle companions. Everyone was glad to see him and the brandy Lachlan had brought was sampled well before Hal had dinner ready.

"Oyster stuffing!" Lachlan Burrell exclaimed with delight when Hal Perkins brought in the turkey, a somewhat spare bird, since food for both man and fowl was rather hard to come by that winter. "I thought the Yankees were occupying oyster-bearing territory."

"Never question Hal's magic," Ed Mattox warned. "Else the genie he keeps in an old whiskey bottle somewhere in one of the hospital wagons might refuse to cooperate."

"This genie is named Asa Blandings, Mr. Mattox," Hal confided. "He runs an oyster boat called the *Belle of Annapolis* between Baltimore and a place at the mouth of the Potomac called Mundy's Point. Coming south he carries supplies from Yankee quartermasters' warehouses and going north he takes on a few oysters, just to keep the Federal gunboats on the Potomac from suspecting him."

"Hal bought quinine from Asa Blandings when I was nearly dead with malaria last fall," said David. "It saved my life."

"And Cherokee cotton sold to Boston factories through the Mexican port of Matamoros paid for it," Lachlan added. "There's a story for you, Ed, but you'll have to wait awhile to write it."

"Like a lot of tales I'm going to write about the old brigade," Mattox agreed. "But right now I'm interested in this Shenandoah Valley turkey before us. Did it really come from your family, Hal?"

"All the way from Reliance, not far from Strasburg," said Hal. "And if it's as tough as the piece I sampled to see whether it was done, you'll swear it flew the whole distance."

Mattox had brought some excellent Havanas, a few of which still found their way into the Richmond salient from Union officers' supplies by way of the established route from Baltimore down the Patapsco River and Chesapeake Bay, ending up ashore at one of the many small landings along the Rappahannock. Sitting around after dinner in the comfortable cabin that was David's quarters and dispensary alike, while a heavy snowfall began to cover the ground outside with a mantle of white, the talk eventually came, as always, to the prosecution of the war.

"What's the reaction in Richmond to Lincoln's Proclamation of Amnesty and Reconstruction a couple of weeks ago at the opening of the Federal Congress, Ed?" Lachlan asked.

"About what you would expect. After all, it wasn't exactly a *carte blanche* invitation to the South to kiss and make up."

"That clause about denying the vote to those who resigned commissions in the Union army or navy to join the Confederate forces pretty much rules us out, Lachlan," David reminded the cavalry officer.

"Along with Jefferson Davis and a lot of former U.S. congressmen," said Mattox. "The main purpose of that proclamation, if you ask me, was to set things up so Lincoln can organize a new state whenever he wants to. All he has to do is arrange for ten per cent of those voting in the elections of 1860 in the South to ask for a new government under Union auspices, take the oath of allegiance and against slavery and come back into the United States before it's too late."

"That's like opening the door with one hand and shutting it with the other," said Lachlan.

"Just the same, it's going to create new border states, particularly in the Trans-Mississippi area," said Mattox.

"They're sure to vote for Lincoln in the 1864 election, too. And you can bet McClellan and the Democrats are fit to be tied."

"Are you saying we could probably get a better peace treaty now than in the end by accepting Lincoln's amnesty proclamation?"

"Lincoln's offer appears to be about the only settlement that would give the Confederacy a chance of ending the war before the South is destroyed and still escape being treated like a conquered nation," said Mattox. "But, if Thaddeus Stevens and a few more in the Federal Congress have their way whenever peace is finally signed, Lincoln's going to have a hard job keeping the faith represented by the offer. And if he's defeated, God only knows what the surrender terms will be—short of making us slaves to the North."

"As of this moment, we'd all be better off without Jefferson Davis and *with* Lincoln," said Lachlan. "But if a report of what I've said appears in the Richmond newspapers, Ed, I'll call you out with pistols at ten paces as a damned liar."

"What's the use of saying again what everybody knows but is afraid to speak aloud—except among friends?" said Mattox. "What say we turn in? I want to make an inspection of the Rapidan earthworks tomorrow."

"It's a good thing you brought your boots, Mr. Mattox," said Hal as he brought in a log for the fireplace. "There's already a couple of inches of snow outside and liable to be twice that by morning."

Hal's prediction proved true—with nearer six than four inches of snow. Not long after revellle and a breakfast of hardtack and bacon, the Stonewall Brigade and Stafford's Louisiana Brigade, who had been part of Stonewall Jackson's forces since the 1862 dash northward along the Valley Pike to seize Front Royal and Winchester, challenged a brigade of Georgians and another from North Carolina. When the Georgians demurred on the grounds that they were not familiar with snow fighting, Louisiana claimed a similar disability and the battle was soon joined.

The Georgians proved quick learners and the Louisianians were soon driven back by a barrage of snowballs

406

against the Stonewall Brigade, who were in reserve. At this point General Walker of the brigade entered the fight, however, to personally direct the turning back of a flank barrage of snowballs by the eager Georgians. Shouting their famous yell, the Stonewall Brigade then moved forward, molding and throwing almost in one motion.

The air was filled with snow, much of it centered upon the commander of the Stonewall Brigade, who for a while became a snowman. But once again the brigade had to turn back when some enterprising Georgians managed to conceal egg-sized stones inside the snowballs, turning them into near lethal weapons.

At this moment, however, the Louisianians, who were concealed in the woods, frantically molding ammunition, came pouring out with a barrage aimed at the Georgia brigade's flank, turning the tide and sending the enemy reeling back. Seizing this advantage, the Stonewall Brigade then poured on the fire, aided by their comrades from Louisiana. The Georgia-North Carolina forces were forced back in disorder and finally sent in headlong flight across the rolling Piedmont hills, practically hidden by the snowballs filling the air in pursuit, many containing rocks.

David was busy at the hospital for about an hour after the battle ended, patching up a few wounds made by the hidden stones. But there were no real casualties and the impromptu battle did much to buoy up the spirits of the somewhat downcast soldiers forced to spend Christmas in bivouac, instead of with relatives, often less than fifty miles away.

All in all the snowball fight was the most exciting event in the southern lines for weeks, until on February 8, the Stonewall Brigade and another unit were sent to oppose a small Yankee probe across the Rapidan. The attack, while not in force, was a sure indication that General George Meade had by no means forgotten about the sector. Nor the criticism that had been leveled at him for failing to stop General Lee from crossing the Potomac back in July and from negotiating the Blue Ridge passes into the Rapidan area shortly afterward. The small victory—seventeen enemy dead and forty-two prisoners—

was a tremendous tonic for the dispirited brigade, once again, as almost always, short on rations, equipment and ammunition.

There was no comfort for the South in general, however, from the knowledge that General Ulysses S. Grant, the Federal bulldog who had taken Vicksburg, Chattanooa, Knoxville and was now starting an advance toward Atlanta, had been called to Washington and placed in command of the entire Federal military establishment with the brand-new rank of lieutenant general.

IV

By mid-March no one could doubt any longer that General George Meade was preparing for one more massive Federal offensive through the Virginia Piedmont toward Richmond. With that news came rumors that a second army was being put together in what was now northern West Virginia by General Franz Sigel. Nor could anyone doubt that its purpose was to move up the Valley toward the important rail center of Staunton to hamper the supplying Lee's troops defending Richmond.

Since Lee could spare almost no one from the positions opposite the Federal lines north of the Rapidan, Lachlan Murrell and a small cavalry squadron were dispatched northwestward toward their old targets of Winchester and Martinsburg, with the twin purpose of discovering just how strong the new Federal army in the Valley was and tearing up as much railway trackage as they could to hamper any movement by the enemy.

The day after Lachlin left camp, John Imboden brought David a letter addressed to the Cherokee officer and bearing the familiar postmark of Chambersburg, Pennsylvania.

"I know Major Murrell has a correspondent in Chambersburg through whom he receives information, David," said Imboden. "And I also know some of it comes from your fiancée in Philadelphia. But he'll be gone about a week, so perhaps you should read it."

The letter was signed by Ellen Porterfield, whom David already knew to be Lachlan's contact in Chambersburg. The message was brief:

Dear Lachlan:

I am writing hurriedly in the knowledge that Pinkerton agents who have been watching the house lately plan to arrest me today or tomorrow. As you know, Araminta is in Washington at the National Hotel with John Ross. Yesterday one of our couriers was taken and I have no way of knowing whether or not the Pinkerton men will force the courier to reveal Araminta's connection with our work, which must obviously come to an end now. But I implore you to warn her somehow and, if humanly possible, arrange her escape from Washington before she can be arrested.

This will be farewell. I have no way of knowing what is ahead for me or for any of us. Save Araminta, if you can.

Yours in the Cause,
Ellen Porterfield.

David handed his old friend the letter and waited in silence while the cavalry general read it through. When Imboden handed it back his expression was troubled.

"We capture Washington newspapers regularly on our forays across the Rapidan to size up Meade's forces," he said. "Every issue speaks of stepped-up activities by the Pinkertons against southern sympathizers in the North, so your fiancée could be in grave danger, David."

"If that courier talks, she will no doubt be arrested. Besides, the last time I heard from her, she said the Pinkertons were always watching the Ross party, when they're in Washington."

"Even if she's arrested, she might be exchanged. We've caught a few Yankee agents, too."

"I can't take a chance on that, John. Lachlan's not available, so I'll have to go into Washington and try to bring her back across the lines."

"Lincoln's proclamation warned that there will be no amnesty for former officers of the U. S. Army or Navy. You won't be on a medical mission either, so you could be considered a spy, if you're caught."

"Araminta is more important to me than life itself,

409

John. You'd do the same if your wife were about to be arrested as a spy."

"I guess so. Got any idea how you'll do it?"

"When I almost died of malaria last summer, Hal Perkins bought quinine for me from an oyster boat owner who runs a regular stolen Union freight service from Baltimore to landings along the Rappahannock. He had to go back the same way and, if I pay him enough, he might take me."

"That could be the best route," Imboden agreed. "Even the Pinkertons would hardly be looking for a Confederate officer to be traveling from Baltimore to Washington."

But when David called Hal Perkins in, a snag developed.

"I could get you aboard the *Belle of Annapolis,* Major," said Hal. "Asa Blandings makes the run from Baltimore to Mundy's Point on the Bay near the mouths of the Potomac and Rappahannock twice a week and the supplies are brought overland on back roads by wagon. But Asa always has to have cash on the barrelhead—in U.S. currency."

"Looks like I'll have to send out a party to capture a Federal paymaster," said John Imboden. "That's the only way we can get U.S. money any more."

"And we don't have time for that." David turned to Hal Perkins. "This would seem to call for your own special brand of magic, Hal."

"That kind of magic is beyond my powers, sir," Hal admitted. "Major Murrell furnished the money to buy quinine for you."

"In U.S. currency?"

"Yes, sir. He said he gets money occasionally still from cotton sold through the blockade."

"Would you know whether Lachlan has received any money lately, John?" David asked.

The cavalryman shook his head. "We haven't had any mail for over a week."

"Then I'll have to search Lachlan's belongings. Maybe we can find some he has hidden away."

"I'll show you the cabin he uses when we're in bivouac," said Imboden. "And then look the other way."

Being part Indian, Lachlan knew how to hide things but David was desperate. With Hal Perkins' help, he finally found five hundred dollars in shiny new coins from the U.S. mint, hidden in an old boot Lachlan had left in a corner. The boot was crusted with mud, part of a pair Lachlan used when moving around the camp on foot, and he had apparently figured that a prowler would hardly look for money there.

"Are you going to request leave?" Imboden asked as David was stuffing the coins into a leather pouch Hal produced.

"No time. It would have to go through channels and Araminta could already be in prison before Old Jube put his stamp of approval on it—if he did at all when I told him what I have to do. I'll just have to go AWOL."

"I'll tell Sandie Pendleton privately what you're doing and have him put through an order assigning you to my command on temporary duty for a cavalry thrust to feel out the Federals north of the Rapidan," said Imboden. "In a week you ought to be back—"

"Or facing a Union firing squad." David's tone was grim. "If that happens, tell Lachlan to see that I'm taken back to Preston's Cove on the James after the war is over. The cove and the knoll I buried Jed Burnet under at Gettysburg are the only two places I've seen in this war where I'd want to rest."

"Don't you dare let the Yankees shoot you," Imboden warned. "Like I told you in Gettysburg, I want you back in Botetourt, where you can look after my health in my old age. Good-by, David. And good luck."

V

Two mornings later, asleep in a rude bunk amidst the rank smell of oysters as the *Belle of Annapolis,* a Chesapeake bugeye with tall raking masts, jib-headed canvas and the ability to sail, it was claimed by its admirers, "in a heavy dew," David was awakened by the sudden sound of a clap of thunder. He'd lain down in his clothes, an elegant claw-hammer with silken shirt and stock, doeskin

411

breeches and boots Lachlan Murrell had kept in his quarters for occasional romantic forays out of uniform. But when he came on deck, he saw that the sky above was clear, the stars shining brightly.

"What's going on?" he asked the shadowy figure of Asa Blandings hunched over the wheel.

"A Federal gunboat's chasin' us, Major," said the skipper. "As soon as I saw him about a half hour ago, I started heading ashore across the flats. These bugeyes draw a maximum of two feet: only way we can scrape over the grounds used by the hand-tongers and pick up enough oysters to make a livin'. Another thirty minutes and I'd have been in shallow water where he can't go, but the wind dropped and it looks like luck's against us."

"What does that mean?"

"Guess you'll have to wade ashore, Major."

"In freezing water? You're crazy!"

"Crazy maybe—for riskin' my neck helpin' the South. But not crazy enough to wind up in no Federal jail. If'n this guy ketches me, I'll say you come aboard to buy oysters down Reedsville way and held a gun to my head."

"But I'm unarmed."

"I've got a gun, Major. And when them Federals come aboard, it'll be in your hand. 'Course you'll be dead, so who'll know whose hand was holdin' the gun in the first place."

David was licked and knew it, but the prospect of wading the near freezing waters of the Chesapeake for at least half a mile with his clothes on wasn't very promising either. While he was debating, briefly, another shot from the one-pounder on the ghostly deck of the Union gunboat, now rapidly overtaking the bugeye, decided the issue when the cannonball thudded into the water a hundred feet astern.

"Over you go, Major," said Asa Blandings, and now David saw the pistol in the skipper's hand. "An' don't worry too much. The water's only about waist deep."

Blandings waved the barrel of the gun toward the shore, where a faint spot of brilliance possibly indicated the location of a human habitation. "That's Pete Wil-iams' dock and he ain't got no sympathy for Yankees neither. Pete's oysterin' but his missus'll see that you get o 'Napolis and the B&O. Just tell Hannah I had to ditch ou. I'll bring the *Belle* into the wind soon's you drop off o the Federals can see me heavin' to. But she'll drift a undred yards or so and them Yankees'll never see you."

David eased himself over the side of the boat; the gun-vales were no more than two feet above the water level o make it easier for the oystermen to lift their catch into he hold. In one instance, at least, Asa Blandings had een as true as his word. The water only came up to his rmpits and was bitterly cold, but he could wade and he et about doing it with alacrity.

By the time the Federal gunboat caught up with the ow hove-to *Belle of Annapolis,* David was halfway shore and warming up somewhat from the effort of vading along the often soft and muddy bottom. He was hankful that he'd kept on Lachlan's fine leather jack-oots, for clumps of oyster shell got in his way through he darkness-shrouded shallows, sometimes tripping him o he had to flounder for a footing in the shallow water efore he could move shoreward again.

Altogether David estimated, it took him an hour to each the rickety dock in front of Pete Williams' clap-oard house on a low elevation ashore and by that time light was already on in the kitchen. When he knocked n the door, too cold and tired to care whether he would nd a friendly welcome or a one-way ticket to a Federal ring squad, it was opened immediately by a tall woman ho reminded him somewhat of the Amazon leading the read riot in Richmond, it seemed now years ago.

"I had to wade ashore from the *Belle of Annapolis,*" e explained. "Asa Blandings said you would take me n."

"Come in before somebody sees you." Hannah Wil-iams took his elbow to help him over the doorsill and nto the warmth of the kitchen. "My! You look like a nuskrat after a storm."

"I won't argue with you there. But I've got to get to Vashington as soon as I can—"

"There's a train from Annapolis at two o'clock, Pete

413

will be shippin' oysters on it," said his hostess. "Get i
the other room and shed them clothes, then wrap your
self in a blanket and come back in here for some coffe
and hoecake. Sorry, but that's all I've got."

"It sounds like manna."

"What are you? A preacher?"

"A doctor," David corrected her as he started towar
the bedroom. "But I feel more like a patient, after a
hour in that cold water."

"We'll drive the chill out of your bones and I'll wash
your clothes and dry them," his hostess promised.

By the time he had peeled off his wet clothes an
wrapped himself in a warm blanket, breakfast was ready
The coffee was real, too, a far cry from the usual brew
southern troops got to drink.

"Pete'll be back with a load of oysters 'bout te
o'clock," his hostess told him. "You can ride into Annap
olis with him and take the train to Washington, if yo
insist on runnin' the risk."

"My fiancée's in danger there. I've got to get her bac
across the lines."

"Don't figure on goin' back the way you come, then
That Yankee gunboat out there's stoppin' oyster boat
every night, tryin' to shut off the flow of medicines an
the like to Richmond."

"We were able to buy quinine from Asa Blandings las
fall, when I almost died with malaria."

"You'll be lucky if you don't get it again," Hannah
Williams told him. "Nothin' like gettin' chilled the way
you were to bring on the ague again."

David had been thinking the same thing. "You don'
happen to have any quinine in the house, do you?" h
asked, but the Amazon shook her head.

"The Yankees have been shippin' it down South wher
Grant was fightin'. Asa must have got what he sold yo
from an army warehouse. Now, get in the other room an
take yourself a nap while I wash some of the mud ou
of them fine clothes of yours and dry 'em by the stove
If'n you get on the train in wet clothes, somebody
liable to wonder why."

Darkness had already fallen when David paid th

river of the hack that had brought him from the railroad tation in Washington to the back entrance of the Na-onal Hotel that faced on Sixth Street across from the lmost equally popular marble front of Brown's. Ara-inta had mentioned in her last letter that on his visits) Washington, John Ross was usually lucky enough to e able to rent the same suite where he had first met her. Ie had decided, therefore, to risk taking the back en-ance and going directly to the suite, rather than pass rough the usually crowded lobby.

The trip from Pete Williams' house on the shore of the -latively narrow Chesapeake Bay a few miles south of nnapolis, Maryland, had been uneventful. Hannah had stored Lachlan's fine clothes to something less than eir former splendor, but made them presentable never-eless. And Pete Williams had deposited him at the ation of the branch railway line connecting Washington d Annapolis.

No one had questioned him or demanded to see the apers, forged ones in the name of Preston Murrell used y Lachlan in his scouting expeditions into areas north the Potomac, that David had found in the clothes he as wearing. Everywhere along the railway line, however, had seen sidings jammed with freight cars bearing ilitary supplies and an occasional flatcar with heavy tillery from the extensive iron works at Baltimore, con-rming the general opinion that a major Union drive uthward was in the making.

The corridor on which the room he sought was located roved to be deserted when he opened the back-stairs e door and glanced down it. Stepping inside, he moved uickly along it and knocked on the door of the suite ohn Ross usually occupied. He had a prepared story of aving mistaken the floor where a friend he was seeking as located, in case the Ross party had not been able to et the same room, but it was Araminta who opened the oor.

"David!" she cried, and moved toward him, but he ushed her back into the room and shut the door before king her in his arms.

Their reunion was of necessity brief and, when he

explained quickly why she had to leave with him, she didn't argue but went to put a few things into a valise, the only luggage they would be able to carry. Meanwhile David went into John Ross's bedroom and greeted the Cherokee chieftain and his wife.

Ross, he saw at once, was definitely weaker than when he'd last seen him almost three years ago on the landing at Parkersburg. Mary Stapler Ross, never very robust, was more frail, too, than before, but the same resolute spirit showed in her eyes.

"Thank God you've come, David," said Ross. "Ever since the papers here carried the story of Ellen Porterfield's arrest day before yesterday, we've been worried that the Pinkerton agents would be troubling Araminta."

"Lachlan was away on an assignment in Martinsburg," David explained. "Mrs. Porterfield's letter to him was given to me and, as soon as I read it, I made arrangements to come to Washington."

"We tried to persuade Araminta to give up what she was doing when we were sent to Philadelphia," said Mary Ross. "But she felt that she had to help the Cause."

"Do you have a plan for getting out of Washington, David?" Ross asked.

"I came here from Annapolis by train without being questioned, but we can't take an oyster boat back to the Rappahannock the way I'd planned. Federal gunboats are stopping them all along the Chesapeake now, so our best bet seems to be to take the train from here to Relay House and connect with the main line of the B&O. Even though Martinsburg is now in West Virginia, I know people there who will find us transportation south. Fortunately I'm quite familiar with the back roads leading into Virginia."

"That sounds exciting!" Araminta had come into the room while he was talking, and her eyes were shining. "When do we leave?"

"I checked at the station when I arrived," said David. "There's a train for Relay House at eight o'clock that connects with the night train for Parkersburg on the B&O. I think we had better leave at once though."

"Don't worry about me," she assured her uncle and

416

unt as she kissed them good-bye. "As long as I'm with avid, you can be sure I'll be safe."

"Where will you take her, David?" Mary Stapler Ross sked.

"To my home in southwest Virginia. Preston's Cove is ot far from Fincastle, the county seat of Botetourt ounty. And it's less that a day's ride from Lexington."

"Why not Richmond, where I'll be near you?" Arainta asked. "I can work in one of the hospitals there."

"General Grant is expected to launch another drive r Richmond, as soon as the weather opens up, and even e capital may have to be evacuated," David explained. There's almost no action in the Valley now and I'd ther know you're safe at Preston's Cove."

They left the way he had come, by the back stairs and ar door of the sprawling old hotel. Araminta was far ore excited than afraid, but David was definitely apehensive until they had safely made the change of ains at Relay House, about halfway between Washingn and Baltimore, and were on a coach of the B&O ain line, roaring through the night toward Martinsburg d, he hoped, safety beyond the lines in Virginia.

On the afternoon of the fourth day after leaving Washgton, David and Araminta, using for transportation a rse and buggy he had been able to buy, through the lp of Confederate sympathizers in Martinsburg, were proaching the farmyard of Hal Perkins' family. Loted in a secluded valley lying between Chester Gap, here the Stonewall Brigade had crossed the Blue Ridge e summer before on the way to Gettysburg, and the rnpike south of Strasburg, it was familiar territory to avid. He had covered almost every inch of it during e marching and countermaching in the summers of 61 and 1862 that had made Stonewall Jackson a gendary figure in military history throughout the world. om Araminta, however, each brawling stream they ossed, each new hidden valley and cove revealed ought new exclamations of delight and wonder.

"I can see why you love this country so much, darling," e admitted. "And why you felt you had to give up your mmission that first year and fight for Virginia."

417

"Wait till you see Preston's Cove and the rest of t
upper Valley. You'll swear you're in heaven."

"Not without you there. I think these past three da
have meant more to me than any three days I ever spe
before in my whole life—and all because I've been wi
you."

"The war can't last much longer than next summe
Then I'll be coming home to you for the rest of our lives

"It still scares me to think of another summer of war
She shivered and moved closer to him. "With Gener
Grant in charge now, the killing is bound to increas
They say he never hesitates to throw masses of men rig
into the mouths of our cannon."

"That's Grant's record, and the North approves it. I'
sure one reason why we were able to get out of Washin
ton so easily and buy this horse and buggy in Martinsbu
was because people in the North think there's not mu
more danger from the South, now that Grant's in com
mand."

Hal's family welcomed the travelers warmly. After
day's rest they started southward up the Valley again, wi
enough food supplied from the Perkins farm for t
journey of roughly a hundred and twenty miles that st
lay before them. Much of the time they were able to fo
low the Valley Turnpike, since Federal troops were n
active in the area at the moment, although they hea
rumors everywhere of an army being assembled west
Winchester around Romney in the new state of We
Virginia.

Only one untoward incident marred the journey, whe
they were caught in a late March blizzard only a day
journey from their destination, while negotiating a narro
country road near Bald Knob at an elevation of almo
four thousand feet. Unable to keep going in the face
a howling snowstorm and with the road temporari
blocked by massive drifts, David was forced to pull o
into a small ravine near the summit for protection.

After several futile attempts to light a fire with w
wood, they gave up and, wrapping one of their thr
blankets around the horse, rolled up in the other tw
under the buggy for protection. When David was awa

418

ned during the night by Araminta moaning in her sleep
nd found her shaking from the cold, he put his own
blanket around her without waking her and stamped
back and forth through the snow to keep from freezing
or several hours until dawn.

Morning dawned bright and clear but, as they drove
the short distance to Preston's Cove, David began to
feel the familiar premonitory signs of headache and ach-
ng in his bones that went with a recurrence of malaria.
Hannah Williams had warned him against that possibility
the night he had been forced to wade ashore from the
Belle of Annapolis. But although he didn't worry Araminta by telling her of what was happening, he had no
doubt that the chill of that night in the Chesapeake had
brought on another siege of the unseen enemy that had
plagued him off and on since the first summer of the war.

As they followed the winding course of the James
River a few miles from Preston's Cove that afternoon,
David developed a shaking chill and a high fever. And
when Araminta drove the buggy into the lovely spot
beside the James River, where his forebears had built
their home almost a hundred and fifty years before, he
was already babbling in the grip of delirium.

VI

The small room was filled with a cloud of steam so
dense that David Preston was not able at first to make
out any details of its construction. When his vision
cleared somewhat, he saw that he was lying inside what
appeared to be a coincal-shaped structure made of woven
wattles, or reeds, plastered over on the outside, for no
light came through except a thin line marking a small
door. The steam appeared to be coming from water
poured upon a rock that had obviously been heated, for
he could see a ring of charcoal, some lumps still glowing,
around it.

He saw that he was lying on a blanket or robe spread
out on the dirt floor and was naked. But although his
body was soaked with sweat, he felt no sense of oppres-

sion from the heat and the steam. Rather, he seeme[d] almost to be floating, with such a sense of relaxation an[d] pleasure that he felt no need to know what had transpire[d] since the last thing he remembered, the bouncing of th[e] buggy down the mountain toward the secluded cov[e] where he'd spent his boyhood years.

Relaxing in the warmth of the steam-filled room, Davi[d] was almost asleep again when the door he had notice[d] in the side of the small structure opened and a gust [of] cold air swept in. It dissipated the vapor long enough f[or] him to make out a blanketed figure, bent over to g[o] through the low doorway and carrying a bucket of wate[r.] The newcomer was obviously graceful and, when th[e] blanket dropped as more water was poured on the ston[e,] sending up a new cloud of dense steam, the lovely sym[-] metry of arm, shoulder and breast told him his companio[n] was a woman—and naked—like himself.

When she moved closer to put one cool hand upon hi[s] forehead, while feeling for his pulse at the wrist with th[e] other, he tried to lift his hand to touch her. Like hi[s] voice, his muscles refused at the moment to obey hi[s] will but something, perhaps the tension in the muscle[s] of his arm at the wrist she was holding, warned her tha[t] he was conscious. And suddenly dropping his hand, sh[e] reached for the bucket and dumped the rest of its con[-] tents upon the hot stone. The cloud of steam filling th[e] room again momentarily obscured her from his visio[n] while she scrambled to wrap the blanket about herse[lf] again.

"How long have you been conscious, David?" Ara[-] minta demanded accusingly.

He tried to speak again, managing only a faint croa[k] as, kneeling beside him, she wrapped the blanket o[n] which he lay about his naked body and, holding him i[n] her arms, pressed his head against the warm fragra[nt] softness of her breast.

"You've come back, darling," she crooned, half sob[-] bing, half laughing. "You were so near death that some[-] times I couldn't even be sure you were alive."

"Where am—?" he managed to form the two word[s]

420

before she silenced his lips with her own and, for a long sweet moment there was no need for words.

"At Preston's Cove," she told him at last. "You went into delirium as we were coming down the mountain. Jake and Ellen helped me put you to bed in what was left of the big hou——"

"I don't understand." He found his voice at last.

"Deserters—Jack called them Yellownecks—came through about two weeks before we got here. When it looked like the Yankees might take this part of Virginia from the west, a lot of Southerners buried their silver and other values under the floorboards of the houses. While the Yellownecks were hunting for it here, the house caught fire, but Jake and Ellen managed, with help from the few neighbors not with the troops, to save the kitchen and part of the breezeway because they're separated from the house."

"And Mother?"

"Losing the house broke her heart, Dr. Buxton says: she died a few days later. Jake tried to send you a message, but you had already left for Washington."

"Mother loved the house, I can understand how seeing it burn would break her heart."

"Jake has a tintype that shows what a beautiful house it was: we'll build it back when the war's over."

"How long have we been here?"

"Two weeks—I think. I've been so busy keeping you alive I haven't kept track of time."

David reached out to touch the wattled side of the hut. "What's this?"

"A Cherokee hothouse—for sweat baths. As soon as we got here, Jake went to Fincastle for Dr. Buxton, but he didn't have any quinine. The doctor gave you up, but I didn't."

"How did you save me—without quinine?"

"When Lachlan and I visited our relatives among the Qualla Boundary Cherokees in the Great Smokies of North Carolina in the summer, we always stayed with Tsali, the medicine man of the tribe. He used to let me go with him to gather herbs and bark for his potions and I learned from him to make the Cherokee Black Drink and

421

some other Indian remedies. So I went into the woods and found some of the ingredients and brewed them into a tea."

She laughed, the most beautiful sound David could remember hearing. "Dr. Buxton called it a witches' brew, but he admits it worked. That and the steam baths I've been giving you here to sweat out the poisons of malaria."

"Sounds like I owe my life to you."

"When you were shaking with chills every third day and burning up with fever the other two, I was sure I'd lost you," she confessed as she bent to kiss him again, a long, warm kiss that sent the strength of excitement racing through his veins, until finally she pushed him away.

"You're getting well fast," she said, a little breathlessly. "Remember, I'm still just your fiancée, not your wife."

"We'll remedy that as soon as I'm strong enough to find a preacher."

"Dr. Buxton thinks we're married already." She laughed, a gay, lilting sound like the girl he'd fallen in love with in Washington almost three years ago. "When I told him how the Cherokees use the hothouses, I could see he was shocked by the thought of even married people taking sweat baths together naked, so I lied a little. But you haven't been compromised, because that afternoon I did marry you in a Cherokee ceremony."

"How did you manage that?"

"Among my people, a promise to live together in love is sufficient. And in case you've forgotten, we did that on the dock at Parkersburg a long time ago."

"I haven't forgotten."

"In the Cherokee ritual, the groom gives the bride a ham of venison to signify that he will always keep their household supplied with meat from the hunt. And the bride gives him an ear of corn, promising to be a good wife and take care of the household. The ceremony is carried out in the Long House that's part of every Cherokee village and afterward the people drink wine together and dance until they're exhausted."

"Just like any other wedding."

"Except that this time I had to go out and kill my own deer for the venison."

422

"With a bow and arrow?"

"Jake lent me a rifle. I hated to kill the buck, he was drinking at the big spring here in the cove. But we needed the meat, and I didn't intend to let you get away from me again."

She stood up. "Do you feel like walking to what's left of the house? It's only a few steps, but Jake's been helping me carry you back and forth."

"I'll try it under my own power."

David's legs were very shaky but, with Araminta supporting him, he made it to the separate building that had served as both kitchen and dining room at Preston's Cove. Part of the breezeway that had once connected it to the mansion itself had escaped damage by fire. Seeing the smoke-blackened foundation and brick chimneys of the gracious old house where he'd been born and lived as a boy caused a wrench at David's heart. But with the girl at his side who had saved his life, when the white man's medicine failed, he was as certain as she was that it would be rebuilt one day in all the gracious loveliness that had characterized the fine old house.

Dr. Buxton, the old family doctor from Fincastle, some twelve miles away, stopped by two days later. By that time the sick man was sitting on what was left of the breezeway, rocking in the warm mid-April sunlight.

"I don't mind admitting I'd given you up before that smart wife of yours took over, David," said the old doctor. "In your case at least, she's a better doctor than I was."

"I guess we doctors could learn a lot from Indian medicine men at that."

The old physician was sipping a mellow old bourbon Jake had somehow managed to hide from the Confederate deserters.

"Quinine comes from the bark of a tree first found in Peru; I can even remember when we prescribed the powdered bark instead of the pure drug extracted from it," he said. "The Indian medicine men probably learned about the effect of cinchona on certain fevers a long time before the Jesuits ever came to South America and took it back to Spain. So, if there's quinine in cinchona bark, it stands to reason other barks would contain it too."

Dr. Buxton took a sip from his glass. "Did your wife tell you I sent a telegram, at her request, to Major Hunter McGuire in Richmond, telling him you're unfit for further military duty?"

"Yes, I was going to ride into town and thank you when I became stronger."

"I'm getting too old for traipsing around the countryside visiting the sick, especially women that think they're dying but aren't. When you feel ready, I hope you'll take over for me here in Botetourt, David."

"I'm still an officer in the Confederate Army."

"Without that wife of yours, you wouldn't be here this time."

"I'm sure of that."

"Then you owe her more than you owe the South, so what's to keep you from taking over from a country doctor who's too old to practice any more? Besides, you could bring the people around here a brand of medicine they've never had before."

"I'm not too sure of that."

"Don't try to butter me up, son. Your wife told me how you saved her uncle in Washington, when that society doctor was going to let him die."

"It could be that she's prejudiced."

"I read the journals. And what's coming out of those schools you studied at in Europe makes us country doctors in America look like a bunch of shysters." Buxton emptied his glass and got to his feet reluctantly. "Think about it, son. I don't need an answer right away, and besides, I couldn't get anybody else if I did. But a man who barely escaped death from malaria twice, like your wife says you did, doesn't owe the government in Richmond anything else."

VII

Spring came early to the valleys of the James and the Shenandoah rivers in the Appalachian mountain chain in 1864. By late April the dogwoods were heavy with buds

424

paper from his pocket. "Here's the Richmond *Enquirer*—only a week told, too."

"I knew that was too good to last," said Araminta brokenly as the stooped, shuffling old physician climbed into his buggy and slapped the lines against the horse's rump to set it into motion. "Why must men make so much of honor, when it breaks the hearts of the women who love them?"

"Because otherwise they couldn't really claim to deserve that love. Is it any different among the Cherokees?"

"Not really," she admitted as they went into the kitchen. "A warrior has to prove he deserves the woman who chooses him; it's part of the ancient law of our people."

"Then you can't really blame me for feeling obligated, can you?"

"I suppose not. How long do we have?"

"I'll need several more weeks to regain all my strength."

"You're going to need it before that," she told him as she turned toward the stove and, lifting a circular lid, stirred up the bed of coals there and poked in another chunk of wood. "Starting tonight we're going to make love at least once every night until you go."

"But—"

"No buts. Cherokee women know how to choose the best time for conceiving by following the cycles of the moon, but I'm not taking any chances. We're going to be sure I'm pregnant before you go, and then, no matter what happens, I'll always have a part of you. Now, sit down and rest while you read the paper Dr. Buxton brought."

The paper was dated April 25, 1864, and mostly described Federal movements north of Richmond, where General Ulysses S. Grant was marshaling the greatest Federal army yet assembled for still another push against Richmond and the army defending the Confederate capital under the command of General Robert E. Lee.

One item that immediately seized David's attention was on the back page, a dispatch from Staunton, Virginia, that read:

FEDERAL TROOPS TO INVADE
SHENANDOAH VALLEY AGAIN!

STAUNTON, Va., April 24—Information reaching this city indicates that an army of about six thousand men and attached artillery is being prepared in the new Union state of West Virginia under Gen. Franz Sigel, commander of that district. Its purpose is undoubtedly to march southward in the Shenandoah Valley, seeking to take Staunton and block the railway line to Richmond as a part of the Union campaign against the capital.

Troops under Gen. John C. Breckinridge, the Confederate commander in the Valley, are moving eastward to repel this attack. The Virginia Cavalry under Brig. Gen. John D. Imboden is now fighting a delaying action in the area around Strasburg to slow the Federal advance, and it is expected that the Cadet Battalion at the Virginia Military Institute will see service in this important movement. Excitement is reported to be high at the Institute because of this possibility.

In Richmond General Lee has stated that he considers a thrust by Union forces into the upper Valley, which has been relatively quiet during most of the present year, to be a serious threat to the defenses of the capital, hence the decision to use the VMI cadets, if such a move seems indicated.

"They couldn't send those children to war," Araminta protested when David showed her the newspaper story. "Nobody could be that desperate."

"Stonewall Jackson took the VMI cadets to the Battle of McDowell in 1862, but at least he kept them in the rear with the supporting units." David hesitated, then continued, "You know Lachlan is with Imboden's cavalry don't you?"

She nodded. "He's written me that he likes General Imboden very much."

"John's a very capable commander but he doesn't have enough men to hold Sigel's army back very long. Everything is going to depend on how fast Breckinridge can march toward the lower Valley."

David's analysis of the military situation was confirmed several days later when Lachlan Murrell, his uni-orm mud-spattered and his horse barely able to stand, ode into the yard at Preston's Cove and dismounted, urning his horse over to Jake to be stabled and fed.

"You look pretty chipper, fellow," he greeted David s he came up the steps to the breezeway. "From the elegram you sent Dr. Hunter McGuire, I expected to see ou planted by now."

"That was your sister's doing." David poured Lachlan liberal drink of bourbon, diluting it only slightly with pring water. "But since I was in a coma from recurrent nalaria at the time, I can hardly blame her."

"Where is Araminta, by the way?"

"Farther up the creek, catching a mess of fish for din-er. She ought to be coming home any time now."

Lachlan grinned. "Don't tell me an upright character ike you is living here in sin with my sister!"

"I'm your legal brother-in-law," David assured him. 'And but for Araminta I wouldn't be here. When the amily doctor gave me up, she treated me with Cherokee nedicine—the Black Drink."

"Good God! She's made an Indian out of you."

"Whatever she's doing, I like it. By the time we got ere from Washington a few weeks ago, a severe malaria ttack had turned me into a babbling idiot."

"I thought malaria only occurred in summertime."

"I got chilled to the bone wading ashore from an oyster oat called the *Belle of Annapolis*. But what brings you his way?"

"I'm on the way back to rejoin John Imboden. He sent ne out into southwest Virginia to see what's holding up General Breckinridge."

"The *Enquirer* says an army under Sigel is moving up he Valley. What about it?"

"Sigel's moving, but cautiously. He's had his ears inned back so many times by irregular Confederate orces that he isn't taking any chances. So far we've been ble to slow him with cavalry skirmishes but he's got a ot more men than John Imboden has. Unless Breckin-idge and John can get together to fight him anywhere orth of Staunton, even a dummkopf like Sigel might be

429

able to catch each force separately and make the Valley safe for the Union."

"I figured it was that serious when I read that Lee had approved sending the VMI cadets into action."

Lachlan gave him a startled look. "Has it really come to that at last? I've been away close to a week."

"So the *Enquirer* piece said. It was sent from Staunton too, so the reporter probably checked his sources."

"John Imboden has a young brother in the Corps, so I'm sure he'd be against using those kids in battle. Besides, after this war is over, the South's going to need the kind of leadership the Institute has often provided in the political sphere. I'd hate to see any of the Battalion get killed off holding back a minor Federal general like Franz Sigel."

Araminta arrived then, with a string of fish, which she dropped to run into Lachlan's arms. "Why didn't you tell us you were coming?" she demanded when she could find her voice again after crooning over him and kissing his bearded cheeks. "I would have killed the fatted calf."

"Your husband did as much with this," he assured her, lifting his glass. "You look wonderful, sis."

"I think I'm pregnant, Lachlan. And we're going to name our son after you."

"I'm flattered, of course. But is that all right with you David?"

"First I've heard of either event," David confessed. "But I'm in favor of both."

The evening passed swiftly, beginning with an excellent dinner of fresh fish, canned corn and dried string beans with hot biscuits and damson preserves.

"One thing I can say for you, David," said Lachlan when he finally pushed his chair back from the table. "You've transformed a social butterfly into a real housewife."

"Love did that,' Araminta assured her brother. "You ought to try it sometime."

"I may, when this is over. How was Uncle John when you left him?"

"He's weakening steadily, Lachlan," said Araminta.

430

I'm content to stay here, it's my world now. But the nation is going to need leadership more than ever after the war is over and Uncle John isn't going to be strong enough to carry the burden."

"The Confederacy is losing everywhere," said the Cherokee officer. "Someone—probably not Jefferson Davis, but someone else—has to realize the Cause is lost and make the best sort of peace he can. And the sooner the better."

"When we start sending the VMI cadets, kids sixteen and seventeen years old, into battle, the Confederacy is scraping the barrel," David agreed.

"A lot of die-hard Southerners are talking of moving in to Mexico when the war's over, said Lachlan.

"I take it that you're going to stick with your people," said David.

"The only place I'll have a vote will be in the Cherokee Nation. Where else can I go?"

"What can you tell me about the Stonewall Brigade?" David asked.

"They're still facing the enemy across the Rapidan earthworks, but I hear the bad weather this spring has been especially hard on them."

"No shoes, as usual?"

"No socks either, until the ladies in General Lee's family knitted some and sent them to the brigade. In fact the Army of Northern Virginia is short of food, clothing, ammunition, medical supplies and doc——" Lachlan broke off and grimaced wryly. "There I go, putting my foot in my mouth again."

"David's already decided to go back," Araminta told him. "I made him stay here long enough to regain his strength and get me pregnant. Now that he's taken care of both, I suppose there'll be no holding him."

"Will you send a telegram to Hunter McGuire for me from Staunton, on your way back down the Valley, requesting return to active duty?" David asked.

"Sure. If that's what you both want."

"It's not what either of us wants," Arminta answered. "But what we know David has to do."

431

VIII

In the basement of a church, about ten miles south of New Market, where an important road ran eastward from the Valley Turnpike through a gap in the Massanutten Range and thence across the Blue Ridge to the Piedmont area of Virginia and Richmond, David Preston was bandaging the foot of a VMI cadet. It was early evening of May 14, 1864, and the young officer was part of a regiment of 215 officers and men from the Virginia Military Institute—plus a detail of thirty-two cadets servicing the two rifled howitzers that had replaced the three bronze guns of the old cadet battery some six months before.

The Cadet Battalion was on its way to join an army of about four thousand men advancing from southwest Virginia toward Staunton to oppose a Federal force of six thousand. General Franz Sigel, the Federal commander, was obviously seeking to seize the Virginia Central Railroad, extending from Covington and Clifton Forge eastward through Staunton and across the Blue Ridge to Charlottesville and the Orange and Alexandria line. And with the vital rail link in Federal hands, not only would supplies for Richmond be cut off but an army could then be moved across the Blue Ridge to form another section in the chain of iron and men being forged around Richmond by General Ulysses S. Grant.

Always an aggressor, Grant was obviously preparing to launch a major attack upon Richmond, with the intention of capturing the Confederate capital and handing as a prize to Abraham Lincoln, facing a not altogether enthusiastic electorate in November. With typical bulldog tenacity, too, Grant had settled down to take the Confederate capital by a frontal assault through the Wilderness area.

David's orders to active duty had been delayed, following the application Lachlan Murrell had telegraphed for him. Telegraphic confirmation assigning him to temporary duty with the VMI cadet regiment had arrived only a few hours before the young soldier-scholars had begun the march to join troops of General John Cabell

reckinridge at Staunton in the last-ditch attempt to stop
the Federal force.

It had been raining almost continuously since the
Cadet Battalion had left its home base four days earlier
with bands playing gaily, the two cannon rolling on
heavily greased axles with hardly a squeak, and the people of Lexington cheering the smartly uniformed cadets
on. Impressive and inspiring though the send-off had been,
however, the spirits of the young warriors, some only
sixteen, had long since been dampened by the rain and
by the certainty that their first taste of actual battle lay
perhaps no more than twenty-four hours ahead.

As David finished the bandage he was applying, a
rather damp cadet runner entered the church and saluted
smartly.

"A message just came for you, Doctor." Like so many
in the southern armies, the cadet had trouble placing
medical officers exactly in the military order of rank.
"General Breckinridge wants to see you at his headquarters near New Market as soon as you can get there."

Wrapping some bacon and a hunk of bread in the
corner of his waterpoof to munch on during the ten-mile
ride to Breckinridge's headquarters, David was soon on
his way. Some ninety minutes later he reported to the
adjutant at division headquarters, just north of the town
of New Market in a two-room log cabin. Through the
open door he could see the commanding general working at a field table, and couldn't help wondering, while he
waited, just why he had been sent for—unless it was a
change of orders assigning him to take charge of the
medical units of the division during the coming battle.

At forty-three, Major General John Cabell Breckinridge was a strikingly handsome man who had already
served as Vice-President of the United States under Presi-
ent Buchanan. He had also run against Abraham Lincoln in the 1860 elections on a platform favoring slavery
and states' rights and, appointed U.S. senator from his
home state of Kentucky after the election, had remained
in the U.S. Senate until December 1861.

Although Breckinridge had worked tirelessly to keep
the South in the Union, when he resigned to take a com-

433

mission in the Confederate Army, his former colleague in the U.S. Government had nevertheless voted to exp him and labeled him a traitor, for which act he w understandably bitter.

David had seen Breckinridge several times while h was in Washington. When he was ushered into the oth room ten minutes after his arrival at headquarters, h couldn't see that the former Vice-President had change much, except perhaps for the grim lines around h mouth.

"Have a seat, Major; I'll be with you in a minute said the commanding general, but it was several minut before he finished reading the two sheets he was studyin and scribbed a signature at the bottom.

"I've been told you served under General Jackso Major Preston," he said at last.

"For two years, sir—from Harpers Ferry to Chance lorsville. I was commanding officer of the First Fiel Hospital of the Second Corps from the first Battle Manassas, until I became delirious from malaria a litt over a month ago."

"And you've been out for some time because of th illness?"

"I was in a coma for almost a month, sir."

"We saw some malaria in winter around Bato Rouge." Breckinridge's eyebrows lifted quizzically. " thought it didn't occur this far north in the colde months."

"The disease is less frequent in northern climes David admitted. "But I had a severe case in the summe of sixty-two and sixty-three, and I believe it remained my system. Anyway I suffered a prolonged chill in Marc and was delirious for some time afterward."

"I'm glad you recovered enough to join us, Major. I' been told that, because of your experience in Europ you were an adviser to General Jackson."

David smiled. "Nobody gave Stonewall Jackson muc advice except perhaps General Lee. But he did use m sometimes as a sounding board when he was working o a battle plan."

"I'm new to this area, so I'd like to use you in som

434

hat the same capacity, Major. General Imboden tells
e the next line of defense to the south, after New Mar-
et, would be at Lacey Spring, where you just left the
MI cadets. Do you agree?"

"Absolutely, sir. If you leave New Market to the
ederals—"

"They already have it, Major. I propose to throw them
ut and prevent General Sigel from marching on Rich-
ond by way of Luray and Sperryville. The question is:
ow best to do it?"

"General Jackson always attacked."

"And you still advise that strategy?"

"Absolutely, sir." David hesitated only momentarily.
But I hope you aren't going to throw the VMI cadets
to the front of the battle line."

Breckinridge gave him an appraising look, but appeared
ot to be offended by his brashness.

"These young men represent some of the finest leader-
ip potential in Virginia, sir," David continued. "The
uth is going to need them badly after the war."

"I also sorely need a victory to bolster General Lee
gainst Grant, and my own spirits as well," said Breckin-
dge. "Do you know what it is to command units in a
ccession of defeats, Major Preston?"

"I'm afraid not, sir."

"I do. First, I tried to head off war through remaining
Congress as long as I possibly could—and my col-
agues rewarded me by voting me guilty of treason.
ext, I suffered defeats at Shiloh, Chickamauga and Mis-
onary Ridge. And now that I have a force under my
mmand two thirds as large as that commanded by an
ept Federal general, I don't propose to be beaten
gain."

Breckinridge turned back to the field table at which he
ad been writing. "I will make this concession though,
lajor; the cadets from VMI will be in the second line."
e signed his name to an order that was on the table
nd handed it to David. "Good night, Major. Please carry
is order to Colonel Shipp with the cadet regiment; he is
 move to join me here immediately."

It was almost midnight when David returned to the

cadet bivouac and reported to the duty officer, Captain Frank Preston, a distant cousin and one of the four tactical officers—called Subs by the cadets—with the regiment. Preston had been wounded in the early months of the war, losing an arm, and had been assigned as an instructor in miltary tactics at the famed Institute.

"So it's to be tomorrow," said the duty officer. "General Breckinridge isn't wasting any time."

"He figures the odds as three of them to two of us. And that's a better situation than the Confederacy usually has in a battle."

"Sergeant-of-the-Guard!" Captain Frank Preston summoned the noncommissioned cadet officer in charge of the pickets guarding the bivouac. "Have the drummer sound the Long Roll; we're moving out at once."

It had been months since David had heard the thundering roar of the drums calling a unit to prepare for action, the signal known throughout the army as the Long Roll. And even though the drumheads were wet from the rain, muting the sound somewhat, he could still feel the same thrill and the same sudden rush of apprehension he always experienced at the sound.

It was still a half hour from dawn when the cadets, after a halt for breakfast and a final inspection of equipment, reached a point almost a mile south of New Market. On orders from General Breckinridge, they moved to the left of the Valley Turnpike and formed a line at right angles to it behind a low ridge called Shirley's Hill. From there, they could see the front line of infantrymen deployed just behind the crest of the hill, while beyond it skirmishers stirred up an occasional crackle of gunfire as they probed the enemy lines a few hundred yards to the north.

The Confederate artillery—eighteen guns, it was reported—were already in place near what was called Bushong Hill, and the two guns of the cadet artillery were ordered to join the main body on the right flank. A cheer rose from the cadets as the caissons swung by, horses at the gallop and riders leaning over to urge them on. David followed, hoping to see John Imboden or

436

Lachlan Murrell before the battle started. He found the familiar stocky figure of Imboden helping to emplace one of the guns making up the Confederate artillery force.

"You're a good omen, David, my boy," the cavalryman greeted him warmly. "With three of Jackson's veterans here today, we're bound to win."

"When they outnumber us three to two?"

"Old Jack would have considered these odds distinctly favorable." Then Imboden sobered. "But I wish we could have a few hundred veterans of the old Army of the Shenandoah and what's left of the Stonewall Brigade here instead of the cadets. My kid brother was on one of those caissons that just rolled by."

"Lachlan told me he was at the Institute."

"So you married the lovely princess? I often heard Joe Stannard tell how that young lieutenant's eyes bugged out when he first saw her at Harpers Ferry the day you came through with the Rosses and Lachlan Murrell on the canal boat. Where's your wife now?"

"At Preston's Cove, what's left of it."

"I didn't know the Yankees had raided in that area."

"Not Yankees—Yellownecks. They burned the house and my mother died from grief a few weeks later."

"Too bad," said the cavalryman. "I remember seeing her in Lexington before the war, she was a real lady. But I'm afraid a lot of houses will be burning soon, when Grant discovers that the Shenandoah Valley has been a major source of supply for our army before Richmond. He blazed a path of destruction through Mississippi to take Vicksburg."

"I'm sure he'll try to starve out Richmond the same way."

"Perhaps we're lucky to still be in the Valley, then," said Imboden.

"I asked General Breckinridge last night not to throw the cadets into the fight—"

"What did he say?"

"He'll start them in the second line; I just hope he'll keep them there."

"Pray God he can. Breckinridge has been in a lot of

battles that ended in defeat, so he probably sees this as a chance to redeem himself."

"He admitted as much last night."

"Can't say I blame him. He tried hard, as Vice-President, to keep the country together, so being drummed out of the Senate as a traitor couldn't have set very well with him. What do you think of the battleground?"

"I haven't seen it since the last time we were here with Old Jack."

"You wouldn't be very safe in going over that hill to look right now, but I can give you an idea of what it's going to be like." Stooping, the cavalryman picked up a stick and began to draw a rough map in the sandy soil. "The Valley Turnpike runs between the North Fork of the Shenandoah River and a winding stream called Swift's Creek. The town of New Market is just ahead of us and this is Shirley's Hill, where the cadets are located."

Imboden drew a cross in the sand to the left. "The start of the battle will no doubt come when Breckinridge orders our men down the far slope of Shirley's Hill."

"The Federals are still in the town then?"

"Two regiments of infantry and about three hundred cavalrymen occupied New Market after I withdrew yesterday afternoon on Breckinridge's orders," said Imbooden. "Sigel has a strong battery farther back in a churchyard, too, but his main body is farther north, supporting the first line."

"Looks like a good situation for one of Old Jack's favorite flank marches."

"I'm going to try just that. If I can make a wide swing with the cavalry and cross Swift's Creek, I might be able to put Sigel into a trap." Imboden drew another line in the sand. "There's a bridge over the Shenandoah River not far away and, if I can break it, the Federals will be bottled up with the river at their backs."

"Jackson would like that setup," said David. "But aren't those streams pretty heavily swollen from the rain?"

"Getting over that creek isn't going to be easy. Wish me luck, old friend. I'm going to need it."

IX

The deep boom of the artillery fire from both sides a little after ten o'clock marked the start of the Battle of New Market. And shortly after eleven, the front line of seasoned Confederate infantrymen went over the hill toward the town, pushing the Federal front line back against the second line, as he had promised. As they moved down Shirley's Hill toward New Market itself, David followed, ready to render medical care to the wounded. No casualties were sustained, however, until the Federal batteries to the north got the range and shells started exploding over the young soldiers.

Four cadets and an officer dropped immediately and a cadet named Merritt was painfully wounded, requiring David's expert medical care. The other three were only slightly injured, however, and, after bandaging their wounds, he sent them to the rear. The officer, Captain A. Goven Hill of C Company, was critically wounded, and David sent him back to the field hospital which, he was informed, had been set up a mile or more to the rear.

As the Confederates continued to press forward, the battle became heated and the Union artillery battery was driven back, forcing General Sigel to retire to a second, and stronger, position. By this time, however, the cadets were near the center of the converted line and in some of the hottest parts of the fighting.

The location of the two streams, both unfortunately too swollen by rain to be forded, had kept John Imboden's cavalry from completing the flanking movement he had planned. Thus the battlefront, for both sides, was confined to a narrow area, increasing the devastation from both artillery and rifle fire. As the Confederate troops pushed forward, seeking to drive the Federals from their position on the heights and capture some of the artillery that was pounding them steadily, the cadets came under even more withering fire from Federal artillery. Several more of the young soldiers were wounded, one youth being killed immediately.

Busy caring for the casualties on the field and several times exposed to enemy fire himself, David had only an occasional glimpse of what was happening ahead. But when he saw the cadet regiment pass Bushong House, where the Confederate artillery had been first emplaced, and move on into an orchard, he realized that in their eagerness, or perhaps because of the changing formation of the battle line, the young men were now in the forefront of the fighting. He was relieved moments later, however, to see the line of cadets take a position behind a fence, where they were protected somewhat from the hail of artillery and rifle fire sweeping the narrow field of action.

Colonel Scott Shipp, the cadet commandant, was wounded just then and David stopped to apply temporary bandaging before the commander could be carried back on a litter, thereby losing touch for a while with the action on the field. Meanwhile a Federal cavalry squadron charged the Confederate line but was beaten back, and shortly after three o'clock, the cadet regiment began to pour its own fire into the enemy beyond the wheat field where most of the action was centered.

The 62d Virginia, advancing on the right of the cadets, who were still protected by the fence, sustained tremendous losses and, had Sigel been able to use his cavalry at the time, he could easily have exploited this break in the Confederate line and perhaps have ended the battle then and there. Fortunately for the South, however, the Federal troops were concentrated opposite the Confederate right flank and, when Breckinridge's troops re-formed and attacked again, two of the Federal regiments gave way. The battle was further complicated, too, when a black thundercloud suddenly burst over the wheat field, turning the already muddy area into practically an impassable bog, where the shoes of the fighting men were almost pulled from their feet.

Inspired by the break in the Federal lines and ignoring the downpour, the officers of the cadet regiment ordered a charge. And carrying high the familiar banner of the Virginia Military Institute, with a picture of George Washington and the seal of Virginia upon it, the color-bearer, an unusually tall cadet, ran well in front. Ignoring the hail of lead being poured down upon them, the ager cadets followed, and, sweeping over the Federal rtillery position with fixed bayonets, captured several uns and drove the cannoneers away.

When the tall cadet standard-bearer, "Big" Evans, 1ounted one of the caissons and waved on the charging adets, they poured after the retreating Union troops. 'hese broke and ran, allowing the jubilant young soldiers) capture Yankees right and left, one cadet bringing in record bag of twenty-three prisoners.

Only when the din of battle died away and word came 1at the Federal troops were in retreat north of New Iarket, was David able to gain much information about 1e fighting, except what he was able to see as he moved bout behind the lines. It was almost dark when he heard 1at Lachlan Murrell had been wounded in the arm and, eing near one of the Virginia regiments at the time, had een carried back to the dressing station of that regiment.

Deeply concerned over Lachlan, David reached the eld hospital of the Virginia troops shortly before sun- own. It was commanded by a highly confident, but ob- iously little-experienced, young medical officer, Captain dward Duggan.

"Major Lachlan Murrell is my brother-in-law," David old Captain Duggan. "I'd like to examine him before ou operate."

"But—he's an Indian."

"A Cherokee, his sister is my wife. Can I examine im?"

"As you wish, Major," said Duggan with a shrug. "But e has a compound gunshot fracture of the humerus. And that arm doesn't come off, he's going to die from sepsis."

"I've seen a few such wounds, Captain"—David spoke little sharply—"during the two years I commanded a eld hospital with Stonewall Jackson."

"Murrell is over there," said Duggan. "I had the orderly ve him some whiskey and laudanum in preparation for 1e operation.

Lachlan, somewhat pale but conscious, was lying on a tter at one side of the makeshift field hospital, which had een set up near a farmhouse in a barn with an attached able. His left arm, bandaged from just below the shoul-

441

der down to the elbow with a bloodstained cloth, hung at his side.

"Has your wound been examined since you were brought here?" David asked.

"The surgeon on the field put on the bandage and marked my wound tag for amputation." Lachlan's voice almost broke on the word. "Will it really have to come off, David?"

"Not if I can help it."

David was looking around at the makeshift hospital and not liking what he saw. Piles of freshly mown hay partly filled the barn and fine particles of dust sifting down from the loft above hung in the air, gleaming like tiny bits of gold in the shaft of sunlight through a west window. From the stable, separated from the main part of the barn only by troughs into which hay was piled for the horses, came the pungent smell of manure.

"If anyone comes to take you to surgery before I get back, don't go," David told Lachlan. "I'm going to survey the farmhouse; it has to be a better place for wounded men than a stable."

He was gone only a few minutes, long enough to tell that the farmhouse, prudently locked, was roomy and clean. What was more, like so many Valley farmhouses, a large kitchen was attached, with a heavy iron range inside for heating water and plenty of wood to stoke the fires, plus a well nearby. Even more important, he found in an outhouse a bag of lime left over from the frequent liming of pastures that was common farming practice in this area, where crushed dolomite limestone was easily obtained from quarries at Buchanan to the south and Loudoun County to the north.

When David came back to the stable after prizing the lock off the front door of the farmhouse, Captain Duggan was still nowhere to be seen, so he ordered the enlisted personnel of the hospital unit to start moving the wounded there. Duggan appeared a few minutes later and, seeing the litters and their occupants being moved from the stable, flushed angrily.

"You can't use the house," he said. "General Breckinridge plans to make it his headquarters."

442

"I didn't know that and you didn't tell me, until I had already started moving the wounded in there."

"Well you can just move them back."

"I've taken over that house as a hospital, Captain. I'm going to use it and I expect you to help me."

When Duggan started to turn away, David realized he was undoubtedly going to report to Breckinridge.

"That's an order," he added. "Fail to obey and I'll put you on report as insubordinate."

Duggan hesitated a moment longer, then turned back. But the look of resentment in his eyes told David his temporary capitulation wouldn't be the end of the matter.

"Take over moving the wounded," he told Duggan. "I'll see about getting an operating table set up in the kitchen. Some of these cases need surgery very badly."

"I still don't see on what grounds you're moving—"

"I'll be brief, Captain Duggan." David was gathering up the medical equipment the hospital afforded while he talked. "A stable is no place for men with open wounds—if you'd had any experience at all in the field, you should know that. Fifteen years ago in Vienna, Dr Semmelweis showed that dead organic matter causes sepsis after childbirth and also in wounds. Chloride of lime can combat the presence of septic matter but not if wounds are treated in a place like this, that is already full of it."

"I never heard of any Semmel——whoever you said it was."

"You've heard of Dr. Oliver Wendell Holmes, haven't you?"

"Of course."

"Holmes said much the same thing—on purely logical grounds from reports of septic cases. I've discovered some lime in an outbuilding and I am going to carry out an antiseptic surgical practice here as far as I'm able—whether you decide to co-operate or not."

Picking up an armful of the medical supplies, David started out of the barn. "I've instructed the litter bearers to take the less seriously wounded men upstairs and put them to bed in the upper room of the farmhouse," he added. "That way we can place the men who need surgery on the lower floors, where we can handle them more easily. One of the orderlies is building a fire in the kitchen stove and we can start heating water in a few minutes."

The next few hours were busy ones for David. He took the patients in order of the severity of their wounds, a practice he had used since he came into the army. In Lachlan's case, the circulation in his left arm and hand below the compound fracture caused by a bullet from a Federal Enfield rifle appeared not to be disturbed, indicating that no major artery was involved, so the cavalry officer had to wait until casualties with more urgent wounds had been treated.

By the time Lachlan came upon the operating table, the pile of arms and legs outside the kitchen door was fairly high and the supply of chloroform almost gone. David examined the wound without anesthesia and was relieved to discover that little treatment was required. The bullet had struck the humerus—the long bone of the upper arm—squarely, splintering a section about two inches long and tearing its way out again through the muscles.

A few bits of uniform had been carried into the wound and these David removed carefully, along with some muscle tissue that had obviously been deprived of its blood supply. This done, he was able to push the loose fragments of bone gently back into place and bind the wound with a dressing moistened in the lime solution being heated in pots on the iron stove, before splinting the fracture so the bone would be held in an approximately normal position.

In preparing a splint, David first tore long strips of cloth and soaked them in a pot of thick starch bubbling on the back of the stove. Then placing the strips on a table to form a long flat splint, a dozen layers thick, he took one end of the strip and started it just over the point of Lachlan's left shoulder. With the lower arm held at right angles to the upper by one of the enlisted men helping him, he next smoothed the strip down along the outer side of the arm, around beneath the elbow and back up on the inner side to end snugly in the wounded man's armpit.

While David worked, the heavily starched strips of cloth had begun to stiffen as the splint dried. And by the

444

ne he finished bandaging the splint snugly into place, it
ready formed a fairly stable support for the broken
ne. And since the lower arm was allowed to hang free
ith only the wrist supported by a sling, its weight, he
new, would overcome a tendency of the muscles to con-
act and cause the ends of the broken bone to override.

Completing the splint, David glanced up to see Captain
uggan looking at the bandaged arm with reluctant ad-
iration.

"Where did you learn that trick?" the younger officer
emanded.

"In Italy. I served for some time with the Garibaldi
rces there after I finished studying in Europe."

"And where did you study medicine?"

"Jefferson Medical College in Philadelphia. Before that,
was a cadet at VMI."

"He was the cadet First Captain," said Lachlan.

Duggan turned away without speaking, but the set of
s shoulders told David the matter of his having taken
mmand of the hospital was not at an end. It was after
ght o'clock before he finished operating upon those of
ounded men who needed surgery. He was drinking a
p of coffee made from captured Union suppies in the
ol air outside the kitchen—which the fire burning in
e range and the steam from the kettles boiling upon it
d turned into something very much like a Cherokee hot-
ouse—when he saw Captain Frank Preston ride into
to the farmyard and tie the reins of his horse to a hitch-
g rack.

As the tactical officer came across the yard to the open
or of the kitchen, David called back to the soldier
the stove to bring him another cup of coffee. Before
ccepting it, however, Preston handed David a letter,
on which was the official seal of the War Department
Richmond.

"This came for you by courier last night at the en-
mpment before we moved to New Market," the one-
med VMI instructor said. "In the excitement of getting
e cadet regiment under way this morning, I forgot to
ve it to you."

"Must be my official orders." David stuck the envelope

445

into his pocket. "I've only been operating under telegraphed order before. How's the battle going?"

"The fighting's over." Frank Preston sank to a bench and drank the coffee gratefully. "The charge the boys made turned the tide and, once they put those enemy cannon out of action, the Federals couldn't stand the heat any longer."

"I doubt if the cadets would appreciate being called boys," said David.

"Maybe not. But two out of every three in that charge were 'rats' and two of those had just passed fifteen. Any way you look at it, May 15, 1864, will always be the most glorious day in the history of VMI."

"Do you know how many casualties you took? I've only seen a few here."

"Five were killed and thirty or forty wounded. The regiment chased the enemy as far as Mount Airy farm about five miles from here, but the Federals retreated across the North Fork and burned the bridges. The battle's over, at least for the time being."

"Thank God for that!"

"This is one time General Breckinridge can claim a complete victory," said Preston. "I'm sorry about Major Murrell; someone on the field told me he'll have to lose his arm."

"He would have if I hadn't taken charge over the protests of Captain Duggan."

"Breckinridge is related to Duggan, I believe. And he isn't going to like your taking over this farmhouse as a hospital, either. I hear he was planning to use it as his headquarters and even had a lock put on it when he came through."

"As far as I'm concerned, that lock was put on when the family that owned the farm skedaddled."

"And what Breckinridge may do doesn't worry you?"

"I've served under Stonewall Jackson, Baldy Ewell and Jubal A. Early. Two of them are still alive, plus Robert E. Lee, and with men like that on your side, who has to worry?"

"Do you think you can save Murrell's arm?"

"A French military surgeon named Ambroise Paré

446

as asked three hundred years ago how he managed to
eat wounds on the battlefield without using either a hot
on cautery or pouring boiling oil into them. "Paré's
swer was: 'I dressed them and God healed them.'
hat's still about the best explanation I know of how a
ilitary surgeon works."

X

Just after David finished making rounds of the wounded
en in the farmhouse hospital the next morning, a courier
rived with an order for him to report to General Breck-
ridge in the town hall at New Market. When he came
to the room, Breckinridge was sitting behind a table
ith General John Imboden on one side and an enlisted
erk on the other. As he saluted, David saw Captain
uggan lounging in one of the dozen or so chairs in the
om. And from the smug look on Duggan's face, he was
ite sure of the source from which any difficulties he
ight have that morning had come.

Breckinridge returned the salute with a rigid formality
at promised no leniency, but the light of amusement in
hn Imboden's eyes told David he had at least one friend
court.

"A serious allegation has been brought against you,
ajor Preston," said Breckinridge without preamble. "I
ve asked you to come here so I can hear your side of
e controversy before drawing up charges for a court-
artial. Do you have anything to say for yourself?"

"First, I would like to know what I'm being accused of,
r."

"Item One," Breckinridge read from a paper on the
ble before him. "It is charged that you assumed com-
and of a military hospital in a time of battle without
thority from me or anyone on my staff. Item two: That
u did so in order to give preferential treatment to one
sualty, Major Lachlan Murrell, and prevented the medi-
l officer in charge of the hospital from carrying out
e treatment indicated for Major Murrell's wounds, thus
dangering his life needlessly. Item Three. That you

447

seized a private house without authority, and broke the lock on the door in order to use it as a military hospital.

Breckinridge looked up. "Have you an answer to these charges, Major Preston?"

"I believe so, General," said David. "To the third charge, of seizing private property for military use, I would say that the needs of the wounded or sick under my care have always been my guide in carrying out my duties as a medical officer. I found that Captain Duggan had set up his hospital in a barn attached to a stable, with no solid wall between. This action constituted a gross medical error on his part, since it was proved medically years ago that contact with animal or human waste is a prime source of sepsis in wounds—"

"By whom was that proved, Major?"

"Dr. Ignaz Philipp Semmelweis was the discoverer, sir. But his theories have been substantiated by American physicians as well, notably by Dr. Oliver Wendell Holmes, one of the leading medical teachers in America. I saw further evidence of how important such sources of contamination can be when I served with the Italian army during the recent war with Austria. And for nearly a year I was a captain in the U. S. Army Medical Corps, assigned to Washington, largely because I carried out the principles of antiseptic obstetrical and surgical practice first prescribed by Semmelweis."

Breckinridge shot a venomous look at Captain Duggan, who seemed to shrivel preceptibly in his seat. "Go on, please, Major."

"As to Item Two, sir, Captain Duggan was present and will testify, I am sure, that I did not treat Major Murrell's wounds until all more serious cases had been attended to. And concerning my authority, I believe I am the ranking medical officer with this army."

"But not permanently so assigned," Breckinridge reminded him.

"It is true that I received no such orders from this headquarters, sir," David admitted. "I am therefore willing to admit that I may have been remiss in my interpretation of the orders returning me to active duty since my illness."

"When did you receive those orders, Major?" Breckin-
ige asked.

"The temporary assignment was made a few days ago,
—by telegraph. I only received my written orders last
ght from Captain Frank Preston of the VMI military
ff. They had been sent to me in care of Colonel Shipp
the Institute and were brought to the headquarters of
e cadet regiment by a courier late last night."

"Before I talked to you, Major?"

"Afterward, sir. Captain Preston forgot to give the
ders to me until I returned to the regimental bivouac
Lacey Spring, so I haven't had time to present them
the adjutant."

"Might I see them now?"

"Of course." From his uniform tunic, David took a
igle folded sheet and handed it to the general. Breckin-
ige read the sheet completely twice and started to hand
back, but stopped when David said, "There is an en-
rsement on the back, sir."

Turning the sheet over, Breckinridge read the eight
ords written there, then handed the sheet back to David.

"Under the circumstances, I will accept as valid your
sumption that your orders authorized you to act as
ief medical officer of this division, Major Preston," he
id. "The hearing is ended."

An hour after David returned to the hospital, John
iboden tied the reins of his horse to the hitching rack
itside and came to the door. He was smiling and, with-
t a word, David went to one of the medical chests.
iking out a bottle of medicinal whiskey, he picked up
o glasses from a sideboard, stepped outside and poured
ieral drinks for the two of them. Lifting the glasses
til they touched, the two men drank a silent toast, then
iboden slapped his leg with his riding gloves and broke
to a loud guffaw.

"I wouldn't have have missed that scene this morning
r the world," said the cavalry officer when he recovered
e power of speech. "As soon as the general dismissed
e hearing, young Duggan took off like a scared rabbit.
reckinridge looked as if he'd seen a ghost, too. Just
hat was written on the back of the order?"

"Only an endorsement." David took the sheet from his pocket and held it up for Imboden to see and read aloud:

HQ Army of Northern Virginia
May 10, 1864

To: Major David Preston, Medical Corps, CSA
Orders above confirmed by this headquarters.

R. E. Lee, Commanding

Beneath the official endorsement was a note in familiar hand:

Glad to have you back, Major Preston. We need experienced doctors like you more than ever in these difficult times.

R. E. Lee

BOOK NINE

Washington

1

The Spotswood Hotel in Richmond hadn't changed much since he'd stayed there two years before, David saw when he took a place at the long bar one afternoon at the end of May 1864, and, resting a well-polished boot on the rail, ordered bourbon and water. He had arrived in Richmond several hours earlier, after seeing Lachlan Murrell, his wound and fracture healing nicely, safely to Preston's Cove, where Araminta could look after her brother during his convalescence.

David was no longer assigned to the VMI cadet regiment, now the heroes of the Confederacy and transferred to Richmond with General Breckinridge and the victorious Valley Army, after their triumph at New Market. Instead, he was on his way to join his old comrades-in-arms, the Stonewall Brigade and Stonewall Division, and had been lucky to find a room at the Spotswood.

Refreshed now by a bath and a freshly brushed uniform, he was looking forward to a leisurely dinner with Ed Mattox and bringing himself up to date on what had transpired since he'd last seen the newspaperman at Gettysburg. Looking around him now as he sipped the bourbon, David could see that the old hotel still had much of the seedy gentility of the past. The same crowd of officers, politicians, salesmen and contract wranglers

451

were there, although the latter had dwindled considerab
since the decision of England not to give further aid
the South without payment in cash or cotton had almo
bankrupted the Confederacy.

He was finishing his first drink and debating orderi
a second when Ed Mattox slapped him on the should
before reaching for the tall, frosted julep the bartend
had put on the bar when Ed came through the door.

"Got the message you left at the paper that you we
in town," Mattox said as they shook hands. "Take yo
drink with you and we'll see what sort of a dinner t
Sportswood is serving."

"The last report I saw, you'd been relieved from acti
duty permanently because of illness," said Mattox whe
they were ensconced at a table in the already crowde
dining room. "What are you doing back here in Ricl
mond?"

Quickly David explained the events of the past sever
months.

"It took courage to put on the uniform again aft
finding probably the only place in this country whe
there's likely to be any peace at all in the immedia
future," said the newspaperman. "But I guess saving yo
brother-in-law's arm made it all worthwhile."

"More than worthwhile. Lachlan plans to go back t
the Cherokee Nation after the war to furnish some bad
needed leadership."

"The Confederacy has just made Stand Watie a brig
dier general so the Boudinot faction will be riding hig
Seen any of your old comrades-in-arms since you cam
back on duty?"

"Only Hunter McGuire—and John Imboden was
New Market."

"Dr. McGuire's been busy building up an ambulanc
corps from practically nothing. I happen to know h
could have had several more promotions, if he'd bee
willing to cozy up to Jefferson Davis and some of Davi
cronies—but not Lee of course."

"Is the general really as incorruptible as he appear
to be?"

"Robert E. Lee's the living symbol of what the Sout

uld have been but hardly ever was. I guess he's one of
e most beloved generals in history, as well as one of the
ost capable."

"I can agree to that."

"Where are you off to next?"

"A place called Cold Harbor, a few miles northeast of
ichmond."

"The last stand." Mattox's tone was grave. "At Spot-
lvania Court House, while you were busy at New
Iarket, Lee pinned Grant's ears back against those
utenant general's stars he's wearing these days. But
e cost was terrible; at the end Old Allegheny John-
ns' Stonewall Division had barely enough men left to
rm a brigade."

"What about the Stonewall Brigade?"

"It was down to less than two hundred men at the
d, with only two officers and no CO. Fourteen regi-
ents, including four from the Valley, were combined
to one small brigade."

"I guess Spotsylvania qualifies as a pyrrhic victory."

"If there ever was one," Mattox agreed. "Now Grant's
ing to make his way around Lee's right flank to join
with an army under Ben Butler at a place called
rmuda Hundred on the James River south of Peters-
rg. And Beauregard—"

"Beauty Beauregard?"

"The same—though he's not quite so beautiful now.
cky Pierre has had some rather unlucky ventures since
rt Sumter and First Manassas. Right now he's watching
e Yankee army at Bermuda Hundred and screaming
: reinforcements."

"That's quite a comedown."

"Yes. But if Beauregard can keep Ben Butler occupied
the James so he can't join up with Grant east of Rich-
nd, the Union won't be able to finish welding that iron
nd they've been trying to create around the capital."

"What about the rumor that General David Hunter is
thering a new force from what was left of Sigel's troops
start up the Valley once again?"

"Hunter's already as far south as Staunton, with only
umble Jones and maybe eight thousand men there to

hold him back. With the Virginia Central Railroad in hi
hands, Hunter can sweep the rest of the Valley."

"A helluva doomsayer you turned out to be," sai
David. "Had any more bread riots in Richmond?"

"Not lately. Everybody's too worn out from hard wor
and short rations to even complain any more—especiall
when the Tredegar furnaces are out of iron to cast int
cannon and half the army's without shoes."

"That never stopped the Stonewall Brigade."

"In the old days Stonewall Jackson could always be de
pended upon to seize enough quartermaster supplies an
munitions every few months to keep his army at least o
its feet with a reasonably full belly. But the kind of wa
fare Grant likes doesn't allow for much in the way o
booty."

"Who's going to win the Union elections?"

"Not McClellan, although he's got the Democrati
Party nomination practically sewed up."

"I wouldn't be too sure," said David. "Araminta tol
me there was plenty of opposition to Lincoln in Phila
delphia."

"And elsewhere." Mattox conceded. "The Radica
don't like Lincoln's amnesty proclamation. The Demo
crats are tired of war. And hardly anybody in the Nort
really wants to give Negroes an equal vote with white
But one good victory could make a hero out of Lincol
overnight; and the way Sherman's moving toward Atlant
he might just deliver that victory before election day
November."

II

David left Richmond before dawn on July 3. Co
Harbor was only about fifteen miles from the center
the Confederate capital. And as he rode northwa
through the area where the Seven Days Battle of Ju
1862 had been fought, the roar of cannon grew loud
with every mile, tangible proof that the battle was movi
toward the climax that was expected daily.

In Richmond it was generally known that Lee w

ving to block Grant's rather obvious plan to press east
the city and turn the Confederate right flank so the
nion forces could join Ben Butler at Bermuda Hundred.
prevent that disaster, Lee had built strong fortifica-
ns along the Chickahominy River to the south and
topotomoy Creek on the north. David had not been
le to find out exactly where General Jubal Early's II
rps, to which he had been assigned, was located, but
judged that, as usual, the Virginia regiments would
most certainly be in the hottest part of the fighting.

As he neared the battle scene, David began to meet
ins of ambulances bringing back wounded men from
e front. From them he learned that the Virginia troops
re not yet involved in the first stages of the climactic
ttle but were still occupying trenches to the northeast
Richmond forming a part of its defenses. By that
he, however, he had come upon a makeshift field hos-
al at Gaines' Mill and settled down to help the over-
rked surgeon, who was trying to cope with a constant
eam of casualties from the battlefront, in places not
ch more than a mile away.

By midafternoon, judging from fragmentary reports
ching the hospital, the full nature of the southern vic-
y at Cold Harbor had begun to take form. When the
ttle started early that morning, Grant's field com-
nders had confidently thrown the blue wave *en masse*
ainst the southern fortifications. The ensuing carnage
s reported to be the worst in the war, perhaps in his-
y, as, stumbling backward in a hail of lead, the Union
ces had given way.

Grant finally broke off the battle shortly before night-
l, by which time 7,000 Union soldiers had fallen before
thundering Confederate artillery and rifle fire. Thus
combined total of casualties in the Spotsylvania Court
use and Cold Harbor campaigns reached 50,000 for
Union, against less than 30,000 for the Confederacy
and all in less than a month.

Work at the field hospital kept David busy through the
xt day and it was the afternoon of June 5 before he
s able to move back toward Richmond and eventually
d his Virginia comrades of the II Corps. When he re-

ported for duty at General Early's headquarters in th
rows of entrenchments protecting Richmond, Joe Sta
nard, now a colonel and limping from a bullet in the l
taken during the retreat from Gettysburg, greeted hi
warmly. A little grayer at the temples and somewh
leaner, Joe had lost none of his sense of humor or h
irreverence for military authority and the strange turb
lent world in which he found himself.

Stannard escorted David to the small 1st Field Ho
pital—only one of the Federal wagons captured at Fir
Bull Run was still miraculously able to move. There H
Perkins, grinning happily, greeted his old commandin
officer, before starting to cook part of a stolen ham. Wi
his usual talent for scrounging, Hal also managed to pr
duce a demijohn of rum and the three—rank long sin
discarded—were soon eating ham, biscuits and fried p
tatoes and drinking hot buttered rum.

"When we heard how you faced down General Brecki
ridge at New Market three weeks ago, we knew you we
back in fine fettle, David," said Stannard. "And the ne
thing we knew, you'd gotten yourself lost during t
Battle of Cold Harbor the same way you managed
wind up in the middle of the fighting at Bull Run, wh
John Imboden and Barnard Bee were retreating fro
Matthews Hill."

"I remember Old Jack giving me the devil for it."

"I'm sure Jackson's spirit was with us yesterday." T
warmth of the buttered rum was mellowing Stannar
thoughts. "If Old Jack had been in General Grant's sho
you can bet he wouldn't have thrown those three cor
right into the faces of our cannon."

The talk went on for hours with so much to discu
and so much of it sad—dashing Jeb Stuart killed
Yellow Tavern on May 11; "Old Baldy" Dick Ewe
though still alive, incapacitated to where he was fulfilli
a routine job of directing the defenses of Richmon
General "Stonewall Jim" Walker and Colonel Willia
Terry; subsequent commanders of the Stonewall Brigac
both severely wounded. But though its number were mu
smaller, the old brigade, David learned, was still part

456

e Virginia troops who had fought so gallantly since ɔse first days at Harpers Ferry.

That night David slept rolled up in a blanket and water- ɔof inside a medical wagon. And when the bugle blew r reveille at dawn, he climbed out in the warm June ɔrning to dress, grab a cup of coffee Hal already had ɔbbling on a pile of coals, and stand with the troops r morning muster and roll call.

The number of the old II Corps was pitifully small, he w as he watched them form in an open field. But the ɪky mountain men of the Stonewall Brigade, scraggly- ired and bearded, uniforms every shade of gray be- ɪuse of the varying strength of lye used to turn the blue captured Yankee fabric to something resembling the ɔnfederate color, were easily distinguishable among the ɪers. There were even a few butternut shirts among ɪm, too, gifts from loving families back home in the ɪlley.

"Think Old Jube has changed much?" Joe Stannard ked as he stood beside David and watched Jubal A. ɪrly—lately appointed to the new rank of lieutenant ɪeral—come to a halt before the massed troops.

"He's weathered some, I wonder if he's mellowed."

"I hope not," said Stannard. "Something must be brew- ɡ when he orders a formation like this."

"Men of the Second Corps, I have good news." Early's mewhat squeaky voice rang over the parade ground. Ve're going back to the Valley."

The announcement brought a cheer and Early made attempt to speak until it subsided.

"Don't get the idea it's just for guard duty though," continued. "We hear that General Grant has ordered ɪnter to eat out Virginia clear and clean as far as his my goes, so the crows flying over it for the balance of ɪ season will have to carry their provender with them." Early paused as a groan went up from the Virginia ɪgade mixed with cries of anger.

"That means Grant plans to keep any supplies from ɪching Richmond and Petersburg from the west," said e Stannard.

"The Yankees are moving toward Lynchburg right

now," Early continued, "and General Lee has given ou corps and the troops of General Breckinridge the task o stopping further Federal movement in the Valley. We wi march at once."

The spirits of the Stonewall Brigade and their fello Virginians were high as the long gray lines turned wes ward in the bright June sunlight. The promise of onc again seeing the Blue Ridge and the fertile Valley beyon gave the mountain men new life, in spite of their sma numbers.

In two days of marching, the II Corps and its attache troops covered sixty-four miles, reminiscent of the day when Stonewall Jackson's Foot Cavalry had marche even greater distances, setting records for infantry. Bivo acked at Louisa Court House, on the road to Charlottes ville, they were cheered by news that a train would b waiting the next day to carry them over the mountains– only to discover that, as so often happened with the rai roads of the Confederacy these days, the locomotive ha broken down.

The march continued by foot, however, and, althoug news that Federal troops had been reinforced by othe units from the West Virginia and eastern Tennessee are dampened the spirits of the marching troops somewha anger took over when they learned that the enemy ha paused in Lexington for a day to burn the buildings o the Virginia Military Institute.

It was an act particularly galling to the cadets, wh were still attached to General Breckinridge's divisior But as it turned out, the delay at Lexington for the war ton destruction of the venerable structures of the schoc cost the Federal forces dearly. By making a forced marc through the rolling foothills east of the Blue Ridge, Early small army came to Lynchburg a day ahead of the Unic forces moving belatedly against them from Lexingtor And, in a pitched battle the next day, the Confederate drove the Yankees westward along the James River t Salem.

With the upper Valley secure, Early's men stopped t draw their first rations in two days, a quarter pound o bacon and a pound of cornmeal each. To the sma

easure afforded by such a Spartan diet, however, was
lded the satisfaction of discovering that captured Fed-
als from General David Hunter's retreating forces, now
irrying for safety in West Virginia, were begging for
mething to eat.

For the first time in many months, probably since the
treat of General Lee's battered but undefeated army
om Gettysburg, the Shenandoah Valley was practically
npty of Union troops from the Potomac to the James,
id Old Jube Early was too doughty a fighter not to
ipitalize on that discovery.

On June 23, their bellies fed and bodies rested as much
was possible in time of war, the II Corps started along
familiar road, the Valley Turnpike, in a campaign
miniscent of Stonewall Jackson's most daring exploits.
'ith it was the division commanded by General John B.
ordon, of which the consolidated Virginia regiments,
cluding the Stonewall Brigade, were now a part. And
ice again this newest Army of the Valley headed north-
ard toward the Potomac River over the route where the
iterans of the famous brigade had performed some of
eir noblest feats of war.

III

At the grave of Stonewall Jackson in a largely burned-
it Lexington, the long gray line filed solemnly past to
lute the man who had led some of them to victory after
ctory in this same Valley. Moving on, July 2 saw Early's
my at Winchester, to the plaudits of the populace and
ill largely unopposed, since Grant had thrown prac-
cally all of his troops against Richmond in the Spot-
lvania and Cold Harbor campaigns. Two more days of
arch brought Early's troops across the Potomac at Wil-
amsport.

Into the fertile rolling fields of Maryland the ragged
onfederates marched to find food aplenty for the first
me in months. Ranging ahead were skirmishers under
eneral John McCausland, an old friend of David Pres-
n's and Joe Stannard's who had, at one time, been com-

mander of the Rockbridge Artillery. Shortly they brough
word to Jubal Early that a force of Federal troops unde
General Lew Wallace had been rushed from the Wash
ington area to oppose his progress. And at the crossin
of the Monocacy River, a major tributary of the Potoma
east of Harpers Ferry, a sharp battle took place on July 9

At the height of the fighting the Stonewall Brigade en
gaged in a flanking march, their favorite maneuver, rout
ing the Federals. And as a result, hurried messages from
the Federal commander to a stunned Washington told o
a Confederate army reported to number 20,000—mor
than twice its real size—approaching the Union capital
In the battles for the Monocacy crossings, however, th
Stonewall Brigade lost fifty of 253, leaving the combine
Valley regiments with less than 200 men.

Using the single medical wagon that remained in con
dition, David's unit had now become a true flying hos
pital. Often he operated in the very midst of the battle
as the opopsing forces seesawed back and forth acros
the rolling meadows and fields of Maryland just north o
the Potomac. Soon the II Corps was approaching the out
skirts of Washington, throwing the Union capital int
confusion and sending trains loaded with refugees flyin
northward to escape from what now appeared to be im
minent danger of capture by the Confederates.

Coming so close upon the news, only a month earlie
of staggering Union losses at Spotsylvania Court Hous
and Cold Harbor, the seemingly inevitable descent upo
Washington by a Confederate army set up a clamor a
through the North for the heads of General Ulysses S
Grant and President Abraham Lincoln. The headlines c
Washington newspapers captured by the veterans of Ol
Jube's army moving eastward toward their goal, the re
cently completed shining dome of the Federal Capitc
itself, topped by the bronze statue of the Star of Freedom
were black with denunciations of Union leadership, bot
military and political, to the considerable glee of th
advancing Confederates.

July 10 found the Stonewall Brigade at Rockvill
Maryland. But by delaying the Confederate advance fc
a day at the Monocacy River, General Lew Wallace ha

own Jubal Early's timetable considerably out of kilter. e forts guarding Washington were garrisoned mainly militia and inexperienced troops hurriedly gathered to pose the advance. Some of them were clerks from vernment departments and, had Early been able to ve against Washington on Sunday, July 10, instead of ng twenty miles away, he could have taken the capital lost without a shot.

On July 11, the Confederate force arrived at Silver ing, Maryland, in the very environs of Washington. bal Early made his headquarters in the beautiful man- n of Postmaster General Montgomery Blair, while troops prepared to attack Fort Stevens, strongest point the defense perimeter protecting Washington. As a ult, the Union capital was in the grip of fear, but tunately for the North, it did not extend to the highest els.

Contrary to his actions on a previous occasion, when coln had ordered McClellan to withdraw a large force m the Peninsula Campaign in Virginia to oppose what eared to be a threat to Washington by Stonewall kson, Lincoln had placed the defense of the capital ctly in the hands of General Halleck, nominally the neral-in-Chief, and Grant, the real occupant of that ition. And although with his many losses in June, nt was hardly free to relieve the capital immediately, lleck and Secretary of War Stanton immediately took thright measures on their own.

When Jubal Early approached Washington along the enth Street thoroughfare leading to Fort Stevens, coln had been at his usual summer quarters in the diers' Home, about halfway between Washington itself the northern corner of the District. Secretary Stanton nediately sent carriages to bring the Union President his family back to the capital, and meanwhile General lleck was busy sending frantic telegrams bringing every erienced military unit available to Washington as idly as possible.

Watching Early, Breckinridge and John Imboden while y studied Fort Stevens, the major fortification blocking ir advance into Washington, David and Joe Stannard

461

waited for the order that would send the II Corps, wi
the attached troops of General Breckinridge, movi
southward for what could be the most spectacular fe
performed by any Confederate general, the capture
Washington.

Already a line of skirmishers was moving into op
ground before Fort Stevens, opposed at the moment on
by a force of Federal pickets well in advance of t
fortification itself. As they watched, the growl of artille
from both sides began to rise to a pitch where the watche
were sure it could be heard at the capitol, less than t
miles away.

"A lot of Union fatbacks are shaking in their boo
right now," said Joe Stannard happily.

"But not Secretary Stanton," said David. "I don't b
lieve he's afraid of the devil himself."

The skirmishers in gray were being met by a ragg
line of blue-clad riflemen and on both sides men we
beginning to fall. Joe Stannard, who was watching t
earthworks of the Union fortifications with his fie
glasses, gave a sudden exclamation of surprise.

"What's up?" David asked.

"The tall man standing at the point nearest us, I cou
swear it's Abraham Lincoln!"

Lifting his own glasses, David focused them quick
When the lean face with the high cheekbones and for
head and the deep-set eyes took shape in the glasses,
whistled softly.

"It's Lincoln, all right. This is just what he'd do."

"Looks like somebody else besides Stanton isn't afra
of the devil himself," said Stannard. "There he goes,"
added as the tall figure disappeared from view. "Son
body must have had the good sense to make him g
down before our skirmishers got within range."

"Think Old Jube will try to take Washington itsel
David glanced toward Early and Breckinridge, where t
colloquy was continuing, the latter gesturing as if he we
arguing vehemently.

"If Breckinridge has the last word, he will. Can y
imagine what it would mean to Breckinridge to wa

o the Senate chamber and arrest many of the same men
o named him a traitor in the fall of 1861?"

"Or start taking gold bullion out of the Treasury."

"And how far do you think Breckinridge or Jubel
rly would get with it?" a new voice asked, and they
ned to see Lachlan Murrell climbing the slope to
ere they stood.

His arm almost healed, Lachlan had joined John Im-
den's cavalry unit once more when they had passed
ough Lexington. And when he insisted upon returning
active duty even with one arm strapped to his side,
vid couldn't refuse him.

"The whole of eastern Maryland is empty behind us,"
nnard protested. "General Wallace's troops retreated
defend Washington after we drove them back from the
nocacy.'

"Besides, Abraham Lincoln's in Fort Stevens," David
ded. "We were just looking at him."

"Early and Breckinridge saw him before you did,"
d the cavalryman. "That's what they're arguing about.
eckinridge wants to storm the fort—"

"Which makes sense," said Stannard.

"For him, maybe. But Jubel is arguing that Lincoln
uldn't have taken the chance of coming this far for-
rd—and what's more Stanton wouldn't have let him—
Fort Stevens wasn't better defended than it looks."

"But does Early have any way of being certain?"

"Take another look with your glasses," Lachlan sug-
ted.

The situation had indeed changed somewhat just in the
minutes David and Stannard had been talking. Al-
ugh the Federal picket line was still falling back, they
re fighting strongly now and a new force was coming
the field to support them. Joe Stannard focused his
d glasses on the new arrivals, studying them for a
ment.

'Those are veterans," he reported. "I can read some
the insignia."

'What organizations?" Lachlan asked.

'Twenty-fifth New York Cavalry, and some from the

150th Ohio National Guard. With at least one compa[ny] from the Second District."

"That means reinforcements from Petersburg," sa[id] the Cherokee officer. "I heard Jubal Early telling Jo[hn] Imboden just last night the latest courier from L[ee] brought a report that Grant now controls the Richmo[nd] Fredericksburg and Potomac Railroad almost as [far] south as Hanover Junction, a few miles north of Ri[ch]mond. He certainly didn't waste any time getting re[in]forcements up here by train."

"A Yankee prisoner my men captured early this mor[n]ing says part of the Sixth Corps is expected by steam[er] from City Point any time, too," Joe Stannard adde[d]. "They're trained fighting men and their presence wou[ld] certainly beef up the defenses of Washington."

"So now it's up to Old Jube to make a decision [on] what to do, and make it fast," said Lachlan Murre[ll]. "Want to make a side bet on what it will be?"

"You sound pretty confident," said David. "Co[uld] you possibly be using some information you have given us to lure us into filling your purse, my friend? [It] wouldn't be the first time an Indian made a fool out [of] white men."

"Cross my heart, I've got nothing up my sleeve."

"One thing's certain," said Joe Stannard, "Stonew[all] Jackson would have gone for Washington yesterday. [Do] you deny that, Major Murrell?"

"No. But we all know by now we can't win this o[ne] and the best we can get is a settlement on reasona[ble] terms—like giving up slavery and returning to the Uni[on]. The Copperheads and pacifists are ready to nomina[te] George McClellan as their candidate and the people a[re] tired of Lincoln's generals losing as many as seven tho[u]sand casualties in one day. So, if the Democrats win t[he] election next November, we just might get what we wan[t]."

"I wouldn't be too sure about the people behind M[c]Clellan, particularly Clement L. Vallandigham," sa[id] David. "Don't forget that he was run out of the coun[try] by the North a couple of years ago because of his Copp[er]head sentiments. And, even if he's back now, he's n[ot] very stable."

464

"What Abraham Lincoln needs most in the election xt November is for the North to become united behind 1," said Lachlan. "And the best way to do that is for South to capture Washington."

"Then you're saying the smart thing for Early to do is settle for making a demonstration here in the outskirts Lincoln's capital, scare the daylights out of the people, I retreat gracefully?" David asked.

"If he's as smart as I think he is, yes. And if Jefferson vis or Robert E. Lee had any way of reaching Early telegraph right now, I'd be willing to bet the wires uld be hot with messages telling Jube to stay as long he thinks safe, but to get back before Grant can cut 1 off."

Very much as Lachlan Murrell had predicted, the nfederate forces skirmished before Fort Stevens on y 11 and captured several wagon trains moving toward shington. By throwing a scare into the residents of ltimore through tearing up B&O trackage between the nocacy River and Maryland's largest city as a final ture of defiance before starting back toward the omac, Early's troops became, for the moment at least, heroes of the Confederacy.

When the cannon stopped booming at Fort Stevens, shington breathed a deep sigh of relief. Capital news-ers made much of the fact that, during the bombard-1t, Abraham Lincoln had displayed his confidence in defenders of Washington by watching the action from earthworks at Fort Stevens.

Much of the North, however, failed to share Lincoln's fidence. The dollar fell to thirty-nine cents in financial rkets and an outcry was raised by both Democrats and lical Republicans. The latter did not trust Lincoln to ly harsh measures to the South when victory finally 1e, and the Democrats couldn't believe victory was sible.

Bulldog Grant, however, still growled at Petersburg, paring to attack Richmond through its underbelly by ting off the supplies flowing to the Confederate capital n North Carolina through Petersburg by way of the ldon Railroad and the Richmond and Danville line,

465

both still in Confederate hands. And, unfortunately f
the South, things were not going nearly so well in
area of Atlanta as they were around Washington.

On the same day that Early was withdrawing from t
Union capital, Jefferson Davis wrote in despair to Ge
eral Robert E. Lee:

General Johnston has failed and there are strong indicatic
that he will abandon Atlanta.

IV

The Federal force hastily gathered for the defense
Washington against Jubal Early did not sit idly he
Major General Horatio Wright commanding the VI a
XIX corps, pursued the retiring Confederates, along w
the troops under General Lew Wallace. Old Jube, ho
ever, was a worthy follower of Stonewall Jackson's stra
gies of war. Fighting small sections of the enemy forc
at a time, he withdrew toward the Shenandoah Valley
way of White's Ford, Leesburg and a cut through t
Blue Ridge with the euphonious name of Snicker's Ga
Nipping at his backside to the south by now, too, we
the troops of General David Hunter, who had return
to the fray after being driven into West Virginia by Ea
as a prelude to his dash toward Washington.

For the Stonewall Brigade and David Preston, it w
an old story many times retold, a game of hare a
hounds with the hare growing weaker and the houn
gaining strength all the while. Taking advantage of eve
opportunity to damage the Federal armies and thus ke
Grant from returning the VI and XIX corps to th
normal positions around Richmond and Petersburg, Ju
Early retreated skillfully. As slowly as he could,
followed the Valley Turnpike southward, the same ro
Jackson had taken in the spring of 1862, after the ne
disastrous Battle of Kernstown. Meanwhile, Gene
William Tecumseh Sherman was tightening a noose arou
Atlanta and a new Confederate commander, Gene

n Bell Hood, had replaced General Joseph E. John-
n there.

With Early's raid on Washington having given a false
ression of strength on the Confederate side, plus the
t that Lincoln's call for a half million volunteers was a
it admission that Grant's one-day loss of seven thou-
d at Cold Harbor had been a strong blow to the
ion, peace feelers blossomed again. Horace Greeley of
New York *Tribune* traveled to Niagara Falls, seeking
contact Northerners asking for peace. Publisher J. R.
more conferred with Jefferson Davis on the terms of
ossible treaty, but Davis would only settle for Con-
erate independence and Lincoln insisted upon the
rn of the South to the Union and the abolishment of
very.

The two sides were still as far apart as ever and, mean-
ile, in the Shenandoah Valley, Early's slowly retreating
ces were pressed hard at Stephenson's Depot, just
th of Winchester. In heavy fighting, a Confederate
ision was defeated when one brigade broke. More
n two hundred were captured and, with the main force
ely escaping a severe defeat, Early retreated toward
asburg, leaving Winchester once again in Federal
ds.

On the same day, in a battle at Peach Tree Creek in
outskirts of Atlanta, a charge of almost 20,000 Con-
erates against a slightly larger number of Federals
s repulsed with heavy casualties, the South losing over
r thousand and the Federals under General William
cumseh Sherman, less than two.

Suspecting that General Wright and part of the Federal
ops pursuing him had been withdrawn by Grant, Jubal
rly launched a sudden attack against Federal forces at
rnstown and Winchester on Sunday, July 24. In the
cond Battle of Kernstown, Early was more successful
n Stonewall Jackson had been two years earlier on
rch 23, 1862, and sent the enemy reeling back as far
Bunker Hill, a familiar spot to the Stonewall Brigade.
To the tired remnants of the brigade and to David
eston, even the small victories were depressing, for
y meant fighting over ground they had held as early as

467

July 2, 1861, less than three months after the wa[r] beginning with the fall of Fort Sumter in Charleston h[ar]bor. It was hard for the weary brigade to rejoice in vi[c]tory, too, with the Liberty Hall Volunteers of the 4[th] Virginia down to one officer and two enlisted men, wh[ile] Company A of the 33d, whose screaming charge at t[he] Battle of First Manassas had started the Federal ro[ut] was reduced to one sick infantryman.

Taking advantage of Federal confusion after the batt[le] at Kernstown, Early struck hard across the Potomac on[ce] again, moving as far north as Mercersburg, Pennsylvani[a,] a few miles beyond Hagerstown, Maryland. Once aga[in] furor was created in the North, but these were me[re] forays, in their way no more significant than had be[en] General Jeb Stuart's famous rides.

General John McCausland's raid on Chambersbur[g,] Pennsylvania, about the same time—in which he d[e]manded a hundred thousand dollars in gold as reparatio[n] for Hunter's burning of Lexington, VMI and other upp[er] Valley points—actually accomplished nothing of signi[fi]cance. Chambersburg was unable to raise the requir[ed] amount of money, so McCausland burned the town, [an] act later used by Federal troops as an excuse for layi[ng] waste to much of the Valley. At McConnellsburg, M[c]Causland once again threw a scare into the thrifty Dut[ch] farmers of central Pennsylvania, before retreating acro[ss] the Potomac.

"If I have to swim that hospital wagon across t[he] Potomac one more time, I hope we can give it a milita[ry] burial in the middle of the stream," Hal Perkins to[ld] David Preston one afternoon late in July as they watch[ed] a regimental blacksmith lower a wheel into a pool, shrink[ing] the red-hot tire he'd just driven upon the wood[en] frame and setting it, hopefully, for some time.

"I'm sure it deserves the honor," David replied.

"More than deserves it, sir. When I took the whee[l] off the wagon you found at Mechum's River Station b[e]fore we started to Staunton by train for the Battle [of] McDowell in 1862, I put it on the one we still have."

"Are you sure?"

"It's got my mark on it. I wonder how many miles it's traveled since you captured the hospital at Bull Run."

"The question is, where do we go from here?"

"Is it true that General Philip Sheridan is taking over the Valley for the Yankees—with instructions to destroy everything that will burn?"

"Sheridan's being put in command of this area for the Union; General Lee notified General Early of it a few days ago. And the Yankees have been threatening to destroy everything in the Valley since shortly after the battle of New Market."

"But that's barbarous."

David knew Hal was thinking of the farm not far to the south, near Strasburg, where much of the uncommissioned officer's family still lived. And of the babies, now toddlers, whose vaccination sores had enabled them to stop an epidemic of smallpox not far from where they were sitting.

"War often gets that way toward the end, Hal. The North is using General McCausland's burning of Chambersburg as an excuse to lay waste to the Valley."

"Forgetting what General Hunter did around Lexington? It doesn't seem right."

"Nothing about war is right, Hal. But in a way, it may be for the best, something like the shot that administers the *coup de grâce* at an execution."

"I was pretty upset when General Jackson had those three deserters shot," Hal confessed. "But when I see that we're down to now because so many have been able to buy their way out of being conscripted, or just plain deserted, I can understand that the general really didn't have much choice at the time."

"That's another trouble about war. It gradually decreases the options open to you, until finally you have no choice except death or dishonor."

"And when you choose death, how many people will remember to honor you because of it?"

From the pickets beyond the edge of the bivouac area came a sudden rattle of gunfire, proof that Federal skirmishers had been detected feeling out the strength of the

469

force bivouacked there. And hearing it, Hal move
toward the wagon to help the blacksmith fit the wheel c
the axle, leaving his question unanswered.

V

On August 1, 1864, General Philip Henry Sherida
a young man already marked for high position, wa
placed in command of the Federal army in the Valle
and moved northward from the Petersburg sector to tak
up his new position. The Confederate Army of Norther
Virginia could better have been called the Army c
Southern Virginia by then, bottled up as it was in the are
around Petersburg by a much larger Federal forc
Atlanta, too, was heavily besieged, and General Hoc
had not proved more successful against Sherman tha
Joseph E. Johnston had been before him.

Numbered from a succession of defeats and depriva
tions, broken only by an occasional flash of news fro
Early's successful forays in the Valley, Maryland ar
southern Pennsylvania, the entire South was in a state c
political paralysis that autumn. Not so the North, how
ever, where the Radicals on one side and peace elemen
in the Democratic Party on the other, were active
badgering a Lincoln administration that was peculiar
sensitive to such attacks, with an election now only
little over three months away.

In spite of the South's terrific loss of manpower in th
Battles of the Wilderness around Spotsylvania Cou
House and Cold Harbor, General Ulysses S. Grant ha
not yet taken Richmond and Petersburg, a failure whi
opponents of Lincoln in the North used as campaig
material against the President. Nobody in either th
North or the South looked forward to the prospect of a
ther winter of conflict but no one knew how to do mu
about it, with Abraham Lincoln and Jefferson Davis st
facing each other like an immovable object and a seer
ingly unstoppable force.

August 7 saw Sheridan assigned to command a ne
military division including the former Middle Depar

ent, as well as the defenses of Washington, the Susque-
anna River and the new state of West Virginia. His
command was to be known as the Army of the Shenandoah, and with it went the freedom to co-ordinate all
operations against Early's Confederate forces, still carrying on hit-and-run operations all along the Potomac and
the lower Valley.

In order to take the measure of his opponent, Sheridan
immediately launched a southward attack from Bunker
Hill, West Virginia, toward Winchester and Jubal Early's
forces there. Meanwhile, at Cedar Creek, just south of
Winchester, Early had entrenched his weary troops to
await Sheridan's attack and determine just how formidable the highly praised new Federal commander would
turn out to be.

In his first attempt, however, Sheridan proved not to
be as daring as the entrenched Confederates had expected.
After skirmishing at Cedar Creek and Strasburg, as well
as near Charles Town, the Union commander withdrew
in order to insure a better line of supplies for his army.
Probing for any sign of weakness on the part of Sheridan,
Early followed him immediately, but, in a sharp fight near
Winchester, was unable to damage Sheridan's forces
seriously.

During August Early performed ably his gadfly role
of stinging the Federals under Sheridan wherever he
could, but actually inflicted little damage. None of this,
however, decreased the dissatisfaction in the North with
Abraham Lincoln's prosecution of the war, as evidenced
by the revelation in Washington newspapers captured
by Early's skirmishing parties of a memorandum the
President had asked members of his Cabinet to sign
without reading:

This morning, as for some days past, it seems exceedingly
probable that this administration will not be re-elected. Then
it will be my duty to so cooperate with the President-elect
as to save the Union between the election and the inauguration; as he will have secured his election on such grounds
that he cannot possibly save it afterwards.

471

This last was a sharp dig at McClellan, the strong
candidate opposing Lincoln and the all-but-certain cho
of the Democratic Party. But it also summarized L
coln's own feelings about the political implications of
coming election.

On Wednesday, August 24, 1864, in a last-ditch
tempt to achieve peace, Lincoln authorized editor Hen
J. Raymond to seek a conference with Jefferson Da
to discuss a settlement, notifying Davis that the w
would end "upon the restoration of the Union and
national authority." Which provision the Confeder
President, of course, refused to accept.

On August 21, Jubal Early, still playing the gad
had driven his army, included the Stonewall Brigade a
the other Virginia regiments, now numbering hardly m
than forty-five men each, in a new move toward Sh
herdstown, West Virginia, with the intention of on
again crossing the Potomac into Maryland and Penns
vania. This time, however, the fords of the Potomac w
well guarded and Early was forced to withdraw.

On August 29, while addressing the Democratic N
tional Convention in Chicago, heady now with the co
viction that they could nominate a candidate to def
Lincoln and end the war at once, August Belmont to
the assembled delegates:

Four years of misrule by a sectional, fanatical and corr
party have brought our country to the verge of ruin.

And on the following day the Democrats adopted
platform for ending the war and placed in nominat
for President, to nobody's surprise, Major General Geo
B. McClellan, with Thomas H. Seymour, former gov
nor of Connecticut, as Vice-President.

The platform stated that:

Justice, humanity, liberty and the public welfare dem
that immediate efforts be made for a cessation of the h
tilities, with a view to an ultimate convention of the Sta
or other peaceable means, to the end that at the earl

cticable moment peace may be restored on the basis of
Federal Union of the states.

Since it was the same basis of settlement for which
praham Lincoln had strived from the beginning, the
ank of the Democratic Party offered nothing new. But
September 1, they at least had their candidate; and
th Petersburg holding out steadfastly against Grant's
stly superior army, while Jubal Early still skirmished
the Valley, the political fortunes of Abraham Lincoln
emed to have reached their lowest ebb.

Then overnight the situation, both political and mili-
y, changed sharply with a telegram to the President
m General Sherman announcing that Atlanta was
airly won." And on the same date, Lee pressed Early
release some of his troops for the support of Peters-
rg and Richmond, a sure sign that Lee considered the
alley no longer defensible against Sheridan's steadily
creasing forces there. In words that virtually sounded
e death knell of the Confederacy, Lee also urged the
noval of exemptions and the increasing of enlistments,
ying:

r ranks are constantly diminishing by battle and disease
d few recruits are received; the consequences are inevitable.

On September 19, Sheridan's army of nearly 40,000
ipped Early's badly divided force of only 12,000 in
e Third Battle of Winchester, forcing the Confederate
its into a general retreat southward up the Valley Pike.
a battle of Fisher's Hill on September 22, Sheridan
ove Early's forces from the heights of Strasburg, push-
 them farther down the Valley. And in this engage-
nt, Sandie Pendleton, who, like David, Joe Stannard
d John Imboden, had been with Stonewall Jackson
m the beginning, was wounded.

An hour after Pendleton was shot, he was brought by
abulance to the makeshift hospital David Preston had
 up just off the road. One look at the young officer's
le face, the bloodstained uniform and the gory bandage
und his groin and abdomen told David that Pendleton

473

was gravely wounded. Opening the medicine chest, removed one of the few remaining tablets of morph and used a hypodermic syringe to give a strong dose the powerful narcotic before making the usually pain first examination. Pendleton opened his eyes at the pri of the needle.

"Never ride a white horse in battle at night, Davi said the young officer, who had risen to the position Jubal Early's chief-of-staff before he was wounded. "K Douglas warned me, but I wanted the men to know th leaders weren't afraid."

"Don't try to talk, Sandie. I'll see about your wound

"They're mortal, I'm afraid. But at least my own m didn't kill me, as they did General Jackson."

The groin wound had struck a vital artery and v still bleeding, though not freely. To control the hem rhage would mean opening the wound and probing the artery, David knew, no doubt starting serious ble ing again. And even if he were able to tie the injur vessel—a not likely eventuality, working in the da without chloroform, the stock of which had long si been exhausted—shutting off the blood supply to the would almost certainly cause gangrene. And judging fr the rigidly of the muscles, as they sought to protect jured internal organs, the wound in the abdominal w undoubtedly included penetration of the abdominal cav in itself alone, almost a sentence of death.

Working as gently as he could, David packed the gr wound with a long strip of cloth to apply pressure to injured vessel there, hoping the lowered pressure in artery from hemorrhage would help prevent much m loss of blood. But knowing the gravity of abdomi wounds of this type and the agony that must surely low before death ended the life of the brilliant yo officer, he could almost wish the vessel would br loose and bring Sandie Pendleton's life quickly and me fully to a close.

Hal Perkins had been helping David and so requi no explanation of the hopelessness of the prognosis. N he spoke and his tone was urgent.

"We'll have to move or be captured, sir," he said

"And leave a dying man to the enemy?"

"I know this part of the Valley very well, sir, Dr. urphy lives at Woodstock, a few miles away, and has ken care of a lot of wounded men in other campaigns. olonel Pendleton will be much better off with him than ing jostled in an ambulance."

David looked up dully. "Or a prisoner?"

"The Yankees are moving fast and may not pay much tention to southern wounded."

"You're right, of course, Hal. Take the colonel to oodstock and ask Dr. Murphy to look after him. And ve the doctor what's left of the morphine; he probably es not have any and at least he can ease Colonel Pend- on's pain."

Once again there was the now familiar confusion of treat. On the way south the next day, David, Joe Stan- rd and John Imboden stopped at Woodstock briefly th Lachlan Murrell—whose arm had now healed and s as good as ever—for the funeral of Sandie Pendle- n, who had died during the night.

Standing in the October sunshine, they watched a small tail of riflemen, almost all of whom had been part of e original Stonewall Brigade when Sandie Pendleton d first joined it, fire a final volley over the grave. And they turned their mounts away from the small cem- ry, the three could easily see the red flare of bonfires ross the Valley, the clouds of smoke rising in the mid- mmer sky—mute evidence that Sheridan's hard-riding valry had already begun carrying out Grant's orders sweep the Valley so clean that even the crows would ve to carry provisions when crossing it.

Nevertheless, Jubal A. Early wasn't giving up the enandoah Valley without a fight. On October 19, he nched an offensive led by the Stonewall Brigade and e remnants of the other Virginia regiments, routing a rprised Yankee force encamped along Cedar Creek at e foot of the Massanutten Range in the neighborhood New Market. Some compared the Confederate victory Cedar Creek to a miniature Bull Run but, with a pos- le major victory in his grasp, Jubal Early hesitated to pursue the fleeing Federals, much to the disgust of junior commanders, and the opportunity was lost.

Early's hesitation may have been prompted by knowledge of the odds against success. Or, like his troo he could have been weary of fighting. In any event She dan was able to regroup quickly and rally his troops throw back the Valley Army with heavy losses, mos in prisoners.

"When Jackson's old legions were destroyed, the e was near," one tired Confederate officer said.

On December 6, the weary and downcast veterans the Stonewall Brigade said good-by to their below Shenandoah Valley and headed for Petersburg by tra Behind them, they left the whole Valley largely un fended and soon to be a scene of pillage and destructi when Sheridan's troops swept it clean as Grant h directed.

"Our numbers are getting smaller every day," said J Stannard soberly as the train bearing part of Jubal Earl army moved down the eastern slope of the Blue Ric toward Richmond by way of the South Side Railro from Lynchburg.

Six months before, Early had used the city as a laun ing platform for his dash to the environs of Washingt itself; now he was giving it up—and with it the Confe erate hold on the Shenandoah Valley that had play such an important part in determining both Union a southern strategy in the continuing—and still undecic —offensive against Richmond that had begun at Ma assas Junction and Bull Run in the summer of 1861.

"Maybe Old Jack was lucky to be cut down at t height of his career," said Lachlan Murrell. "He d secure in the knowledge that he was obeying God's w as he saw it. And he was saved the realization that t Cause he loved has failed, as much because of bumbli generals and crooked politicians as for any other reaso

"I have an idea some of the trials that lie before may be even worse than those behind us," Joe Stann added glumly.

"Not for me," said David. "I understand now wl Jackson meant in his last words, when he said, 'Let

oss over the river and rest beneath the trees.' There's
cove in Botetourt County where a vengeful U.S. Con-
ess can't find me and I can't get there a moment too
on, once the fighting is over."

"Take my advice and go there now," said Stannard.
know you came back because of the Stonewall Brigade,
t with so few of us left, it hardly seems worth the
uble."

"We Virginians volunteered for this war at the start and
'll see it through to the end."

"Pray God the agony is over soon then," said John
boden, who was with the others. "When I remember
at this Valley was like the time we marched through
on the way to Manassas Junction that first summer and
the wasteland it's becoming now, I realize what a
w and horrifying dimension has been added to war-
e."

"I've always thought of Sandie Pendleton as belonging
the age of chivalry," said David, remembering a freshly
ed grave at Woodstock. "But though outmoded, it
uld still produce a spirit like the Spanish cavalier—if
ould remember the words of the song."

"I remember," said Joe Stannard and began to sing
tly:

> "The Spanish cavalier stood in his retreat
> "And on his guitar played a tune, dear,
> "The music so sweet, we'd oft-times repeat,
> "The blessings of my country and you, dear."

"Sandie fitted the song, so maybe it's just as well that
life ended while there was still a touch of romance
t in warfare," said John Imboden. "But I guess men
e Ulysses Grant and Philip Sheridan have just about
stroyed that, too."

477

BOOK TEN

Appomattox

I

Christmas 1864 was anything but pleasant for the we
remnants of the Stonewall Brigade in the trenches gua
ing Petersburg, about twenty miles south of Richmo
They had arrived there on December 9, and learned
most immediately that the wanton destruction Gene
Philip Sheridan was wreaking upon their beloved Shen
doah Valley could hardly be compared with the path
flame, pillage and destruction General William Tecums
Sherman had blazed in his march across Georgia fr
Atlanta to the sea.

The Federal Congress and Lincoln—the Republic
and the President having won a clear sweep in the el
tions of November 1864—were electrified a few d
later by the news that Sherman was engaged in the en
lopment and capture of the city of Savannah, Georg
All of which meant that the Confederate States of Am
ica had now been divided from west to east by Sherma
march from Atlanta, after having been split from north
south on the day following the fall of Gettysburg
Grant's capture of the final river bastion of Vicksbu
Now, it was reported, Sherman was preparing to slice
the stricken South once again, by moving northw
along the eastern seaboard.

With the enemy no more than a stone's throw av

m the Petersburg trenches, any head raised above the
rapet was likely to earn a bullet for itself. And although
e pits had been dug for the protection of those man-
g the trenches night and day, they were at best poor
otection against the frequent rounds of mortar fire
bed by the enemy into the fortifications.

One spectacular occurrence had enlivened somewhat
summer before for both sides. Federal sappers, former
al miners, had dug an extensive tunnel beneath the
tersburg defense lines at one point and detonation of
ssive charges of powder in the tunnel on July 30,
64, had created a deep crater. The Union troops
igned to develop the break in Confederate lines where
crater exploded, had been so astonished at its size
depth, however, that they had milled about in it
her than crossing through the break. And while they
itated, the Confederate defenders had poured a galling
into the massed blue-clad troops struggling in the
oths of the crater, with over 4,000 Yankee casualties
ulting.

In the trenches, the remnants of the Virginia regiments
upied themselves as soldiers in winter quarters have
e since warfare began. They "drilled, reorganized,
ached, prayed, sang and played cards and so whiled-
ay the gloomy days waiting for the bloody springtime,"
the words of one of the participants. Most of all they
fered: from near starvation, from cold, from lack of
thing and shelter and, inevitably, from disease. Colds
ned rapidly into fevers, fevers into pneumonia and, all
frequently, pneumonia into not always unwelcome
th.

With medical supplies almost nonexistent, David Pres-
and Hal Perkins did what they could for the sick
the occasional casualty. Meanwhile, of the several
roaches to Petersburg, only those on the southeast
ained open much of the time, with the Boydton
nk Road and the South Side Railroad the only major
ries left for the movement of supplies and ammuni-
into the city from the south.

On February 6, 1865, the Stonewall Brigade was in-
ved in fairly active fighting when Federal troops tried

to extend their grasp on Petersburg as far as Hatch(
Run, south of the city, aiming at the Boydton Plank R(
and the South Side Railroad. The brigade took a beat
and some dispirited veterans surrendered, but the ma
casualty was Joe Stannard, who was brought to Davi
hospital wagon, functioning as a makeshift field hosp
to the very end, with his left arm shattered.

Pale from suffering and shock, but with bleeding c
trolled by a tourniquet Stannard himself had twis
about his upper arm—using a handkerchief to surrou
the arm and a stick to twist and tighten the Span
Windlass—he'd been able to make it back to the hosp
under his own power.

"I hope your scalpels are sharp," Stannard told Da
as he was examining the arm.

"They are, but we don't have any chloroform left."

"What about whiskey?"

David glanced at Hal, who nodded. "There's plent

"Break it out then, Hal," said Stannard. "I've be
waiting a long time for an excuse to get dog drunk, a
this is it."

By the time David was ready to operate, Joe St
nard's voice was already thick from the effects of
entire pint of whiskey.

"Don't feel sorry for me, doc," he said. "In Lexing
I'll be a hero, so I'll get a lot of legal business out of t
amputation. Besides, all a lawyer has to do is turn pa
of legal volumes, sign subpoenas or checks, and for tl
one hand is enough. This way I'm out of the war w
honor, but if General Lee had to order General Gord
to make another attempt to break out of this ring arou
Petersburg, I could have wound up being shot."

II

On February 16, 1865, the 5th Virginia sent a petit
to Jefferson Davis, asking the ailing President of
Confederate States of America to designate the five V
ginia regiments as an individual unit to be known as
Stonewall Regiment. Nothing came of the request, Da

ng occupied at the time with the larger business of
ing to hold together a Confederacy that was being
ieezed into an area east of the Tennessee border and
Shenandoah Valley of Virginia, south of Richmond
l north of Savannah, with Sherman already beginning
move northward to shorten its length in the North-
ith line.

At the end of February, General William R. Terry's
gade of about twelve hundred men, served by the 1st
ld Hospital, was assigned a position opposite the deep
le of the Petersburg crater, its surface already begin-
ig to be covered with vegetation. But, for the most
t, the salient was inactive and there was even an in-
mal truce between those defending it on each side.

On March 25, the division commanded by General
in B. Gordon, including what was left of the Stonewall
gade and the Virginia regiments, made a last attack
on the enemy forces. Certain that the Confederates
re powerless, the Union troops were caught napping
l the yelling Southerners—perhaps the last time the
ious rebel yell would be heard during this war—over-
. the Union lines at the beginning of the attack.

But then, as had happened so many times before,
rything seemed to go wrong. The advance was not
owed through, giving the Yankee forces time to re-
up and turn a heavy fire from both rifle and artillery
Gordon's center and both flanks. The shattered rem-
ts of the Stonewall Division were forced back into
Petersburg fortifications and the 5th Virginia, which
l petitioned Jefferson Davis asking special recognition
the Virginia regiments, underwent the ignominy of
ng its colors.

The cold, ragged troops retreated to their former posi-
is without even having captured any badly needed
plies. And at the end of the brief, but bloody, assault,
feelings of the Stonewall Brigade, now numbering
y about two hundred men, were best summed up by
iember of the 2d Virginia who wrote his family: "We
ild not even find courage in despair. All was lost and
future seemed without aim or object. Death and the
ve alone appeared inviting."

On March 25, General John B. Gordon once again a concerted attack on the Union line guarding the east side of the perimeter of fortifications surrounding Pete burg. It was a desperate venture intended to force Gr to protect his right flank by withdrawing troops from northern perimeter. If successful, southern forces Petersburg and Richmond might have been able to br out of Grant's band of iron and launch a push westw to join, for a final stand, with the only Confederate ar of any size left in the area, led by General Joseph Johnston, in North Carolina.

Although Sheridan, having finished laying waste to Shenandoah Valley and destroying most of Early's for there, had already moved eastward to help Grant, Confederate attack of March 25 showed, for a few ho all the promise of the earlier one at Hatcher's Run. once again, the initial success was lost from inability push the attack far enough to consolidate the two forc The harried Confederates were finally driven back w a loss of 4,000 killed, wounded and captured, compa to 1,500 for the Union—a major defeat for an alrea reeling force.

In the last days of March and the first of April, G eral Robert E. Lee began preparations for a retreat we ward along the Appomattox River, while the No started the final closing in upon Petersburg, whose would open the road to Richmond and insure the capt of the Confederate capital. Yet, in such a dire state, so found time for more pleasant—and unfortunate—p suits.

General George E. Pickett, whose fame had burgeo after the gallant, but futile, charge at Gettysburg, entrusted with the task of holding the vital Five Fo Junction point on the White Oak Road southeast Petersburg. With 10,000 men against 10,000 Un cavalry and 12,000 infantry, the odds were not w Stonewall Jackson would have considered about even

Lee had given Pickett specific instructions to hold F Forks at all hazards, protecting the road to Ford's De and preventing the Union forces from striking the So Side Railroad. Yet, when Union forces under Sheri

acked the Five Forks area on April 1, Pickett was
ending a shad bake—or fish fry—at the rear. Before
reached the front to take command again, the vital
ction point had been lost and Union troops were surg-
over it in victory.

The engagement at Five Forks allowed the last rail-
d to Petersburg to be cut, leaving Lee no longer able
provide food for his army. At the same time, his
erves had been exhausted and, when Grant struck
ously at Petersburg on the morning of April 2, 1865,
Confederate lines broke badly.

The retreat from Petersburg began that same day,
ving Richmond, twenty miles away, defenseless. Riding
orse he had requisitioned in the final hours of confu-
a, David Preston followed the creaking hospital wagon
ven by Hal Perkins. Neither of them was at all sure
wheels would even make it to North Carolina, if Lee
uld manage to perform the miracle of joining his
ops with those of General Joseph E. Johnston, said to
in the neighborhood of Greensboro or Durham.

One consolation was that Joe Stannard was safe, sitting
de Hal Perkins with the stump of his amputation
nd to his side to protect him from pain of the muscle
tractions that always made recovery from an ampu-
on painful. And since the wagon bore the yellow
kings that distinguished the medical corps, and during
battles around Petersburg the Union troops had
ays respected those markings, David was not really
ried.

III

pring had once again painted the Southland in green
gold and white. The sun shone warmly in Richmond
the morning of April 2, 1865, and people turned out
ost en masse for divine services. They were even
erful, for weren't the dogwoods bursting their buds?
en't the trees green and flowers popping from the
? And wasn't it certain that somehow, by some means,
eral Robert E. Lee, that military magician, would

still manage to turn imminent defeat into victory?
almost had to, for just a few months before, Lee
finally been placed in supreme command of Confede
forces on all fronts, a position Jefferson Davis, ailing
and querulous, had refused him until then.

Reports reaching Richmond from Petersburg spok
heavy fighting, but that, too, was an old story. The
ter of guns from the south was occasionally audible
Richmonders made their way, on foot or on wheels
church. But the sound of cannon had been much lo
two years earlier when McClellan had come in sigh
the Confederate capital.

Pickett was there in the breach, was he not? Ga
Pickett who had led the charge at Gettysburg. Also L
street, his wound healed, still irascible at times but al
courageous. So, too, A. P. Hill, stalwart warrior in his
undershirt, for who in Richmond could know this
in the day that Hill was dead by the time church
tolled, killed that very morning by a single Union
man as he sought to reach the Boydton Plank Road
rally the men fighting at Hatcher's Run to protect
South Side Railroad.

That same vital railroad, its tracks stretching east
toward a junction with the Richmond and Danvill
Burkeville, marked the remaining route of escape fo
embattled Army of Northern Virginia. Withdrawing
of the Appomattox River, as the lines that had
around Petersburg for nearly a year started cavin
around him, once Pickett's men at Five Forks had
forced to fall back while their commander was atten
a fish fry, Lee's only hope of escape for what was le
his army was to move westward to the junction with
Richmond and Danville line. From thence a rapid
southward was conceivable, allowing Lee to join J
ston's army in the Carolinas, although it, too, was alr
being pressed from the south by the forces of Ge
Sherman carrying his campaign of plunder and fi
northward.

When Lee's forces broke out of the Petersburg defe
and started their evacuation of the town, it was to
eral Philip Sheridan that Ulysses S. Grant gave the

outdistancing the retreating Confederate army and cutting the Richmond and Danville Railroad before they could reach it. Even before the fighting for the perimeter forts of Petersburg subsided to an occasional rifle shot, Sheridan's cavalry was off and running, followed by three infantry columns under General George G. Meade. Lean, tough, contemptuous of the foe they were seeking to destroy, Sheridan's men were only concerned now with swiftness of movement. For speed was of the essence. Relentlessly they harried the flanks of the retreating Confederates, seeking to get ahead of the tired and shuffling gray lines before they could break through into North Carolina.

Cut up into small units, Lee's forces shrank steadily from desertion as they retreated westward. But Grant, having seen apparent victory turn into defeat more than once in the Wilderness and again at Cold Harbor, had no intention of letting Lee consolidate his forces with those of Johnston, the only other body of troops of any size left in the Confederacy.

Kneeling at prayer in his pew at St. Paul's Church in Richmond as the service began, Jefferson Davis felt a tap on his shoulder. And when an aide silently handed him a telegram on which were printed the words, "I think it is absolutely necessary that we should abandon our position tonight," Davis didn't even need to see the signature at the bottom of the message to know what it meant. No longer did Davis have either the strength or the independence to argue with the general whose courage, devotion and skill had almost singlehandedly held the Confederacy together for almost a year after eventual defeat had been certain.

By 11 A.M. that night, Davis and most of the Cabinet had left Richmond. And as the train pulled out, flames set by the departing troops to destroy what few stores were left in the city had already spread to other structures. Soon they would destroy most of the once proud Confederate capital, the target of Federal armies for four years, during which the hundred-mile strip between Richmond and Washington had literally been carpeted with the bodies of Confederate and Union dead.

485

On April 3, Davis and the most of his Cabinet we at Danville, Virginia. By that time, the forces led Robert E. Lee had almost reached Amelia Courthou where they had expected ample supplies to be store only to discover that Philip Sheridan had already cut both the vitally needed supplies and the route to t south.

Lee's immediate goal in the retreat from Petersbu had been the small junction point of Burkeville, whe the South Side Railroad joined the Richmond and Da ville line. There the troops retreating from Richmo were supposed to join him for the final dash towa North Carolina, but they never made it.

General John B. Gordon's division, reduced now to little more than a regiment in size but still containing t remnants of the once proud Virginia regiments and t Stonewall Brigade, was guarding the rear and the l flank of the retreating Confederate army. By the seco day after the Battle of Five Forks and the debacle the Sheridan's men had reached Jetersville, a small ham on the Richmond and Danville Railroad slightly less th forty miles from Petersburg. Meanwhile, Lee's forces h been plodding eastward toward Amelia Courthouse, abo ten miles away, with Gordon's ragged, hungry and tir men fighting skirmishing battles almost every mile.

David Preston's hospital wagon was the only medi facility available and though often in the midst of fighti with bullets whistling through the canvas cover of t wagon, it had still managed to keep from being capture Hal Perkins was working with David, so Joe Stanna his stump still strapped to his side, drove the single m now pulling the wagon.

Even then there were sudden flashes of hope a southern defiance. When Federal cavalry general J. Irv Gregg was captured by Gordon's men, the Union offic was forced to ride at the head of the tattered colum where he could be seen by his own men and thus wo be a target for the first bullet if they attacked. At Jete ville, Sheridan had paused long enough to begin entrenc ments, into which Meade's infantry came a few hou later, with the intention of forcing a final battle betwe

Confederate troops less than a dozen miles to the
rth and the main body of Grant's pursuing forces as
n as they arrived.

Approaching Amelia Courthouse, however, Lee did
t know of the Federal presence there. Nor did he know
t Sheridan was riding ahead to cut off any Confederate
vement to the south toward North Carolina. Mean-
ile Grant had not stayed to celebrate his victory at
ersburg, even though Abraham Lincoln had been on
teamer at City Point, not far away, and had ridden
o Richmond later in triumph. Riding hard like his
tenants and his troops, Grant was only about twleve
es away, and joined Sherman that same night.

Even then, Lee surprised his old antagonist one last
e, with a night march from Amelia Court house toward
mville on the South Side Railroad, the only route now
n in the direction of Lynchburg and possibly the Blue
ge.. Discovering the breakout of the Confederate
ops on the morning of April 6, Grant sent his infantry
rching westward to maintain pressure on the Con-
erate rear, while Sheridan once again circled south
west of Lee's desperate army, seeking to cut them
from Lynchburg and any possible march to the south
ard North Carolina.

As Joe Stannard drove the hospital wagon onward,
s of Confederate disorganization were everywhere ap-
ent. A welter of guns, ammunition and anything dis-
dable had been piled beside the road by weary soldiers
ore they melted into the countryside to escape the final
tle and certain destruction. The Virginia troops, still
operating but badly battered unit, plodded on, but, at
mall place on the Appomattox River called Sayler's
ek they came at last under a slashing Federal attack.
ighting desperately, the old 27th Virginia lost its
ors, the first time the unit had lost face since the regi-
nt had been mustered for the seizure of Harpers Ferry
r years earlier. And there they were confronted, too,
the report that, among the thousands of Confederates
ced to surrender at the climax of the Sayler's Creek
tle, was General Richard Ewell, stumping up to de-

liver his sword to a Federal officer and no doubt spout
profanity all the while.

From a vantage point on the top of a hill within si
of the vicious fighting below at Sayler's Creek, Robert
Lee was reported to have turned away sorrowfully w
the words: "Half of our army has been destroyed."

The remnant of the Confederate force still moved w
ward along the Appomattox River, which, too deep
ford, was a protective barrier for the weary men, p
ticularly since they burned bridges as they moved, ke
ing the Federal troops on the south side. Then, late t
afternoon, Yankee soldiers reached one bridge while
was still burning, and, putting out the fires, poured acr
to the northern bank. Once again, they attacked the r
of the dying giant that had been Lee's vaunted Army
Northern Virginia, the same army that, as recently as
months before, had administered a stinging defeat
Ulysses S. Grant at Cold Harbor, east of Richmond

Reaching Farmville that night, Grant sent a note
General Lee, asking him to surrender and, in Grant's o
words: "Shift from myself the responsibility of any furt
effusion of blood." Still fighting their way westw
toward Lynchburg, however, the Virginia troops, a p
of General Gordon's now shrunken division, made a f
sortie on the Appomattox Road but to no avail. A
when on April 9, at Appomattox, only 8,000 Confeder
soldiers mustered for the morning report of the Army
Northern Virginia, it was obvious that defeat was
evitable.

Even then, it seemed, the exhausted Virginia tro
must face yet another fight with Sheridan's Federal for
David's hospital wagon went, as usual, with the tro
sent westward under command of General Fitz Lee
General John B. Gordon, along with what had come
be known as the "Light Brigade." Made up of tro
from General A. P. Hill's III Corps, it was comman
by Colonel Kyd Douglas, who had been promised
rank of brigadier general by General Breckinridge,
cently become Secretary of War in Jefferson Davis' Ca
net, but had not yet received order authorizing the p
motion.

robing westward and meeting no particular resistance, ⸱glas' troops, with the Stonewall Brigade and the rest he Virginia regiments, reached a point some distance ⸱y from the main body. David's hospital wagon had ⸱e as usual with the troops but he ordered it pulled to ⸱top, until he could determine where medical help ⸱ld most likely be needed. As he and the wounded Joe ⸱nnard stood watching, Colonel Kyd Douglas rode up ⸱ dismounted.

I just heard a rumor that General Lee is at Appomat- Courthouse discussing terms of surrender with Grant," ⸱said.

⸱oe Stannard looked westward to where a few cavalry- ⸱, obviously Federal, since the South had no spirited ⸱ses like the ones upon which they were mounted, were ⸱ng across a field.

'I hope *they* know that," he said, pointing his good ⸱ toward the distant troops. "What's left of the old ⸱newall Brigade is out there and I'd hate to see even ⸱ of them get killed if the war has really all but ended."

'I'd better get over there and see what's happening," ⸱ Douglas.

'We'll go with you," David told him. "If there's any ⸱ting, it's obviously going to be west of here, and that's ⸱re the casualties will be."

'Did you think it might end this way that night when ⸱ were watching the Federal camp from Sitlington's Hill ⸱McDowell?" Kyd Douglas asked as he rode beside the ⸱gon.

'Not with only eight thousand men remaining in the ⸱ny of Northern Virginia."

'This is one time I'd like to see the Yankees melt away ⸱in like they did during that night," said Douglas. "But ⸱'s not going to happen either."

Ahead of them a sudden burst of firing was heard ⸱ Joe Stannard urged the mule pulling the wagon up ⸱ slope they were ascending. At the top, however, he ⸱denly reined in behind Kyd Douglas and David Pres- ⸱, for massed before them was a solid phalanx of blue- ⸱d infantrymen with a dozen or so Confederate skir- ⸱shers from the "Light Brigade" and the Valley regi-

ments standing between them and the hill upon wl
the wagon stood, obviously waiting for the final cha
It didn't come, however; instead, while they watched,
Federal force, like a phantom army, turned and mc
away out of sight.

"Maybe you got your wish, Colonel Douglas," D:
said softly. "The enemy seems to have disappeared."

"What the hell's going on?" Joe Stannard exclain
but neither of the others could answer. Then Hal Perk
who was standing up on the wagon seat where he c(
see better, spoke.

"An officer's riding up behind us, Major Preston,"
said. "It looks like Major Murrell. I heard he'd been
tached to General Gordon's staff."

"What's going on up here, Colonel Douglas?" said
Cherokee officer, pulling his horse to a sliding stop a
yards away. "General Gordon wants to know whe
you're in command of the army or General Lee? *Lee*
surrendered."

The other three looked at each other solemnly, ha:
believing what they had heard; then Joe Stannard spc

"Old Jack would have wanted it this way," he s
"The Stonewall Brigade fired the last shot in the war.

IV

The next day, General Lee's final order to his tro
was published:

After four years of arduous service, marked by unsurpa
courage and fortitude, the Army of Northern Virginia
been compelled to yield to overwhelming numbers and
sources. I need not tell the brave survivors of so many h
fought battles, who have remained steadfast to the last,
I have consented to the result from no distrust of them.
feeling that valor and devotion could accomplish notl
that could compensate for the loss that must have atten
the continuance of the contest, I determined to avoid
less sacrifice of those whose past services have ende;
them to their countrymen.

By the terms of the agreement, officers and men can return their homes and remain until exchanged. You will take h you the satisfaction that proceeds from the conscious-s of duty faithfully performed; and I earnestly pray that a rciful God will extend to you His blessing and protection. With an increasing admiration of your constancy and de-ion to your country, and a grateful remembrance of your d and generous consideration for myself, I bid you all an ctionate farewell.

One further ceremony remained, the final official pa-le on Wednesday, April 12. For once rain was not ling, although the day was chilly and cloudy, but of the e regiments that had made up the original Stonewall gade, only two hundred and ten men were left. In a al tribute from their fellows, these were elected to head neral John B. Gordon's division as it crossed the Ap-nattox River toward the waiting ranks of Federal ops to lay down their arms.

Many of the men were limping, a few had to use crude tches, and Joe Stannard walked with David Preston ide the hospital wagon driven by Hal Perkins. As the ous brigade marched past their captors to lay down ir arms, a command rose from the blue-clad ranks and Union troops who had fought some of the war-weary erans for the entire four years of the war, snapped to sent Arms in tribute to the vanquished.

At this recognition of their valor, even in defeat, the ered remains of the Stonewall Brigade squared piti-y thin shoulders and lifted heads to face the front. rching to the designated spot in military order, they ked arms, removed the cartridge boxes they were rying and hung them upon the stacked rifles, before ling whatever standards were left. Many of these were hout colors, which had been removed and stuck away he pockets of the former color-bearers.

The war had ended and the Stonewall Brigade had rched into eternal fame as one of the most revered ting units in the history of America. Marching with n unarmed, as a medical officer, David Preston felt his throat fill with an emotion of pride greater than a he'd ever experienced before.

If there was any glory in war, he thought, it must this: the courage of the vanquished in the face of th victors, marching steadfastly toward a future which co only be difficult for all of them, with their homes of already demolished by flame, their families decimated disease and privation, but in spite of everything—still proud Stonewall Brigade.

V

Two days later, on the evening of April 14, 18 President Abraham Lincoln was shot by actor John Wil Booth, while attending a play at Ford's Theater. Linc died the next morning and, with him, the hopes of Confederacy for a continuation of the generous ter upon which General Lee had laid down the arms of Army of Northern Virginia at Appomattox Courtho three days before.

Vice-President Andrew Johnson, now elevated to highest office, announced, while asking Lincoln's Cabi to continue with him, that: "The course which I h taken in the past, in connection with this rebellion, m be regarded as a guarantee for the future." The fact mained, however, that Lincoln's announced tolerance connection with a program for readmission of the rel lious states to the Union had almost cost him re-elect and only Sherman's victories at Atlanta and Savan had saved him from the ignominy of being defeated. N of which augured well, of course, for Andrew Johns being able to control the Radical element in the Cong demanding dire punishment of the former Confede states.

David Preston learned of the tragedy in a Sund morning newspaper at Lynchburg, as he was head westward, toward Preston's Cove. Lachlan Murrell left immediately after the surrender for the Cher Nation to assess the situation there.

The next day, riding through the pass giving acces

e Cove, David paused to observe the quiet beauty of
e scene that lay before him. On a plateau halfway up
e mountainside, a small herd of sheep was grazing,
ile lower down the meadow itself was an oasis of green
at almost seemed to be a mirage. On the small lake
med by the dammed-up creek a didapper, as the small
ring birds were called, plunged beneath the surface in
skittering dive that sent tiny wavelets spreading out in
er widening circles until they disappeared. Leaving a
ray of droplets as the small bird emerged with its prey,
hining minnow wriggling in the warm April sunlight.

The detached kitchen and dining room of the big house
re still standing beside the ruins of the main house,
t the lush growth of spring grass and the bright colors
blooming weeds and flowers had already softened the
unt outlines of the chimney and foundations. A wisp of
oke came from the chimney and a slender, graceful
man came to the door and stepped out on the breeze-
ay.

Turning to a crib standing in the warm April sunlight,
e lifted a baby from it and David's heart suddenly
gan to sing. Holding the baby she turned to look
ward the low pass that gave access to the protected
ve, as he was sure she must have looked hundreds of
es during the past months.

And seeing her and the baby, he kicked his heels
ainst the gaunt sides of the mount he had ridden from
pomattox following the ceremonies of surrender. Shout-
g his happiness as he urged the horse forward, he rode
wn to meet his wife and his child, while she stepped
wn from the breezeway and started to run toward the
ad, bearing the child in her arms.

The war was ended for David Preston, as it was for the
onewall Brigade. And for both a new life was already
gun.

493

FTERWORD

was early August 1866 and the sun shone warm and
ght on the green countryside as a small party of people
Brandywine Cemetery at Wilmington, Delaware. Be-
d them workmen had already began to fill in the grave
ere the body of John Ross, Chief of the Cherokee
tion, rested beside that of Mary Stapler Ross, his wife
until further arrangements could be made by the Chero-
e National Council.

'I'm not sure I wouldn't rather for Uncle John's body
stay here," said Araminta as she took David Preston's
n for the short walk to the carriage in which they had
den behind the hearse. Beside them walked Lachlan
rrell, already soberly conscious of the responsibilities
death of the Cherokee leader had put upon his shoul-
's.

Ross had died on August 1, 1866, in the city of Wash-
ton, fifteen and a half months after the surrender of
neral Robert E. Lee at Appomattox Courthouse had
rted the chain of events which had ended shortly with
official surrender of the Confederacy, in which Chero-
e General Stand Watie had achieved the distinction of
ng the last Confederate general to give up—on June
, 1865.

The months following the end of the war had been a
ficult time for Chief John Ross, ailing and depressed
the death of his wife at her home at 708 South Wash-

ington Square in Philadelphia on July 20, 1865, a ye
earlier. Even though gravely ill, Ross had felt it his du
after forty years as principal chief of the Cherokee N
tion, to negotiate as honorable a peace as possible. A
particularly one that would assure the future of the N
tion and prevent its division into northern and southe
sections, as the Boudinot faction and Stand Watie a
vocated, a device that would effectually destroy the un
for which Ross had spent most of his life fighting.

Ross had resisted, too, the attempt of the Fede:
Government to punish the Cherokees for their brief trea
with the Confederacy, now that the understanding
Lincoln and his friendship were no longer an influen
toward amelioration of the bitterness that followed t
war. He had almost collapsed at the Murrell home ne
Park Hill in Indian Territory, after going to a coun
held at Fort Smith in which the government sought
bring all the Indian tribes into a single nation, with
white governor, something Ross had managed to fig
during much of his life. But though vilified by governme
agents and by those in the Nation itself who oppos
him, he had succeeded and the Nation was still intact,
lands safe, at least for the moment.

The final Cherokee Treaty, signed in July 1866, w
the best John Ross, often from his sickbed, had been ab
to negotiate with the Federal Government. It complete
nullified the treaty with the Confederacy of 1861, abo
ished slavery, as was being done in all of the former Co
federate states, and granted amnesty to those who ha
fought against the Union, as well as rescinding the co
fiscation of Cherokee land, a most important element
the final settlement.

The events of the turbulent year had been too mu
for John Ross's failing body, however, and he had di
on August 1, 1866, his successor being William Pott
Ross, a Princeton-educated Cherokee who supported t
dead leader's plans for the Nation. A friend of the Murr
family, William Ross was already leaning upon Lachla
Murrell for the support that presaged a high place o
day for the former Confederate officer and VMI graduat

The Institute itself, too, was being rebuilt at Lexingt

he beautiful Shenandoah Valley of Virginia, where lay
body of its greatest hero, General Thomas Jonathan
onewall" Jackson and where General Robert E. Lee,
oved and admired as much in defeat as in victory,
ild soon be taking over the reins of Washington Col-
e, to which one day his own name would be added.

UTHOR'S NOTES

a novel of this scope, covering the four years of the erican Civil War in Virginia, Maryland, Pennsylvania the District of Columbia, plus the day-to-day story ne of the world's most famed fighting units during the odiest combat periods in history, it would be imsible to list the hundreds of references consulted. I n, however, to acknowledge my indebtedness to cerspecial studies which have proved invaluable in reating the great events in the campaigns of General newall Jackson and the brigade that was officially ed for him.

Among these are: *Four Years in the Stonewall Brigade* John O. Casler (Guthrie, Okla.: Privately printed, 3): *Stonewall Jackson and the Old Stonewall Brigade* John Esten Cooke (Charlottesville, Va.: The Uniaity of Virginia Press, 1954); *They Called Him Stone-* by Burke Davis (New York: Holt, Rinehart & aston, 1954); *I Rode with Stonewall* by Henry Kyd aglas (Chapel Hill, N.C.: University of North Caro- Press, 1940); *Lee's Lieutenants* by Douglas Southall eman, 3 vols. (New York: Charles Scribner's Sons, -4); *Reveille in Washington* by Margaret Leech (New rk: Harper & &Brothers, 1941); *The Civil War Day Day* by E. B. Long with Barbara Long (Garden City, (.: Doubleday & Company, Inc., 1971); *The Chero-*

special indebtednes
Commander by John S
, and New York, D. Van
masterful and probably the f
major campaigns; and to *The St*
James I. Robertson, Jr. (Baton R
State University Press, 1963), a scho
study of the Stonewall Brigade from its inceptions to
end at Appomattox. The various Civil War battle
pamphlets of the National Park Service History S
have also been invaluable, particularly for the fine r
of the various campaigns, even though they are in
public domain, I am especially grateful for the permis
of the Park Service to reproduce some of them.

Of the major characters appearing in *Stonewall
gade,* only David Preston, Araminta, Lachlan Mu
Joe Stannard, Ed Mattox, Hal Perkins and a few o
are fictional. The remainder are historical and all ba
and campaigns follow as closely as possible the cours
actual events. The bread riot in Richmond occurre
described, though with roughly a year's difference in t
The account is recorded in *A Rebel War Clerk's D*
by John Beauchamp Jones, Philadelphia, 1866.

More than anything else, I am indebted to one of
greatest military tacticians of all time, Thomas Jona
Jackson, Jr., and to the gallant Virginians who began
war as the 1st Brigade at Harpers Ferry in 1861, num
ing over 4,000, and ended it at Appomattox, Virginia
the Stonewall Brigade, with only two hundred and
men left.

*Frank G. Slaughter, M
Jacksonville, Flo*

July 8, 1974